W9-BXE-181

YOU CAN NEVER TELL

Also available by Sarah Warburton

Once Two Sisters

YOU CAN NEVER TELL

A NOVEL

SARAH WARBURTON

CROOKED
LANE

NEW YORK

Copyright © 2021 by Sarah Warburton

All rights reserved.

Published in the United States by Crooked Lane Books, an imprint of The Quick Brown Fox & Company LLC.

Crooked Lane Books and its logo are trademarks of The Quick Brown Fox & Company LLC.

Library of Congress Catalog-in-Publication data available upon request.

ISBN (hardcover): 978-1-64385-736-7
ISBN (ebook): 978-1-64385-737-4

Cover design by Melanie Sun

Printed in the United States.

www.crookedlanebooks.com

Crooked Lane Books
34 West 27th St., 10th Floor
New York, NY 10001

First Edition: August 2021

10 9 8 7 6 5 4 3 2 1

For my parents, with love.

Dear Grace,

You're not even two years old, way too young for the lessons I have to share. You're still learning to say simple words like *Daddy* and *dog*. I describe everything we do as we do it, like the narrator to a film we're living. *Modeling*, it's called, by speech therapists and child development experts in parenting books. It's the way I put words together as I demonstrate the action—phrasing a question, then providing the answer. "Shall we make lunch?" "Let's see what's in the fridge." "Do you want juice?" "After lunch, it's time for nap." And so on.

And all the while you putter around your play kitchen, dropping wooden blocks into a small pot and feeding your baby doll or offering a block to the bewildered dog.

At the end of each day, between your bath and bedtime, your daddy reads you a book with stiff cardboard pages. Tonight he chose a simplified version of Cinderella. You patted the pumpkin and laughed when he waved his finger like a wand and booped you on the nose.

You don't know that you have a godmother. Not a fairy one who could transform vermin and vegetables into a coach-and-four. The woman we asked to be your godmother was something different. She was the Baba Yaga of legend, the Countess of

Bathory, the stuff of nightmares. And for a while, I called her my friend.

Maybe comparing her to larger-than-life figures makes her sound intriguing, even appealing, but that was her power. She mimicked emotion, she created the illusion of relationship, and she blinded with her charisma.

Charisma isn't the same thing as character. I know that now.

She's the reason your father still wakes up screaming. If the world could be pressed into a cardboard book, the evil witch could be identified by her smirk and her long nails, but your godmother wasn't a witch. She was a predator, a wolf in sheep's clothing, the spider inviting a fly to her parlor. And I fell into her web.

Looking at you now, your eyes drooping, your little body curled around your stuffed rabbit, I can't imagine the time you'll be old enough to hear the truth. Maybe this story will keep you safer and make you wiser. But I'm afraid that words aren't strong enough for that lesson. People's words can't be trusted. Not everyone is who they pretend to be. Your father shouldn't be reading you Cinderella; he should be reading Red Riding Hood.

That's the reason I listen to true-crime podcasts while you nap and your father's at work. I'm part of a sisterhood, scarred in a way no one can see, but I'm not alone. I used to think we told stories as a way to hold back the dark, but now I think stories are a training ground, an opportunity to do a dry run through danger. If Hansel and Gretel had read their fairy tales, they might have recognized the witch before ending up in a cage.

Here's the truth, Grace. You have two sets of loving grandparents, two amazing aunts, a mother and father who adore you, and a godmother who's a serial killer.

That's the story I don't want you to hear. Not now. Maybe not ever.

But the world won't keep it a secret. On my phone, I have the newest episode of my favorite true-crime podcast queued up, waiting, and I can feel the pressure building. This is the first time I'll hear my story told start to finish by someone else. These hosts—Helen and Julia—sound like friends, but now I wonder what they'll think of my choices, what version they'll share.

How do you know you're living a true-crime story? Maybe the better question is, how do you know you'll survive?

1

Helen: This is a story about friends.

Julia: Friends like us.

Helen: Not exactly like us.

Julia: Hey, I've always said I'd kill for you.

Helen: And you're the one I'll call to help bury the bodies.

Julia: But if I did the killing, wouldn't I be the one calling you?

Helen: That kind of thinking is exactly why we won't get caught. Anyway, on this episode of *Crime to Chat*, we'll introduce you to an idyllic neighborhood, a storybook life, two friends—and the twisted, bloody secrets underneath it all. But first, let me tell you about some of our amazing sponsors, who make this podcast possible.

1

AFFIRMATIONS ARE JUST lies we wish we could believe. But that didn't stop me from using them.

The drive from New Jersey to Sugar Land, Texas, was mere minutes less than twenty-four hours, so I'd had ample time to practice, mentally chanting positive thoughts as if they could conjure a sunnier future. I couldn't say whether or not they would, but the words did fill the space in my head where regret and fear usually bloomed. They'd gotten me through the drive, through the delivery of our furniture, all the way to this, our first morning in the new house.

If I repeated them faithfully enough, maybe I could forget that these unpacked boxes were all that remained between me and actually starting over.

My therapist back in Jersey had prescribed antidepressants, but first he'd made me promise to embrace his ideas for cognitive behavior modification. The first one I'd tried was keeping a bullet journal of goals for each day, then updating it with a record of what I actually did. For weeks, bullets written in brightly colored ink promised that I would take a walk, try a new recipe, call a friend. Finally I'd given up, leaving the pages blank.

Because writing *stayed in bed* for over a month was even worse than actually doing it.

So affirmations were my new thing. Along with everything else. My whole life was new.

I started to slice open another moving box while positive mantras ran through my head instead of thoughts. I didn't want to remember that tomorrow Michael would go off to his new job and I'd be alone, unemployed, with nothing but these affirmations to guide me.

I am excited about the new house. I am excited about Texas. I will find a job. I will make new friends. Buck up, Kacy. Everything will be good again.

And the box cutter nicked my thumb, cutting right through the stupid affirmations. Mentally chanting them never made me feel better anyway. But it did help keep the past at bay.

I popped my thumb into my mouth, but not before leaving a dark smudge across the label *Tremaine: Kitchen.* Somewhere we had Band-Aids, buried in a box along with antiseptic spray and ankle wraps. The movers who'd packed us up kept it tight. Every box labeled by room only, no *Tremaine: Medicine Cabinet* or *Tremaine: Bedside Table.* They could have saved time by labeling every single one *Tremaine: Former Life.*

Did I really need a Band-Aid? I pulled my thumb out and a dark bead formed immediately, swelling until it ran down the side of my hand. "Michael?" I called. "Do we have a first-aid kit somewhere?"

No answer. And that wasn't like my engineer husband. Sometimes it seemed like an unanswered question caused him physical pain. Pressing my index finger against the wound, I stood and called out again. "Michael? Where's our first-aid kit?"

This new house was one story, open floor plan, nowhere to hide, and only a handful of places where he wouldn't hear me calling. I started searching. The hall bathroom door was open, no one in the room that "would make a great nursery," according to our realtor—but I found him in the master bedroom closet.

He was running his hands over the seam of a box, and it took me a moment to realize he was pressing the tape back into place, resealing it. I didn't need a closer look to guess the contents. I could read them in the way he rose to his feet with his hands out as if to ward me off. Michael had almost opened the only box without a label.

My finger skidded off my bloody thumb and I held it up in explanation. "Do we have a first-aid kit?"

"In the car." He reached down and tore a bit of packing tape off the box. Then he pulled a tissue from his pocket and took my hand in his, inspecting it. "Not deep. Just sharp edged like a paper cut and in a bad place. We'll close it up, and it'll be fine."

The whole time his hands kept moving, folding the clean tissue into a pad that he pressed against the cut, wrapping the tape firmly to apply pressure in just the right place, tucking under any loose edges so that my makeshift bandage was neat and orderly. When he was done, he raised my hand to his lips for a quick kiss. "All better."

"Thanks." Tomorrow he would go to work. Tomorrow. I'd be by myself in this house. Without a job, without a friend, without a plan. *I am excited about the new house. I am excited about the move. I will find a job. I will make new friends. Everything will be fine.*

The affirmations made my breathing weirdly rhythmic, and Michael noticed. He noticed everything about me now. His hands went to my shoulders, and he pulled me close against his chest. His old T-shirt smelled like cotton, cardboard, and the shaving cream he used. The safest smells in the world. "It's going to be okay," he whispered into my hair. "You don't have to decide anything now."

"I need something to do. I want to work."

"So you can start the job search. But there's no pressure. You can take your time, explore your options."

"But no one's going to hire me, not in my field."

"Maybe you could apply under your maiden name. Or try something different. They say the average person has dozens of job changes." He rubbed my back, and I had to fight the urge to pound my fists on his chest. This wasn't a problem he could engineer away.

He sensed the tension in my body and let me go. "What happened wasn't fair. But we can't change it. If you want to work, we'll figure something out. Maybe start small, see what's out there, make some contacts."

The last thing I wanted to do was meet people, have them looking at me and judging me. And I was an art historian. That's not a field with tons of openings to begin with. All those years, all that work, for nothing. But none of that was Michael's fault. He had married someone optimistic and ambitious, not a lump who lived in a blanket fort for five weeks. Not someone who burst into tears at every trigger word like *painting*, *art*, or even *friend*.

He'd never doubted me, and he'd made this move to give me a fresh start. I had to get my shit together. I owed it to him. Not that he'd ever say so.

But then he added, oh-so-casually, "You know, the firm has a support group for spouses. Maybe there's something like that in the neighborhood too."

And there it was, the thing he'd been wanting to tell me. Just meet one person. Just one. Find a friend, a coworker, a boss. One person to trust. Of course, I knew it took only one person to lie, to smear your name, to blow up your life. I couldn't imagine "making friends," not anymore. Michael probably just wanted me to find someone to take the pressure off him. But that wasn't fair either. That's something else I'd learned—trauma could bring out the worst in the wounded. I wasn't as nice as I used to be.

I am excited about the new house. I am excited about the move. I will find a job. I will make new friends. Everything will be fine. Michael loves me, and I love him.

Looking past Michael, I saw the box sitting on the closet floor like an anchor to our old life. "That's one of mine. Leave it. I'll deal with it later."

His mouth tightened, and I knew how much he wanted to tape that box up and throw it out.

But the past couldn't be sealed up so neatly. Not then, and not now.

* * *

Once Michael went to work the next morning, the house was quiet in a way our apartment in Jersey had never been. I could hear the air conditioner, but it only made the vaulted ceiling and open floor plan seem more cavernous.

I'd put the kitchen together—our small selection of pots and pans, our matching set of mugs, everything in the right place ready for our new life. Four chairs were arranged neatly around the kitchen table. I'd broken down the empty boxes and stacked their flat carcasses by the front door.

There was plenty to do, too much and not enough. Boxes of sophisticated professional clothes in the bedroom, pieces of the self-created uniform I'd worn at the museum, and boxes of books in the study, building blocks of my capsized career. And we had artwork, still flat-packed, ready to hang. Our bare walls were all painted the same silvery gray, made warmer by the greige undertones.

But I didn't feel the warmth, not even when sunlight broke through the window treatments left by the previous owner. Someday I should replace the heavy double-layered fabric with something lighter, more contemporary, or at least more cheerful. Michael had draped a multicolored blanket crocheted by my grandmother over the back of our sleek gray sofa. Maybe he was trying to brighten things up too.

My phone buzzed. Mom calling to check in. I sat on the sofa and answered.

"How are you?" she asked. Just like Michael, everything she said had an undertone of pity.

"Great. Busy putting things in order." The words came out of my mouth like I was reading from a script. I really just wanted to put my head on my mother's shoulder and cry. But I didn't want her to worry any more than she already was. I pulled the blanket down over my lap and twined my fingers through the crochet holes.

"And Michael, does he like his job?"

"It's his first day, so I don't know yet. He said the people at his interview were nice. How's Dad?"

"Oh, you know. He's in a state because of the weather. Too much rain and his tomatoes are rotting. He was supposed to go fishing with Bill, but normal people don't like to sit out on the river in a rainstorm, even though I hear that's when the fish get frisky. Anyhoo, that's not why I called."

Then she stopped, clearly waiting for me to ask, *Why did you call, Mom?* So I did, clutching one floral crochet square in my hand.

"I was talking to Theresa, you know, down by the florist? She says her sister runs an art gallery there in Sugar Land. I told her you had a PhD in art history and museum experience, and she said you should go right over and introduce yourself."

My heart started pounding. "I can't—"

"I know you're scared, honey. But you can't let one bad person keep you from going after your dreams. When Molly's band broke up, she found a new one. And it's been two years since Charlotte's divorce, and she's dating the nicest guy. You've got your whole life—"

"Mom, it's not the same!"

I'd never raised my voice at my parents, not ever. And the shock of it was enough to shut us both up. I could picture my mother holding the phone to her ear, just as I was, while we listened to silence.

And then I was sorry, so sorry. Mom wasn't wrong. My sisters had suffered setbacks, but they'd kept going. I knew she was trying to help, just like Michael. Everyone wanted to fix my life and make the pain go away. *Or maybe*, said a mean voice in my head, *they just want you to shut up and suck it up.*

I am excited about Texas. I will find a new job. I can make a new life.

"What's the name of the gallery?" My question was an apology. A plea that she wouldn't give up on me.

"Marville Fine Art Gallery." And, in my mother's subdued tone, I could hear that she wasn't angered by my outburst; she was worried.

"Okay, Mom. Thanks." I pushed the blanket off my lap and stood.

"Let me know how it works out. Love you, sweetie."

"Love you too."

A job in a gallery. *Interesting.* And I hadn't found anything interesting in weeks. I used to work in a museum, designing exhibitions, but a gallery would be nice. There'd be art, maybe some acquisitions, maybe some shows. I could start building a new résumé, a new life. But my heart was still beating too quickly, and the little flame of hope flared into panic. Any job would want my references, my history.

I pulled out my phone, about to do something I'd promised everyone—my therapist, Michael, my mother—that I would stop doing. But I couldn't resist the awful pain of picking a scab, so I typed *Kacy Tremaine* into Google, the same way any diligent employer would.

And the familiar words jumped out: *disgraced employee, missing art, real-life* Goldfinch?, *declined to press charges,* and *gross misconduct.* That was me, the art thief who'd had a change of heart, the girl who was lucky she wasn't in jail. I didn't have a conviction, but I did have an arrest warrant. Even dismissed charges were part of your permanent record. I *looked* guilty, even though I wasn't. *I will find a job.* So much for that affirmation.

Could I just go back to my maiden name or pretend to be someone else? Sure, if I also wanted to drop evidence of my degree, my work history, any of the things necessary to actually get a job in my field. Either I was myself—with the skills and experience and baggage of my past—or I was no one. At least I wasn't a liar. Not now, and not back then when it all went down.

I typed another name into the Google search, *Aimee McFadden*, my former best friend. And among the dozens of hits, I found her like I always did. New posts, new pictures; her life was clicking along right on track. She had everything she wanted.

She'd just had to ruin me to get it.

2

ALL THE BOOKS were on the study shelves, our clothes were hanging in the closet, and I was in the car on the way to dinner with one of Michael's new colleagues. And his wife. They lived in the same planned community as us, Bluebonnet Skies, but in a different neighborhood that would take us twenty minutes to reach. Plenty of time for me to freak out.

I will make new friends.

Fear bubbled in my stomach, and I glanced at Michael. Under the passing streetlights, his face looked relaxed, happy even. I didn't tell him I was freaking out. No special key or self-help book or magic phrase could make my issues disappear like a magician whisking away a cloth. All the white rabbits in my brain were dug in and panicking.

But Michael liked his job; he was excited about it. When my future plans exploded back in Jersey, I had holed up in our apartment like I was waiting out the apocalypse. One of us had to troubleshoot the life we were living, and I clearly hadn't been up to it. So he contacted a headhunter.

Michael had picked up a nice Sangiovese to bring with us, and I clenched the neck of the bottle like I was throttling it. We were here because of me, because I had trusted the wrong person. Now I had to make it work. I would meet these people, and we would have a lovely evening. But first I had to prepare.

"So it's Elizabeth and . . ."

"Wyatt. Like Wyatt Earp," Michael answered.

"Very Texas."

His lips quirked up. "Except they're from Canada. I think I've only met three actual Texans since I walked into the building."

"And what does she do?"

"I'm not sure. Since they're here on his visa, I don't know if she's allowed to work. But she can tell you about the spousal support system."

"Sounds governmental. The SSS."

"The Social Security Service." Then the humor ebbed from his face, and he reached over to pat my knee. "You're going to be fine. These are nice people. They want to meet you."

"Right." I couldn't tell him that it wasn't Wyatt and Elizabeth that worried me.

All the houses in the neighborhood were brick and stucco, set on tiny manicured lawns. We pulled into the driveway of one almost indistinguishable from our own. The neck of the wine bottle was slick from my tight grip.

Maybe this was what we needed, couple friends. But that was just another reminder that it had been *my* best friend, my choice, that ruined everything. I slipped a hand into Michael's, and he gave it a little squeeze before ringing the doorbell.

Everything in the foyer was fast and familiar—shaking hands, slipping off our shoes, you have a lovely home, thank you for the wine—and then we were ushered into the kitchen, where barstools were arranged around a central island. There was a little grill in the middle surrounded by plates of veggies and sliced meat.

Elizabeth tucked a strand of smooth blond hair behind her ear. "I thought we'd do indoor hibachi."

"Sounds good," Michael said, and I nodded.

"Let me give you the five-cent tour." Wyatt winked in a way that said he was playing at being a grown-up, just like we were. A fraction of tension left my shoulders.

Their house had been designed by the same builder as ours, the same builder as everyone else's in the whole planned community, but theirs was two stories to our one. We dutifully followed Wyatt around the first floor, where the kitchen connected to the formal dining room, and up the stairs, where a spare bedroom had the same "pre-nursery" look our extra bedroom did.

Then we trooped back down. Wyatt invited Michael out into the garage, where he was experimenting with brewing his own beer, and they disappeared, leaving me with Elizabeth.

The thing about making friends is that you need a person with some rough edges. It's like Velcro. If there aren't any little hooks, you'll slide right off. Standing here with a stranger felt like being a kid when your mom goes to visit a friend and they send you into the backyard to "play" with whatever other child happens to be there. A two-year age difference, a gender gap, even a girl who likes video games while you still like dolls and you'll both end up staring at each other in mild disappointment and silent boredom.

So I started cataloging all the little things about Elizabeth, looking for an entry. Her nails weren't polished, just short and sensible. She'd hit the sweet spot between casual and "making an effort" with slinky black trousers, no-show socks, and a scoop-neck fitted tee in royal blue. A trio of rings hung from a silver chain around her neck. She caught me looking and lifted one up to show me. "Do you like it? My two best friends each have one." The golden rings looked handcrafted—one yellow, one white, one rose gold. It's hokey, I told myself, like the grown-up version of a braided friendship bracelet.

But I couldn't help reaching out and stroking the cool metal. "Beautiful. Do you get to see your friends often?"

She smiled, one of those women with a natural grin, and said, "We catch up over Christmas, and we try to do a girls' trip once a year. But my friend Meagan just had a baby, and I think schedul-ing's going to get trickier. We're always FaceTiming and texting. You've got to have other women in your corner, you know?" She opened a drawer, took out an oven mitt, and slipped it on.

"Yes," I agreed, but I wasn't really listening. Those women were on the dark side of the moon in Canada. I was right here, perfect friend material. I leaned against the kitchen counter, try-ing to look casual.

Elizabeth opened the oven and slid out a baking sheet with something wrapped in foil. Setting it down, she asked, "So, have you thought about what you'll be doing? I mean, while Michael's at work?"

"I'm not thinking about that yet. Still getting adjusted after the move." What I didn't say was that thoughts of the future sent me spiraling into the pain of the past. I couldn't get a job because of what happened, not without lying. I couldn't make plans without risking a panic attack. My mind was a rat in a maze with an electric shock at every dead end. I spent every minute "not-thinking" about things.

Now my silence had gone on too long, but Elizabeth let me off the hook. As she deftly unwrapped the foil, revealing browned rolls, she said, "You should take your time getting settled. But when you're ready, there are lots of galleries in EaDo, the arts district 'east of downtown.' Didn't you work in a museum?"

The expression on my face felt like a grimace, but I hoped it was appropriate. "Yes. And you, what do you do?"

She smiled, lifting the entire mass of rolls into a waiting bread basket, then flipping the end of an embroidered linen towel over the neat stack. "I was with an interior design firm in Toronto, but I haven't picked anything up here in Houston. I got an offer from a place downtown, but the commute would have killed me. I'm thinking about starting something out here, picking up a few small design jobs, taking things slowly."

"So you're allowed to work here?" I blurted out, then my cheeks grew hot. "I mean, with Wyatt's visa and everything?"

To my relief, she laughed. "I am. At least right now. They changed the rules, but they could always change them back."

How similar was interior design to art history? Maybe I could go into business with Elizabeth. As I followed her to the table, I noticed details like her cookbooks, bright, vibrant, and arranged so the contrasting colors were next to each other—lemon yellow, cilantro green, tomato red, white with cobalt-blue letters—and a polished wooden bowl of oranges on the counter just far enough away to seem casually placed. If there had been an orange cookbook instead of a yellow one, would Elizabeth have put lemons in the bowl?

She set the bread on the table and turned around, taking in my empty wineglass. "Let me top you up."

The tannins were puckering the back of my throat, but I nodded and let her take my glass. "Thank you." I had to say something else, something interesting. "Did you grow up around here?" *Stupid.* I knew she was Canadian. We had literally just discussed the visa situation. "I mean, had you ever been to the States before?"

As she deftly twisted the wine stopper out of the bottle, she said, "I grew up outside of Manitoba. This is the furthest south I've ever lived, but we visited Disneyland once, when I was little. How about you? Where's your family?"

This was the world's most boring conversation, and I was losing her. There's a chemistry to friendship, you have to be in flow, and I was so much in my own head that I couldn't relax.

"Northeast."

She nodded, handing me my glass, and we stood there in silence, not a comfortable one, for just a moment too long. Then she said, "Let's call the boys and eat."

* * *

The dinner itself was fine. Since Michael and Wyatt were both there, we had enough conversation without a big effort from me. They talked about work—Michael's favorite topic—and the neighborhood, and some women's group called the Bluebonnets. We learned about changes in the homeowners' association and about Elizabeth and Wyatt's passion for camping and skiing.

Elizabeth was skilled at steering Wyatt away from engineering and back to more general topics. I used to excel at that dance, roping Michael into interacting with people at art exhibitions and museum galas. Then we'd go to dinner with a bunch of engineers, and I'd be the life of the party. That Kacy seemed like a different person now.

I caught Michael glancing at me from the corner of his eye. I wasn't participating enough, and he'd noticed. There was a momentary lull, so I asked a surefire winner. "How did you two meet?"

And it worked. Wyatt looked to Elizabeth, waiting for her to take the lead. She rested her hand on his arm, and the gesture had a graceful yet practiced look. "We met at university. McGill in Montreal. I was working on a degree in design with a minor in accounting, and he was in the electrical engineering program." She paused and I saw her fingers tighten on Wyatt's arm, signaling his turn to speak.

He said, "In addition to the degree requirements, I had to take an elective from a list of 'complementary studies.' Maybe it was the same for you?"

Michael laughed. "I had a whole bunch of required 'nonengineering classes.' Americans believe in general education. Freshman comp was the worst experience of my life."

Worst experience of my life. I didn't look at him, but every cell in my body froze. He was joking—it was a throwaway phrase, I knew that; my rational mind argued his case. But on a visceral level, the *worst experience of my life* had been the past year. Hadn't it been his worst experience too? Or at least worse than any first-year composition class, even one that featured poetry writing and performance?

Wyatt grinned. "Things could have been worse for me, that's what you're saying. So, I was taking a course on the sociology of something—"

"The sociology of work and industry," Elizabeth took over. "It was kind of about the history of the workplace as technology and industry changes. I was already thinking about going into corporate interior design. I sat down next to a cute guy who was taking notes on his laptop like his life depended on it. By the end of the first class, he had this look of absolute panic on his face, so I introduced myself and asked if he wanted to study together."

"When a cute girl offers to translate whatever the hell sociology means, you say yes," Wyatt added.

"And I kept him." Elizabeth gave his arm another little squeeze before letting it go and picking up her fork. She speared a thin strip of beef, which sizzled as it hit the cast-iron grill. "How about the two of you?"

"Online," I said, before Michael could open his mouth. "We met online."

I remembered the details of his profile like the facts on my own driver's license. *About me:* Above-average intelligence and below-average social time. *About you:* Hoping for same. *Perfect date:* Ask what we'd like to do, Research and get to know each other, Imagine the possibilities, Plan for the future, Create it together, Test for weakness, Improve every day.

Ask. Research. Imagine. Plan. Create. Test. Improve. Now I knew it as the "Engineering Design Cycle," but then it had seemed like this guy had the answers I needed, a way to impose order on my crazy life. His profile picture was just the top of his face, like he was peeking over a wall into the frame. It was so weird. But I liked his eyes. And I'd just been on twenty thousand dates with assholes who translated "Love adventure . . . where shall we go?" as "Totally slutty . . . let's do it in your car."

On our first date, we met at a gastropub, and as soon as I saw Michael, all my nerves melted away. It was so easy. Whatever pseudoromantic ideas I'd had about butterflies in my stomach and the fizziness of falling in love vanished in the enveloping warmth of the absolute comfort I felt with him. On our very first date I forgot to be nervous. I ate my fries and his too, and he never looked away from my face. Later I couldn't remember what we talked about. I only remembered feeling like I'd been holding my breath for months and it was finally safe to exhale.

I didn't feel that way now.

Our toasting forks had long handles capped with wooden knobs at one end and three prongs like tiny pitchforks at the other. There was a platter with strips of beef, bell peppers, onions, jalapeños, and some thick white strips of cheese.

"Halloumi," Elizabeth explained. "A good cheese for grilling." We speared the food and set it on the hibachi between us. The air above the grill wobbled in the heat.

This wasn't the kind of food you ate when you were hungry; this was a meal for conversation, a thoughtful choice to share with a couple you'd like to get to know. Wyatt and Michael seemed perfectly matched—nice guys who were also electrical engineers, problem solvers with even tempers who wouldn't get bogged down in social nuance or drama.

After a few tries, I speared a bell pepper and let it slide onto the grill. This would have been such fun if I'd been able to relax. We'd talk, I'd make a joke, and we'd all laugh, throwing our heads back. After all, we were two carefree couples—young, good jobs, nice homes, no kids. But I was so unsure, doubting every social instinct I'd ever had.

I stabbed a strip of beef, but then it didn't slide off the fork onto the grill. I gave it a shake, and my hand hit the edge of the hot surface. Only for a second, not enough for a real burn, but the fork and beef went flying, right onto Elizabeth. It was a nightmare. She was splattered with marinade, and we were all asking if she was okay.

"I'm fine, just fine." She waved us away and scooped up the beef, still impaled on that freaking fork. Then she looked at me, and I could have sworn I saw real concern in her eyes. "Kacy, how's your hand? Do you need some aloe?"

I could have said yes, let her find some burn ointment, apologized for her shirt, and we'd have been talking and taking care of each other. This could have been the moment when we started to become friends, real friends.

"No, no, I'm fine. Excuse me." I pushed back from the table, unable to look at Michael's worried face or meet Elizabeth's eyes. On Wyatt's tour, I'd seen a bathroom, and I prayed I would get there before the first sob broke free. I could feel it, swelling under my breastbone, worse than any burn, blurring my vision even as my hand found the doorknob, and I didn't have time to turn on the bathroom light before I was crying hard, so hard my legs couldn't hold me up.

I slid down the closed door until I sat with my back against it, alone. My body ached with this sorrow, sobs rattling my core. I was broken, really broken. If Michael had met me today, we wouldn't be married. I couldn't make a friend, not today, not ever. I wasn't failing just at finding work; I was failing at life. No magic affirmation could hide the truth, and no pill was strong enough to cure me.

Worst of all? Sooner or later, I would have to leave this bathroom.

2

Helen: So, this is a case I've been wanting to do for a while. It takes place in a suburb of Houston, somewhere you wouldn't expect anything bad to happen.

Julia: But we know awful things can happen anywhere.

Helen: Sad but true. Sugar Land was voted one of the best places to live in the country. Best place to raise a family. A little more conservative than Houston—affluent, middle class—but if you thought it's all cowboy hats and big hair, you'd be wrong. Sure, there's big oil money, but it's extremely international, with companies pulling in talent from countries around the world. I found that in 2011 Fort Bend County, where Sugar Land is located, was ranked the fourth most diverse county in the United States. And the area is resilient, coming back from natural disasters like hurricanes and flooding.

Julia: I like the words *international* and *diverse* more than the words *natural disaster*. You're telling me this is one of the best places to raise a family?

Helen: Like *Leave It to Beaver* good.

Julia: But we're not that kind of show.

ON THE DRIVE home, I sneaked a glance at Michael's face. His profile was absolutely composed. If I'd been thinking when I fled the dinner table, I would have run water in the sink or flushed the toilet, anything to cover up the sounds of crying. Instead, after I pulled myself together, splashed water on my face, and opened the door, there was an awkward hush over the table that made it clear everyone had heard. Michael must have made an excuse to keep our hosts from knocking on the door and asking the dreaded question: *Are you okay in there?*

So I returned to a table where the hibachi had been replaced with a dark-chocolate cake dusted with powdered sugar and a room heavy with things our hosts were too polite to say.

While Wyatt asked Michael about some work-related thing, Elizabeth offered me coffee. Caffeine was the last thing my shredded nerves needed, but I would have accepted anything to restore forward momentum to our evening. After Elizabeth served me a cup of coffee, a slice of flourless cake, and a halfhearted invitation to the next Bluebonnets meeting, Michael and I made it to the front door, thanking our hosts, promising to return the favor, and (in my case) avoiding direct eye contact.

And Michael still hadn't said a word since we'd left. Not one. He wasn't angry, I told myself, just analyzing the evening, trying to find the trigger, the moment that had set me off. If he could figure out what had happened, he could fix it. That was the way he thought. And we'd been working through a whole list of solutions: time off, a therapist, medication, this entire move to Texas.

But what if there wasn't a fix? Maybe I was broken for good.

Everything in this master-planned community had been carefully constructed, from the landscaping with its gently curved green spaces to the arching streetlights guiding us from one neighborhood to the next. Life should be this smooth, this easy. We passed under a light, and I could see how tightly Michael's lips were pressed together.

"I'm sorry," I said, but I wasn't sure if the apology was for the bathroom incident, the entire evening, or the disappointing person I'd become.

He didn't answer.

I wrapped my arms around myself and leaned my head against the window. I knew his silence didn't mean anger, and I didn't expect him to change the way he processed things, but I felt so alone. This was why I needed friends.

Only a few months ago, I'd have texted Aimee. Just a lightning exchange of one-liners and I'd have relaxed. Once I felt heard and understood, I'd have been able to give Michael the space he needed without making it personal. But now I hated myself, and I thought he probably hated me a little too.

I wished it were all Aimee's fault, but I'd been the one who trusted her.

If I closed my eyes, there were dozens of memories waiting. The side of her face as she drove us through the heart of Manhattan. Sitting on the railing of a rooftop bar, toasting with vodka gimlets and then almost choking with laughter. Her hands, draping a light scarf around my neck and then turning me so the mirror showed us both. She made me feel smart, funny, beautiful.

At the museum, standing in front of a piece by a new artist and knowing, just knowing that the two of us were feeling the same thing. I loved Michael so much, but art had never meant to him what it meant to me. What I'd thought it meant to Aimee.

She and I had been hired at the same time, and there'd been a moment when we might have been rivals, when we were both the new girls at the museum, both about the same age, both polished and northeastern and trying to prove ourselves. And then she had leaned forward and whispered, "I hate this part, when we're strangers on our best behavior. Let's just be friends already. Are you in?"

"Absolutely." I felt the thrill of an unexpected windfall, something changing for the better.

She'd looked me up and down. "Want to go clubbing after work? I'll be your wingman . . ."

I shook my head. "I've got a . . . I'm seeing someone."

"Are you seeing him tonight?" When I shook my head again, she grinned. "Good. Then you can be *my* wingman."

I'd been dating Michael for almost two years, but I'd never been the kind of girl who went clubbing. Quiet wine bars, book readings, gallery openings. But the club lights flashed like a dazzling interactive light installation, and my pulse got caught up in the beat of the music. We danced, and when a guy came up to us, I knew it was a test. Back in college, my friends and I had a policy—"no woman left behind." Aimee and I were new friends. Would she ditch me for some guy?

But as the music shifted seamlessly from one track to another, she shrugged him off like a jacket and came over, breathless, with beads of sweat along her hairline. And she kept choosing me, after each meeting at work, for road trips to see performance art, in her lightning-quick replies to my every text.

Together we had been so powerful.

I hadn't just lost my best friend. I'd lost my best self too.

Michael slowed down, and I opened my eyes to a blur of blue and red lights. Before I even wondered if we were going too fast, I saw the cop car was already stopped behind the pickup he'd pulled over. Somebody else was having a bad evening too.

We crept past, and the dark asphalt streets ahead of us were empty under the steel streetlamps. Everything was quiet, each neighborhood locked behind a matching brick wall like separate kingdoms. Somewhere behind us the curved highway vibrated with oscillating traffic, but looking ahead, you'd think the entire world was intent on getting a good eight hours of sleep.

Michael kept driving about ten miles under the speed limit, even as the red and blue lights retreated in our rearview mirror.

"You need to find a doctor here." His voice was definite, and it snapped my attention back.

"Dr. Johnson said—"

"Dr. Johnson isn't here. You're not getting better."

"It takes time. The medicine—"

"Maybe you need a different dose."

I bit back my answer, but my eyes filled with tears. You'd have thought I was all cried out. Michael didn't want to hurt me, but he did want to fix me. And any reminder of my brokenness stung. Besides, what if he couldn't engineer this problem away?

The silence between us was expectant, and I realized he was waiting for me to say something. "I'll call tomorrow. For a referral."

"Thanks," he said quietly. I knew he was disappointed, just like me. This evening should have been easy. We could have been at the start of something really fun, a new friendship.

Instead Michael would still see Wyatt at work, maybe they would even be friends, but Wyatt's friendship would be tinged with pity. He and Elizabeth were probably already talking about it while they loaded the dishwasher and wiped down the counters. "He's a nice guy, but Kacy . . . what do you think is wrong with her?" Maybe they'd think it was drugs, or a death in the family, or just call me crazy.

And they'd look at each other and shrug, glad to forget about my problems. But Michael would forever be "poor Michael" in their minds.

A nice guy with a messed-up wife.

*   *   *

The next day Michael was back at work and I was home alone, stuck with my own company and a shame hangover from the previous night.

I attacked the last of the moving boxes as if I could redeem myself. This house was bigger than our old apartment, and our furniture looked as unmoored as I felt, with just a little too much space between a chair and its end table. Our bookshelves were filled with my art books and Michael's engineering texts as well as the history books we both loved. But the shelves themselves sat isolated, like a single painting in the middle of a wall.

Maybe I just hated open-floor-plan homes. Even when I tried to fill the empty spaces, it didn't work.

The kitchen cabinets were uncrowded, each glass set inches away from the next. Our master closet was the size of a loft in Manhattan, every article of clothing dangling untouched by the one beside it.

And as I stood in the middle of all that space, the only box left was the one Michael didn't want me to see.

The one with any reminder of Aimee.

When you break up with a guy, there's sometimes that dramatic scene where you dump his stuff into a cardboard box and meet up for a hostile exchange of goods. Your crappy T-shirt for my water bottle. My second-best running shoes for your favorite CD. And maybe I cracked the case on the way over, because who even listens to CDs anymore?

But there's no protocol like that for ex-friends. And we hadn't broken up, not exactly.

I had known she'd started seeing a new guy. There were long gaps between texts I'd sent and her replies. Aimee would show up at work not quite as put-together as usual. And she wouldn't tell me who it was.

Now I pulled the box forward and plopped down on the floor next to it with a sense of inevitability. Unless I threw it out, this box wasn't going anywhere. I worked my fingers underneath the packing tape and peeled it back. Inside, there was a jumbled mass of memories—exhibition catalogs and rolled promotional posters, a handful of random postcards and Polaroids, bits and pieces from my life in the museum. I couldn't help reaching for the photos, fanning them out like a losing hand of cards. One showed the placement of an alabaster statue, another had a grouping of oil paintings, and in another a woman stood with her arms spread wide. I knew she was showing how much space to leave between installations, but she looked like she was waiting for an embrace. I'd trusted her. I'd loved her.

But by this time she had begun sleeping with the museum director, a bald-headed guy twice her age who was also the CEO of the North Atlantic Museum Trust. And she'd been embezzling. And taking a few pieces of art. Which I had learned when the theft was discovered and Aimee framed me for it.

Some part of me felt like I was still standing in the director's office, trapped in the nightmare. On one side of the room, the director, the museum's lawyer, an insurance adjuster, and Aimee—all with identical frowns of cold judgment.

On the other side, me.

If there had been any more proof than a suspicious email trail Aimee had created and her own lying testimony, I would be in jail. But after the only truly valuable piece of artwork mysteriously reappeared and the money was written off, I had been dismissed with a permanent mark on my reputation. A local reporter had shared enough details to blacklist me socially and professionally. If I had been guilty, I could have understood being fired, even being made a pariah in print and online. But I knew I was innocent. And so did Aimee. She was the part I just couldn't understand.

Had we ever been friends? Why had she driven me to the ER when I cut my hand on a sharp piece of tile and then waited while I got stitches? Those late-night calls, the little "just thinking of you" gifts—from an article torn out of a magazine to a funky piece of artisan jewelry to a bizarre flavor of chocolate to postcards addressed, stamped, and mailed even though we saw each other daily (our private running joke). None of that had been necessary if all she needed was a fall guy. It was like the man who meets your parents and talks marriage only to ghost you after sex.

I looked at Aimee's glossy lipsticked smile, her dark arched eyebrows, the angled bob framing her face, the face of a liar, and twisted the photo in my hands.

A knock reverberated through the house, filling the empty spaces. I dropped the picture and stood, tensed for flight, even though I knew it was probably a delivery or something. But as I hurried out of the bedroom, the knocking continued and the doorbell rang, one sound, then the other, frantically, relentlessly alternating.

I opened the door as a young woman in a light-pink hijab pushed past me. With one hand she pulled me back into the house; with the other she clenched a cell phone. She had a small white dog yapping in the crook of her arm, and she still managed to elbow the door shut behind us. She was frantic, her eyes wide.

I recognized her as the woman who had walked past me the other morning with the same small dog prancing on the end of a leash in one hand and a little boy with a huge backpack clinging to her other. She had smiled at me, and for a second her whole

face had been a perfect circle under her sky-blue hijab. Today her
eyes were round with fear. She dropped the dog, who began spinning as well as barking, and her fluttering hands were everywhere,
clutching at my arm, raising her phone to her ear, motioning me
to lock the door, to move away from the windows, until finally we
sank into chairs at the kitchen table.

"I'm sorry." She gestured to the front door. "But I couldn't go
home."

"What is it? What's wrong?" My thoughts raced. Could it be
an animal in her house? An abusive husband? A home invasion?
"I'll call the police."

I half rose from my chair, because my phone was still in the
closet, but she stopped me. "They know. The police are at my
house now."

She spoke a stream of words into her own cell phone, a language that to my ignorant ears sounded like water spilling over
stones.

"What happened?" I asked, my fear subsiding a little. If the
police were already there, someone was handling the crisis, whatever it was. But I didn't understand why she was here instead of
there, talking to the cops.

She lowered the phone. "I'm sorry, so sorry. These boys, they
stole a car and drove it all over, the police chasing them right past
the school and where the children play. I got the neighborhood
alert about it on my phone while I was walking Bibi. But when I
got home, my garage door was bent like this"—she held a flat hand
angled sharply over the phone—"and the car was still right there
in my driveway. The policeman said the kids crashed the car and
ran away. 'Joyriding' "—she made one-handed air quotes—"but
they know the kids and it's not the first time, so they are looking
for them, and I could go into my house, but with my garage door
like that, how do I know—" She paused again, listening to the
phone, and then spoke another run of that beautiful language into
it, becoming more emphatic near the end. She repeated one word
that sounded like *hasana* three times before holding the phone out
to me. "My husband."

I took it and a male voice with a slight British accent said, "I
apologize for the inconvenience. I am on my way from work, but

it may be thirty minutes before I arrive. May I ask a favor of you? If you will wait, I will pick up Rahmia there."

Rahmia lifted Bibi and smoothed the little dog's ears back. The edges of her headscarf fell forward, obscuring her face, but her hands trembled slightly.

"Of course," I said. "It's no trouble at all."

"You are very kind. Rahmia does not want to be alone right now. I will be there promptly, and I greatly appreciate your generosity."

I handed the phone back to Rahmia. She spoke softly into it and hung up, rolling her eyes at me. "My husband is such a worrier. But it's just me at home until school lets out. And the police, they say my house is safe, but how do I know?"

Rising to my feet, I asked, "Would you like some tea?" The electric kettle gleamed on the counter, because I'd unpacked and put away all the kitchen items, but then I remembered I hadn't bought any tea. Texas was so hot.

Rahmia said, "That would be very nice, but I don't want to be any trouble."

"No trouble at all." I opened the pantry, hoping for a miracle. And there, on the nearly empty shelves, was a small cardboard box with spices, matches, toothpicks, and mercifully a few random tea bags.

"I only have green tea," I said apologetically.

Rahmia smiled at me. "You are so kind." Her hands kept moving, ruffling Bibi's fur, then smoothing it back down.

I took two cups from the cabinet, dropped in the tea bags, and filled the kettle. The ordinary routine of hospitality was calming. I found it much easier to be a hostess than a guest. Just remembering last night made me flush, and I fiddled with the kettle a little longer than necessary until my face didn't feel so hot.

"We're new to the neighborhood. Have you lived here long? Does this kind of thing happen often?"

My questions sounded abrupt, but Rahmia didn't seem to mind. "My son, Emir, and I have been here almost two years, but Ali has been here longer. We had trouble selling our house in Detroit. This is a nice neighborhood, but you have to be careful. Not just here—everywhere. I thought it might be safer here, but right after we moved, there were home invasions, where people come and"—she slammed a fist into her other hand—"just knock down the door. That's what I thought when I saw the car smashed into my garage. If a person is home, they get shot. Ali says it's drugs and it happens closer to the city, inside the 'loop,' he says, but strange things have happened here too."

I was having a little trouble following her. "Like what?"

She leaned forward, tipping Bibi onto the floor. "Twice the police have found cars on the side of the road, the keys still in them, engines running, but the people"—she opened her hands wide—"gone."

My confusion must have shown on my face, because Rahmia lowered her voice and spoke with exaggerated slowness. "The drivers are missing. When the police go to their homes, they are not there either. They were driving their cars; they pulled over and disappeared. No one knows what happened to them. Empty car, empty house, just gone."

The kettle squealed. I was suddenly glad it was a bright sunny morning and my front door was locked.

3

Helen: Let me set the scene. Then we'll get to the crime. This area of Sugar Land has a large number of planned communities, entire neighborhoods often designed by a single builder with their own schools, playgrounds, swimming pools, grocery stores, and aesthetics. Really manicured landscaping, wide sidewalks, and those little sprinkler parks—

Julia: Splash pads.

Helen: —and these planned communities have stringent homeowners' associations. They set the rules like whether you can have a basketball hoop or when you need to mow your lawn.

Julia: That seems kind of authoritarian.

Helen: The idea is that one house can bring down the property values for the entire community. And since dues can be as high as a thousand dollars a year, all the residents are invested in making sure everyone follows the rules.

Julia: Okay, even creepier. Like your neighbors are now informants. [whispering] I'd like to report an untrimmed tree.

Helen: But you have to figure the people who move there like it that way. Of course, it doesn't mean that nothing bad ever happens. I was going over police reports for the neighborhood we're considering, and there's the usual tame suburban stuff. Traffic violations and petty theft. The neighborhood actually has its own designated deputy from the sheriff's office. Here's a fun fact: he gave faux tickets to anyone with valuables on their front seats or with their car doors unlocked.

Julia: So he'd try car doors to see if any of them were unlocked. Creepy.

Helen: Or really earnest.

Julia: It's a little too "Big Brother."

Helen: But there's also some darker stuff. A meth lab within two miles of an elementary school rated in the ninety-fifth percentile. A home invasion. Car theft. So what happens in a case like the one we're describing, when a perfectly nice, HOA-run neighborhood suddenly finds itself the site of a murder house?

Julia: You're jumping ahead. First we have to meet our murderer.

4

AFTER RAHMIA'S HUSBAND, a handsome man with heavy brows, picked her up, I paced around the empty house, looking for tasks that required little thought—retaping the box with memories of Aimee so Michael wouldn't worry, wiping down the counters, moving books from one place to another.

In Jersey, I'd never felt alone like this. Our apartment was surrounded by other apartments, and I was never more than a thin wall away from another human being. And we'd had a doorman at the entrance, a person always there to keep me safe.

Now I checked and rechecked the alarm system until Michael got home. He was tired, I could see it in the heavy way he set down his bag, but as I told my story, the life came back into him.

"She just barged in?" He looked around, as though evaluating the safety of our home.

"She was scared. And I know her." By sight, anyway.

"You need to be careful about opening the door to strangers." Did he think I couldn't be trusted home alone? It wasn't like I'd just open the door to anyone.

"I know her. She's not a stranger." I wrapped my arms around my middle for reinforcement. Letting the wrong person in. That was something I'd done, to myself and to Michael too.

"Okay." Maybe Michael regretted coming on so strong, because he said, "It's still light outside. Let's go see what happened."

"I'm not sure where they live."

"We'll figure it out." He took my hand and gave it a squeeze. "I've been sitting at a desk all day. It'll feel good to stretch my legs."

Even this late, the indigo sky glowed with lingering daylight. If we had been in our Jersey neighborhood, the streets would have been crowded with people coming home from work or heading out to night jobs, on their way to meet friends or lovers, running to the bodega, walking a dog, in motion, always in motion, in throngs. In this neighborhood, there was so much space. Back in Jersey, my parents also lived in the suburbs, but in an older neighborhood without these broad sidewalks and blank, cookie-cutter houses.

A car passed us with only a single person inside, a woman driving, her face set in a tight mask of concentration. And it was almost a full minute before another car came along, this one with a man driving and a child alone in the back seat. And then another moment before a third went by, an SUV with tinted windows. Out on the highway, these vehicles packed together like people on a city sidewalk, but as they peeled off down their exit ramps, each went its separate way to soccer practice or Scouts or home for a sit-down dinner.

Now we had space to walk holding hands, swinging them a little without worrying we'd be knocked apart by a Segway or cursed by a commuter. Ahead of us, a car pulled up to our street's block of freestanding mailboxes, and a woman leaned out to unlock her box and withdraw a handful of envelopes. Then she drove a few houses down, pulled into her driveway, and got out, juggling the mail and a briefcase and her keys. A man jogged past on the opposite sidewalk, and in the distance I saw a teenager walking a shaggy dog. Michael and I weren't alone, but nobody jostled us or drove us together. Everyone was an island.

Michael and I crossed over Windswept Court and walked only a little ways before we saw it, a brick house like any other. The only sign of trauma was the garage, bowed in just as Rahmia had described it. Streaks of red paint marred the pale metal of the garage door, and bits of broken plastic glittered on the driveway.

Other than that, her house was indistinguishable from a house we'd passed on the previous block. The same builder had designed them all, the same landscaper had planted crape myrtles and box-wood, and the same homeowners' association had mandated the colors of the front doors and the height of the lawns.

Michael tugged my hand. "Look." He nodded to the street, and I saw black rubber streaks where the car must have skidded out of control.

"How fast do you think they were going?"

He paused, considering. "Not too fast. The door's banged up, but if they'd been going full tilt, a car could have smashed right through." Calculations must have been flashing through his mind like one of those mathematical word problems I could never solve.

Then one of the curtains in the front windows twitched, and I was suddenly self-conscious. Even when I saw it was Bibi, pop-ping up and down in the window under the edge of the curtain as she leapt, I tugged Michael's hand. Rahmia had felt like a poten-tial friend. I didn't want her to think I was some kind of stalker, checking up on her story.

As the daylight ebbed away, the lighted windows seemed to brighten, each a pinhole theater, inviting our gaze. In one, a ver-milion wall displayed an oversized poster of Marilyn Monroe. In another, a man watered plants, the circular front window framing him like a piece of performance art.

Everyday activities by everyday people, surrealistically ordinary.

We'd been walking in silent harmony, I thought, like we often did as a kind of transition, a space between our workday and our time together at home. But then Michael asked, "Did you get a recommendation from Dr. Johnson?" and my whole body tensed.

I'd forgotten. *My head was still so slow, and I'd opened the box from Aimee, and then Rahmia came by, and*—all the excuses spi-raled through me, fueled by shame.

"I didn't." I could hear the edge in my voice as clearly as Michael surely could. It wasn't his fault, it was mine. But, god-dammit, I was doing the best I could.

He didn't say anything, and that felt like a reproof.

On our walk home, we passed more ordinary, happy people with easy, uncomplicated lives, or at least that's the way they seemed—a jogger with a red baseball cap, a lady with a baby in a front pack and a collie on a leash, and a couple about our age, taking a walk like we were. They were on the other side of the street, so we gave each other half waves and swift smiles.

The man raised his chin, and I thought he'd probably say *Hey* instead of *Hi*. The woman had wildly curly red hair, and she smiled at me like we were in on a secret.

I couldn't smile back.

There were secrets, I thought, as Michael unlocked our front door. Secrets inside every house. Not the kind you could see through a window.

*　*　*

The next morning I woke to the movement of the bed, the disruption of the covers, and drowsed through the sounds of Michael showering. I could stay in bed all day. No one would miss me or pity me or say, "Have you seen Kacy?" But yesterday, I'd started to succumb to that siren song.

I'd gotten back under the covers and lost half a day, and it had only made things worse.

Once Michael's off to work, you'll have nine hours to huddle under your blanket fort. There's no reason to get up. There's nothing out there for you.

But I recognized that whisper, and I flung back the bedsheets. Aimee was an external saboteur, but just like in a horror movie, this call was coming from inside the house. Or, more precisely, my head. I couldn't be my own worst enemy anymore.

Michael came out of the bathroom, already dressed in a neatly pressed shirt and trousers, his hair still damp and his neck flushed. He grinned, and I knew my own hair must be a tangled mess, but he liked it. He asked, "What's your plan for today?"

My days used to be so full, packed with meetings and tasks for work and list after list of activities that might fill any free time. I missed being overscheduled.

"I'll find a doctor." I stood and started smoothing the bedclothes. Michael knew what kind of doctor I meant.

He took the other side of the coverlet and helped me pull it up neatly. "How about the SSS group? When do they get together next?"

Michael's new company was great about supporting spouses. The Spousal Support System had sent a thick packet of information home with him, just for me. Book clubs, organized outings, conversation groups in a dizzying array of languages. Gregarious women who had traveled the world and were conquering Sugar Land with confidence.

Not a chance I could handle that.

My overwhelm must have shown in my face, because Michael said, "Or something lower-key like that neighborhood group Elizabeth mentioned? Don't they have a meeting or something today?"

Right. The Bluebonnet women's group. "Maybe. I'm not sure. Are you done in the bathroom?"

"You could call her and get the details."

"We'll see." Now there was a slight edge to my voice, and Michael let it drop. He didn't need to organize a playdate for me. If I decided to go to this meeting, I was capable of finding out where it was.

After all, I'd gotten out of bed.

But I didn't want to send him off to work with distance between us. And Rahmia had made me feel a little bolder. It had been easy, talking with her. Or at least, listening while she talked. A group might even be less intimidating, because all the attention wouldn't be on me.

"I'll probably go."

He grinned. "I might be home late. Have a good time."

After my shower and coffee, I found the information. Actually, a child could have found the information. The group had a website, and their meetings were open to anyone. Usually their monthly meetings were held at the neighborhood's clubhouse, kind of a cross between a park pavilion and a community center funded by our HOA. But this meeting was the "Fall Kickoff" at the Sugar Land Country Club.

For a second I thought about forgetting the whole thing, telling Michael I couldn't find it, anything. But honestly, why should it make any difference whether I was braving a crowd of strangers in a casual or an upscale setting?

Opening that box, thinking about Aimee, had just brought it all closer to the surface. The entire story of my crappy past year filled me to the brim. It was all I could think about, all the time.

And if I wasn't careful, if I relaxed for even a second, I would vomit it all out. A group setting seemed safe.

I just wanted my existence to be less effort. A conversation that I didn't have to edit, an evening where I wasn't trying to prove anything. When Michael and I met, I'd just said whatever I wanted, and he did the same. Now he was so worried about me, and I was so desperate to appear okay, that we were performing our relationship instead of participating in it. I couldn't keep pretending to be okay; my poker face sucked. I had to get better for real.

Fortunately, there was time before the meeting to scroll through the list of mental health care providers covered by our new insurance. Screw trying to get a recommendation. I was going to make the very first appointment I could get.

*   *   *

I am friendly. I am brave. As I stood in front of the country club, my affirmations didn't change the truth. I would rather have faced death by firing squad a thousand times than attend even one women's club meeting.

I started at the welcome table, draped in bright blue and adorned with brochures, forms, pens, and several vases of faux bluebonnets. Two women sat behind it, one dressed in turquoise, the other in fuchsia, colors that would have made them stand out like tropical birds against the black-and-white palette of New York. I hesitated, wondering if I'd made another mistake, but then one saw me and smiled. "Come on over! If you're looking for the Bluebonnets, you're in the right place."

Haltingly, I approached, and the bright smiles and brighter colors seemed to intensify. The woman in fuchsia had dark hair pulled back into a fat ponytail, tied with a silken scarf. "You're new?" she asked.

When I nodded, she lit up like I'd made her day. "We are so glad you found us! If you'll go ahead and fill out a membership form and a name tag, Christy'll take your dues and give you a welcome bag." She pushed a little package across the table, and then her gaze shifted past me and she shrieked, "Ginny? Oh my God, it's been ages!"

I took my papers and moved down the table to an empty space. Was this the way I'd make connections? Maybe in a year, I'd be the one catching up with an old friend, although I couldn't imagine myself shrieking about it. Quickly, I filled out the forms and handed them to Christy, who also swiped my credit card.

"Don't forget your name tag," she reminded me as she pulled a blue-and-white-striped gift bag from under the table. "And here's your welcome bag. We'll be meeting in the big assembly room off to that side. Help yourself to coffee and something sweet before you go in."

The gift bag dangled awkwardly from my hand, the stiff paper too big to be jammed into my purse. Taking a deep breath, I walked toward the coffee station. I exchanged a quick smile with the woman filling her cup from a shining coffee chafer urn, but she left to rejoin a cluster of friends.

As I started filling my own cup, someone behind me asked, "Kacy?"

The coffee sloshed, staining the white tablecloth.

I turned to see Elizabeth, wearing the same kind of flowy trousers and dressy T-shirt she'd worn the night of our disastrous dinner. Her pleasant expression looked deliberate. I couldn't help but wonder if it had flickered when she'd first recognized me, or if she'd thought about avoiding me.

She was standing next to another woman, easily twice my age, whose silky halter top and oversized hoop earrings were what my mother would have deemed "not age appropriate," a phrase leveled equally against women her own age and my younger sister.

Elizabeth motioned me closer. "It's good to see you. This is Sandra. Sandy, Kacy and her husband just moved here."

Sandra didn't make a move to shake my hand, but she gave me a little nod. "Just moved here from where?"

Before I could answer, a woman shouted, "Five minutes, everyone. Get your coffee and grab a seat."

Perfect timing. Now it was natural for me to trail Elizabeth and Sandra into the big assembly room. A dozen tables for six were set up, and I slid into a seat next to Sandra. On my other side were two women in the middle of an animated conversation. Instead of a centerpiece, glossy origami paper was fanned out on the heavy white tablecloth. I reached out to touch the square closest to me, sleek with blue and purple waves of color.

The president—a sensible-looking woman in a crisp button-down shirt—welcomed everyone. After a few opening statements and a quick reference to this meeting's "fancy digs" that drew knowing chuckles, she introduced the speaker.

The lights dimmed, and as slides filled the screen, I was acutely conscious of the women around me. On one side, I kept catching a hiss or giggle from the never-ending whispered conversation. On the other, Sandra and Elizabeth kept their gaze on the speaker.

In this roomful of strangers, I was so lonely for a real friend.

Finally the speaker finished. As the lights came back up, the president took her place. "Don't go anywhere, ladies. You may have been wondering about the paper in the middle of the table. We're making origami stars to support literacy awareness. After you ladies transform these little squares into gorgeous works of art, I'll collect them, our volunteers will give them a shiny coating and some hanging loops, and we'll have them up for sale around the holidays. All proceeds go straight to building literacy here in Sugar Land. Directions are up here on the screen. And this whole month we're collecting books. I'm putting a big ole bin on my porch, so you can drop them off anytime. Thank you so much for all you do!"

She stepped down, and the noise level in the room swelled to fill her absence. I reached for a sheet of paper, finally confident that this was an activity I could do well. One of our museum events had been origami based, and I'd loved the way following the directions transformed a two-dimensional sheet into a mini sculpture. A glance at the instructions confirmed that this star wasn't terribly complicated. I had just made my first fold when Sandra said, "Liz, I can't figure this out. Can you get me started?"

Maybe Elizabeth winced when Sandy used her nickname, but she still said, "Sure. Why don't I make the first three folds, and then you can pop it out into the star shape?"

Elizabeth pulled a few pieces of paper closer and began to fold them. The two women to my left hadn't touched the origami. They had turned their chairs away from us to better talk with people from the other table. I popped my first star into shape and felt the same warmth I'd felt yesterday when I'd helped Rahmia. This was what I needed, to be proactive, to participate, and not just in this literacy project.

I steeled myself, glanced up at Sandy, and asked, "So, how long have you lived here?"

A slight arch to her eyebrow indicated that my question was a little too abrupt, but she said, "About seven years. There have been so many changes to the neighborhood. You wouldn't even have recognized it back then. Where did you buy?"

If Michael and I had been renting, would she even deign to speak to me? I told her my neighborhood, and she countered, "Not the Sullivan house?"

I hesitated, confused.

Resting her hands on top of the stack of paper, she asked, "Are you three houses past Windswept Court? A one-story?"

Nonplussed, I nodded. She was building up to something.

She widened her eyes, blinking like that would make her seem guileless. "You're very brave to live there. I'd just be too creeped out."

"What are you talking about?" Even as the words came out, I regretted them. This was exactly what Sandy hoped I'd say.

Fanning the papers out with idle fingers, she asked, "You know what happened to the guy who lived there before, don't you? I mean, didn't they have to disclose it or whatever?"

Elizabeth's lips thinned, and her hands moved even more quickly, folding the papers with sharp creases and passing them to Sandy, where they were piling up.

"I don't know what you're talking about," I said shortly, using a little extra force to sharpen my next pleat. She didn't need to know we'd bought it from a young couple whose father had recently died.

"Well." Sandy leaned forward, abandoning all pretense of doing work. "The old man who owned the house *died* right there in the bedroom."

Before I could say anything, Elizabeth tapped the half-folded stack of stars. "People die everywhere, Sandy."

"Not like this. They say he slipped and hit his head, there was blood everywhere, and he wasn't found for *three days*. The carpet was ruined. I just couldn't live in a house where something like that happened."

"Oh please. I'm not afraid of the dead." And my sharp retort not only shut Sandy up, it gave me a little thrill. This kind of low-stakes sparring made me feel like myself again.

While we'd been crafting and chatting, the president had been making the rounds, and she reached our table just as the three of us fell into an awkward silence. "I see we have a new member! I'm Michelle, president of the Bluebonnet Women's Club."

"Hi, I'm Kacy." She was too far away for a handshake, so I gave a little wave.

"Welcome, Kacy. I'm glad you found us. If you need anything, I know these two will take care of you. We like to pair up old members and new members." With a wave of her own, she moved on to the next table.

Elizabeth looked at me and smiled, but it was just a little too tight around the edges. Nice to know I was making friends so easily.

I had seven paper stars in front of me, and the stack of origami paper between us now seemed wildly optimistic. The two women next to me turned their chairs back around. One of them said, "Sandy probably knows."

Sandy dropped the star she'd almost popped into shape and leaned forward. "I probably know what?"

"Whose kids stole that car."

She shook her head. "Definitely from the apartments. The house they crashed into, wasn't that near you, Kacy?"

Without thinking, I said, "Two houses before Windswept. The car smashed right into the garage. It really scared Rahmia."

"Rahmia?" One side of Sandy's mouth pulled up in a half sneer.

The air conditioning suddenly seemed colder. "My neighbor, the homeowner. She was walking her dog, and when she got home, the police were there and the car, but the kids were gone."

"Was it a terrorist thing?" That would be where Sandy's mind went. As soon as she heard an Arabic name, she'd stopped worrying about the juvenile delinquents and moved straight to blaming the victim. I knew way too much about that game.

"Or a hate crime?" Elizabeth added.

I could feel my agitation rising, as if all the trauma of the whisper campaign against me were starting up against Rahmia. "How? It's just kids who stole a car. I think it was the road, the way it bends around. They lost control."

Sandy's lips pressed together, like it was a flimsy cover story and she for one wouldn't buy it.

And that made me keep talking. If only I could make her see Rahmia's round face, her fear, the way she lavished love on Bibi. But I feared Sandy wouldn't look beyond Rahmia's hijab. "She's really nice. I've seen her walking her son to school."

Maybe Elizabeth thought she could defuse racism with logic. "There are always kids setting off fireworks on the playground or spray-painting the bridge. Plus, almost sixty percent of our neighbors are East Asian, and I haven't heard about any problems. This was just a random accident."

"That's right, you both live in the *new* section of Bluebonnet." Sandy's nose pinched like she could smell the nouveau riche stink on those of us relegated to the melting pot of this lush planned community. "I just think there might be more to the story. You can't tell about those people, can you?"

Heat rose in my face, and before I could check the words, I said, "Oh, I can tell a lot about *some* people, bitch."

Sandy gasped, and my hand flew to my mouth. Elizabeth's hands were still, the women next to me stopped talking, the whole table was staring.

I grabbed my purse and strode to the door, barely keeping it under a run. The tables closest to the door didn't spare me a glance, they hadn't heard what I said, but I wasn't kidding myself. Anyone who hadn't heard me firsthand would hear it second-hand from Sandy. And this wasn't a swear-out-loud kind of place. Instead of making Sandy look bad, I'd made myself look worse. Vulgar, young, déclassé.

Racist bitch, I thought viciously. I wasn't going to burst into tears, but I might burst into flames. I wanted to drive at top speed, I wanted to scream, I wanted to crash.

There. I spotted a haven, a ladies' room, and veered into it. Before I got behind the wheel, I needed to splash some water on my face, calm down. I couldn't lose control, but I couldn't hold it all in.

The restroom was empty, but I didn't want to run the faucet. I didn't want water cooling my face. A lone coffee cup smudged with peony-pink lipstick sat on the marble counter top. Without hesitation, I snatched it up and hurled it at the wall. It caught the edge of a brass sconce and shattered, spraying bits of china every-where. And before I could catch my breath, from behind me flew another cup, exploding like the first.

I whipped around.

In the doorway stood a woman with curly red hair pulled back into a loose knot and her hand just lowering from the cup she'd thrown.

She looked familiar, I knew I'd seen her somewhere, but in my shock, all I could do was gape.

In a husky voice, she said, "Nobody should have to bust shit up alone."

4

Helen: We've talked before about how underrated women are as killers.

Julia: It's true. I mean, there's this idea of being nurturing—

Helen: Or just not as physically strong—

Julia: That poison is a woman's weapon—

Helen: Or a coward's. Like you have to be brave to shoot or whack someone?

Julia: I think only the Mafia whacks people.

Helen: But the truth is there are plenty of examples of female serial killers—Belle Gunness, Myra Hindley, Aileen Wuornos, Genene Jones. And just like Ted Bundy or Dennis Rader, they were hidden in plain sight. If they had acted like serial killers—

Julia: Whatever that means—

Helen: Then they wouldn't have had so many victims and they would have been caught sooner. Nannie Doss, Lydia Sherman, and Belle Gunness were active for over a decade each. From everything I've read, nobody was even looking for a serial killer linked to any of the murders they'd committed. They were just living their lives. That's the thing: female serial killers—like all serial killers—have to blend into their community to escape detection. These women have friends, husbands, neighbors, even kids.

Julia: Serial killers, they're "just like us." Creepiest new feature in *Us Weekly*.

Helen: And the serial killer we're talking about today was no different. Family, friends, neighbors—she had it all. And then she met Kacy Tremaine.

CHAPTER

5

THE WAITING ROOM was nothing like the one I'd been to in New Jersey.

My old therapist's waiting room had been New England Creative, but this one was Manhattan Hardass. The walls were a soft white, the carpet a neutral gray, the furniture darker gray and chrome. All of it matched everything else—the floor, the lamps. There was also a receptionist hidden behind a sliding frosted window. Even though I was the only person here, she spoke in hushed tones, passing me an electronic tablet with all the forms to sign and assuring me Dr. Lindsey would be with me soon.

The only sound was the air conditioning, shushing like a white noise machine. No magazines on the table, no brochures advertising support groups or shiny new medications, nothing. This waiting room was a cryogenic chamber.

I turned my phone over in my hands, remembering the aggressive rush I'd felt yesterday. Swearing and breaking things had made me feel more like my old self than months of medication. Even if my old self had been soft-spoken and careful.

Last night I'd told Michael the whole story, and it had filled me with triumph rather than shame. He must have thought smashing things in a bathroom was better than sobbing on the floor of one, because he just laughed. "You probably said what everyone was thinking. If this club doesn't work out, there's always the one through my work. And who *was* that woman?"

Lena. Lena Voss. Born and raised in Arkansas but a Texas resident for two decades. My neighbor.

But I hadn't known that right away. All I'd known was that I wasn't alone, that someone supported me, even in my rage. She'd put a hand on my shoulder. "You're okay now. Whatever happened, just fuck it." The fragments of our coffee cups still rocked on the china-dusted floor as we strode out into the lobby.

"Is everyone looking at me?" I'd whispered.

"Nope. They're all too busy worrying about their own selves. But you could smile a little. Don't want anyone to think I'm marching you to your death."

Lena had pushed the big front door open, and the frigid air conditioning gave way to a heavy wall of humidity. Across the expansive parking lot, other women were heading for their cars, and one of them gave Lena a little wave.

That simple wave triggered my memory. I said, "You live in my neighborhood. We saw you last night, my husband and I."

Her laugh would have been a full-bodied and uninhibited guffaw on anyone else, but it seemed perfectly sized and natural as breath for her. "Well, nice to meet you, neighbor. I'm Lena, and you are . . . ?"

"Kacy. We just moved in."

"So this is your first Bluebonnets meeting, and you're already throwing dishes. Who pissed you off?"

"Sandy."

"Ah, figures. That woman acts like she's auditioning for *Desperate Housewives*. Don't let her get to you. There's a little drama at every meeting, but it always blows over."

I wanted to believe her, to believe in drama that was fleeting, not life ruining. I wanted to be confident and strong, to look to the future. Apparently I couldn't get there on my own.

Maybe Dr. Lindsey could make that happen.

My former therapist had his office in an old Victorian with battered hardwood floors and white plaster walls. The furniture was well-worn leather and mismatched end tables, and Dr. Johnson matched the decor. He wore Mr. Rogers–style sweaters and often had a pair of glasses on his face and another pushed back on his head. His beard was pure white and he occasionally brushed it with his fingers while I was talking, as if reminding himself it was there. He sat on a chair by the door and I sat on a sofa near him and mostly cried. Sometimes he passed me a tissue. When our time was up, he would say something vague and I'd leave.

The only thing of substance he'd given me was a prescription. But I hadn't expected any more help than that. The problem wasn't imaginary. Unless he could turn back time, appear at the museum and warn me about Aimee, denounce her and exonerate me, keep me from being so stupid, so trusting, so naïve, there wasn't anything he could do for me.

But six months and a big move later, I was still a certifiable basket case. At least, until yesterday. I tapped out some new affirmations on my fingers. *I am strong. I speak up. I am not afraid.* I hesitated, tapping my fourth finger before choosing the obvious. *I am ready for therapy.*

"Remember," Michael had warned. "You don't have to commit to Dr. Lindsey. We're going to find a therapist that you connect with, one that can help."

I had connected with my old psychiatrist, more or less. Something about his clichéd contemporary Freud appearance and non-threatening passivity gave me the space to fall apart. I didn't feel self-conscious or like I had to present a false front. He didn't expect better of me, like my dad, or want to coddle me, like my mom, or suffer all the collateral damage like Michael. He was just there.

And I was still the same.

I took out my phone, but the internet didn't pull up. No signal. Was this building made of solid lead? Even the wireless networks were locked. Every single one. Maybe it was the universe cutting me off from my online stalking addiction. No matter how many times I checked up on Aimee, all I got was a stomachful of envy, hatred, and grief. The residue still coated my insides, and I dropped my phone back into my bag.

Then a little light blinked by the receptionist's window, and the door opened. A man walked out quickly, without looking around, tunnel-visioning his way across the room to the opposite door. He opened it and was gone.

"Kacy?" A woman leaned through the still-open door. She was older than me, maybe ten years or so, wearing the kind of professional outfit I knew well. Black trousers, silk blouse, slim blazer. Her hair was a sleek bob, shining in a brown as neutral as her waiting room.

Dread pooled in my gut. This was it, the moment before she knew my pathetic story, the gap when I might still be anything— a woman who suspected her husband of cheating, a recovering drug addict, a high-powered professional with a bone-deep sense of ennui.

I am strong. I speak out. And then with a rush of heat, I added, *I bust shit up.*

I rose to my feet, and she held the door wider. "Come on back."

* * *

The first session had gone as well as it could have; at least, that's what I told myself. After warming up by answering some questions about my medication, my eating and sleep, I'd plunged into the story of me and Aimee, the same one I'd been running over and over in my head for six months. How I'd thought we were friends, what the first signs of betrayal were, how stupid I felt, how I couldn't trust my own judgment, so maybe everything that happened really was my fault. Sometimes in the rush of my words, I almost expected her to sympathize with me, or at least acknowledge how terrible Aimee was and how much I'd suffered. But all Dr. Lindsey did was make mild noises that encouraged me to keep on talking.

The time was up before I knew it.

She shut her notebook, and we looked at each other. Was she going to make a pronouncement? *In my professional opinion, you are a whiny, screwed-up excuse for a human being and you should get the fuck over it.*

But what she actually said was, "Let's set a weekly appointment, if that works for you?"

When I nodded, she stood up and opened the door to the hallway. "Sharon at the front desk will get you scheduled."

On the way home, I ran errand after errand—picking up new towels and blackout curtains, stopping by a plant nursery for some mint to place by the back door, and wandering through the largest grocery store I'd ever seen. But there was only so long I could stall. I didn't have anywhere else to be, and the empty house was waiting. After my emotional purge in the therapist's office, I felt hollowed out, laid bare. And it wasn't only my own ghosts waiting there anymore.

When I told Michael what Sandy had said about the previous owner, it hadn't bothered him at all. "First, it's just gossip," he'd pointed out. "And besides, what matters more? That he lived a happy life here, or that he died here? It's only because these houses are so new that people are freaked out about living in a place where someone died. In New England, you couldn't find a place where someone hadn't."

Lying next to him in our bed, it had seemed like he was right. The hardwood floors in our bedroom gleamed innocently in the moonlight. I wasn't squeamish, and there was nothing creepy about our house.

But now as I drove into our neighborhood, I wondered if those gorgeous hardwood floors were exposed only because the carpet had been so soaked with blood. I didn't want to go home, but I'd run out of errands. Turning onto my street, I was blinded for a minute by the glare of sunlight off Rahmia's windows. I pulled into my driveway, turned off the engine, and hesitated. The temperature rose so quickly in the car that I got out, leaving my bags in the trunk. Nothing I'd bought was perishable.

I'd walk to the mailbox, or maybe farther. Maybe I'd just keep walking until Michael came home. Or longer. How long could I go before I outwalked my own thoughts? Telling my story hadn't erased the memory of Aimee, but it had given me a glimpse of life without that emotional burden.

And it would still be empty.

Once at the block of mailboxes, I opened the little door to ours and pulled out the mass of paper jammed inside—a rolled-up glossy magazine, a few advertising fliers and a postcard, and an envelope addressed to "current resident."

As I shoved everything back into the box so I wouldn't have to hold it while I walked, I got a better look at the postcard. I yanked it back out and held it in both hands. Not a coupon for pizza or the promise of a free car wash. The front of the postcard displayed the Martina V. Umana Museum, the place where I'd spent so many hours curating, encouraging, and creating art. Longing and grief flooded me. They thought I was a thief, a liar, and they'd still kept me on some kind of mailing list? *You're fired, but don't forget to attend our next exhibition.*

But how had they gotten my new address?

I flipped the postcard over.

In Aimee's spiky handwriting, I read, "Don't you wish you were here?"

Hands shaking, I tore the card, over and over again, as if I could destroy Aimee and the museum and the entire past year. Tearing it wasn't enough. I wanted to burn it and then bury the ashes.

Leaving the mailbox open and my key hanging out of its lock, I wheeled around and smacked right into someone. Hard.

I cried out, dropping the scraps of paper from my nerveless fingers.

Then strong hands grasped my shoulders and a familiar voice said, "You're okay. Take a breath."

Blinking to clear my vision, I saw Lena, her brow furrowed, her red hair brilliant in the sunlight.

"I'm not crazy," I couldn't help saying. "I'm really not."

"Well, damn," she said with a grin. "Then I guess I'm the only nutjob here. You might need these." With a quick motion, she shut the mailbox door and dropped my keys into my hand.

I clenched them convulsively. "It's just this woman, my friend—"

"Let's walk it off. You can tell me everything."

And in a rush, I did.

Maybe talking about Aimee with the therapist had loosened the jar lid, but as I walked with Lena past one blank-faced brick house after another, the whole story came pouring out: not just what Aimee had done, how it had ended, but also the way we'd met, funny things she always said, weird little inside jokes we had.

"Aimee used to send me postcards, not because she was traveling but just because," I told Lena. A bright picture of a cat or an art print from the museum gift shop. Almost every week one would appear in my mailbox, stamped and addressed in her distinctive handwriting and bearing a single question. *Have you ever sat on the sill of an open window? If you were a lipstick, what color would you be?* No signature. None needed. Just a way of saying hi or surprising me even in her absence. And I'd send her a postcard back with my answer.

Another thing I'd lost when she did what she did. Another sharp blade to my gut when I got this new postcard. "She sent me another one, just now, as a jab. That's why I was so upset."

"What a bitch," Lena said.

That's the reaction I'd wanted from the therapist. Now that I was getting it, something contrary inside me still wanted to make excuses for my former friend. Instead, I just shrugged like *What can you do?*

"She totally betrayed you. She should be in jail."

"Maybe karma—"

Lena stopped walking and grabbed my arm to hold me still. "Screw karma. That's like waiting around and hoping an anvil will fall on her. No, she's a disgrace to all women and she needs to pay."

I knew this was feeding the worst parts of myself, but my anger felt so hot, so strong, so different from the soul-sapping exhaustion of being hurt. I was tired of being a wounded animal. "You know, when she was standing there in the director's office, accusing me, I couldn't believe it. It felt like she'd killed my real best friend, the one that did all that nice stuff. Because that person felt real. I loved her, and now she's gone, and the murderer looks just like her."

"It's the mind games that make women the worst. My mother—" Lena looked away. "Well, she was one of those women who hates other women, but she could play all their games. Just like Aimee. And Sandy. And too many people who don't get what's coming to them."

"I'm sorry." Maybe I hadn't been grateful enough for my own mother, her even-keeled unconditional love. The only thing she wanted me to do was be happy. And that was the area where I'd failed her the most. "Do you have any brothers or sisters?"

"Nope. Only child."

That was another thing I should have felt grateful for—my sisters. I knew if I needed them, if something happened to Michael, if our house burned down, I'd always have a place to go. But a sister both was and wasn't a friend. We weren't the same age or in the same stage of life or even in the same zip code. We had the same laugh and the same parents, but we were all three very different people. Maybe we would have been friends if we hadn't been related, but being sisters meant we wouldn't ever *just* be friends.

Of course—given what happened with Aimee—wasn't that a reason to be thankful? Friends might disappear, but my sisters would be stuck with me for life. Whether they liked me or pitied me or found me exhausting.

I don't know what my face looked like, but Lena said, "Screw her. We're friends now, and we'll be fucking unstoppable."

And it was okay, I felt okay, like whatever I said, whatever had happened, it didn't matter now. There was a future where I wasn't alone.

By the time we finished walking a loop of our neighborhood, I could feel sweat beading at the back of my neck and under my arms.

As if she could read my mind, Lena said, "It's hot as hell out here. I guess you had four seasons up north? We've just got two— scorching and bearable. That last one won't come around again until November."

"I don't think I can make it three more months."

"You'll have to come over and hang out by the pool. I make a mean margarita."

We'd reached the block of mailboxes again, and I slowed down, suddenly a little shy. "I'd like that. Can we exchange numbers?"

After the awkwardness of entering her number into my phone and sending a text to give her mine, I said, "Thanks. I mean, I really needed—"

"Hey." She held up her hands as if to ward me off, but with a grin. "That's what friends are for. And you're going to be seeing a lot more of me."

I nodded and held my phone up as if proving that I'd be in touch. Then I turned, but I'd gone only a few steps when I realized Lena was following me.

Stepping to one side, I slowed down so she could catch up and glanced at her questioningly.

She laughed, that deep, rolling laugh. "I forgot to ask where you live. I'm the second from the corner."

I knew in my head we were just in the honeymoon stage of friendship, too early to really know anything about each other, but I couldn't stop the feeling of joy that rolled over me. There would be so many coincidences that made us seem fated to be friends. And this was the first.

We were next-door neighbors.

6

After I waved good-bye to Lena, I unloaded the curtains and towels from the car and carried them up to the front door. Beside it was a package that hadn't been there when I'd parked an hour ago.

I set down the bags, unlocked the door, and picked up the package. It was a shoe box not wrapped in tape or sent through the mail. My name was written on the top in black permanent marker, and my heart started to beat a warning.

Aimee wasn't here, she couldn't be, but I glanced up and down the street. Whoever had left the box had come and gone while Lena and I were walking. No one appeared to be watching, but the malicious postcard was still on my mind.

I removed the lid and found a note, written in a precise, dark script:

Kacy,

I'm sorry I missed you. I thought you might enjoy making more origami stars. We're collecting them through the end of the month. Please call me if you'd like to work on them together.

Best, Elizabeth

She'd included her phone number at the bottom of the page, and underneath the note were two neat stacks of origami paper.

I could imagine Elizabeth choosing each word carefully, hesitating as she decided what to say. Her note was as sleek and controlled as her blond ponytail, and I didn't know what to make of it.

Was this a thoughtful gesture because she'd noticed I enjoyed the origami, at least until Sandy ruined everything? Or was she implying that I should have done more work before swearing and storming off?

Pressing the lid back onto the box, I set it on the kitchen table. First I'd finish unloading the car, and then I'd put away the groceries, wash the towels, hang the curtains, and plant the mint I'd picked up at the nursery. Then, if there was any time left, I'd think about the origami. I wouldn't think about unboxing a new piece of art, the excitement of a new exhibit, even poring over a museum catalog. Those feelings were all mixed with Aimee now, tainted. A life of washing towels and gardening was all I had. It would have to be enough.

By the time I rescued the mint, it was limp from the intensified heat of the car. I carried it straight through to the backyard and set it down so I could search for the hose and a trowel.

*   *   *

All the backyards in our neighborhood were enclosed by high fences with gates facing the street. To get from one yard to the other, you had to go out through the front gate and then back through the other one. Our own backyard was a rectangle, barely twelve feet deep and a few feet wider than the house itself, planted with a hardy green grass. "St. Augustine," our realtor had said. "Shade-tolerant carpet grass." She might as well have been speaking a foreign language, but Michael nodded and asked some follow-up questions about our new automated sprinkler system.

Then, through a loose slat in the fence, I caught a glimpse of blue water in Lena's yard, promising the cool relief that no shade could deliver in this humidity.

Giving up on finding the hose, I ran the mint under the spigot, blasting it a little too hard. When I turned off the water, I heard Lena say, "That you, Kacy?"

I turned and glimpsed her distinctive red hair through the gap in the fence. "I'm trying to plant some mint."

"Need any help?"

"I can't find a trowel." Although, after looking, I wasn't completely sure Michael and I even owned one.

"Hold on, I've got one."

She moved away from the fence, and I set the dripping plastic pot down. A few mint leaves, bruised by the force of the water, released their scent, the sole hint of coolness in the heavy, humid air.

In only a second, Lena was back. "Heads up!" and a small hand trowel flew over the fence, glinting in the sunlight.

"Thanks." I bent and jabbed the trowel at the tough ground, hacking out a small hole. I thought Lena might go back to what she'd been doing, but instead she stayed by the fence, where the slats were too narrow for me to see anything except the shadow of her presence.

After a minute, I felt like I should say something else, so I added, "We've been talking about a garden, so I thought I'd start with a little mint. Think it'll grow all right?"

"Oh sure, mint will be fine. But the ground here is like gumbo. Red clay and really erratic water. Depending on what you want to grow, it's probably better to do raised beds. Some stuff grows like crazy, but root vegetables struggle."

I set the mint into the hole and pressed the earth around it. "Michael's worried about the sprinkler system. He thinks a vegetable bed might not need the same schedule as the grass."

"Brady's working on that too. We should get those guys together. Why don't you both come over tomorrow night? We'll grill and hang out by the pool."

For the first time in months, I felt flushed with success. "We'd love to. Look out, here comes your trowel back."

As it spun end over end into the yard next door, catching the light, I almost smiled.

This would be something to share with Michael. I could make friends, good ones.

* * *

Michael was tired that night, although he tried to hide it. He agreed to dinner the next night, and we watched television together snuggled up on the sofa. I didn't tell him about the postcard.

Before I went to bed, I turned my bottle of antidepressants upside down so that it stood on its cap next to my sink. In the morning it was a simple visual cue to take my pill, or a reminder that I hadn't. Dr. Lindsey had mentioned tapering off, but vaguely, like it was something we might work up to. Now I thought about walking in the sunshine with Lena, and giving up the pills seemed almost possible. At the same time, panic fluttered in the base of my stomach. I didn't ever want to feel the way I had six months ago. Never again.

In bed, the pillow was cool against my cheek, and I fell asleep almost immediately, barely registering that Michael was reading something on his phone beside me.

When I woke with a start, it was still dark. While the black-out curtains I had hung kept any light from seeping in through the bedroom windows, the skylight in the bathroom let in just enough moonlight to make out the outlines of the doorframe, the dresser, the crease where walls met floor and ceiling.

I couldn't make out the floor itself; the dark wood was swallowed in the night. Now I couldn't forget Sandy's words: *There was blood everywhere, and he wasn't found for three days.* And I couldn't pretend that image didn't haunt me. I should have asked Lena about it when we were walking. After all, the dead man had been her neighbor. Maybe she'd tell me Sandy was lying; maybe he'd died peacefully of old age. Maybe there was nothing to be afraid of.

But my mind offered up another half-dozen reasons for fear— the abandoned cars and missing people Rahmia had described, the home invasions and traffic accidents and smash-and-grab robberies at gas stations and Aimee out there laughing.

Beside me, Michael's breathing was so quiet that I put a hand on his back, just to feel its rise and fall, but instead of being lulled back to sleep, I could feel the last shreds of drowsiness leave my brain. I was keenly awake, and the idea of lying in bed seemed intolerable.

I slipped out from under the covers, snagged my phone from the bedside table, and padded quietly out of the room. Because of the open floor plan, half of the house stretched like a corridor from the front door to the back, arching over the living room, dining room, kitchen, and family room.

As my fingers patted the wall, feeling for the light switch but turning on the ceiling fan instead, light filtered through the sky-light in the kitchen, sinister light, the kind in an old horror movie, the kind edged with pools of darkness where things could hide.

And I noticed for the first time a small red light facing the bedroom, blinking in the corner where the back wall met the ceiling, like an eye watching over the exit. It must be part of the security system. I groped for the light switch, flipped it on, and turned off the fan, leaving it to run down in lazy circles. The red beam wasn't noticeable with the overhead lights on, but the little white box that held it definitely looked like part of our alarm system. Nothing to worry about.

Two o'clock in the morning. Too late to still be up, too early to rise.

I picked up the box of paper Elizabeth had left and sat down on the sofa. Somehow, after only a week, my body had adjusted to the one-hour time shift. If Aimee was awake, it was an hour later for her, and she might be coming in from a club, kicking off her heels and dropping her keys, checking her phone . . . but there my imagination failed. Who would she be texting now? The only thing that used to make my insomnia better had been knowing I wasn't alone, that there were two of us awake, our texts glowing fireflies to hold back the dark.

Now I had to stop kidding myself—I hadn't known Aimee then, and I didn't know what she might be doing now. She could be slipping out of the museum director's bed; she might be working late with only the security guard for company; she might be online, hunting for someone else to scam; she might even be scouring the internet for any updates on my inactive social media accounts. I should have deleted them all, but if I had, I wouldn't be able to see anyone else's. Correction: I wouldn't be able to see *hers*.

After a false start, my hands remembered the motions, slowly smoothing and creasing, as a new picture formed in my mind— Aimee thinking about me in these wee hours, hunting down my new address, writing a postcard. Malicious, yes, and creepy, but it was weirdly satisfying to know I wasn't alone in post-stalking her, that she hadn't just chosen me as her scapegoat and then forgotten me. If I'd gotten that taunting note a few days ago, I would have been devastated. I would have been back under the covers, wishing the world away.

I ran my nail over the one sharp angle of the origami, then tugged it until I was holding a perfect paper star.

Maybe I could imagine a tomorrow made sweeter knowing that my happiness might make Aimee crazy. Lena's voice, rough edged with anger, echoed in my mind. *She's a disgrace to all women, and she needs to pay.*

Aimee had sent that postcard to hurt me, but all she'd done was make me angry. Finally, after all this time, the heavy sadness in me was giving way to fire.

There wasn't anything to stop me from sending a postcard of my own.

*   *   *

The next night we were hanging out in Lena's backyard and I sat at the edge of her pool, the August air warm and heavy, the water like cool silk on my calves. I swirled my foot, sending eddies across the surface.

Lena was getting another pitcher of margaritas, and the first two I'd had were already softening the edges of my world. Over the top of the high fences, the sky was a deep indigo and the moon was up. A bug lantern on the far corner of the yard crackled, and the scent of citronella overpowered even the lingering aroma of charred beef.

Michael was walking along the fence line with Lena's husband, Brady. They stopped to investigate the loose slat between our two yards. Michael had a lower tolerance for alcohol than me, and from his expansive gestures, I knew he was buzzed.

Brady wasn't as tall as Michael—he and Lena could probably stand eye to eye. His hair was as close-cropped as if he'd been shorn on an army base, and his biceps strained the sleeves of a Sugar Land Skeeters T-shirt. "Do you like baseball?" he'd asked when he saw me noticing it, and when I faltered, not wanting to offend him with the truth, he laughed. "No worries. This isn't a team you support for its stats."

Now he and Michael came over to me, their strides in sync despite the difference in their heights. Brady caught my eye and winked, like we were in on some kind of joke. Maybe I frowned a little, and he smirked, saying only, "Let me see what's taking Lena so long with those 'ritas."

As he disappeared into the house, Michael slid out of his canvas shoes and sat down, dangling his own hairy legs into the pool. I kicked him gently and he bumped me with his shoulder.

"What were you talking about over there?" I asked.

"The way the sprinklers go, there's a space they don't hit, by the fence, so you either have to water by hand or it just dries out. We were thinking about putting a tiered garden there and rigging up a kind of irrigation thing, old-school like the Egyptians used."

"You were talking about the Egyptians?" Oh, it felt so sweet to be amused, to be having a good time. I'd missed this feeling.

"They had this reservoir drip irrigation system that would keep the beds moist without rotting out the fence like a spray of water would. But you'd need to do both sides."

"So you're having fun?" I knew he was, but saying it would mean I'd found us quality friends.

"Sure. He's an interesting guy." Michael leaned over and drew something on the surface of the water, a sketch absorbed even as his finger moved.

Brady came back onto the patio with a fresh pitcher of drinks. "She'll be out in a sec. Hey, Michael, I think I've got some lumber and stuff in the garage. Let's see what all we'll need." He set the margaritas down on the wrought-iron patio table. "Think this'll keep you busy while we're gone, Kacy?"

Before I could do more than grin, Michael was on his feet, water rolling down his calves. He slipped his wet feet into his shoes and followed Brady through the front gate.

All the salt was gone from the rim of my glass. I was ready for a refill, but I didn't want to stand up. Leaning back on my elbows, I could see a few stars above the haze of neighborhood lights. The air stirred, warm on my neck but cool where Michael had splashed me on his way past. Up north this time of year, I might have sensed a slight chill of autumn after the sun went down. A few trees might show the first signs of changing color, but here in Texas, it was swimming pools and margaritas.

"You look comfortable." Lena had come out without me even noticing. Michael probably wasn't the only one who was buzzed.

Good thing we didn't need to drive home. The thought struck me as funny, and Lena smiled back at me as she picked up my glass and refilled it.

She sat down beside me, her hair slipping free from its pony-tail. She pulled it loose, shaking her head, and I remembered wanting to ask her about the previous owner of the house. I started with, "Sandy—"

With the hair elastic in her teeth and one hand holding her hair in place, Lena said, "That bitch."

I stopped, startled, as she wrapped the band around a pony-tail from which wiry strands still escaped. Then she said, "Sorry, that's just how I think of her in my mind. That-bitch-Sandy. What about her?"

"She said somebody died in my house and it was kind of gruesome."

"Please. Any excuse for drama. You want me to spit in her iced tea?"

I must have looked confused, because she laughed again, the sound rolling across the backyard. "Brady's heading back to her place tomorrow. She designed her own tile backsplash, and now she hates it. Just hates it. But somehow it's our fault for not pointing her in a different direction. Which—news flash—I did, but she didn't listen. It's the great custom light installation fiasco of last year all over again. Dumb and mean is a bad combina-tion. I swear, if she gives us grief about the payment, I'm cutting her off."

"So she was lying about my house?"

"Yeah, the former owner died, but he was old. No big deal."

The lime from my margarita puckered the back of my throat, but I asked, "What was he like?"

"How do you mean?"

"Did you ever see him?"

"He was fine. Kind of a pain about us bringing our trash bins in on time and leaving work vans in the driveway. But once one of our packages was misdelivered, and he brought it over. Not real friendly, but whatever."

Watching our feet slow-kicking back and forth in the water, I found Sandy's malice, our house's history, and even my own past blurring. What did it matter? I had nothing to worry about. This moment was enough. It was perfect.

And maybe Lena felt the same warm glow, because she clicked her glass against mine. "Compared to that guy, y'all are a definite improvement."

5

Helen: Now we have to discuss the facts of the crime. This couple killed over a dozen victims that we know for sure, both men and women.

Julia: That's weird, right? Because serial killers usually stick to a preferred gender or victimology. They're what you'd call "resistant to change."

Helen: Understatement! In fact, Dean Corll, "the Candyman," took exception when his accomplice showed up with a girl victim instead of a boy, and that fight led to his death. The Gallego couple preferred teenage girls, the Moorhouse Murderers killed women, as did Infante and Villeda and the Hillside Stranglers, while the Moors Murderers—Ian Brady and Myra Hindley—preyed on children.

Julia: Crimes of opportunity.

Helen: Definitely. They'd drive around until they saw a potential victim.

Julia: Someone easy to overpower.

Helen: True. That wasn't the case with the team we're discussing today. They preyed on men, women, young—well, teenagers—and old. That's a big reason nobody suspected a serial killer was operating in the area. No common victimology. Some of their victims were strong. Like Marcus Fontenot. He was ex-military, and even though he was older—

Julia: How old was he?

Helen: [sound of papers] He was . . . over seventy. Here it is. Seventy-five. But he was a big guy. Six feet even.

Julia: Not the easiest target.

Helen: And that's so strange. One of the earliest targets was a young woman, another was a teenage boy, but some victims like Marcus would be a struggle to subdue.

Julia: Assuming he had enough time to struggle.

Helen: That's the thing. Maybe it seemed less dangerous, being approached by two people—

Julia: Especially when one's a woman—

Helen: Exactly. He let his guard down.

CHAPTER

7

Now days had gone by since I'd told someone—more than one person—about my past, and no one seemed to care. No tar, no feathers, no public shaming. So, when my phone buzzed with a text and then another, I didn't panic. Sitting at the kitchen table with my coffee, I sipped it deliberately, savoring. I had a new number, a new life, a new friend. My phone wasn't a coiled snake, poised to strike.

In the weeks following Aimee's betrayal, an article had been published in the local paper, a statement had been made by the museum, and suddenly I was receiving hate texts and prank calls. A hundred messages from strangers made it clear they thought I hadn't gotten half the punishment I deserved, and each had a special reason I should be ashamed—not only of what I'd supposedly done, but of my very existence. Entitled, sheltered, spoiled.

And then they'd call me lucky for getting off unpunished.

Lena hadn't given a shit about any of that, and the first new text on my phone was from her. *Just making sure y'all stumbled home okay* and a winking emoji.

I texted back: *Margaritas=happy. Thnx . . . next time on us.*

Then I opened the text from the unknown sender and read: *Hi Kacy, The Bluebonnets are working on a fundraising event for the literacy project and I thought your experience might prove helpful. We have our first committee meeting over lunch today. Is there any way I might pick you up at eleven? I apologize for the short notice and appreciate your help. Elizabeth*

Well, maybe freaking out at a dinner party and swearing at a social gathering was the right way to win friends. And Lena had accepted the true me. This could be my chance to break through with Elizabeth. Committee meetings and event planning were familiar territory from my old life. Before I could overthink anything, I responded: *Sounds good. I'll be ready.*

Two hours, three outfit changes, and an application of makeup later, I slipped into the passenger seat of Elizabeth's sensible SUV. Her blond hair hung loose and sleek, and her eyes were shaded by Chanel sunglasses. She looked impeccably unapproachable.

But it was too late to back out. I pulled the door shut, and she said, "I hope you don't mind, but we're meeting downtown. It's about a half hour away."

And just like that, my nerves returned. This wasn't Lena, with her devil-may-care approach to life. This was Elizabeth, who maybe liked me, maybe wanted to be friends.

Or maybe just pitied me. After all, I'd sobbed in her bathroom and sworn at the Bluebonnet meeting. One more strike and I might be out of chances.

We drove out of the neighborhood, two lanes becoming four, and entered the highway, where the number doubled again, with lanes entering and exiting, funneling cars over and across the whole city. Even though we weren't in the heart of Houston yet, buildings unrolled on either side as far as I could see, just as many and as tall as up north, but with more sky arching above. The vastness of the sky only made the sheer number of houses, apartments, offices, and hospitals that much more staggering.

Big as Texas was, there were plenty of people to fill it up.

As if she knew what I was thinking, Elizabeth said, "There's so much new construction, even in our neighborhood. The builders promise that people can get their kids into the existing schools, but then we end up rezoning and the protests start."

"Is that something you think about? The schools?"

Her sunglasses hid her expression, but she hesitated before saying, "Not yet. But it never hurts to plan ahead."

So we were both still on the threshold, not newly married, no babies. Maybe someday we'd be signing our kids up for preschool together, but not yet.

Not yet.

The restaurant was just as big as everything else in Texas, but it wasn't a steakhouse or Tex-Mex theme. The blown-glass art-work, the airy interior, and the eclectic menu made it sophisticated yet accessible.

And the women we met were just as polished and warm. Inés was the wife of an Argentinian surgeon, a "visiting scholar" at the medical school; Rachael was a graphic designer, pregnant with her first child; and an empty chair right next to me was reserved for Alondra.

Rachael said to us, "She texted me her order and said we should get started. You know how it is—a new case, a big-deal client—but she'll be here. Eventually."

"She's a lawyer?" I whispered to Elizabeth as we sat down.

"Criminal defense," she whispered back. "Always busy but really nice."

I unfolded my napkin, sipped my water, and kept quiet, let-ting the conversation and the business of ordering flow around me. If I messed this up, who knew if Elizabeth would give me another chance, let alone the Bluebonnets.

As Rachael asked Elizabeth about someone I didn't know. Elizabeth looked away and knocked her napkin on the floor. Inés took that opportunity to ask me some easy questions—where I'd moved from, what Michael did—and I turned them right back on her until our drinks were poured, our menus had been removed, and the server departed.

Rachael glanced down at her phone. "Inés, you know that car we were talking about, the one with Louisiana plates?"

Inés glanced at me, making sure I was paying attention. "First, we noticed it on the way to see the alligators at Brazos Bend State Park."

"Getting our steps in." Rachael flashed me her slim wrist-watch, which must be a fitness tracker too. Even pregnant, she was tracking her steps? These women were hard-core.

"And that car looked brand-new, but it's been parked on the side of the road for almost a week. I drove back around yesterday just to see, and there it was." Inés widened her kohl-rimmed eyes like she was telling a ghost story.

Elizabeth's smooth brow furrowed. "Maybe the people were camping?"

Rachael shook her head and held up her phone. "They were *dead*. Police just found them hacked to *pieces*."

Inés gasped, and Elizabeth said sharply, "That's not funny."

"I'm not laughing," Rachael snapped back. "It just hit my news feed. They were on their way back to Louisiana after visiting her folks in Rosenberg. Nobody knew to look for them on some country road, and even if they had, the bodies were way back in the swamp. Some pieces were missing because the gators—"

"That's enough!" Elizabeth's voice was so loud that a table of men in suits looked over at us, and Rachael blushed, one hand dropping to her pregnant belly.

"I didn't mean . . ."

Inés patted Rachael's arm. "It's okay, sweetie. Maybe this is not the best talk for lunchtime, but you can tell me on the way home."

Actually, I wouldn't have minded hearing a little more, but instead I said, "Is this how all your committee meetings go?"

Not a great joke, but enough for Rachael and Elizabeth to both smile weakly. Inés laughed and bumped my shoulder. "Wait and see, Kacy. Wait and see!"

Elizabeth pulled a trim notebook from her purse. "So, where shall we start?"

This was the moment of truth. Either I'd say nothing and they'd forget I existed, so I might as well have stayed home, or I'd open my mouth and say something stupid. *I'm confident and competent. I can do this.* I'd planned dozens of events—openings and fund raisers and receptions—but I'd planned them with Aimee. We'd spent hours matching the music to the canapés to the art to the type of attendees. If the art was off-putting, should the music be avant-garde and discordant, or soothing like Norah Jones? Would young professionals prefer a DJ or a big-band, retro vibe? And the budget was always the bottom line.

Inés started throwing out ideas—a fashion show, a lavish gala, a ball—and I couldn't help asking, "What's the budget?"

The women all exchanged a little smile that made me feel stupid, and then Rachael said, "These women—and Alondra, especially Alondra—are extremely talented at getting donations."

"But it's a good question." Elizabeth's tone was a little too sharp, and Rachael's eyes widened in surprise.

Inés jumped in. "But the better question—more fun, at least— is the theme."

Surely it wasn't my imagination that Elizabeth seemed on edge around Rachael? But Inés spoke rapidly, throwing out fantastical ideas, from a carnival to a time traveler's ball.

We were all laughing at the idea of a junior-prom theme when another woman, tall with a round face and blunt-cut bob, strode purposefully through the restaurant. She dropped into the chair beside me and held out her hand. "Hi. Alondra."

Surprised, I put my own hand into hers for a brisk shake as she looked around the table. "Thanks for meeting downtown, ladies. I know it's a little out of your way. Catch me up."

Alondra sipped her iced tea, made a face, and flagged a waiter. "I'd like a water without ice or lemon and a Whitmeyer's single-barrel neat." Then she glanced around the table and arched an eyebrow as if to ask, *Am I drinking alone?*

Inés set down her iced tea and nodded at the waiter. "Prosecco, please. No, a spritz. What's the one?"

"Aperol spritz," Rachael said. "Wish I could." She patted her stomach.

Alondra turned her attention to me and Elizabeth. "Ladies?"

I hesitated, and Elizabeth said, "I'm driving." There was a bite in her tone, but Alondra just shrugged. I shook my head no.

She wrinkled her nose. "So are we stuck with the club? The acoustics were awful last year. Everything else was fine."

"We can do better than fine." I sounded like my old confident self, and Elizabeth smiled, relaxing a little. "You're more familiar with the area than I am. What kind of options do we have?"

As the conversation started up again, I could absorb myself in the merits of one location over another, the idea of a themed event, even cracking a few jokes that made Elizabeth laugh. Now Alondra was the one watching, but I could see Rachael and Inés glancing at her after every suggestion.

The server came back with our meals, and as he worked his way around the table, Alondra leaned close to me, her gaze piercing. "So, new girl. Where you from?"

"Jersey."

"Moved when?" Her question came right on the heels of my answer.

"A few weeks ago."

"Profession?"

"My husband's an engineer."

"And you?"

"I'm not . . . I mean . . ." I trailed off, hoping she'd change the subject. There was a difference between talking about my past on purpose and being interrogated about it. And the rapid-fire question-and-answer session made my breath shallow and my pulse race.

Elizabeth said, "Kacy worked at a museum." *No, no, no, not my personal history.* My nails bit into my palms. Better that this polished attorney think I was just some no-ambition tagalong to my husband.

Alondra didn't take her eyes off me. "One I've heard of?"

She wasn't going to stop, not until I answered. "The Martina V. Umana Museum of Modern Art."

"I heard you stood up to Sandy." Alondra's expression hadn't changed, she hadn't moved at all, but I felt as though she'd leaned forward and was staring directly into my soul.

"What?" My cheeks grew hot at the sudden pivot, and I was conscious that the other three women were completely silent. "I guess, I mean . . . you heard about that?"

Her eyes crinkled in a smile that seemed to relax her entire body. "I hear about everything. Nicely done. Rahmia's done more good in a few months than Sandy will in a lifetime."

I might have asked what she meant, but she called out a question across the table, leaving me feeling as though the rapier that had pinned me to my chair had been withdrawn. I moved my salad around my plate until Alondra asked me a softball question about hors d'oeuvres and the conversation returned to the event.

Inés and Rachael were still working on a shared order of tiramisu when Alondra stood up, her black coffee "to go" in one hand and the other on the back of my seat.

"So, does this committee have positions? I vote we make the new girl chair. You up for it, Kacy?"

"Sure." But I knew I didn't sound sure. If Alondra really did hear about everything, how long before she heard about me? A simple internet search would reveal that as far as the world was concerned, I couldn't be trusted. It had felt so good to talk to Dr. Lindsey and even better to be honest with Lena. But my own coworkers at the museum hadn't believed I was innocent. How could I expect these strangers to trust me?

I twisted my napkin in my hands. "Or maybe . . ."

"How about cochair?" Elizabeth offered.

"Excellent." With a wave, Alondra was gone.

On the way home, the traffic seemed to increase every minute. Elizabeth frowned, her hands clenched around the wheel. "So we'll probably end up at the club, but you and I should visit two or three other places and get estimates."

We drove in silence for another mile. One difference between Elizabeth and Aimee was this pause. Elizabeth answered my question and then waited, letting me think. Aimee used to answer and then jump into the empty space, filling it with suggestions, sometimes serious, more often not, spinning our conversation off course. Because it wasn't about getting the job done; it was about bonding, living in the moment.

Then Elizabeth said, "We'll also need to get the invitations worked up. With your art background, maybe you'd enjoy that?"

"Sounds good." And it did. That was something I could handle.

"Once you have them ready, we use the Fort Bend Copy Center. After you email it to them, call to make sure they've got it. They're pretty old-school."

"About the money . . ." My words sounded artificial, wavery.

"You can either pay and submit a receipt or get an invoice and they'll give you a check to take back. We've got it set up so each check gets countersigned."

"You can't be too careful." So there was no way I could be accused of embezzling, no opportunity that could be misconstrued.

"Was this the kind of thing you used to do?"

"One of the things."

"Houston's got a ton of art museums. Do you want to go back to work?"

And a flood of sorrow rose in me, as if by lowering my guard I'd given it leave to suffuse my entire body. But this time I wasn't braced against it, wasn't fighting, and instead of bursting into tears or running away, I let it spread out along every limb, warm and heavy. I was tired of pretending I wasn't sad.

"I can't." I didn't raise my head, not wanting to look at Elizabeth. I spoke slowly, careful not to let too much emotion spill out, placing one word in front of the next like walking a tightrope. "My best friend at my last job framed me. They think I stole some paintings and embezzled money. There wasn't enough proof to bring charges, but I don't think I can work in a museum, or gallery, or maybe anything like that again."

After a few minutes of studying my hands and waiting, I raised my head. Elizabeth was looking steadily at the road without expression. I couldn't tell what she was thinking. Did she believe I was innocent? Did she think I was guilty of lying, stealing, or oversharing? There was no way to know without asking, and I realized it didn't matter.

I was tired of hiding my past, and I wouldn't apologize for it.

Not anymore.

8

WEEKS PASSED. WHILE the news screamed stories about the murdered man and woman found in pieces under the live oak trees of Brazos Bend State Park, Michael and I fortified our home. "It's safer to park in the garage and shut the door before you go into the house," he told me after the news reported another driveway robbery—on top of the home invasions and the convenience store shootings and the drug busts and speculations about the missing drivers of at least two other abandoned vehicles. Somehow I'd thought we had left big-city crime behind when we moved to the suburbs, but as the fourth-biggest city in the United States, Houston's presence dominated our almost-idyllic neighborhood.

One weekend Michael and I pulled down the wallpaper in the kitchen, spraying and scraping it off the drywall where it had been glued. In the paint store, I saw kits for a faux finish called Venetian plaster. While I deliberated with the can in my hands, Michael came up behind me, and I held it so he could see the directions. Squinting, he said, "Sounds like a lot of work, but if you're up for it, maybe do the small bathroom first. It could use a refresh."

He wasn't wrong. The burgundy-and-pine-striped wallpaper looked like something the old man had chosen alone, while the cream paper with pale-pink flowers we'd stripped from the kitchen might have been the choice of a long-ago wife. Now we'd designated one of the bedrooms for guests, and the other, currently empty, would probably be a nursery.

Someday.

We bought creamy paint with a buttery undertone for the kitchen, spray-on texture to cover the flat surface of the drywall, drop cloths and sandpaper, rollers and more wallpaper remover, and the Venetian plaster too, even though it involved about sixteen different steps.

I had the time.

I'd exchanged texts with Elizabeth, the subtext of her words impossible to decipher. She wasn't an emoji user, and her messages were precisely punctuated so that even an invitation to meet for lunch read like a mild reproof.

My morning walks hadn't synced up with Rahmia either. I'd seen her and her son on their way to school, their hands clasped and Bibi dancing before them on her leash, but they'd all been too far away for more than a distant greeting.

But Lena had texted over and over—we'd hung out by her pool and gone to the nursery to get more plants for the beds Michael and Brady were building, and late every afternoon we walked together around the neighborhood, sometimes finishing with a dip in her pool. We talked nonstop. I'd learned that Brady had a background in engineering but preferred "being his own boss." He ran a home improvement company with a fleet of vans, each stocked for a specific task: locksmith, HVAC, roofing, plumbing.

"So he's like a contractor?" I asked on one of our walks. The air was thick with heat and humidity, and we'd followed the concrete sidewalk past the entrance to Bluebonnet Skies and were headed toward the elementary school.

"Pretty much, except he specializes in residential. Hey, let's turn here." And Lena veered to the right, following a branch of the sidewalk that took us under the power lines in an open space between the two brick walls that enclosed separate neighborhoods. "Those master builders are cheap as shit."

"And he's certified in all those things?"

"He's certified in enough, and he fills in the gaps with other professionals, guys who don't or can't run their own businesses. I used to do the scheduling, but we've got it mostly automated now. My degree's in accounting."

At my expression, she burst out laughing. "I know, you didn't see that one coming, did you? Everything in this world comes down to love or money, and I figured there was only one of those I could get certified in. Brady's crap at planning. I handle all our books, I drew up the master lists for each van, and I set up our computer scheduling for employees and customers."

"You're a good team." I wished Michael and I had something like a shared business, something concrete that I could point to and say, *See, we were meant for each other.*

"Damn straight. Brady has less than zero patience for the high-maintenance types we deal with like that-bitch-Sandy." She pushed a damp curl away from her face. "Did I tell you now that we've redone the kitchen and that fucking backsplash three times, she's trying to renegotiate the price? I swear, last week I spent more time in her damn house than mine."

Better Lena than me. I'd avoided Sandy at the last Bluebonnet meeting, but the memory of calling her a bitch to her face made me warmer than the late-afternoon sun. We approached the drainage ditch we called the "bayou." A sign warned that alligators might be present, but all I saw from the wooden bridge that spanned the water were cattle egrets, bright white even in the shadow, and the sun gleaming off the dark turtles that clustered at the shore.

"How do you have time for the Bluebonnets?" I asked.

She shrugged. "I go to the general meetings, drop our ad in the newsletter, and make sure I'm at the fund raiser. But you won't find me choosing flowers for the fashion show or getting blitzed at book club."

"Why do you go at all?" Lena didn't seem like the kind of person who did anything she didn't want to do. I tried to imagine her at a downtown restaurant, sipping cocktails and debating fund raiser themes, but I couldn't. She was Carnival and those women were Easter Sunday.

"I'm waiting for them to need me. When they get back home and something goes wrong in their perfect little lives, I need them to think about me. Me and Brady." Lena pulled her hair back off her neck and tilted her face up to the sun, all without slowing her stride. "Those bitches will gossip and backstab and God knows what all, but when they have to choose, they'll pick one of their own. Especially the kind of work Brady does where people are all up in your home. They see me at a meeting, makes them think they can trust my people in their house. Like we're friends."

Practical. Almost chilling how practical it was. "Some of them are nice. Elizabeth—"

"You made a friend. Sweet." The corner of her mouth twisted.

Okay, that sarcastic edge was weird. "You'd like her."

"I know her." Lena looked away from me, our steps in sync even as the long silence stretched out. "She's fine. Uptight, but fine. It's okay, honey, I'm not looking to make friends, but you do what you want. Just promise me one thing?"

"What?"

"Don't go all Stepford on me." She didn't smile, and I couldn't tell if she was kidding.

*   *   *

One day thunder rolled through the air, and it rained hard and fast, too much for the gutters, rain sheeting down over our back door.

My phone pinged: *2 wet 2 walk. Come hang out?*

Even the few steps between my front door and Lena's were enough to send rivulets of water down the back of my neck. I let myself in, calling out a greeting, and as I slipped off my wet shoes, the air conditioning and the damp made me shiver. Lena's house was a two-story, designed by the same builder as ours but with a larger dining room and formal living room, which had been transformed into an office. Right inside the front door, there was a huge desk of golden wood and a desktop computer for "business stuff," but I'd never seen her working there.

I followed Lena's answering greeting and the smell of something rich and inviting into the kitchen. She said, "I've got a pot of beans on for soup, and I thought we'd bake some bread, if you're up for it."

"Sure." I thought of my favorite little corner bakery in Jersey, where the man behind the counter wore a white apron and the glass shelves displayed loaves and rolls of every shape. "Isn't it hard?"

"Not if you know how." She pointed to a glass jar on the counter, filled with what looked like library paste. "Sourdough starter. That one goes back twenty years, from one my aunt uses. She always says that as long as you've got dried beans, flour, and a starter, you're not too far from a good dinner."

"Hey, if you say so, I'm all in. But I have absolutely zero culinary talent." I went to the sink to wash my hands.

Under Lena's direction, I mixed the flour and salt, then added the starter, stirring until I had a shaggy mass of yeasty, tangy dough in my bowl.

"Won't the starter die now?" I could see a few bubbles around the edges of the jar.

"Nah. I'll just stir in a cup each of flour and water and let it sit overnight. Here." Lena reached under the counter and pulled out another mason jar. With the same wooden spoon, she scraped about half of the starter into the new jar. "You take this one."

"I can't. I'll kill it."

"Don't be stupid. Just leave it on your counter until tomorrow morning, then stick it in the fridge. Every two weeks or so, give it a stir, toss or use about a cup of it, then add another cup each of flour and water, like I just did. Simple. The only thing you'll kill is the part you throw out. But you'll love this bread so much you'll be using your starter all the time."

She pulled a roll of masking tape and a marker from a drawer, wrote a label, and stuck it on the jar, where I read *Live Starter from Lena*. "We didn't have a bunch of money, but we always ate well. My aunt was doing farm-to-table before it was ever a thing. I saw a jar like this on Pinterest, fancied up with a 'friendship starter' label. How many of those do you think get tossed out?"

I wrapped my hands around the jar and raised it to my face, inhaling a smell like good beer. It turned out that if you wanted to make sourdough, you either needed to start three days ahead of time or have an heirloom starter like this one, from Lena's aunt to Lena to me. I said, "My mom was a school nurse. She was always pretty tired, so dinners were quick and easy. Fish sticks, mac and cheese, soup from a can. She didn't make anything like this."

More than the food, I remembered sitting around the table, the kitchen light shining down on my mom, my dad, and the three of us girls. That place felt safe. Even if you didn't clear your plate, even if you hated vegetables with a fiery passion, even if your sister flicked peas or kicked you, our kitchen table was a place the darkness couldn't touch.

Could I ever create something like that with Michael? A haven. A family.

Then Lena patted an open expanse of counter. "Time for the fun part. We're going to beat the shit out of this dough."

But my mind wasn't on baking anymore. "Will you pass this starter on to your kids?"

For a second, her face went blank, and then she blinked and squinted. "Kids? Not my thing."

She shook flour onto the counter and dumped the glob of dough onto it. With a rough motion, she tore the mass in two and pushed one a little closer to me. "First we knead it, then we'll let it rise. Watch." With force, she pressed and turned and thumped the dough, frowning at it. I got the feeling she was irritated with me.

But where could I have done something wrong or crossed the line? I tried to imitate her motions, pushing with the heels of my hands as the mass became smoother and more resistant.

Then she asked, "So, babies in your future?"

I thought about the feeling of sitting around the kitchen table with my sisters and my parents, the way Rahmia's head had tilted down to hear her son. My own niece and nephew. The way Michael and I woke each morning in a bed big enough for a brood of kids and a dog. We had room in our house, room in our lives for more now, and I said, "Maybe."

"Well, good for you." She didn't look at me, even though the practiced motion of kneading made it clear she could do it in her sleep. Maybe she was one of those people who hated kids. Maybe she thought I was just another silly Stepford wife after all.

The air was chilly between us, and her strong hands flipped and pounded the dough. She glanced at mine, still marred with streaks of unincorporated white flour.

"You've got to give it more force." She reached out and took my dough, clenching it in one hand as she raised it and smacked it against the counter top. Then she flipped it, folded it, and dug the heels of her hands into it. The dough that had seemed so resistant to my hands just succumbed to hers.

She battered it rhythmically for another few minutes and then knocked it back to me. "There. Now we wait."

Of course, Lena wasn't good at waiting. Less than fifteen minutes later she'd turned off the beans, left the dough on the counter, and was driving me to "some taco truck Brady said is the *best*."

The rain had blown past, and the sun seemed to turn the standing pools of water on the roads to steam. We sped over the interstate and exited into a part of Houston I hadn't seen before.

The access road took us under the overpass, and in the darkness I saw a cluster of men, one an older man in a battered army jacket despite the heat, holding a sign that read *Hungry. Please help*. Lena's gaze darted to them. "Ex-military," she said softly, and I wondered if she would pull over. The light changed, and we came to a stop beside him. He was about my father's age, but the lines in his face were deeper and his shoulders more stooped.

The man drew closer to us, holding the cardboard sign in front of him with trembling hands. I fumbled for my bag and found it empty of cash. As I met his eyes and shook my head, his resigned expression didn't change. He simply turned his attention to the next car in line, and when the light changed, he stepped back onto the pavement.

I wanted to do something, find something to help, but with a spray of water from our tires, we were back into the blinding sunlight as Lena skated through the intersection on a yellow light and went barreling down a side street lined with strip malls pocked with empty stores.

I couldn't tell the difference between side streets and alleyways, but without so much as a peep from a GPS app, Lena whipped the car around one turn and then another, explaining, "Brady says it's always in this area somewhere. At least for now. You find the best taco truck one day, and then it disappears. People move on or get shut down, then another one pops up."

She pulled into a parking lot that seemed to back up to one of the derelict shopping strips. I couldn't even tell what kind of stores they were from the yellowed doors edged with rust. One was propped open, and I could almost make out someone standing at a checkout, but whether it was auto parts or groceries or secondhand furniture was impossible to say.

A group of people, mostly men, were clustered around a battered white truck with a green awning. Street food was something I missed from the city, and eagerly I followed Lena. The tarry smell of wet asphalt yielded to the tantalizing odor of caramelized onions and browned meat.

We ordered tacos, the good street kind with carne asada or carnitas in thin double folds of corn tortilla and fresh spicy veg on top. The man who took our order nodded, calling it back to a younger woman with the same arched eyebrows and angular shoulders. His daughter? Sister? They were busy, efficient, their hands moving without pause.

Only a few minutes later we had our Styrofoam clamshells and two full-sugar bottled sodas back in the car, because "It's too damn hot to eat outside," Lena had said. She wasn't wrong. Intensified by the concrete and the chrome of cars and construction trucks, the heat rolled through everything, clogging our lungs. How could that woman, just a girl really, endure working in that truck, where the heat from outside must be met with the heat of the grill?

Lena had already eaten half a taco, and I picked one up slowly, my appetite fading.

"Listen," she said, "about earlier. Have kids, whatever. But you swear to me that we'll still have fun." She frowned at the other half of her taco.

I felt a warm glow. Lena, this force of nature, needed me. "Of course we'll have fun. We're friends. And that's all in the future anyway."

She cut her eyes at me. "I can't talk to fucking Brady the way I talk to you. It would suck if you just disappeared into some mommy-world."

"That would never happen," I promised, and she relaxed.

As I bit into my taco, a car drove past us, stopping at the open door of the mystery shop. Cilantro caught in my fingers as I watched a figure, bundled head to toe in a black hijab, exit the passenger side and hurry up the concrete steps to the open door, where she stopped, as though afraid to enter.

"What are you looking at?" Lena asked.

"Nothing." I turned back to face her, but not before I saw that Rahmia, polished suburban Rahmia, had appeared in the doorway. With a furtive glance, she'd drawn the woman inside.

The world seemed strange, unsettled. I didn't understand any-one, least of all myself. I rewrapped the remaining tacos in alumi-num foil. "Let's go back the way we came. I want to give these to the man under the bridge."

"That's not the quickest way home," Lena protested. "Just give your leftovers to Michael."

But I couldn't forget meeting the man's eyes, the resignation in his posture, the darkness under the bridge. I didn't know what his life was like any more than I knew what was happening in that shadowy storefront beside us now. But I had read the words on his sign. *Hungry.* And I had food.

Maybe I couldn't understand everything, but I could believe what he was telling me and try to help. "Seriously, Lena."

"Fine." She buckled her seat belt and put the car in gear. "Fucking bleeding heart."

Then she winked at me, and everything was okay again.

CHAPTER

9

WHEN MICHAEL HAD his first business trip, just two nights, I was acutely conscious of the exact amount of time I'd have to fill. The first day's plan was simple. I'd pick up Elizabeth, we'd stuff the formal invitations for the fund raiser, and then we'd check out one of the proposed venues and have an early dinner there.

Outside her house, I raised my hand to knock, but the door opened before I could. The Elizabeth I saw was not one I knew. She was wearing yoga pants and a boatneck T-shirt, but her feet were bare and her hair looked tangled and uncombed. Her eyes searched my face, and she reached out with both hands for mine and drew me inside. "I'm so sorry. I meant to call. I can't—I mean, thank you for coming, but I'm not ready . . ."

She trailed off, and we stood, her icy hands clasping mine for a minute.

"It's no problem," I said. Her eyes were unfocused, as though she was also nervous about looking at me. What could be wrong? Not drugs, not Elizabeth, and she wasn't visibly injured. I didn't give a shit about the Bluebonnet business, I never really had, but I definitely gave a shit about Elizabeth. "Let's sit down," I said gently. "You can tell me all about it."

"Oh God." She dropped my hands. "I didn't even offer you coffee or—"

"It's okay." I tried to make my voice as soothing as possible. "I'm fine. Let's just sit." And I walked over to the white leather sofa and sat down, patting the spot next to me like I was trying to coax a timid child.

"Okay." She didn't look convinced, as though the role of hostess was still tempting her. I knew how easy it could be to escape into the rote lines—won't you have some coffee, have you seen the new construction, are you going to book club later. But something was wrong, wrong enough for Elizabeth to need my help.

"Sit down," I said more firmly, and she finally did, perching gingerly on the far end of the sofa. It was the kind of sofa you sank into, an expanse of cushy leather, but Elizabeth sat bolt upright as if she were in a straight-backed wooden chair. "What's wrong?"

She darted a glance at me, and whatever she saw in my face must have reassured her. "Wyatt and I, I mean, we've been trying for about a year. And it hasn't worked. It did, almost, once, but then—" She opened her hands as if the almost-baby was slipping through them, and when she looked back at me, her eyes shone with gathering tears. "And then two weeks ago, I took the test, and it was positive." Her voice lowered on the last word, as if even saying it aloud might jinx it.

"That's great." I kept my tone cautious, because she didn't look great. Now that we were sitting down and I could study her, I could see a chalky-green tinge under her skin.

She nodded, looking down at her hands, clenching and unclenching them in her lap. "I'm bleeding." The words were so soft I almost didn't understand, and I leaned in closer.

"Have you called your doctor?"

She nodded, but she still didn't look up.

I reached out, touching her arm. "What do you need?"

Her restless hands stilled; then she turned one up to take mine, clinging to it. She faced me, tears overspilling now, wetting her cheeks. But she was so composed, so still. If not for the shiny tears and the tightness with which she held my hand, I wouldn't have known how afraid she was. "He said not to come in. He said—" She took a deep breath. "He said it might be normal, but if it wasn't, there wasn't anything he could do."

Before I had a chance to think, I'd pulled her close, and she was crying now, really crying, on my shoulder, while I whispered comforting but meaningless phrases. My mind kept working. I didn't know anything about this, didn't have any experience, but I hated the doctor who'd told her to wait and see. What kind of shit advice was that? And I hated myself a little, too, for taking Elizabeth at face value.

If anyone should have understood the difference between the way someone looks and the way they feel, it should have been me.

When the worst of the storm abated, Elizabeth pulled back, wiping at her eyes and apologizing. That's something I also understood, how embarrassing it was to be vulnerable.

"Listen," I said, "do you have another doctor? Because even if this is normal or he can't do anything, you deserve a doctor who'll listen to you. Is this your GP or your ob-gyn?"

"My ob-gyn. If this time didn't work, he was going to refer us to a fertility specialist, but he didn't think it was necessary yet."

"How about your GP, would you like to call him?"

Elizabeth half smiled. "It's okay. You're right, she'd be a better listener, but if something's wrong, she can't—" She gulped the end of the sentence down hard, her eyes creased with the effort of holding back tears.

"Okay." Wyatt and Michael wouldn't be back until the next night, and this house was so quiet, even quieter than my own. I couldn't leave her alone. "Tell me if I'm out of line, but would you mind if I hung out here? We could watch a movie, order pizza, just take it easy. Hell, we can even stuff those stupid envelopes. I mean, with Michael out of town, it's not like I've got anywhere to go . . ."

And she nodded, visibly relieved. "Yes. If it's no trouble, I mean, if you don't mind. That would be great."

When I texted Michael—*have Wyatt call E*—I saw I'd missed a message from Lena about baking and another one about walking. I sent her a reply—*sorry off grid today*—and my phone buzzed again immediately: *what's going on?*

Elizabeth looked up, and I felt her watching me as I answered: *tell you later.* Another incoming text felt like an intrusion, so without even looking, I silenced my phone. I could see the messages popping up, but I turned my attention completely to Elizabeth.

Right now, she needed me. Lena would have to wait.

*　*　*

Later that evening, I ordered out for pho from a nearby Vietnamese restaurant, figuring that chicken noodle soup would be nourishing and comforting. As we ate, I was relieved to see the color returning to Elizabeth's face, even though she steered clear of the jalapeño and sriracha I added to my own plastic bowl.

When we finished, the fragrance of lemongrass lingered in the kitchen. Elizabeth rose from the table and moved to help me clean up, but I waved her away. "What's the point of ordering delivery if you're still going to play hostess?" I teased.

"Fine," she answered with a grin. "I'll go relax on the sofa while you do the heavy lifting."

Just then, her phone buzzed with a text. She glanced at it and reached for the back of a kitchen chair to steady herself.

"Sit down," I said. "What's wrong?" The ringer on my phone was turned off, and anything might have happened. Maybe a car accident. Michael and Wyatt, speeding back from the oil fields, wrecked and bleeding by the side of the road.

But Elizabeth shook her head, one fist pressed to her mouth. "It's Sandy," she said. "Marcia was supposed to pick her up for scrapbooking, but she didn't come to the door or answer her phone. Marcia's got the keypad code to open her garage, so she let herself in. But I just can't believe—"

"What happened?"

"She's dead."

The last Styrofoam container still clutched in my hand, I stared at Elizabeth, seeing instead Sandy with her bright clothing and supercilious expressions. Now she seemed fragile to me, always trying to look younger, attacking other people to make herself feel stronger. "How?" I whispered.

Elizabeth sat down at the kitchen table and wrapped her arms around herself. All the color she'd regained had ebbed away. "She slipped in the shower. That's where Marcia found her."

I stuffed the last of the trash into the bin and came to join her. "Was that Marcia?"

She shook her head. "Rachael."

After the history between me and Sandy, I didn't expect I'd be getting a text about this. "Are they organizing meals or collecting for flowers or . . ." I didn't know what else might be needed.

"She lived alone. We'll probably do flowers, but it's too early yet."

I felt conflicting pangs of pity for the woman who'd died naked and alone and pangs of irritation for Sandy who'd been so mean, so narrow-minded, and whose carelessness was putting Elizabeth's health at risk. "Go sit on the sofa." I patted her shoulder. "I'll make you some tea."

But the lush leather sofa, the steaming mugs of mint tea, and the mindless drone of the television didn't dispel the specter of Sandy, her neck at an unnatural angle, bleeding out alone on the bathroom floor.

10

I WOKE CONFUSED, WEARING my clothes, my nose filled with the rich smell of the leather sofa. Elizabeth and I must have fallen asleep watching a marathon session of mindless television. I could hear a key turning in a lock, a door opening.

And Michael calling my name.

My eyes fluttered open, and the first thing I saw was Elizabeth, asleep in the recliner, and the television display, frozen with a message asking *Are you still watching?*

Something heavy hit the ground in the foyer, and I sat up as Elizabeth stirred. Wyatt was already crossing the room, kneeling beside her, smoothing her hair. "Are you okay?" he asked.

"I think so." She leaned into him. "Kacy was here."

Michael stood by the door with an unfamiliar suitcase, probably Wyatt's, at his feet. When our eyes met, he smiled.

For the first time in ages, it felt like everything would be okay.

*   *   *

No new texts from Lena the next morning, but when I went out to check the mail, she was on the sidewalk, coming back to her own house with a bundle of envelopes in her hand. Seeing her, I felt a smile forming on my lips, but then I remembered the seven unanswered texts. Why hadn't I replied? Maybe she'd be hurt. Maybe I'd messed this up.

I stopped, and we stood facing each other at the end of her front walk. The sunlight glinted off her red curls, and with a quick smile, she said, "Hey there."

The flutter of panic in my chest subsided. All that fear was just my crazy talking. Lena and I were good. "Want to walk with me?"

She waved the sheaf of letters. "Business day. Too much crappy paperwork. Tomorrow for sure."

"Definitely. Tomorrow." I started to walk past her, but she didn't step aside.

"Where were you yesterday?" Her tone was light, casual, but her gray eyes were studying my face intently.

"Over at Elizabeth's. She needed help with that committee thing." Unbidden, Elizabeth's pale face rose in my mind. My expression felt artificial, a mask I was trying to control. Could Lena tell I was lying?

She didn't say anything, and her silence seemed deliberate. The force of her attention had been so bright, so welcoming, that by withholding it, she'd thrown me out in the cold.

"Did you hear about Sandy?" I asked, hoping to shock this stranger into becoming my friend again.

She nodded, her mouth a tight, unnatural line. Still she didn't speak, but she didn't leave either. We just stood there awkwardly.

Finally I blurted out, "I know you're busy with work, but if you ever want, we could use your help on the committee." *Please say yes.*

"Hard pass." Another beat, and she glanced down at her phone. "Speaking of work . . . I'll catch you later."

Again, I felt uneasy, like I'd done something wrong. But Lena was always so open, so forthright. If she had a problem with me hanging out with Elizabeth or thought I was keeping a secret, wouldn't she just say so?

The next day, she texted like nothing had happened. She and Brady came over for dinner at our place, and then the guys went back to disassembling the fence and putting together the tiered garden they'd been planning.

While Lena and I sipped pinot grigio, we talked about our childhoods, places we'd lived, things we loved. She had a million stories about clients, descriptions of homes Brady's company had worked on, and zero sympathy for Sandy. But I was too grateful to care. I listened and laughed and watched Michael setting a timber tie in place, his shoulders tensed with the effort, his smiling eyes relaxed.

At one point in the evening, my phone buzzed, and I glanced down at a text from Elizabeth: *Thank you again for your help. Feeling so much better. Doctor says everything is fine. It's still a secret, but I'm happy that you know.*

Relief flooded me. I was glad Elizabeth was okay, glad I knew her better. But her secret was mine now, something I couldn't, wouldn't tell Lena.

And secrets killed friendships.

* * *

Later on an early-morning walk, I saw Rahmia and Bibi coming back from dropping Emir at school. For once, I was on the same side of the street. I waved, and Rahmia quickened her pace to reach me.

"Kacy." I loved the way her entire face lit up. "It has been so long!"

"I thought I saw you downtown last week," I offered, "in one of those strip malls just past the Beltway."

Rahmia's eyes widened for a second, and her smile disappeared. As I remembered the way the cloaked figure had hurried into the darkened storefront, shame blossomed in my gut. Just because Rahmia was friendly didn't mean we were the kind of friends who shared secrets. She probably thought I was a creepy stalker.

"But I could have been wrong," I stammered. "You know, when you're thinking of someone, you see them everywhere. And I was thinking it had been a while since we'd talked."

"It has been a while." She still appeared guarded, thoughtful, but we fell into step together.

"How is Emir?"

Just as I'd hoped, Rahmia relaxed, the tension ebbing from her face. "Oh, he is a handful! The school, they give the kids colors like a traffic light for how they behave, and Emir is red for talking, red for laughing, red, red, red. My husband says we need to give him consequences at home too, but I think he's already getting punished at school, so why should he suffer twice for the same crime?"

I laughed, trying to imagine the worst thing that tiny, impish Emir could possibly do, and Rahmia laughed too, but ruefully. "Finally, after so many red days in a row, I asked him, 'Emir, why can't you just behave like all the other kids?' and do you know what he said to me? 'Don't worry, Mama, I only do a bad thing once. Someday I will have done all the bad things there are in the world, and I will bring you home good green marks every day.'"

I laughed again, and I felt stupid for imagining Rahmia had been skulking around a derelict strip mall. Of course I was mistaken. I'd made a lot of mistakes.

Some secrets had nothing to do with me.

* * *

My appointments with Dr. Lindsey had continued weekly, but they seemed a thing apart from the work of living my life. My biggest problem with therapy was the persistent feeling that I wasn't doing it right. I understood how to write a paper on a piece of art, how to organize an event, how to make small talk or introduce a speaker. But my desire to make a good impression was constantly at war with my longing to let out all the pain. And as my pain lessened, my eagerness to act like everything was okay increased.

So building a friendship with Lena, getting to know Elizabeth better—it was more than deepening personal relationships; I was also gathering "gold stars" to prove I wasn't, had never been, the problem.

But I was still carrying Aimee's postcard with me. And I'd picked up a blank one depicting the skull of a Texas longhorn. I would send it once I decided what to write. If that friendship could be a lie, what guarantees did I have that these new ones would last?

"You know," I said to Dr. Lindsey, "if I could just understand why she did it, I'd feel better. It's not like she had a gambling problem or a drug addiction; it's not like she was desperate for money—"

"You assume she wasn't desperate for money," Dr. Lindsey said mildly.

"Well, there have to be easier, less cruel ways to get cash. Lower risk in every way. What makes a person behave like that?"

Dr. Lindsey tucked a strand of glossy hair behind one ear. "So you think understanding Aimee's motivation might make it easier for you to get past the fallout of her actions?"

I thought over her words for a minute, then nodded. "Yes. I just keep turning it over and over, trying to make sense of it."

"What if you aren't ever able to make sense of it?"

I shifted in my seat. What was she trying to say? That people were unknowable? That she didn't know the answer either? What the hell was I paying for if there weren't any answers to be had?

"You're frowning," Dr. Lindsey noted. The air conditioning seemed to be getting colder, and the quiet hush of the building roared in my ears.

Wrapping my arms around myself, I felt like a fractious child. "It's just, didn't you go to school for this? To understand people and their motivations? What would you ask her if she were here?"

Dr. Lindsey shook her head, her blunt-cut bob swaying. "Aimee isn't here. The only person who's here, the only person I'm concerned with, is you. Let's say you did understand her motivation and it made you feel better, releasing you from this pain and anxiety. What then?"

I didn't understand. Her face was intent, and I could feel my heart fluttering like it had in the museum director's office before I was fired. This was just another exam I was going to fail. "You want me to imagine what she could say that would make it all okay? Some motivation that would be good enough?"

I knew I'd said the wrong thing. Dr. Lindsey didn't look disappointed, not exactly, but she took a moment before speaking, and I could tell she was thinking of how to rephrase her question so even an idiot like me would understand.

My eyes scanned the room again. If only she had a clock. If I just knew how close I was to getting off the hook. I'd come in thinking I was doing well, and now I just felt stupid again.

And Dr. Lindsey sighed, a small one, but audible. "Our time is up, Kacy, but I want you to think about this. If I could wave a magic wand and make Aimee disappear, if everything she'd done had still happened but she was just gone—not still working at the museum, not posting on the internet—how would your life look then?"

I thought of the postcard in my bag, still blank, ready like a curse I planned to work. If there were no Aimee . . . my mind was blank.

I barely registered Dr. Lindsey walking me out to the waiting room, my trip down the elevator, even driving home. A world without Aimee might stretch to the horizon like the Texas sky.

* * *

I was in our hall bathroom, stripping the paper with orange-scented spray, when suddenly the floor seemed to buckle and I fell heavily against the wall, groping for something to hold me up. My fingers found the towel rack, but it pulled loose and fell to the ground as I spun around, vomiting into the toilet. *Shit.*

When my stomach was empty, I went to the sink, washing my hands and rinsing out my mouth. My brow was sweaty, and I splashed water on my face.

Food poisoning or the flu?

The smell of the orange-scented spray that promised to dissolve wallpaper paste seemed overpowering. I left the supplies there on the floor beside the fallen towel rack. Lying down when you were sick wasn't like lying down when you were depressed. I'd have a big glass of water and a nap on the sofa.

By the time Michael got home, I was feeling better, but not better enough for the fumes. I'd tried once, but it had made my stomach clench and roll again.

"Let me take a look." He was in the bathroom a long time before he shouted out, "Kacy, come here."

I heard the fan going as I approached, and the orange chemical smell seemed a little less potent, but Michael wasn't stripping the wallpaper or rehanging the towel rod. Instead, he seemed to be peering inside the wall, where the brackets for the rod had pulled out a chunk of plaster. His fingers were inside the drywall, groping around. Then he drew back his hand and held it out flat in front of me.

A camera no bigger than a nickel. Tiny, barely more than a lens and a computer chip.

"Who did this?" I touched it with a fingertip, carefully, like it might sting me. Then the implications rippled through me as though I really had been bitten. "Someone was *watching* us?"

"I don't know." His face was grim. "But I don't think it's recording right now. Looks inert."

He set the camera down carefully on the counter and picked up the towel rack and the two brackets that had held it, each a circle secured by four screws. He set the bar and brackets together off to one side.

Then he started patting the floor, collecting the screws.

Frozen, my stomach churning again, I wrapped my arms around myself tightly. We'd been living in some creepy stage set, and every social media troll could be watching a live stream of me panicking right now. Maybe Aimee was watching. Could she have done this? *I am calm. I am in control. I can handle this.* Michael was concentrating, trying to figure out what was going on. I couldn't lose my shit.

But I was. *I am freaking out.*

My knees almost collapsing, I crouched down to be closer to Michael or to hide my face, and together we found one screw, then two, another and another, until the seventh. And that was it. Along the edge of the counter, under the door of the linen closet, behind the base of the toilet. Only seven screws.

Michael said, "The lens must have lined up with a screw hole."

I'd heard of peepholes in public bathrooms, but this was our house. It felt like someone was standing right behind me, staring at the back of my neck. "Call the police. We should call them. Or the alarm company? Unless someone there did it."

Michael frowned. "I'm going to check the master bath."

Just then, my phone buzzed with a text: *Y'all want to watch the game?*

And he paused. "Is that Lena? See if Brady's home. We could use some help."

I texted back: *Having an issue. Can you & Brady come over? There in a sec.*

And a few excruciating minutes later—barely enough time for Michael to take off a single towel rack from the master bathroom—the front door opened and Lena called out, "Where are you?"

"Down the hall," I shouted back.

She and Brady crowded into the bathroom while I explained what we'd found.

Lena bent to get a closer look at the camera. "Shit, that is messed up. You okay, girl?"

I nodded, afraid now that if I opened my mouth to say anything, only a bawl of fear and grief would come out. This house wasn't safe, it wasn't. Nowhere was safe. Michael was trying to get answers, and all I could do was fall apart.

She put a hand on my arm and gave it a squeeze. "We'll figure this out. Brady, y'all install nanny cams and things. What do you think?"

"Looks like it was wireless. A little camera like these can't transmit very far. But it shouldn't have been recording. Even the best batteries on something like this won't last longer than a year." Brady flipped it over. "I seriously doubt this thing was still active. To be a long-term spy thing, it would have had to be hooked into a power source."

Lena patted me on the shoulder. "Probably it was just the old man. He always seemed like a total pervert."

Before I could ask who'd owned the house before him, Michael appeared in the hallway, another camera in the palm of his hand. "Found this one in the master bathroom."

"Where?" I asked, but he didn't answer.

Brady took it and held it up to the light. "These aren't cheap. How many are there?"

"Two at least." Michael pointed to what looked like a tiny hair sticking off of one corner. "And I'm not sure it wasn't spliced into the electrical system. Could this be a wire?"

The bathroom was too crowded with people, and our reflections in the mirror made it seem like dozens of people were looking at me, watching me, spying. "Could there be a camera behind the mirror?" I *knew* it wasn't a one-way mirror, that was stupid, I knew our study was on the other side of that wall, but my face was getting hotter and my breath was shallow.

"No." Michael, absorbed in examining the camera he'd found, didn't even look at me. "We'd see a nonreflective spot."

"Okay, let's start checking the rest of the house." Brady dropped the camera onto the bathroom counter next to its twin. "We'll do a visual today and a real RF scan tomorrow. I should probably buy a sweeper for the home electronics truck anyway. I can add it as an optional additional service."

I blinked to settle my eyes, but the LED glare of the lights in the windowless bathroom and the lingering fumes made this seem like a bad dream. I needed a way to make it okay, to solve it. "I'm going to find the packet of manuals and contracts that came with the house. Maybe it was some guy with the alarm company or something."

"Don't worry." Lena put her hand on my arm. "Brady's on top of all this electronic stuff. Like he said, the batteries are probably dead anyway. Seriously, that old guy was a psycho. I bet he was doing something perverted, but it's all okay now. Fucker's totally dead."

In a kitchen drawer, I found the warranty information for our air conditioner and furnace, the instructions for our stove, and the HOA agreement. There was a company listed on the alarm, the same company we'd called to set up monitoring when we first moved in.

Lena opened the panel of our alarm system. "Everything here looks normal."

"What about that red light?" I pointed to the little box in the upper corner of our back wall. "There's another in the master bedroom. Let's rip those down."

"Hold up." She grabbed my arm as I started to drag a chair over. "That's part of your alarm system. Should just be a motion sensor, a laser across your back wall. A good idea when you've got these high privacy fences like we do. You can call the company, but if you rip 'em off, you'll have the police here double time. Let Brady take a look."

The feeling of being watched—no, scrutinized—struck me again, and I felt a wave of dizziness just as Michael came out of the back room.

"You look pale. When did you last eat?"

"I had lunch . . ." I hadn't told him about getting sick. "I threw up earlier. Too many fumes from the wallpaper stuff."

"You need to keep the fan on, and maybe open the door to the garage to suck some of it out." He ran a hand over my forehead, and I leaned into the comforting warmth of his fingers.

"Is there any way to tell where it was transmitting?" If these cameras were live, if they still worked, Michael would have called the police. He was calm, and I could be, I had to be, too.

"I don't know. We'll keep looking tonight, and then I'll do some research."

Brady shouted something from farther down the little hallway, and Michael ran to join him. They'd found another.

This wasn't one anomaly; it was a major issue with our house.

When I looked at Lena, she was watching me with a steady gaze. "You were sick earlier?"

"A couple hours ago. I'm sorry, I should have said. I don't think I'm ill. Just fumes."

She didn't smile or look away as she considered me. Then she seemed to snap out of it. "You probably need to eat something. I've got soup at home, or we can order pizza if you think you can keep it down." And I could feel the warmth of her concern again.

At the thought of food, Chinese food specifically, my nausea subsided, but my unease remained like a cloak over my shoulders.

Four cameras total. The two bathrooms and one in each of the small bedrooms. One had been hooked into the ceiling fan, the other into an outlet near the baseboard. Who wanted to monitor people's ankles?

So many thoughts flooded my mind, from the charitable—fancy child monitoring system—to the heartbreakingly awful—human trafficking and porn.

Before bed, Michael checked every outlet, every screw, every piece of hardware anywhere in our master bedroom and bathroom. Over Chinese food, he and Brady had ordered an RF scanner with overnight shipping, but tonight we were on our own.

I'd eaten enough lo mein and scallion beef for eight people, and I felt great. Strong, powerful. The blackout curtains made it impossible to see or *be* seen, I told myself. The cameras were some leftover artifact from the past, nothing to do with us.

When I fell asleep, I dreamed I was in the darkened museum after hours. Only the security lights were on, and the corridor I followed took me in a loop past the same three rooms over and over.

In the distance, I could hear the footsteps of a security guard and the jingling of the keys of his belt. Then I remembered I'd been fired, I wasn't supposed to be there, so I hurried around a corner, only to find myself just ahead of him, but in the same hallway with the same three galleries.

One was completely dark and seemingly empty; another had a found-art installation, long paper spirals formed from recyclables hanging from the ceiling, spinning slowly with the air conditioning. And the final one had a statue in a spotlight, a riff on *Winged Victory*, a woman without a head, formed from stiff paper instead of carved stone. The folds of her chiton gathered around her smooth, taut belly, and I heard Aimee's voice behind me: "If you can't imagine a world without me, maybe you need a belly as big as the world?"

I woke again before dawn, and as I sat on the sofa facing down the red light of the motion sensor, my fingers folding paper stars, everything seemed so clear. How had I not thought of it before?

I must be pregnant.

6

Helen: Of course, we're not talking about a single killer. I think that could have skewed the victim profile too, since there were two perpetrators.

Julia: Well, what other serial killer "teams" do we know about?

Helen: The most famous in the Houston area would have to be Dean Corll, known as the Candyman or the Pied Piper. His two partners—Brooks and Henley—were both teenagers, and together they lured over twenty-eight young men to their death. A fracture in their relationship led to Corll's death and the revelation of his crimes.

Julia: It's always the infighting that breaks up the band.

Helen: A few years later in Los Angeles, the Hillside Stranglers were active. Cousins Kenneth Bianchi and Angelo Buono raped, tortured, and killed ten women and girls. This is another case where the older individual—here Angelo Buono—might have influenced his younger partner. After their tenth murder, Bianchi followed his ex-girlfriend to Washington State. Less than a year later, he kidnapped and killed two university students, and the police caught him.

Julia: But all of these serial killers are men, and we're talking about a husband and wife.

Helen: Don't worry, my friend, we've got precedents for men and women killing together all over the world. Gerald and Charlene

Gallego murdered ten people in California in the late seventies. Rodolfo Infante and Ana María Ruíz Villeda killed eight women in the early nineties in Mexico. David and Catherine Birnie murdered four women in the mideighties in Australia. And in England the most famous serial-killing couple has to be the Moors Murderers—Ian Brady and Myra Hindley. And the debate is always power dynamics, whether the husband or wife was driving the action.

Julia: If there was a sexual component, I'd have to say the husband. Also, ick. Super ick.

Helen: And that's certainly something that defense attorneys have claimed. Charlene Adell Gallego testified against her husband; Ana Villeda claimed she only watched the murders.

Julia: The couple that preys together, stays together? So if she said, "No more killing; I'm out," maybe she'd be her husband's next victim.

11

I DIDN'T SLEEP AGAIN, instead filling the box on the sofa with multipointed stars. My little stack of glossy paper was getting low. I'd been experimenting with how many points I could put on a star and whether I could adjust them after I'd popped them into shape. Somehow, despite my experience as an art historian and museum employee, art had been something I'd only studied, not anything I'd thought I could make.

But these little paper pieces, sort of "proto-art" or maybe even just a "craft," were easy for me, comforting to my hands, and the more of them I made, the more natural it felt to manipulate them and deviate from the pattern.

And they dissipated my anxiety.

My fingers folded and creased as I let my mind roam.

Michael and I had talked in a general way about having a baby. Initially, while we were dating, we'd had the "do you want kids" talk. When we bought this house, it had been obvious to assume one of the two extra bedrooms would be the nursery.

After the night last week that I'd spent with Elizabeth, when Michael had made his way back from the trip to West Texas with Wyatt, we'd discussed it. How scary it would be to lose a child. How much we hoped everything would be okay for our friends. Wyatt had said they've been trying for about two years. The next step was a fertility specialist.

I thought about Elizabeth, her colorful kitchen, how careful she was—not just in life, but with people. She'd be a good mother.

And then I imagined my own child. Coloring papers or folding them into shapes. Swimming in Lena's pool. I'd been four when my younger sister, Molly, was born, but all three of us girls babysat when we got older. I knew something about kids. Maybe I'd be a good mother, too.

Michael would sure as hell be a good dad. But I didn't want to present him with a "maybe." He was an only child, a planner. I knew he'd been thinking about what his parents getting older would mean for us, weighing the pros and cons of moving (a bigger paycheck, a clean slate for me) against the distance it put between us and them.

And it was a Saturday. He wasn't the kind of guy who slept in, but it was still super early. If I was careful, if I didn't wake him, I could duck out, get a test, and be back before he woke up.

*   *   *

Later Michael meticulously dissected one of the tiny cameras we'd found the day before, while Brady came back and swept the house with an RF detector. I followed him through every room, watching him run it along the edge of the ceiling and sweep every inch of the wall. The thing beeped and vibrated but didn't find any other cameras.

"Does that mean there aren't any?" I felt like my body was humming with its secret, even though I hadn't taken the test yet. The directions said to do it first thing in the morning, and this was a test I didn't want to fail. Even though I was saving it for Sunday morning, the world around me was opening, blossoming like a flower. These cameras were relics of the past. I should be afraid, I was sure I should be, but I wasn't. They were like Aimee, like the thousand prying eyes of strangers on the internet. They couldn't touch me.

"None that are transmitting." Brady lowered the device and met my eyes. "Seriously, the batteries in those things were dead, and little guys like that don't transmit far anyway. My money's on the old guy."

"Lena said he was a pervert?" I was playing the part of a normal person, asking for reassurance, and Brady seemed just as eager to give it as Lena had been yesterday.

"Could be. Or maybe he was just paranoid. Put these in to monitor his own house. I've seen stranger things. You wouldn't believe what kind of electronics and lights and stuff people want rigged up in their homes." He winked.

That would explain why we hadn't found any cameras in the master bedroom. Instead of imagining the former owner of our house helplessly bleeding out on the bedroom floor, now I pictured him sitting there hunched over a monitor, watching every room in his own house from a central command station.

In the afternoon, I called our home security service, and over the phone they walked me through testing the system. When I armed it to "away" and waved my hand through the invisible beam against the back wall, the alarm sounded, a comforting wail.

So that red light on the wall wasn't an eye to spy on us but a watchdog to keep us safe.

Sunday morning I woke up early again from a dream about a paper baby, all sharp folds and creases, made from fliers from the museum where I had worked but so delicate I couldn't pick her up without crushing her.

Slipping from the bed, I tiptoed into the bathroom. With trembling hands, I opened the box and followed the directions, counting out the minutes second by second, until the symbol bloomed in the wand's plastic window. *Pregnant.*

"Michael?" My voice wavered. I was on the edge of the precipice, the last moment *before*, when everything else would be *after*. And Elizabeth was still on my mind, her fear the proof that even a *yes* could become a *no*, that I might be on the brink of nine months of *maybe*. Maybe baby. Keeping this secret, holding it in, might be a way of protecting Michael from the uncertainty.

But I always told him everything.

"Michael?" Louder now, and I leaned out of the bathroom so I could see the bundle of covers under which he huddled. And suddenly I couldn't wait, I wanted this bright future, and I ran to the bed to wake him with kisses.

*　*　*

That afternoon, instead of going to Sandy's memorial service, Michael and I went over to Lena and Brady's. I'd donated for a floral arrangement, but now death seemed far away, overcome by the joy of impending new life. This time we brought the food, a bag of tacos from our new favorite place. My nausea had risen in the morning, but unlike every other stomach upset I'd ever had, it subsided when I thought of food. Before Lena even brought out the margaritas, I'd already eaten two tacos, and I held up a hand. "Not for me, thanks. Just started a new medication."

"Plain water, then, or fizzy?" Her tone was light, like this was no big deal, but her gaze had sharpened. Despite how laid-back Lena seemed, not much got past her.

And even to my eyes, Michael was vibrating with excitement. He and Brady had taken down enough slats from our fence to fit the tiered garden and had jerry-rigged sprinklers from each yard to cover it. Brady said something, and Michael laughed, shaking his head.

The corners of my own mouth curled up, and the glass of sparkling water Lena handed me caught the light as the bubbles rose.

Lena sank into the chair next to me and clinked her glass against mine. "Here's to us."

"And the boys." My eyes were still on Michael, bending to tamp down the earth around a plant on the top tier. There was something so competent yet tender about him.

"Sure." Lena raised her glass in their direction, and Brady looked up and waved back. "Here's to the guys."

Then she cut her eyes at me. "But we run this world. Here's to them and cheers to us. *All* of us."

She knew.

* * *

Pregnancy anchored me in my body, making everything beyond its borders—the past, the thoughts of others, my future plans—hazy and unimportant. In my second trimester, I felt powerful, supercharged with energy.

Lena and I continued our daily walks, and I made an effort to check in with Elizabeth. As zen as I felt with the new hormones surging through me, I could still see the fear beneath Elizabeth's stretched-thin calm. I called and messaged her on the slightest pretext—about the Bluebonnet fund raiser, about a story I'd seen on the news, even for directions to a store she'd mentioned. Lena might have said, "Your GPS not working?" But Elizabeth always responded warmly, and usually followed up, and soon I didn't even think before reaching out.

The evening of the Bluebonnet fund raiser for childhood literacy went off without a hitch with a predictable but fun "favorite literary character" theme. Michael had deferred to me on our costume, so I was dressed all in purple with a name tag that said *Crayon*, and he wore a pale-blue pajama top with the name tag *Harold*. Princesses, Austen characters, Sherlock detectives, and animals ranging from bears to mice to dragons laughed and danced around us, and I felt so buoyant that I didn't miss the champagne.

That morning Michael and I had found out we were having a girl, news I wanted to tell Elizabeth in person.

I scanned the crowd until I saw her standing by a table of silent-auction items, her blond hair shining against the dark-brown dress she wore. Slipping between the revelers, I came up and grabbed her hand. "A girl," I whispered. "It's a girl."

She hugged me, so quickly the embrace was over before I realized it had happened. Then she bit her lip, glanced around as if confirming that no one was listening to us, and whispered back, "We're having a boy."

I squealed, and she shushed me, but her eyes were sparkling. "We're not telling people. Not yet."

"Let me throw your shower," I offered.

"I don't know." She shook her head, reaching up to straighten her name tag, which read *Toad*. Somewhere, Wyatt must be in a green shirt, styling as *Frog*. "It seems like tempting fate, celebrating too much, too early."

"You don't have to have it tomorrow. You've got five more months."

"Have yours with me," she blurted out, and then her hand flew to her mouth. "I'm sorry. That was stupid. You want your own shower. You deserve your own. I just thought if there were two of us . . . but that was selfish."

I wasn't even listening to her apology. "Yes."

"What?" She looked at me, her eyes wide.

"Yes, let's have a joint shower. I mean, can we? We can't throw our own."

She waved her hand, as if that detail didn't matter at all. "Really? You won't feel cheated?"

"I'll feel lucky." And as the party swirled around us, I could almost forget that this life hadn't been my original plan. Things were better, sweeter, than I had expected.

And this time, I hugged her.

12

Elizabeth was right to wave away my question of who would host our shower. Turned out that was another benefit of belonging to the Bluebonnets. Inés and Rachael took the lead, although to their credit, they tried to recruit Lena too. I was entering my third trimester, just a few weeks behind Elizabeth, on the day of the shower.

To Lena's disgust, there was a decorate-the-onesie station, a guess-the-baby-food-flavor game, and a poster of celebrity baby pictures for people to identify. Lena busied herself rearranging the plates of tea sandwiches and bouquets of cake pops and refreshing the rainbow sherbet punch.

The worst part was when Elizabeth and I settled into chairs between the two gift tables, differentiated only by slightly more pink or blue tissue paper. As we took turns opening presents and holding up tiny outfits, oohing and aahing and thanking the gift giver who *just couldn't resist,* Lena stayed on the edges of my vision.

I looked up from a bag full of board books to thank Rahmia, but I couldn't find her friendly face in the throngs of women. At last I saw her standing by the door, talking on her cell phone, her expression uncharacteristically grim. I set the bag down by my chair and nodded to Elizabeth to open hers.

Finally the only gifts left were our matching towers of rolled diapers festooned with rattles and baby socks and bath toys, swathed in cellophane and bows. "Diaper cakes," Elizabeth had whispered to me. "You can't unwrap them or all the diapers will unroll and it'll be a big mess."

I felt like we'd been sitting for hours. As the semicircle of gathered women began to disperse, I stood, brushing the last bits of pink confetti off my lap, and scanned the room.

"Hey there, what did I miss?" someone said behind me. I turned to see Alondra. She gave me a hug as brisk as everything she did and handed me an envelope. "Gift card. Figured you didn't know what you needed yet. Who are you looking for just now?"

"Rahmia."

"Ah." Alondra nodded toward the back door. "Rahmia was outside on the phone when I got here. Sounded like she might be wrapping up."

My throat was dry and my cheeks were starting to ache from all the grateful smiling. I nodded at the punch bowl, and Alondra walked with me. I dipped up two glasses of the sticky-sweet punch and handed her one, which she sipped before wincing and setting it down unfinished.

She said, "I've been trying to get her to join the Bluebonnets, but she's too busy. I'd hoped she would be one of our speakers, but she doesn't want the attention."

"What?" I tried to piece together friendly Rahmia, exasperated by Emir, and the shadow I'd thought I'd seen in the shopping complex with the words Alondra was saying.

Then Alondra looked past me and raised her voice. "At the very least, we could do some fund raising."

And Rahmia herself came up beside me, smiling at Alondra. "Nag, nag, nag."

"What is she talking about?" I asked Rahmia.

Alondra answered. "Rahmia works with the local branch of the International Women's Resource Center. Listen, I've got to get some water or something. No offense, but that punch is like drinking a lollipop."

As she left, I turned to Rahmia. "I didn't know about this."

Her hands fluttered as she said, "Alondra makes it too big. I just help where I can."

"You help women, like with a women's shelter?"

Rahmia sighed. "Let's sit. You shouldn't be on your feet so long." She drew me back to the twin chairs, sitting in the one where Elizabeth had been. "So, it started because I am lucky. I *wanted* an arranged marriage; I didn't have to have one. My sister and her husband met in medical school, but I was tired of waiting for my family. I knew Ali from before; we'd been in grade school together. And even when we went overseas to our different colleges, we both spent summers with family. Ali had started his PhD, and I had just finished my master's, so the timing was perfect for our engagement."

"I don't understand what this has to do with your work." My eyes felt gritty, and I reached up to rub them. The fluorescent lights and the beam of everyone's attention during the gift opening must have made me more tired than I'd realized.

Rahmia patted my arm. "Just that I am lucky. I have a husband who loves me, and our marriage is happy. Not everyone can say that. Some women, they come here and maybe their husband locks away their passport, keeps their money. Maybe he isn't kind. But if they don't already speak English well, or if they have no money of their own, or once they have kids, they have no way to get help if they need it. So that is what I was doing."

"That's great work. You should speak at a meeting, tell people about it!"

She shook her head. "I don't want to cause trouble for Ali or to put our family at risk. Interfering in a marriage is dangerous, but I feel strongly these women need help and the law here does not protect them. When I need a legal question answered, Alondra helps me out. Unofficially. Because sometimes the only help we can provide is unofficial help."

A shadow fell across us, and I looked up to see Lena, a wrapped gift in her hands.

Hastily, Rahmia rose to her feet. "But I have been talking too much. This is your party. Have fun." With a wave, she headed across the room.

I started to stand, but Lena dropped into the empty chair. "Freaking Bluebonnet baby shower. I swear, if they'd let me throw this thing solo, we'd be having some real fun." She passed me the box. "I didn't want everyone gawking at this. Were you just about to die before it was all over?"

Laughing, I said, "Yeah, I hate being on display." I loosened the tape and smoothed back the paper even as Lena started to twitch with impatience. Amused, I actually took a little longer than necessary to unwrap the package, a fancy video baby monitor.

She leaned close and pointed to the description on the box. "It's got enough of a range that you can even hang out at the pool with me and still keep an eye on the nursery. You can make sure the baby is safe. And you can install an app on your phone so you won't be tied down. No worries."

"It's great. I love it."

Sitting back in her chair and stretching out her legs, she grinned. "Good. Because even a baby isn't going to keep us from having fun."

* * *

As the days passed, my body kept changing, and although I felt bigger and heavier, my confidence, the sense of being rooted in a community, stayed with me. And despite my larger size, Lena and I walked every day. She was still the friend who could make me laugh easily, who made me feel unselfconsciously free. Our walks past the mailbox and around the neighborhood were slower, but we spent just as much time together.

I never did send a revenge postcard to Aimee, not even after another one arrived from her. This time Aimee had chosen a black-and-white print of a seamstress's dummy in front of a window overlooking Brooklyn in the thirties. In black permanent marker next to my address, she'd written, *Is this what you wanted to be when you grew up? Soz ~A*

Before I realized what was happening, laughter bubbled up inside me. Aimee had no idea. She didn't know I was pregnant; she didn't know I had friends; she didn't know I was chasing happiness and it was right within my grasp. Lena twitched the postcard out of my fingers and flipped it over to read it. "That fucking bitch."

"It's okay." The sun was warm, without the slightest edge of winter. Aimee would be wearing sweaters, or she'd be shivering in too-thin blouses.

"It's not okay. Bad enough that this psycho loony framed you and got you fired; now she's stalking you? Someone needs to teach this bitch a lesson."

7

Helen: So now we've got a baby in the mix.

Julia: I'm sorry, I need a minute to freak out. Because the baby shower? Thrown by a killer. Seriously, how creepy is that?

Helen: After the baby was born, she even babysat. They left their three-month-old infant with a couple that had killed over a dozen people, picking off the homeless, the elderly, the undocumented. There's a huge homeless population in Houston, but there's also a robust safety net of shelters and social workers. Even commuters pass the same faces every day. If a cluster of people went missing, someone might notice. But our killers plucked one from Harris County, one from Spring, one from Galveston, always staying below the radar.

Julia: And I know what our listeners are thinking. Maybe the authorities hadn't noticed a serial killer was in the area, but how could their neighbors, their best friends, have no idea?

Helen: We've talked about this. Serial killers can be incredibly good at compartmentalizing. They can be charming; they may have spouses, friends, even kids of their own. Ann Rule wrote a book about working the phones at a help line with Ted Bundy. This couple is so good, so very approachable, that they are literally taking people off the side of the road without a fight. They just don't look scary.

Julia: That super-nice couple that is so very helpful, those neighbors that "keep to themselves," the guy you carpool with, the woman with the adorable dog . . . they're all suspects?

Helen: I'm sorry, babe. I know you like your murderers nice and obvious. But if every serial killer were a creepy loner, they'd never find any victims.

Julia: Bad guys should totally wear name tags.

13

F OUR MONTHS OLD, and Grace still woke at least once a night. I heard her stir on the baby monitor and opened my eyes just enough to check the time, two hours past midnight and three since her last feeding. I'd perfected the art of sleepwalking down the hall, nursing her in the glider, and returning her to her crib without fully waking up myself. When I rolled out of bed, I realized it was empty. Michael must still be out with Brady.

But it was a weekend, and they'd been drinking. Lena was out of town, and I hadn't felt like tagging along with Grace to watch sports and not drink beer.

He'd probably be in the bed by the time I got back.

I scooped up Grace's little body with its flailing arms and settled into the chair, tucking a pillow underneath her for support. Grace nursed quickly, her eyes never opening, one hand clenching and unclenching next to her cheek. When she let go with a brief sigh, I raised her to my shoulder, patting her back firmly without jarring her. If I returned her to the crib without burping her, she'd be restless or even awake. But if I did everything right, I might get three or even four more blissful hours of sleep.

My cheek rested against her soft head and my own eyes were closing when I heard her expel a bubble of air and then another. I kissed her fuzzy hair and took a last inhale, gathering myself for a smooth transfer from my shoulder to her crib.

But then, in an instant, I knew we were not alone. A sharp scent cut through the sweet smell of infant and the haze of sleep deprivation and mind-drugging love. The smell of sweat. And I heard panting, harsh and rough.

Every nerve in my body flared to life with a single impulse—*flight, flight, flight.*

The door to the nursery flew open, but it was only Michael standing there, illuminated by the glow of Grace's night-light and the baby monitor. His eyes were wide, unfocused, his face so pale it was almost green. His shirt was streaked with dark stains like he'd been working in the garden. He scanned the room, but not methodically as if checking to make sure everything was safe. His gaze darted from corner to corner as if he might surprise a danger lurking there, waiting to attack when he looked away.

"What's wrong?" I shrank back, clutching Grace to my chest.

But he shook his head and raised a finger to his lips.

"But—" I tried again, and he shook his head fiercely.

He held up a hand—*wait*—and left the room.

The tiny bundle in my arms was so warm, the little arms limp and the face slack, satiated with milk. Not even the tension hardening my muscles, not even the way I scooted back as if I could find extra protection against the window, made Grace stir. If something, someone, was in the house, I wouldn't follow Michael, not while I was holding my baby like my naked heart in front of me.

I glanced around the room. Everything seemed so unprotected. I was the first thing you'd see if the door opened, and the crib was the second. Carefully, I lifted Grace, not sure if I would hide her on the floor of the closet or under the crib, but the door opened and Michael was back. This time he had a pad of paper in his hand and a pen, silver and glittery.

He bent and unplugged the night-light and the monitor with a single movement. As my eyes blinked, trying to adjust to the dark, he pulled me into the closet.

My heart pounded against Grace, snug and oblivious between us.

Michael pulled out his phone, and in its dim light I read, *Say nothing. No lights. I'm not sure who's listening or watching.*

I reached for the phone, but he shook his head, mouthing, *Not safe*.

Suddenly, even in the enclosed center of my home, I felt completely exposed. And Michael looked wild, his eyes wide, his hands shaking. I reached up to touch his forehead, thinking *maybe he has a fever, maybe he's on drugs*, and he closed his eyes, leaned into my touch with a ragged breath that was almost a sob.

I shifted Grace to one arm and took the pen, my writing awkward and wobbly as I scrawled, *What's going on?*

He slipped the cell phone back into his pocket, but in the dark I could hear the pen moving over the paper. He pressed the pad back into my hand and raised the cell phone. I read: *He might be watching, but we have to get to the car. Danger! Trust me!!*

The last three words were underlined so hard that the pen had torn through the page and there was a dark smudge on the paper beneath them.

Grace gave a little cry, and I realized my grip had been tightening. "Okay," I whispered. What else could I say? If there wasn't any danger, humoring Michael wouldn't hurt. If he was high or sick, I'd have to get him into the car anyway to get him to the hospital. And if there was danger and I didn't listen to him, whatever happened next would be my fault.

He nodded curtly; then the closet went dark, and the sound of writing came back. But I could guess what he was worried about. If he really thought someone might see us inside the house, he'd definitely be worried about someone seeing us leave. And we couldn't just sneak through the darkened rooms in silence, slip into the garage, and then go driving away to safety.

My car wasn't safely in the garage like usual. I'd parked on the driveway. *Stupid*. His car was blocked in, and mine was right under the spotlight of a streetlamp. As one of us opened the driver's side and the other one tried to get Grace in the car seat, we'd be lit like actors on a stage.

The faster my pulse raced, the more I wanted to retreat with Grace, keep her safe, curl my body around hers.

In the dark, Michael was a shadowy form like the literal embodiment of the monster in the closet. If he was sane, if he was still the Michael I knew, then I also knew what he was doing. He was scribbling down a plan on the pad. The thrum of danger, waiting, and not-knowing was worse than anything. I put my hand over his. "Just—" I started to say, but he shook me off and put his fingers over my mouth hard. I felt the paper notepad pressed into my hands, and I had to bite back the words.

He held up the phone again, the light quavering in his shaking hand.

We have to go. It's Brady. Don't let him see. Go fast to the driver's side. I'll take Grace.

And then underneath: *No talking. I love you.*

Those last three words scared me most of all. They were tacked on the end like a "just in case" postscript. This was the moment when all those vows on our wedding day would be put to the test. You think you will love and honor someone, but how do you really know until the chips are down? Grace's small body radiated warmth as I raised her up and kissed her.

The light was out again; the closet was pitch-black, but backlit by my memory, I could still see Michael all our years together. When the world believed Aimee's lies, his faith in me had been absolute, and I'd never known why I deserved it or how I could repay it. I'd said something about that once, and he'd told me, "In marriage, it's not a question of repaying. Where you go, I go. We're a team."

I took another deep breath of Grace's head and lifted her onto Michael's shoulder.

Once her comforting weight was gone, I felt chilled, unmoored. But Michael's hand found mine. He pressed the car keys into my hand, and with a finger he tapped out *one, two, three.*

We ran, fast and silent, flattening ourselves against the wall, past the open maw of the hall bathroom, then into the expanse of the kitchen. Shouldn't we set off the alarm system to bring help? Shouldn't we call the police? Each internal question triggered another burst of adrenaline, but I had committed. *Follow Michael. Follow Grace.* Our house had never seemed so big, each window a point of exposure, each light fixture a potential camera.

Michael hadn't hesitated, opening the door single-handedly and sprinting to the car, and my panic drove my feet faster until I was light-headed. *Driver's side.* He'd said to go to the driver's side.

I'd been clenching the keys so tightly that it hurt to loosen my grip, and when I tried to find the car key, my nerveless fingers fumbled and almost dropped them, but I hit the lock.

Michael opened the passenger side and hissed, "Let's go!"

And I was in the driver's seat, starting the engine as he slammed the door shut, backing up before he was fully seated, driving away from our house, its windows dark, its front door open, while Michael still clutched Grace against his chest.

As the house retreated behind us, he twisted around, maneuvering her into her car seat.

Gently, I wanted to tell him. *Be careful.* It wasn't safe, hanging over the headrest, driving with Grace unsecured, any of this. But nothing was safe anymore.

Grace's belt clicked, and Michael dropped back into the seat beside me.

As I glanced at him, the car bumped up against the curb, and I wrenched the wheel, bringing us back onto the road. It was all I could do to control the car, to keep us moving straight, away from the danger. We were out of the neighborhood before I could draw a deep breath, still clenching the wheel so hard my hands hurt.

"Where are we going? What happened?" I looked at Michael, his face pale and almost gaunt, as if he'd lost twenty pounds in an evening. Like me, he'd left his seat belt unbuckled, the first time I'd ever seen him without one, and that was almost the scariest thing.

"The police station." His voice was heavy, and he reached out with one hand to touch my knee, as if for reassurance.

And then he started to cry.

I'd never seen Michael cry, not really. He'd gotten quiet, or choked up, or hunched over—but racking sobs, the kind that stole your breath and made it stutter, never. I kept driving, my heart pounding and the wheel in a death grip.

What could have happened?

"Please, please tell me what's wrong."

But his fingers only tightened on my knee as he fought to choke back the tears.

When we arrived, the world around the parking lot was dark, but the building glowed like the warm windows of a lighthouse. I was drawn to this antidote to the fear and darkness, and I parked directly in front of the building, underneath an arching security light.

I turned off the engine and put my hand on top of Michael's, the way I'd longed to. He was silent now. "You want to go in?"

Whatever he'd witnessed, whatever had happened, it couldn't be worse than this fog of ignorance. Every horrible thing I'd seen in a movie or news program scrolled through my mind, but it was all locked inside Michael's head, and he still wanted to protect me. That's the way he was. He thought we were in danger—Grace and me—and he'd taken us to safety, but now he'd have to tell us why, and he was afraid. Not just of what had happened but of what it might do to me.

"I'm okay." I squeezed his hand. "We're okay."

And with a shuddering sigh, he nodded and opened his car door.

The dome light came on, and when I reached automatically to unbuckle the seat belt I wasn't wearing, I saw it. My hand, smeared with something dark; more on the knee of my gray sweatpants. I rubbed my fingers together, my breath coming short with horror. Viscid, wanting to stick to itself, to bind my fingers together, transferred from Michael's hands to mine.

Blood.

He hadn't just seen something; he'd *done* something. I shouldn't have driven my husband here, delivered him up to the police when he was covered in blood. If he turned himself in, I'd lose him.

But Michael was already opening the door of the station, and as I flung my car door open, a mewling sound from the back seat reminded me. Grace was there.

Shit.

Shaking, I wiped my hands on my pants, scrubbing hard, but they still didn't feel clean. I opened the car door, some part of my mind chittering, *You're transferring DNA; you're contaminating evidence; you'll get blood on the baby; you're a bad wife, a bad mother.*

I wouldn't lift her out of the car seat and carry her, vulnerable and exposed. I'd take the whole carrier out of the base. She'd be cozy in her little bucket, with an awning I could pull down to keep her hidden and sturdy plastic sides protecting her.

And the blood on my hands wouldn't get anywhere near her body.

Unhooking the car seat was agony, my fingers fumbling across the release, but finally it popped free and I slid it out of the car. I had to set it down for a second to get the handle into position, and by that time both her eyes had fluttered open and she was staring at me intently.

"Everything's okay," I said softly. *Please, please go back to sleep. Don't cry, don't want to nurse. Just please, please, go back to sleep.*

Her brow furrowed. I couldn't even convince a baby.

Instead, I pulled the awning as far forward as it would go, hefted the weight of the seat, and followed Michael into the station.

Inside, the officer behind the glass, a slight woman with a neat brown bun, looked at us, at Michael and at me, clutching the handle of Grace's car seat. "Can I help you?"

I could almost see the thoughts behind her assessing gaze: *Domestic abuse? No visible trauma. Robbery? They would have called 911.*

"Michael?" I asked.

His face was fixed and grim. "I need to report a murder."

14

WHILE I WAS still trying to draw breath, to ask a single question, they took Michael into some other room. Scrambling to follow him, I dropped Grace's carrier on the floor with a thump, but she cried out, and in the seconds it took for me to look down at her, my husband was gone.

We waited. First in the waiting room, where the air conditioning blew too cold and the fluorescent lights were harsh and impersonal. Behind the glassed-in desk, the officer bent back to her work, not glancing up at us. Outside the world was dark, still sleeping, only a few sporadic cars on the road, a set of headlights punctuated by darkness again.

And I didn't know what Michael had seen, what he had done, who was dead. Was it Brady? Persistent tendrils of fear were choking me, slowing my heart, so that I struggled to breathe.

The chill and silence of the front room were oppressive. A police station in downtown Houston might be hopping at all hours, but early in the morning in this suburban corner of Sugar Land, all the scary things were tucked out of sight.

I couldn't sit down; my body wouldn't stay still. I paced around the chairs, arranged in formation to face the glass-fronted window where the front-desk officer sat, and past a display case featuring historical memorabilia, medals and ribbons, and contemporary awards, gleaming chunks of glass and polished wooden plaques.

Two years ago I would have been reassured by the sight of a police car, but now that Aimee had framed me, I knew I'd be flagged as "troubled." Any good policeman, one worthy of an award-winning department, would think twice before trusting me.

Grace wasn't sleeping, but she wasn't fussing anymore either. She watched me stride past her again. I approached the desk, and the officer looked up. Squinting, I read *D. Navarro* on her name badge. She was only a little older than me, her face all rounded curves of cheek and chin, a friendly face. She had seen my husband with his bloody hands, but I wanted to promise her that he wouldn't, couldn't have done anything wrong. There was no scenario on earth that I could imagine in which Michael had hurt anyone.

"Please." I searched her face. "Please, can someone tell me what's going on?"

"I'm sorry." She actually sounded sorry, but there was firmness in the set of her lips that left no room for negotiation.

"How long will I have to wait?"

"I can't say." She glanced at her computer, ready to get back to whatever she'd been doing before I interrupted.

I'd bet she *could* say, but she wouldn't. She had all the answers and I had nothing. Michael didn't need her faux friendliness right now. He was still in danger, being interrogated in the bowels of this building. And someone was dead, the thought as dangerous as a downed power line. If I got too close, if I started to wonder who or how, to think about that blood, I'd be overwhelmed. Grace and Michael needed me, so I shoved those thoughts away, the unknown victim flickering at the edge of my consciousness, stripping my nerves raw.

For all I knew, they'd blame him, my Michael, who'd been so terrified, so determined to protect me and Grace. The next time I saw him could be through bars. It was up to me to keep that from happening. He needed a lawyer, and there was only one I knew personally. Why hadn't I taken two seconds to grab my cell phone?

"Is there a phone I can use?" I wanted to keep talking, to persuade Officer Navarro, to make her like me, but I shut my mouth tight after the question. Nothing I said could help me or Michael, not when I was completely in the dark.

"Sure." Maybe it was my imagination, but she looked relieved to give me an affirmative answer. She pointed to the hallway just past the display case, and I saw an alcove I hadn't noticed. My brain was so tired, so stressed, so stupid. What else had I missed?

I nodded my thanks and turned, saying over my shoulder, "I'm just going to get something from the car." For a second I wondered, if I picked Grace up, would it look like I might flee? But no one had asked me any questions or seemed to care what I did.

I lugged the baby carrier to the passenger side of the car and set it down. The black sky that arched over the electric lights of the city had bleached gray. Dawn was only a couple minutes away.

In the glove compartment I found it, the Bluebonnet Women's Club directory, just where Elizabeth had told me to keep it. "You'll be driving to book club or craft group or a fund raiser meeting and you'll need to check an address," she'd said, "or you'll be out and you'll want to meet up with people, and you'll be glad it's there. I'm never at home when I need mine."

But I didn't flip through it by the dome light. I had my back to Grace for only a second before I seized the book and got out of the car. I didn't even want to blink for fear something might attack us. I hauled her back into the station, all the way to the courtesy phone, and only then did I flip through the book for the home number I needed. I knew I would wake Alondra, but I dialed anyway.

As it rang, my nerves winched tighter and tighter. And when the call hit voice mail, I dialed again. And again. The fourth time, a woman answered, snapping, "What?"

"Alondra?"

"Hold on."

And then Alondra was on the phone, listening as I gasped out words that didn't make any sense, "Michael" and "murder" and "police station."

The only question she asked was, "Which one?"

I hung up the phone, exhaustion flooding me instead of relief. Alondra would take care of Michael, and I'd take care of my baby. Normally Grace could go longer than two hours, but she was already chewing on her fist.

Returning to Officer Navarro, I asked, "Is there a place, I mean, someplace private, I could nurse?"

Right on cue, Grace made a gurgle that ended in a complaint.

The officer smiled. "Sure. We've got a community room that nobody's using right now. Come on through."

She buzzed the door open, and I hefted Grace's carrier and walked in, listening hard, but I didn't hear Michael's voice anywhere. When Officer Navarro met me in the hallway, I asked point-blank, "Are they going to question me? Or at least tell me what's going on?"

Her friendliness faded a little, as if she suspected that I'd used Grace to try to get some information, but then another cry, sharper, came from the carrier to bolster my story. "I really can't say." Officer Navarro reached out a finger to stroke Grace's hand. "I mean, I don't know. Let me show you to the community room, you can get this little one fed, and I'll follow up with Detective Clark."

Alone in the spacious "community room," where a few plastic chairs were scattered about and a series of inspirational posters aimed at children lined the walls, I unbuckled Grace from her car seat, trying not to look at or think about the smudges on her pajamas from Michael's bloody hands.

As I'd feared, her diaper was squishy, but she didn't smell and I hoped it was only wet. She was already making her little complaining, grunting cries, but she wasn't wailing full throttle. I shut the door to the hallway and chose a chair not in the line of sight from the room's small window. Although the police station was probably riddled with cameras.

Even a starving baby will rebel against tension in your body, fight and wail. And Grace had to eat. I didn't know how long we'd be here, but my nerves were raw and throbbing, and if she started to howl, I didn't know what I'd do. Break into a million pieces, shatter, howl myself.

I squeezed my eyes shut, took one breath, slowed it down, and took another. Carefully, I tucked Grace under my T-shirt. She tensed, and I tensed, and she arched her back with a shrill cry.

One more breath, my slowest yet, and I crooned the first few bars of my mother's favorite lullaby: "Too-ra-loo-ra." Finally, she latched on, and my entire body was flooded with visceral relief.

How had we gotten here? The evening had been so ordinary, so normal. I closed my eyes, remembering. After dinner, Michael had taken Grace for her "bath," really just a wipe-down with a warm damp cloth run under her chin and around the folds on her arms and legs. I'd cleared the table, savoring the way the light slanted through our front windows. Early evening, and my family was home together. Everything felt so right.

He'd brought her back and given her to me. If all went well, we'd have an hour or so until she needed to be fed again, and then if I was smart, I'd go to bed early.

But this night she'd reared up and started rooting on my shoulder, patting with her little hand and making insistent grunts. She wasn't going to wait an hour. She wasn't going to wait fifteen minutes.

"Do you want to watch something?" I'd asked.

"Sure." Michael picked up the remote, but before he could do more than click the television on, there was a tap at our back patio door. My arms tightened around Grace, but then I saw it was only Brady.

Michael tossed me the remote. "Back in a few."

I'd found a channel showing old sitcoms, and to the syncopation of the familiar dialogue, I positioned Grace. She latched on and nursed with greedy gulps, her tiny fingers curling and flexing.

The sound of Michael's and Brady's voices from the backyard was comforting, and it made me miss Lena. She'd been gone only a few days, but it would be another week before she was due to return. How quickly I'd become accustomed to having a friend right next door. I looked down at Grace's little face, her eyes not fluttering shut as they should have been but wide open, impossibly bright, staring at me. She'd stopped nursing and was just looking, like she'd never seen me before.

She didn't resist or protest as I lifted her to my shoulder, patting her on the back softly, and then a little more firmly until she burped. Then she pushed up again, twisting to look at me. No chance she'd be going to sleep anytime soon. If she insisted on three hours of this "quiet alert" stage and then I fed her again, maybe, just maybe, I could get to sleep by eleven, then feed her at three-ish in the morning, then get another few hours of sleep before rising at a normal hour.

I went to the back door and looked out. The yard was shadowy, the sun too low now to light it. Michael was kneeling on the ground, examining some part of the tiered garden structure, and while I couldn't see Brady, I could hear him shout from the other side of the fence, "Try it now."

Then an arc of water rose from beside Michael, curving up and over the top of the garden, falling on the tiers I couldn't see, the ones on Brady and Lena's side.

"Add the pulse," Michael shouted back.

And the water changed from a smooth arc to a series of dashes, the flow of the water interrupted even as the arc remained. With a whoop, Michael stood and stepped back to admire his work.

I turned Grace to face the yard. Maybe she would see the light shining on the flashing water, or just her father and his eager, excited face.

Then Brady pushed back through the fence. "Looks even better from this side."

"Now we just have to get your part rigged up." Michael glanced back and saw me there. "Hey, isn't it cool? We'll have at least one from each side, like a water display. It has to be high-powered enough to sustain the arc, but not so much that it batters the plants."

"Looks like the water feature at the Galleria." Elizabeth and I had walked there just last week, pushing the babies past the designer stores, looking down at the skating rink, and people-watching, observing shoppers from all over the world.

"Or a mini Bellagio." Michael slipped his arm around me and kissed the top of Grace's head. I leaned in, loving the way we made a complete group, ready for our portrait.

Brady was watching us, a strange expression on his face, but when I met his eyes, he looked like his usual self again. "Success like this calls for a toast. You in?"

"Go ahead." I felt like curling up with Grace, snuggled on my own sofa, in a safe world. Without Lena, Brady was too bulky, too boisterous, just too much.

Now in this cold police station, I would have given anything to be back in that moment with Michael's arm around my shoulder. If I could have done it all again, I'd have said, "No, don't go with Brady." I'd make Michael stay home, and we'd have been safe. None of this would have happened. We'd have spent the evening together on the sofa; we'd wake together in our own bed; the world would have been right.

This community room was frigid, I was tired, and the little plastic chair was sending spasms of pain through my lower back, counteracting the weight of the hours I'd been awake and the stress dragging down my limbs. I kept trying to force my brain to work, to pick through my memory for the key that would make the police give Michael back to me.

I ran through the math again in my mind, the things I would say when they questioned me, hoping the numbers would add up to something that would save my husband. Michael had gone off with Brady at nine o'clock; I'd nursed Grace and put her down at eleven. He hadn't been home when I heard her fussing at two in the morning. But sometime between two and three, he'd come back in, and this nightmare had begun. A little over five hours. They hadn't been driving, there hadn't been anyone else in the house, but something terrible had happened. Not only that, but Michael had been afraid that someone would be watching us. Was it Brady? Or had the mysterious someone killed him?

No, this whole thing was crazy. Michael could never have been involved in a murder. Never. Nobody was dead. This was just some kind of misunderstanding.

Nursing Grace in an empty room with my head bowed and my whole body arching in and over my baby like a shell, I felt like I was in the right position for praying. I fell back on the one I'd prayed as a child: *Please, God, please let everything be okay. Please, let this be okay.* I was praying for Michael, alone somewhere and traumatized; I was praying for myself, frustrated and helpless; I was praying for Grace, who deserved a peaceful life with parents who were in control. And I had a sense I was praying for someone unknown. Someone whose blood stained my sweatpants.

I wasn't braced against the flood of feeling, the deep well of sorrow, that I tapped into. I tried to choke it down, but my throat was full of the wail I couldn't utter.

Finally, Grace's frantic nursing stopped. I tickled her cheek, but instead of resuming, she pulled off and gave me a loopy, milk-drunk smile. Cuddling her against my shoulder, I patted her back until she gave a little burp. I tucked Grace back into her seat, feeling a pang of guilt as I maneuvered the buckle over her swollen diaper. Maybe the police station had a spare one somewhere.

When I stepped out into the hallway, I wasn't alone. Coming directly toward me from the lobby was Brady, his hands cuffed in back, his head raised defiantly. Two officers were following behind him and another was leading the way down the hall, but all I could see was the familiar face. His T-shirt was too dark for me to make out any stains, and his jeans were black as well. I fell back a step into the doorway of the room, moving Grace's seat so she was behind me.

And he noticed. Of course he did. This time his gaze held mine and his wink was slow, knowing. Then he bared his teeth in a smile.

CHAPTER

15

THROUGH THE FRONT windows of the station, I could see the sun had risen and cars were taking people to work or to school or to the shops, but Grace and I were stuck in limbo without Michael. At least he wasn't alone now. Nothing short of my first sight of Grace had ever been as welcome as Alondra, walking through the door in her pencil skirt and matching blazer. She looked like a professional badass, and her brisk nod of greeting had warmed me more than the broadest smile. When she disappeared through the doors into the bowels of the station, I knew someone was finally on our side.

After a long time, such a long time, while other people and officers, all strangers to me, passed through the lobby, Alondra came back. Her hair was just as sleek, her pencil skirt uncreased, but there was tension in the corners of her mouth and eyes. And Michael wasn't with her.

I stood, accidentally brushing the handle of Grace's little seat, and I heard my baby stir. "Where's Michael?"

Alondra drew me back down so that we were sitting beside each other. She kept her hand above my elbow, a tight grip. A few seats away, an elderly man watched us with unabashed interest.

Alondra lowered her voice. "They haven't charged him with anything, but they're going to detain him for a while. It could be all day. And they want to question you."

"What will I do with Grace?" I couldn't leave her behind, but bringing her with me would divide my attention, a part of my consciousness always hovering over her. And I needed to be fully focused for Michael's sake, and my own.

"I think at her age she can go into the interview room with you if she stays in her carrier, or they'll have an officer sit with her."

My heart started to pound even harder, and I opened my mouth to protest, but Alondra held up a hand. "I've heard Michael's initial statement, and before we go any further, I want you to tell me quickly and quietly exactly what happened last night."

"I was nursing Grace." I paused. "I mean, Brady came over." But that wasn't right either. "He knocked on our back door, and he and Michael worked on the garden. They showed me they'd fixed the sprinklers." Those flashing fountains seemed a thousand lifetimes ago. "Then Michael went over to hang out with Brady, and I nursed Grace."

"So he was only gone a few minutes?"

Grace sighed in her sleep, and I let myself watch her, taking in her round cheeks, her plump uncovered legs. Uncovered because I hadn't grabbed so much as a blanket or a Binky as we fled. "No, this was the last feeding before I went to sleep. I got up again at two, and he wasn't home. But while I was rocking her, he came back. He . . ." I wasn't sure how to describe the urgency, the fierce pantomime. "He wouldn't talk; he cut off the lights and took me, us, into the closet. He said—he wrote down—that we might be watched, that we had to run to the car. We couldn't go to the garage because I'd parked in the driveway, blocking him in." I stopped. Alondra must think I was out of my mind. Because we didn't live this kind of life. The worst thing that had ever happened in our neighborhood was kids joyriding. Michael and I had been next door a hundred times. Maybe I was insane. This couldn't be real. "He took the baby, and we ran through the house to the car. We drove away, and he said to come straight here."

"Did he tell you what happened?"

I shook my head, ashamed to look at her. Alondra would never just obey a man blindly. She would have demanded answers; she would have stormed into Brady's house and saved the day.

But then I saw a dark smear against the light-gray fabric of my sweatpants. Michael's hands had been bloody.

My whole body flashed hot, then cold. "Please, please just let me see him."

Abruptly she hugged me, awkward and angular but real. When she pulled back, she met my eyes. "We're going to get through this, but you have to hold it together. If I end up representing Michael . . ." She shook her head. "I may need to pull in someone else from my office. But that's a concern for later. Right now, your next step is answering some questions. And I'll be with you. First, they may read you your Miranda rights—"

I yelped in protest, my whole body recoiling. I should have known that the innocent got blamed and framed, that no one would believe me or Michael, it would be just like before, only instead of embezzlement, this would be something bloody. They'd take Grace away, they'd throw me in jail, they—

Alondra gave me a little shake. "Hey, it's protocol. And they might not. But even if they do, it doesn't mean they're charging you. You won't have to answer a thing, not a single thing, unless I give you a signal. Look at me. Focus." She gave me a small, unmistakable nod. "I'm here for you. Okay?"

She waited until I nodded back, and then she said, "Okay. So they may read you your rights, they may give you papers to sign, but I'll look at each and every one first. Then they'll want you to tell them the events of last night, just the same way you did for me. You'll have to repeat parts and tell them out of order, they may go over the whole thing several times, but don't get flustered. Don't guess or try to speculate. Just say that you don't know and stick to the facts you're completely sure about."

I felt so alone. "When can I see Michael?"

She shook her head. "Don't worry about that right now. The only thing you need to focus on is this interview. Then we'll get you and Grace out of here."

"Whatever happened, they know it was Brady's fault, right?" Brady had been the one in handcuffs, and he could be lying his ass off this very minute, trying to put all the blame on Michael.

Alondra stood, and as I rose to my feet, she said, "I know you have questions. Let's get through this interview, and then we'll deal with what comes next."

I followed her back into the depths of the station, lugging Grace in her carrier. There were two detectives waiting in the hallway—a man about a decade older than me and a woman with close-cropped hair and a narrow face who looked about my age. While they were introducing themselves as Detectives Haley and Clark, I couldn't help looking past them, yearning for a glimpse of Michael. I could hear the hum of voices, but they belonged to anonymous strangers, not my husband.

The detectives exchanged glances, and the man held open the door to a bland room with a table, a few chairs, and a camera set up in the corner. The woman, Detective Clark, motioned me in, and Alondra followed right behind. So it would be just us girls. Maybe this detective thought she'd have rapport with me?

She motioned to a chair. "Please have a seat. Do you need a glass of water or a cup of coffee?"

I shook my head. Nothing Detective Clark gave me would set me at ease. I still remembered every detail of the case in Jersey, how the oily detective's questions all implied I was guilty, everyone knew it, I was a thief and a liar, so I should just come clean. Eventually he'd even threatened me, but there wasn't any evidence. I'd gotten off that time, but I knew the truth. This detective was not my friend either.

Setting Grace's carrier gently on the ground, I sat. Alondra's expression was impassive, but she studied me intently. I must look as strung out and terrified as I felt. I'd never had much of a poker face, and it was taking all my effort to remain upright and lucid. I didn't have enough energy left to try to hold anything back. Maybe criminals were better at compartmentalizing or multitasking. Maybe they just believed their own lies. I had to hope that truth and Alondra would save me.

The questions Detective Clark asked were like the "active listening" questions I got from Dr. Lindsey. I'd describe what happened, from the time Brady knocked on our back door to the time Michael and I pulled up in front of the police station. And then she'd ask about a small part of it again, repeating what I had said. "So, Mrs. Tremaine, you said Michael left with Brady at nine?"

"Yes." My mind whirled. Wasn't that what I'd said? Had I misremembered the time? My voice sounded weak, thin, untrustworthy.

The detective always followed up. "And what time did you say you went to sleep?"

"Asked and answered, Detective." I was so grateful for Alondra, fierce and awake, while my next-to-sleepless night and caffeineless morning were catching up to me. This interview room, these nice-for-now questions, everything made me feel caught in a mixture of my worst memories and a waking nightmare.

"I'm just trying to nail down the times, counselor. We all know it's not easy to keep track of that kind of detail, especially for a new parent, who might be a little sleep deprived."

"Actually . . ." This woke me up a bit. "Actually, I was really aware of the time. Grace's on a three-hour feeding schedule right now. Sometimes she goes four hours, but I always know when her last feeding was before I put her down, because that helps me know how long she's slept." *And how long I've slept.* "I fed her at eleven and then went to sleep myself. She's not good about taking a bottle, so when I heard her at two, I got up to feed her. And I checked the time, and it had been three hours. On a regular night, if everything went well, she might even have slept for four more after. Once she went five. And that would have put us between six and seven, which is when I've been getting up. She's pretty regular." I looked at Alondra. "I even fed her here at six. And she'll want to be nursed again in about an hour."

Alondra said, "Any other questions about my client's grasp of time?"

Detective Clark gave a little half smile that acknowledged she'd pushed me and Alondra too far. "Let's talk about your neighbors."

I sat up straighter. Maybe I could tell from the questions she asked what exactly had happened, what they suspected.

"How long have you known Brady and Lena Voss?"

"Almost a year and a half now, ever since we moved in."

"And how would you describe your relationship?"

"Friendly?" I sounded like I wasn't sure. "We're friends." Although I wouldn't describe myself as Brady's friend. Especially not after seeing him in the hallway. It was terrifying how easily I'd accepted he was a murderer. He must be. "I'm friends with Lena."

"And your husband, he was friends with Brady."

"I guess." How much did she know? If I said *Yes, they were friends; they worked in the yard and went fishing together*, would Michael be implicated in whatever Brady had done? But if I downplayed it, or worse, lied and the cops found out, that might make it look like there was something to hide. As if she could sense my distress, Grace let out a sharp cry. I glanced down, and her eyes were wide open, searching my face.

"You spend a lot of time together."

I didn't look at Detective Clark and instead watched Grace as she tried to find her mouth with her fist. She shouldn't be hungry, but she was looking for comfort. "Some. I mean, Lena and I go walking almost every day, and then we all hang out a couple of evenings a week."

"What kind of things do you do?"

"We have dinner, sit around their pool. Lena taught me to bake. Michael and Brady built a tiered garden thing. They've been running it around the fence, and they're making changes to the sprinkler system. Hacking it, they say. That's why Brady came over last night, like I said. They got the sprinklers on the first raised bed so they looked like a fountain."

Grace gave up on her fist and squawked again.

The detective made a noncommittal *hmm*. "And when was the last time you saw Mrs. Voss?"

I reached down and guided Grace's fingers toward her mouth, but she arched away and let out another cry. She wasn't going to put up with this much longer, and I wasn't sure I could either. "Lena? Wednesday. She was going to see her aunt in Texarkana. She's supposed to be back next week."

"Have you heard from her since she left?"

"She texted me a couple of times." I reached for my phone, but Alondra put her hand on my arm, and I stopped, as I remembered I didn't have it anyway. Was she worried that something on my phone could be used against Michael? "I think the last time was yesterday morning."

Detective Clark addressed Alondra. "We'll need to see those texts."

"We'll review your request after the interview." Alondra's voice was cool.

"Who told you about Lena's trip?" Detective Clark shuffled some papers, as if she had all the answers written down and I was getting everything wrong. Then another thought sent shards of ice into my heart. Was Lena okay? Maybe Brady had sent those texts. If I weren't in this room, I'd call her. I desperately wanted to hear her voice.

"Lena told me. She's okay, right? Have you talked to her?" Grace's cries were coming faster now, scraping me to the bone. I bent down and unsnapped her from the carrier, lifting her to my shoulder, where she nestled into my neck.

"Had she mentioned this aunt before?"

"Yes, she had. Her aunt practically raised her."

Detective Clark made some notes on the papers in front of her. Then she said, "Can you think of anywhere else Lena might have gone? Any places that were special to her? Any friends or other family she might have visited?"

Another jolt to my system. *They don't think Lena is at her aunt's house, and there's blood on my sweatpants, and, oh please God, don't let it be Lena's.* We'd spent so many hours talking, talking, talking, and about what? I knew her opinions on every television show we'd watched, on the merits of triple sec versus orange juice, and I knew tons of details about her childhood, but they were vague, unpleasant. "I know she grew up in Arkansas. I think her aunt was the only family she was close to. She wasn't on social media, except for the business."

"No idea where else she might have traveled?"

"She said she wanted to go someplace tropical for a second honeymoon. She and Brady didn't get a real first one, and she wanted to go someplace like Hawaii or the Virgin Islands." Not a cruise. I could hear Lena's voice in my head: *Floating cesspools of forced fun? Hard pass.* But she'd liked the idea of an all-inclusive resort. With Brady, anyway. Even the thought of his smile with its bared teeth made me shudder.

"No idea who else she might have been in contact with?"

"She never really mentioned anyone else. She . . ." How could I explain who Lena was without sounding like I hadn't known her at all? "She lived in the moment. Even when she talked about the past, it was just a fleeting thing, unspecific. Her business, her husband, their clients, the Bluebonnet Club, that was pretty much her social world."

"What's the Bluebonnet Club?"

"It's a social group. We raise money for charity."

She gave a little nod, and I felt like a complete dilettante. Helpless to save Michael or Lena, too stupid for a real job, just a lightweight. As if she could read my thoughts, Alondra winked.

Of course, the club was where I'd met Alondra. And no one would consider her a bored housewife.

"Have you tried to get in touch with Lena?" I asked. "Isn't she at her aunt's house?"

The detective didn't respond, and Grace squirmed against my embrace.

"Alondra," I whispered.

"Later," she mouthed back. Then, a little louder, she said, "I think my client has been more than cooperative. Given that she and her daughter have been here since two this morning, and given that she is neither a witness nor a suspect, don't you agree that it's time to send her home?"

I expected Detective Clark to protest, but instead she raised an eyebrow at Alondra. "I think you may be right, counselor. As long as Mrs. Tremaine remains available to assist our investigation as needed and refrains from speaking to the press, I think she should be clear to return to her home for now."

The thought of a shower, a fresh diaper for Grace, snuggling together under a blanket on our sofa, sounded like such sweet relief that it took a moment for the poison to hit my system.

Refrain from speaking to the press.

Not the press. Not again.

16

I HELD BACK MY questions, not wanting to ask in front of the detective, even though my anxiety was rising. Alondra walked me out into the lobby, and then I turned to face her. "What about the press?"

Alondra's mouth was a grim line. "Sooner or later the news will get out. Reporters will contact you."

"But I don't even know what happened."

"I know." Alondra put a hand on my arm. "And as soon as I can tell you more, I will."

"So I'm supposed to just go home and wait?"

Alondra looked apologetic. "Actually, right now the police are searching your house."

"What?" Anger flooded me. That detective had said I could go home, but she must have known I couldn't. "Why?" My box of paper stars, the postcards from Aimee, Grace's nursery, all being touched and tossed about by strangers. "I want to see Michael." My words quavered, but the longer he was away, the more I ached to see him, to know he was safe.

Alondra lowered her voice. "That's not going to be possible this minute. Right now, he's assisting the police."

"Alondra, what happened? I have to know. There was blood, and I saw Brady—"

She glanced around the room as if confirming that no one was too close to us. I'd never seen Alondra cautious or tentative, but it was one more unsettling thing in a nightmare series of events. "You can't talk about this, not with anyone. Not your mother, not your doctor, not your priest. Do you understand?"

I nodded, barely registering what I was promising. Nothing mattered but Michael.

"The police have arrested Brady for murder."

My insides went hot, liquid. Brady, my best friend's husband. Brady, who'd never really put me at ease. But Michael had worked next to him in our yard, relaxing in his presence the way I did around Lena. Had Brady taken advantage of that trust? "The blood—what happened? Who's dead? Michael didn't do anything."

"I can't tell you about Michael's statement, but it resulted in the arrest."

"But Michael's okay? They haven't charged him?"

"They haven't charged him yet."

"When can I see him?" I could hear the pleading sob in my voice, but I didn't have the energy to be ashamed.

"He's not here. He's gone with the police to walk them through the crime scene."

The crime scene . . . "Lena's house?"

"And he's given permission for them to search your house as well."

My house. Our safe space with Grace's nursery and all my books and our kitchen table. "But I didn't . . . nobody asked me."

"They only needed permission from one of you, and they talked to him first." Her voice was so controlled, so even. That was the kind of strength and self-possession I wished I had. Instead, everything I learned was another blow that sent me reeling, until I couldn't believe I wasn't huddled in a fetal position on the ground.

But Grace was at my side in her car seat. One little leg bent and straightened out at an angle, her bare, uncovered toes flexing in the chill air. I had to be strong for her, hold it together, not break down. But I wasn't prepared, not as a wife whose husband was being interrogated nor as a mom who hadn't brought a diaper bag or a Binky. Grace probably already needed a new diaper, and if she'd had a blowout, she'd have to stay in her soiled outfit. Maybe we were free to leave, but the truth was, we had nowhere to go.

"So Michael's not even *here* anymore?" My voice was rising, taking on a hysterical edge.

"You can meet him at home as soon as they've finished their search." She checked her phone. "Almost done."

I shook my head hard, then ran my hands through my hair and tugged, trying to clear my mind, to make this world seem real. A world where Lena might be dead, Brady might be a killer, Michael might be in custody.

"Kacy, I have to say something, and it's important. Are you listening?"

I wrenched my attention back to Alondra. She said, "This is going to hit the news cycle. Maybe in the next few hours, maybe in the next few days. You need to be prepared for that. Is there somewhere else you can go, someone you can stay with?"

"I can't go home?"

"You can . . ." Her brows were furrowed. "But you might need another place, a quieter place to stay. It's hard to tell how these things will play out. Is there somewhere else you could go?"

I thought of an impersonal hotel or Elizabeth's small house. "Not without Michael."

Her lips thinned, and I could almost hear the words she was holding back. *That's what you say now, but wait until things get worse.*

Then she glanced down at her phone. "All clear. You can go home."

For now.

*   *   *

I had to drive our car back to the house. In the harsh glare of full morning, I could see details that I hadn't noticed at night. The smudge on the gray plastic inside the passenger's side door that might be blood. Another one on the driver's seat, where Michael's hand had touched my knee. I'd been awake since two, my nerves felt scraped and raw, and I wanted to burn the clothes I was wearing. Even sweet Grace stank, her diaper bloated, her outfit creased and stained.

When we turned into our neighborhood, everything was cartoonishly bright. The elementary school was just getting ready to start, and I could see Rahmia and Emir walking with Bibi, shining like cotton candy in the sunlight. On either side of the street, groups of children were running, walking in a cluster around an adult, racing each other on bikes or scooters. I was spilled ink on this storybook picture, a refugee from a noir film stumbling into a Disney song. Nice moms like these didn't spend the night in a police station. None of my neighbors had blood on their outfit.

I was driving slowly, ridiculously slow. I didn't even have my wallet. No identification at all. But there were documents in the glove box. They might get me for driving without a license, but I could prove where I lived. And honestly, if I got a ticket for a minor driving infraction at this point, I'd just laugh.

I could feel the dread creeping up on me as I approached the turn onto our street. There was a breath, just a second, when I was making that turn past Rahmia's house and I thought maybe everything would be normal. A flash where I could imagine Michael and Grace and me safely at home.

And then I saw the cars crowding both sides of our normally uncrowded street. A police car, a white van, a news van with a roof-mounted satellite dish, more cars. And people going in and out of Brady and Lena's house, carrying plastic tubs. A tent was set up over the front of their garage. And there were reporters, one standing with a microphone on the opposite side of the street, a cameraman nearby.

Stunned, I eased my foot off the gas, and as I drifted to a stop in the middle of the road, I saw the barricade. A policeman in uniform caught my eye and waved me off to the right. I turned onto Windswept Court driving past the mailboxes, following the road around until it joined up with my street so I could approach from the other direction of the loop. Things didn't look any better from this side, but the barricade didn't block my driveway. An unfamiliar car did.

I parked on the side of the road, two houses down from my own, three from Lena's.

Afraid now, afraid of being stopped by the police, of being barred from seeing Michael, of being on the news, I picked up the garage door opener and took Grace out of the back seat.

Walking quickly, I left the sidewalk and with purpose crossed my neighbor's yard, positioning myself as close as possible to the garage. When I hit the button, it felt like three dozen people snapped their heads around to stare at me, but as soon as there was enough space, I ducked under, sliding Grace's seat with me, and sent the door crashing down again.

Were the police still inside? Would they be expecting me?

At the door to the laundry room, I called out, "Hello?"

Michael answered, "Kacy?"

He was in the kitchen. I raced to find him, leaving Grace rocking in her little car seat in the hallway.

My husband looked like he had lost thirty pounds. He was wearing gray industrial sweatpants a size too big and a navy-blue T-shirt with *Sugar Land Skeeters* on it. A stranger's clothes, and when I threw my arms around him, I could smell industrial detergent over the sour stench of sweat. He hugged me so hard that for a second I couldn't breathe, but the pain was proof that this was real, we were together.

Then I pulled back to look at his face, and I was afraid all over again.

17

ALONDRA HAD SAID not to discuss the case, but as soon as I saw Michael, every warning evaporated. I touched his cheek, his stubble scratchy against my fingers. "What happened?"

In the eight hours since I'd seen him last, the lines around his eyes and mouth had deepened, and his shoulders were hunched. "I can't," he muttered.

I hugged him again, pressing myself against the cheap T-shirt issued by the police. "They wouldn't tell me anything."

He looked into my face with an intensity that scared me. "If they charge me and we've discussed this at all, you could be charged too."

Stumbling back, I knocked down a kitchen chair, its crash echoing through the house. "Charge you? Why would they charge you?"

From the hallway, I could hear Grace's tentative cry.

"I don't know what the police are going to do. But if we talk, you could be charged as an accessory. That's what your friend the lawyer says." He shook his head, the way he always did after running a personal risk analysis. "We can't take that chance."

"Nobody's going to charge us. Nobody will even know."

"She said spousal privilege is waived if we've talked. I'm not going to put you in danger." I knew he'd walk away rather than change his mind.

"Michael . . ." But I couldn't speak over the swell of pain under my breastbone. Then he wrapped me in his arms again, hugging me until I almost couldn't breathe. "You have to tell me. You have to."

He tried to turn away, but I grabbed his arms so hard my hands hurt. "Who's dead? What did Brady do?"

"I can't tell you." He ducked his head, trying to avoid my gaze, but I clung to him.

"You have to. I'm your wife. I love you, no matter what." Michael had never said *no* to me, not when I'd insisted.

He ran a hand over the back of his neck, shifting from foot to foot. I knew he wanted to follow the rules and make the best, smartest choice. But he loved me, and I wasn't letting go. Finally he inhaled and said, "We were drinking, watching the game, and I heard something upstairs. Brady got a funny look on his face, and he said, 'Wanna see something cool?' " Michael's gaze was distant. "So I followed him up, and—"

Still looking intently at the floor, over my shoulder, anywhere but into my eyes, he said, "There was a woman, tied up, in the room at the end of the hall, the one they said was storage. It was . . ." He shook his head like he was trying to shake away the memory. "There was a bed, a camera, and video monitors. She'd rolled onto the floor, and he'd . . ." Michael pulled away from me. "I was too late to help her. And . . ." He swallowed hard. "And on one of the screens, I could see you. Asleep."

Grace let out another wail, but I was frozen in the realization that Brady had been watching me, watching us, for months.

"I thought he'd kill me and then come for you. I couldn't . . ." Michael turned away again, his shoulders vulnerable, his voice muffled and thick. "I told him whatever he wanted to hear, and as soon as I could, I came home."

"Five hours," I whispered. Five hours when I'd been sleeping and Michael had been fighting for our lives. What would I have done in his place? Screamed, fallen on my knees beside the woman, run? Any of those choices would have gotten me killed. But how had he been able to convince Brady to trust him? I'd always been able to read Michael, and now I studied his face, but it was a locked door.

In the hallway Grace was crying now, and Michael turned, almost running toward her. I followed him, the details of what he'd told me swirling. He stopped in front of the carrier and bent down. Grace's sobs abated as she stared at him. He reached out with both hands, then hesitated and let them fall to his sides. "I can't. You do it."

Quickly I unsnapped Grace from her carrier and picked her up, letting her nuzzle into my neck. Michael had shoved his balled-up hands into the pockets of his sweatpants. His face looked older and worn, and in the ill-fitting clothes issued by the police, he seemed almost like a stranger playing the part of my husband.

The blood on his hands, the woman . . . "Was it Lena?"

"What?" He did look at me then, his eyes rimmed with red.

"The woman. Who was it?"

He shook his head. "Not Lena. Younger. And she had brown hair. Like you."

And then he did step closer, his face crumpling again. Shifting Grace to one side, I pulled Michael close, feeling the dampness of his tears against my neck. He'd been so strong for so long, long before this terrible night. Now he needed me, and I was going to be just as strong for him. We were a team, and we'd get through this together.

*   *   *

The next few days were a nightmare, caught between piercing fear and unrelenting tedium, the grinding certainty that terrible things were on the horizon but all I could do was wait. Wait as the police summoned Michael for another round of questioning, wait as the reporters filled our lawn, wait until the next awful surprise.

The police had gone over our house, every inch of it, and they had found cameras in the security system, hidden in the white boxes that housed the motion sensors. "Why didn't they interfere with the alarm?" I'd asked the technician who'd carefully disman-tled the box.

He shrugged. "Plastic housing was big enough for both. And your system's hooked into the landline, but these cameras are wireless."

The tech team searched every corner of our house, and the scanners they used made Brady's look like a child's toy. For all I knew, it might have been. We'd invited in the very person who'd installed the cameras, and we'd believed every lie he'd told us.

No wonder his special sweeper hadn't found them. He'd probably rigged it to beep whenever he wanted.

And now our house had holes and gashes, missing pieces removed by the police, and the parts that remained were tainted and untrustworthy.

They'd even dug up the tiered garden Michael and Brady had built. Now the lumber was piled to one side, the plants in a wilted heap beside the mound of loose earth the police had dumped back into the hole. Maybe it did resemble a fresh grave, but at least I knew it was empty.

I did what I could, fixing concrete things that didn't distract my mind from the vortex of questions. I had the locks changed and the alarms rewired and rearmed, for all the good those security features had ever done us. I bought a rosebush and stuck it into the space where the garden used to be. I hauled the lumber to the curb. And now Grace and I were waiting again. Just like we had been for days.

But no, it was more than waiting. I had summoned all my strength to talk to my mother, to tell her the barest outline of what had happened. And then I spent twice as long talking her out of flying to be with us like she had after Grace was born. "You can't do anything right now, Mom. Nobody's sick. We're okay," I said, even though I wished to my bones that she was right next to me, wrapping me in a hug, making it all go away. But I wasn't a child. Letting my parents come down would only put more people I loved in an untenable position.

I called Michael's parents, too, hoping to spare him some of the trauma of reliving the story. But of course it didn't work. He was their only child. They had always been kind to me, they probably even loved me, but they needed to hear this from him. Which meant he had to explain to them why it wasn't a good idea for them to try to travel, how he would be fine and how we had a good lawyer. And I listened as he minimized his own fear and pain to assuage theirs. When he hung up, I'd seen the shadow of his father's oxygen tank and his mother's tremor in the way he swiped a hand across his eyes.

Now he was at work, negotiating with his bosses to keep his job. "Don't worry," he'd told me. "It's not like I have a public position, and what I do is pretty specialized." But he had been worried, and so had I. People got blamed for things that weren't their fault, people got fired without cause, and maybe his company wouldn't want to be mentioned, even peripherally, in conjunction with something as awful as this.

"It'll be all right," I'd said as he left, and he'd nodded. But I couldn't tell if he believed me or if I was just another burden, one more person whose feelings he was protecting, one more person whose needs were smothering his own.

So Grace and I were alone, and I had to shore up our home, make it safe again, try to block the holes and keep the water from rushing in.

I missed Lena. I missed knowing she was only one house down, that any moment of doubt or fear could be brushed away by her quick laugh, that I was never really on my own because I had a *Come right over, I'm on my way, Let's do it* kind of friend. Now I didn't even know if she was dead or alive, a murderer or a victim or both.

I set Grace down on the quilt my mother had made her and tapped the stuffed play arch to make it swing. Then, crisscrossing my legs like a child, I sat next to her and tried to think. I'd need spackle to cover the holes left where cameras used to be. And paint. Was there paint in the garage? Even if there was, the heat had probably spoiled it. Maybe I should get the whole house painted. My breath was coming quick and shallow.

Despite the midday sunlight streaming in through the window and Grace kicking and cooing beside me, I wrapped my arms tightly around myself. How could we stay here? Maybe we could start over again somewhere new. We could get a cottage with a ready-made garden, Michael could telecommute, maybe we'd pick a place close to my parents. My eyes were squeezed shut, but that didn't stop the tears from running down my cheeks.

We couldn't sell this house, not so soon after buying it. We couldn't afford to. And who else would want it after what Brady had done?

Then I heard something. A tentative knock on the front door, not the banging I might have expected. Michael had already disconnected the doorbell. I'd suggested one of those video doorbells, but as soon as I did, I realized we'd never be able to trust any camera-related item in our home again. The police had taken

Grace's baby monitor, we'd taped over the cameras on our laptops, and Michael had smashed our Alexa with a shovel and thrown the shattered pieces in the garbage.

The knocking paused, as though someone was listening for a response, then started again. I didn't get up. No one I knew should be coming to the door. The reporters weren't allowed on our front step. And even the police called first.

Looking down at my phone, I saw I had received a message, but I'd muted calls and notifications. Elizabeth had texted me: *Are you free?* And then fifteen minutes later: *Coming over. Bringing lunch.*

The knocking stopped, but I leapt to my feet and raced to the door, jerking it open just as she stepped off our porch. "Wait, sorry, I didn't see your text. Come on in."

Elizabeth had Theo in his car seat hooked on one arm and a heavy diaper bag over the other, and she looked like she might have apologized or hesitated, but as a reporter broke free from the pack in front of Lena's house, she hurried in after me.

I locked the door behind her and motioned her through the kitchen and into the family room, far away from the front windows. Sure enough, I caught a glimpse of movement on the other side of the door, but thanks to Michael's wire cutters, no doorbell sounded. And they'd already been warned about knocking on the door. Alondra had been positively terrifying.

Elizabeth set Theo's seat down carefully. His dark lashes curled against his rounded cheeks, and one hand made a loose fist while the other relaxed open, the palm smaller than the pad of my thumb. "I brought some sandwiches. I thought, if you weren't busy, we could have lunch. But then I didn't want to wake Grace up with the doorbell."

As if in answer, Grace gave two strong frog kicks and crossed her eyes at the star dangling from the play arch over her head.

"The doorbell doesn't work anyway. How have you been?"

The words seemed so banal, so ordinary. Something I might have said to anyone at any point in my life. But this was the first time I'd seen Elizabeth since everything happened, and I wasn't sure why she had come. Did she wonder if I knew more than I was saying?

She glanced at the sofa and then instead sat on the floor in a single, fluid movement, still so poised, even though her hair looked like she'd scraped it back into a ponytail with her hands, and she wore no makeup. "I'm fine. I'm worried about you. Everything sounds so awful. Wyatt said Michael was going back to work, so this is your first day alone. Has it been like that outside the whole time?"

I nodded, a lump in my throat. I'd been so busy holding it together for Michael and being calm and soothing for Grace that sympathy almost unhinged me. I sat next to the baby quilt and ran a finger across Grace's feather-soft hair. Maybe she just felt sorry for me, the naïve wife, a trusting idiot who didn't ask enough questions.

Elizabeth straightened a corner of the quilt and set the play arch swinging again. "Do you need help with grocery shopping? Or anything, really? I could organize some meals—"

"No thank you!" My words came out more strongly than I'd intended. But the last thing I wanted was for women I sort of knew to come into my house with pity in their eyes or worse, morbid curiosity.

Elizabeth flushed. "Of course. I wasn't thinking."

Worse than Elizabeth's discomfort was the voice I could hear in my head. Aimee's raspy tone: *Those vultures want to pick your bones clean. They'll be feasting on you at every gossip session for a month.*

"And the reporters, they're always there?"

"Since I got home after . . ." I didn't want to say *after my husband showed up covered in blood and we fled in terror to spend the night at the police station.*

She frowned, her lips pinched together. "That's ridiculous. I'm going to—" She shook her head. "Later, I'll make some calls. Tell me about Grace. It's only been a week, but she looks like she's growing."

For the rest of the day, we pretended nothing was wrong, absorbed in the babies and the food and the comfort of each other's presence. We were still there on the floor when Michael came home from work.

"How did it go?" I asked automatically, and then flinched. He wouldn't want to talk about this in front of Elizabeth. Maybe he'd been fired; maybe we'd be homeless. He gave me a wan smile and shrugged, and the only thing I could tell from that was what I already knew. My husband was exhausted.

As Michael fumbled for words and I struggled to tell Elizabeth how grateful I was, she got Theo settled in his car seat and put her packet of wipes, her baby's play quilt, and the remains of our lunch back in her bag. Then she gave me a quick, fierce hug, and without another word, she hefted the car seat and left, not sparing so much as a sideways glance for the reporters on our lawn, not even the one I recognized from CNN.

Without her comforting presence, the room seemed darker. I asked again. "How was it?"

"Okay. Just like I said. Everything is okay." He took me in his arms, and for just a second I let myself relax, even though I knew things couldn't have been that easy. Oh, I really wanted to believe in this lucky moment. Michael wasn't fired, we still had a paycheck, our family was intact. For now.

But I couldn't shake the fear born of a thousand true-crime dramas that he still might be charged. And that was the big legal fear. The personal one was that he'd already been tried and found guilty in the eyes of everyone in Texas.

My peace didn't last a second longer than our embrace.

8

Helen: So this is where things get weird. According to everything I could find, the police hadn't identified an active serial killer at this point. Some of the cases were classified as missing persons, some hadn't been reported at all, and only Frankie Watts, victim number two, and one couple, Jessica and Damen Weber, had been discovered and were being investigated as homicides.

Julia: It's like they have no respect for victimology. You can't just switch back and forth from chopping up individuals to dismembering couples.

Helen: That's probably why the two cases weren't linked initially. Watts was a murdered runaway from Dallas found in Humble, and the Webers were a Louisiana couple traveling back from a visit to family. First their car was found abandoned on the roadside; then their bodies were found in Brazos Bend State Park. A higher-risk kill, different victimology, but similar MO.

Julia: And no one was looking for a serial killer, so there wasn't anything to stop Lena and Brady Voss.

Helen: That's right. In fact, the time between victims was getting a little shorter, so if anything, it looks like there would have been more murders. But instead, on October third, the next-door neighbor Michael Tremaine went to the Vosses' house for a drink. The couples had been friends for over a year. They had dinners together, the guys had worked on a garden project together, and

Lena Voss was godmother to the Tremaine's baby. But on this
night, Lena was out of town.

Julia: Or so Brady said.

Helen: That's the story, anyway, and the reason Michael went over
while his wife stayed home with the baby. The guys had a couple
of beers, and then something happened. In Michael's statement,
he says he "heard a noise and from upstairs, a sound like something falling." Brady jumps up and runs upstairs, Michael follows
him, and he gets there right after Brady kills his last victim, Shelby
Jackson.

Julia: And Michael just walks in on it?

Helen: Apparently it was some kind of a murder room, all covered
in tarp with cameras and video monitors on the walls.

Julia: We have to talk about those later.

Helen: And according to Michael, Brady kicks the dead body
back into the room, grabs him—

Julia: Grabs Michael—

Helen: Yes, grabs him by the arm, pulls him into the room, and
slams the door. Then Brady dismembers the body, wraps it in the
tarp, and they carry it down to Brady's garage and load it into
one of the trucks there. During this time, Brady has a couple
more drinks, and when the body's packed in the truck, he asks
Michael if he wants to dump it. Michael delays, telling him the
moon's pretty bright, that they'll have better luck the next night,
and that he thinks there's a place under the bridge that might be
good.

Julia: Basically bullshitting.

Helen: And this is as good a time as any to take a break and talk
about the internet speculation. People are wondering: Why did he
stay there so long? Why did he help Brady? Why didn't he call the
police right away or run screaming?

Julia: Because we all think that's what we'd do.

Helen: But you can never tell. No one knows what they'd do.
There aren't many people who'll ever be in a situation where your
friend, your neighbor, invites you into a house where you've been
a hundred times, you're drinking and hanging out, and all of a
sudden you walk into a crime scene and your friend says, "Hey,
hold this ax." So I know it's exciting for people online to spin these
conspiracy theories and speculate that the guy who reported the

crime was involved, but I think there are some extenuating circumstances. I mean, first, he's in shock.

Julia: Well, you'd have to be.

Helen: For all the reasons we just said. This isn't a situation he ever imagined he'd be in. And second, he was in danger. Real, immediate, personal danger. Brady's bulky, strong; it's clear from the setup he's done this before; he's literally holding a weapon. I know it's not action-movie material, but the truth is that if Michael had tried fight or flight, either way, he'd be dead.

Julia: Victim number eleven, Marcus Fontenot, was ex-military, a really big guy.

Helen: Exactly. And there's another reason we didn't talk about yet. Those cameras and monitors. You and I know the police found cameras in the house next door and footage from lots of houses in the neighborhood. Michael claimed that earlier they'd found some of them in his home, but they looked old and the batteries were dead and they swept to try to detect any others, and they just figured it was something to do with the former owner. But Brady was there where they looked for the cameras. He's the one who did the electronic sweep.

Julia: He *pretended* to do an electronic sweep.

Helen: We know that now. And I bet—I mean, Michael's an engineer, he's no fool. When he saw the video setup in that room, he had to think about his own home. Where his wife and baby were. So he's in shock, he's afraid for his life, and he's afraid for his family. So he goes along with Brady, buying time so that he can get out of there. Which he does. He goes back, gets his wife and baby, they drive to the police station, and that's how Brady's caught.

Julia: And the internet speculation—he must have known, he must have been involved, why was he there so long? He was there for over five hours.

Helen: But not five full hours of murder. Not that fifteen minutes or whatever makes it better.

Julia: Like how long is too long?

Helen: But that's where the speculation came from. The bottom line is that if he hadn't gotten out of there, hadn't gone to the police, I definitely believe more people would have died before Brady was caught.

Julia: Brady *and* Lena. Up to this point, they were killing as a team.

Helen: And that brings us to our next questions. Why did Brady approach Michael in the first place?

Julia: Because Lena wasn't there.

Helen: And what exactly happened to her?

18

T HE NEXT MORNING Michael headed off to work, squeezing
into his car jammed next to mine in the garage and driving
away with his head ducked as though he could avoid the press. I
wished I had somewhere else to go, something else to think about,
some escape I could call my "responsibility," some job to take me
out of these four walls. We had hardly spoken to each other since
he'd gotten home from work yesterday, instead moving through
the house like two wooden dolls. The daddy doll loaded the dishwasher, the mommy doll bathed the baby, and then they sat stiffly
on the sofa until it was time to lie in bed.

Not sleep. I thought I might never sleep again.

Now Grace lay on her quilt, kicking her feet in time to my
fingers tapping on my coffee mug.

The police had asked me so many questions about Michael,
and I had so many of my own. But I was afraid. Not of what the
police were implying—I knew Michael, knew him to my bones.
He left his email open on his computer, I knew the password to
his phone, he called to let me know when he'd be late. I'd never
wondered if he was where he said he was; he'd never kept secrets.
Until now.

This was Michael, who'd rubbed my back for hours the day
after I'd been fired. Who'd never snapped at me or told me to pull
it together. Who'd taken a new job and moved all the way across

the country for me. And all the little things—how he kept a box of granola bars in his car to hand out to the homeless, how he texted me links to sweet or funny stories, how he didn't hold a grudge, his anger always gone by the time the sun rose. And he hated true crime—dramas, podcasts, even news stories. While the world was wondering what had happened to the young mother and her two kids or if the roommate knew more than she was saying, Michael would just remark that the whole thing was "so sad" and then turn his attention back to making his immediate life better.

I, on the other hand, had wasted so much time wondering what it meant that the coworker had lied to the police or judging the husband for having had an affair. And what had I gotten out of it? I sure wasn't any more informed about human nature. Look at how easily Aimee had deceived me. And almost two years later, I didn't know her any better or have a deeper understanding of why she'd framed me.

As for Brady, either he was a complete monster, one who'd been in my home, eaten my food and fed me his, and seen me before, during, and after my pregnancy, all without raising any red flags, or my husband was lying. More than lying. Complicit, murderous.

Because one fact wasn't in dispute. A dead body had been found in the house next door. And now my husband had secrets, such heavy ones I was afraid they'd break him.

My stomach was full of acid, my coffee cold, as I sat on the sofa watching Grace stretching her arms and legs, blissfully oblivious. I'd get the spackle from the garage and start patching the holes in our walls. I'd fix the damage I could fix. In a minute.

Then from somewhere outside I heard a harsh grinding, a machine roaring to life with an earsplitting squeal. My breath caught, and I ran to the window. Through the gap in our back fence where the tiered garden used to be, I caught a glimpse of a yellow hard hat and orange safety vests. Construction workers in Lena's backyard.

I flung open the back door and stepped out. Even at this distance I caught a whiff of ground concrete and heat. They were busting up the pool.

"Hey," I shouted, waving my arms. But my voice was swallowed by the din of destruction. And then one of the workers flung a gray tarp over the gap in the fence, cutting off my partial view.

The rosebush I'd planted was blanketed in a spray of dust, white like concrete or bone. Of course it wasn't bone. I knew that. But the dead girl was everywhere I looked, behind Lena's second-floor windows reflecting the morning light, behind the fence that shielded the side of the Vosses' house from ours. There was only one reason I could think of. They were looking for more bodies.

The same pool where I'd swirled my foot through the water, the same pool where I'd felt the dawning of hope, connection, friendship, and a future.

I couldn't look.

Wheeling around, I fled inside and collapsed on the sofa, wrapping my arms around myself.

Grief ran under and through my fear for Michael, like dark veins through marble, different from anything I'd felt before. With Aimee, I'd been unprepared, blindsided by her betrayal, grieving a friendship that had never existed. But this was something deeper.

How could anyone be so violent, so vicious? Aimee had destroyed my career; Brady had destroyed lives. There was a time I hadn't understood the difference, but now the obliteration of a second chance, another day, a future was all too clear. This wasn't a scar across the growth rings in a tree trunk; it was the whole oak burned twig to root. Families left with nothing but memories. The way I would have been if Brady had killed Michael.

I could imagine Brady as a killer. The easy way he struck up rapport, the way he used a wink to make a moment slightly uncomfortable and then grinned, as if taking pleasure in it. At least, that was the way it seemed now. Back then, the grin had seemed to say, *Just joking, everything's okay.*

And I wasn't grieving just anonymous lives; I was grieving Lena. Every day without that distinctive knock on the door, every hour without her haphazard texts, every minute wondering what had happened to her.

The vibrations from the machines ran through me, reverberating as strongly as my breath. If it was this powerful in my body, it must be too strong for Grace; it might damage her hearing. But she was quiet, arching her back a bit as if trying to discover the source of the sound that filled our home. I picked her up. We'd go to the far side of the house, the nursery.

There I could still hear the noise, but it didn't buzz through nerve and sinew. I set Grace in her crib under her mobile with its trembling paper stars. She looked surprised, and then her brows drew together. She already knew what the crib meant, and she wasn't sleepy.

"Just give me a second," I told her. "I'm trying."

I ran back out and scooped up her bouncy chair, a roll of paper towels, and the spackle and putty knife I'd set out earlier. She was almost crying when I got back, but once she was settled in her chair with its arch of cheerful stuffed shapes, her world was all right again. I wished I could fix everything that easily. But the hole in the nursery wall next to the light switch was proof. I'd let her down. I hadn't seen the signs of danger. All I could do now was repair the visible damage.

Tentatively, I spread a little spackle, but it just fell inside the wall. I'd need something to give it support. I tore off a sheet of paper towels, wadded them up, and stuffed them in the cavity. This time the spackling compound stuck to the paper towels, and I spread it out across the edge of the drywall.

My own grief was a hole, the absence of Lena. And I could imagine only two choices, both of them paths that led to darker places. The first was that she had never gone on a trip. The police had checked with her aunt, and not only had Lena not visited, but there'd been no plans for nor talk of a visit, not according to the aunt. Those texts Lena had sent me didn't mean she was alive. They could have come from anyone.

No, not anyone. From Brady.

The thought I was avoiding, coinciding with the first path, was that Brady had killed Lena, the same way he might have killed a dozen others. That he'd used her phone to buy himself some time or delay suspicion. That he'd disposed of her body before he'd started dismembering the young woman, the one Michael had seen. After all, a killer who could do that to a stranger, a human with whom he had no history, would be more than capable of doing it to his wife.

My hand trembled, and the edge of the putty knife scored the spackle. I scooped more up and pressed it on, then scraped it smooth again, willing my hand to be steady.

My friend with her flaming hair, her larger-than-life personality, her laugh that rolled like thunder, was dead and buried somewhere she might never be found. That was an absence that couldn't be filled, a loss I couldn't wrap my head around.

But there was a second path, one the police were also considering. I could tell from the questions they'd asked, the way they'd walked me through my calendar, examined my texts with Lena, asked about specific dates and places.

Lena could have been involved as well. No, not *involved*; that was just my mind trying to mitigate her responsibility. Lena, my friend, might be a killer like her husband.

This patch was as smooth as I could make it, but the texture wasn't the same as the wall around it. I picked up the plastic tub and read the directions. *Let dry, then paint.* Grace had dozed off, her head lolling on its side. I'd see if we had the right color.

When I opened the garage door, the heat rolled over me. Paint cans from the previous homeowners were lined up against the wall, along with a box of leftover tile and some spare shingles. Our garage wasn't neat and orderly like Lena and Brady's. Some unopened boxes still sat in a corner, along with the bikes we'd brought but hadn't ridden since the move, Grace's stroller base, and a jumble of miscellany—an old pair of Michael's running shoes, a battered tool box, empty packaging and old Christmas decorations and unused gardening tools and bug sprays.

Our neighbors' garage had been spotless and well lighted, just like the inside of the trucks Brady's contractors used. Each truck had a laminated inventory of its contents to be checked before every call. That was Lena's doing. She was the reason Brady kept expanding his business. She was the reason Michael and I didn't own a power drill. I knew exactly where she kept hers in its designated slot in her highly organized garage.

Some of the questions the police asked had been about their relationship. Had she seemed afraid of Brady? Did it seem like she was excessively willing to please him?

But that was nonsense. Lena hadn't been afraid of anyone, and she sure as hell hadn't seemed in thrall to Brady. If anything, she had been the one driving their business and arranging their home. Maybe he'd resented that and one night he'd just lost his temper. Maybe she'd learned what he was doing and he'd killed her to keep her quiet. Maybe.

I thought uncomfortably about my older sister, Charlotte, how surprised I'd been to hear her marriage was over. Maybe I didn't know anything about relationships. Maybe the friendship I'd thought I had with Lena had been a lie like my friendship with Aimee. Maybe she hadn't chosen me because she liked me. Maybe she'd been stalking me.

I was standing where two paths diverged, but this wood wasn't yellow, it was pitch-black. One path would plunge me off a cliff; the other would dump me into a swollen river, and there was no way back out again. And there might be a killer out there, wearing the face of my friend.

Snatching the handle of the can marked *INT* and a screwdriver from the toolbox, I hurried inside, locking the door behind me like I'd never done before.

The press was there on the front lawn of Lena's house and ours. I couldn't flee the noise of the destruction next door by walking Grace around the neighborhood in her stroller or even checking the mail. And all those people out there—the crime show commentators, stringers from the national news, and maybe just some true-crime junkies—they didn't have any answers for me, only more speculation.

Just like I probably was the subject of speculation for my neighbors.

I set the paint and screwdriver in the nursery next to the spackling gear. One hole down, at least half a dozen left. I might be able to fill them all before Michael came home.

My phone was suddenly a leaden weight in my pocket, its stillness further proof of Lena's absence. I could check the news, see if anything additional had been published. Had the police found more bodies, had Brady confessed anything, did they have any idea what had happened to Lena? I could feel the eagerness inside, right alongside the sick fear that I'd see what I'd seen the last time I checked. The front of my own house.

Nothing I wanted to know had been released. If this were a television program, some investigative journalist or freelance detective would have bribed their way into the police station or found a jailhouse informant. Instead, the people on my front lawn were searching for answers I didn't have.

And we paid to live in this stupid neighborhood with its manicured lawns and trash can curfews. If we could get fined for putting our recycling bins out too early, surely these vultures weren't allowed either.

I couldn't do a damn thing about the police, but the news crews would have to go. Furiously, I searched on my phone for the homeowners' association number and called, only to get a voice mail. Should I identify myself? Would it make me look guilty to complain? Before I could chicken out, I blurted, "I'm on Evening Primrose and there are reporters everywhere, blocking the street and making noise. Do something about it."

I hung up, my face hot. I hadn't identified myself, but I'd taken action.

Grace squawked, waking to the realization that she was hungry, and I bent to scoop her up, my heart pounding against her. She'd just finished nursing when I heard voices on the street outside, then a knock on the door.

I peeked through the beveled glass at a figure on the front step and a police car in my driveway.

My mouth dry, Grace dozing in my arms, I opened the door to an officer in uniform, about ten years older than me. In a thick Louisiana accent, he asked, "Miz Tremaine?"

When I nodded mutely, he offered me a business card. "I'm the designated officer for this community."

My arms tightened around Grace.

But then the officer removed his sunglasses. His eyes, under heavy black brows, were kind. "I understand you've been having some trouble with the news people. Now, I'm all for free speech, but the HOA has some regulations in place to keep the streets from being clogged up."

"That was fast. I just called." Maybe I shouldn't have said that, but something was rising in me. My call had made things better. First I'd get rid of the reporters, then I'd work on the bigger problems.

He nodded. "I've been meaning to get out here. We've had a couple of calls. There's plenty of families with young children or those who just plain don't want their homes featured on television. And this street's pretty narrow. And right now nobody's living next to you anyhow, which means the burden of that harassment is falling on you and your little one. You're entitled to some protection, in my book."

As he was talking, Rahmia came down the opposite side of the street. I hadn't seen her since the night everything happened. Now her eyes widened, and her steps slowed as she walked past. She probably thought I'd fooled her, just the way Lena had fooled me.

That was our life now. Even the nicest constable in the world couldn't make things okay. Clearing the reporters would only remove the visible proof that all my neighbors, all of Sugar Land and Houston and beyond, all of Texas had a taste of what had happened, and now they were thirsty to know more.

I knew Michael was innocent, I knew trauma could heal, and I knew it was up to me to get us both out the other side. If finding the truth was the only way through this nightmare, I would get those answers, and the rest of the world could choke on them.

9

Helen: So why did Brady Voss get caught? Up to this point, he'd been committing murders and he hadn't even had a close call. He wasn't devolving, he was making smart decisions, varying his hunting grounds, his victim types, and his disposal sites.

Julia: Pacing himself. Twelve victims chosen from six different counties, all spaced about six to eight months apart.

Helen: There's actually no reason to believe he wouldn't have— couldn't have—continued what he was doing. Maybe even for years. All he had to do was keep on keeping on. But then he invited Michael Tremaine over—

Julia: Do we know that?

Helen: According to both Michael and his wife's testimony, Brady invited him over that night. Now, we do know for the past year they'd been getting together a couple times a week, working on some garden projects and yard construction and hanging out. Maybe Brady was "grooming" Michael?

Julia: And his wife's not around . . .

Helen: We'll get back to that in a minute.

Julia: So Brady thought he'd have a "guys' night out" for murder?

Helen: It's happened. Consider the Hillside Stranglers, cousins Bianchi and Buono; or the Tool Box Killers, Bittaker and Norris, who met in prison; or the Railway Killers, childhood friends Duffy and Mulcahy.

Julia: But it's a huge risk. You can't just come out and say, "Hey, wanna commit some hideous crimes together?" He must have started by dropping little hints.

Helen: Making comments he could laugh off as a joke.

Julia: And that's the kind of thing that makes you wonder, why didn't Michael pick up on the weirdness? There had to be a creepy factor.

Helen: Even if we allow for how charming a serial killer can be, you also have to wonder why Brady thought Michael might say yes. I mean, the other thing about serial killers is they're supposedly good at reading people, right? Picking out likely victims. So why did Brady pick Michael as a potential murder buddy?

Julia: Do we have his testimony?

Helen: At first he didn't say anything. Later he said Michael knew all along what he was doing and wanted to give it a try. But we also know Brady's a lying liar.

Julia: We know what Michael says happened that night, but the video evidence only shows the center of the room. There's no way to see the whole picture.

Helen: All those recordings are why the police knew there were more victims to find, why they knew Brady was guilty, but it's also why they weren't one hundred percent sure about Michael.

Julia: If I were his wife, I'd want to be more than one hundred percent sure.

CHAPTER

19

JUST BECAUSE I'D decided I needed answers didn't mean I could get them from Michael. When he walked through the door after work, I asked, "How was your day?" Simple, innocuous, a question from the *before* time.

But he hesitated, bracing himself, his shoulders rising. "Fine. The project I'm on involves lots of computer time. And traffic was a bear."

"Not on our street, though."

At his uncomprehending look, I added, "We have a neighborhood constable. Apparently reporters are not approved by the HOA, so he cleared them out."

Did he almost smile, or was that wistful thinking on my part? Suddenly, fiercely, I missed Michael, my best friend, the guy I looked forward to talking with at the end of every day, on the drive home from an event, after the credits rolled at the movie theater. "I also spackled some of those holes. Grace helped. How about you; did you talk to anyone?" Before, he would have told me who he'd seen, what they'd been working on, if they'd gone out to lunch.

Now he just shook his head. And I imagined Michael hunched over his computer, trying to lose himself in the familiar work, while all around him people wondered, maybe even whispered: *Have you heard? Can you believe it? Could you imagine?*

After a dinner neither of us actually ate, Michael went to the bedroom to lie down. Grace and I spent the evening alone. After I fed her and sang to her, I crept into bed beside him.

In the dark, I could hear his measured breathing, familiar and rhythmic. But was he asleep or just pretending? I couldn't tell.

I dreamed again of the museum, its exhibition halls empty, lit only by the emergency lights. Somewhere Grace was alone and in danger, and I had to find her.

I ran through a room filled with spinning paper curls cut from newspaper that caught in my hair, another with paintings of the houses in our neighborhood, a dozen almost exactly the same, each with a different title: *Domestic Abuse no. 1* or *Bankruptcy Study 33* or just *Death (violent) 5*—a house that looked like Lena's. But I hurried past.

Finally I entered the room with a modern take on *Winged Victory* again, a contemporary woman in jeans and a loose tunic wrapped in folds around her torso. Her wings weren't marble but onyx, polished to catch the meager light, with long feathers angled sharply inward. This wasn't Nike, goddess of victory, resolute despite the strong winds buffeting her. This was a grave marker, the angel of death.

I faltered. At her shoulders and neck, the stone was unfinished, rough and raw. There was a plaque at her base, one I'd never seen before, and I took a step forward, squinting to make out the engraving. Two words—a name? But it was smudged with something dark. I reached out to wipe it clean, and then I heard someone cry out.

I wheeled around. Michael stood behind me with an expression I'd never seen on him before. He smirked, just like Brady, and then he gave me a slow wink. "I'll get the baby," he said, and disappeared.

I woke with my heart pounding, every muscle tensed to the point of pain.

Someone was whimpering. Michael. His forehead furrowed, his hands pushing the bedclothes away, his head shaking: *no no no*. I reached out for his arm, to wake him, to reassure him and myself as well, to bring back my husband with his kind eyes and his unflappable calm. But when my fingers touched his skin, he shuddered and swung his arm out, catching me right in the face and knocking me back. Shocked, I slid off the bed with a cry, and he sat up, gasping. "What? What is it? What's wrong?"

"Nothing. You were dreaming." Speaking felt strange, like I'd had a shot of Novocain, and I blinked back the tears in my eyes.

But he turned on the light, squinting at me. "Kacy?"

"I'm fine." My voice sounded funny too, but I couldn't tell if it was the moisture in my throat or the ringing in my ears.

"You're hurt." But he didn't sound sure; he didn't recommend an aspirin or an ice pack. He just sat there, bolt upright, his hair mussed and his eyes glassy.

"Everything's okay. Just go back to sleep," I said.

And like a marionette with its strings cut, he collapsed, asleep.

Everything wasn't okay, Michael was acting so strangely, and it felt like the shadow of my smirking dream-husband was still with me, giving me that ominous wink.

* * *

The next morning Michael came into the kitchen, and I hastily lifted my mug of coffee, wishing I could hide my black eye behind it. He stopped, stricken. "What happened?"

"Last night—"

"*I* did that? I thought it was just a nightmare. I'm sorry, honey. Let me see." He took my chin in his hand and tilted my face upward. "Does it hurt?"

I shook my head, savoring the warmth of his attention. "It's just a fancy bruise. No big deal."

"I'm so sorry. I took a sleeping pill, and then I dreamed . . ." He let go and turned away. Even in sleep, he hadn't been able to escape what he'd seen. And now he felt guilty for hurting me on top of the guilt he already felt. And I'd seen for myself how terrified he must have been, and I wished with every atom of my being that I could banish those fears and promise him safety.

"Do you want to talk about it?" I asked, knowing what his answer would be.

He opened the cabinet, but instead of taking out his coffee mug, he just stood there with his back to me.

Of course he didn't want to talk about it. He didn't want to think about it. He wished it had never happened, or that it had happened somewhere else, to someone else. And I knew firsthand how little medication could do here. A pill could dampen the anxiety, force you to sleep, but it couldn't erase the past or dispel your demons.

"Would you talk to someone else? A professional?"

"Maybe." With a flick of his hand, he shut the cabinet. "I'm going in early to work."

"Do you want coffee to go?"

But he was already scooping up his computer bag and heading to the garage. "I'll get something on the way."

"I can phone Dr. Lindsey's office for you," I called after him.

The only answer was the slamming door.

In the silence, I could feel the tension seep from my body. I'd never had to be on guard like this around Michael. From the outside, nothing had changed for us, not really. Michael and I loved each other and Grace. Michael still had his job and we had a lovely home, but the foundations of our faith in humanity were crumbling, and that made everything look as bleak as a post-apocalyptic landscape. If we hadn't seen the truth about our friends, our closest neighbors, how could we be sure about each other?

I was going to find out everything I could about this case and any others like it. The police wouldn't tell us anything, the journalists were scrambling, but they didn't know any more than I did. What made a person a killer? Why would Brady have killed Lena, if he'd killed Lena? And how could Michael and I not have known?

Did I really know anyone?

* * *

On an ordinary morning, Michael would have asked how I planned to spend the day. I'd had my answer all ready: "Taking Grace to Mother Goose Story Time at the library." And I would. Because I wasn't a liar. I just wasn't volunteering the whole truth.

He hadn't asked anyway.

I pulled out of the driveway, pausing to savor the sight of a street free from reporters and white vans, but I couldn't pretend things were back to normal. Yellow crime scene tape still crisscrossed Lena's front door, and an unmarked police car was stationed in the driveway. As I turned onto the main street, I saw Rahmia on her way back from dropping Emir off at school.

Under her pale-green hijab, her face was serious, and even Bibi seemed subdued. Rahmia glanced at my car, and then her eyes widened like I'd been marked with crime scene tape: *Danger*. I glanced in the rearview mirror, where my shiner was still abundantly clear, and I could see her concerned face retreating into the distance.

At the library, I went up and down the shelves with Grace in her stroller—really just a lightweight set of wheels and a handle that snapped onto her car seat. I filled the bottom with books about murderers and the murdered, the psychology of violence, psychopaths and how to recognize them. All the things someone like Dr. Lindsey must have studied. On one of these pages, there had to be an answer.

But after I checked them out, I realized I couldn't take these books home. Even having them in my car was risky.

I texted Elizabeth: *I need help with something. Can I come over?*

Of course. Don't use the buzzer, just knock. Theo must be sleeping. Elizabeth wasn't a walk-right-in kind of person, unlike Lena. None of us were anymore. Even before Brady, there had been stories of home invasions, people tied up while their houses were ransacked, people shot as they answered the door, people followed into their garages.

So it was a relief to knock softly on Elizabeth's door and hear her undo the dead bolt. I set Grace in her car seat just inside and ran back to get the armload of books.

Elizabeth looked from my face to the stack in my arms. "What's going on?"

I could feel a flush rising. Would she think I was a freak, a voyeur getting off on the grisly details of other crimes, no better than the women who whispered about me in the supermarket or texted each other any new tidbit they'd heard? There wasn't any excuse I could think of, nothing I could say except the truth.

"I have to know, have to understand more about what happened. But if I do this at home, I'm worried it will upset Michael."

She tapped her own cheekbone. "Your eye, what happened?"

"I fell out of bed. Last night." After Michael hit me. But in his sleep. There was no way I could explain that wouldn't sound like a lie. Even what I'd just said sounded so fake. "It looks worse than it is."

One corner of her mouth tightened. She didn't believe me.

"Really," I added. "I was having a bad dream, and I started flailing. I must have caught the edge of the nightstand."

"Okay," she said. Had she bought my sort-of-true story, or was she just reluctant to push the issue? Either way, she added, "Tell me what's going on with these books. You want to understand what Brady did? Like the details, or"—her gaze fell on the top book—"what?"

"Why he did it. And about Lena." *And Michael*, I thought but didn't say. If I didn't know anything about people, if I made friends with liars and thieves and murderers, how could I trust my judgment about my husband? Despite my doubts, my heart yearned for Michael, the way he'd rubbed my back when I wouldn't get out of bed in the depths of my depression, the careful, surprised way he'd held Grace that first time, and the way he'd clutched me close when we'd gotten home from the police station. I believed him. I trusted him. But I'd been wrong before. "I want to know what might have happened with Lena," I added hastily.

I couldn't tell from Elizabeth's expression what she thought about Lena. Dead, complicit, got-what-was-coming-to-her, or some combination of the three. Then she gave a little nod, and I knew that whatever Elizabeth's opinion of Lena, she was on my side. "I can help, if you want. I mean, I'm still not completely sure what you're looking for, but I'll try to help."

*   *   *

By midafternoon, Elizabeth and I hadn't found anything that gave me answers. I could imagine Dr. Lindsey asking, "Now what answer could there be that would satisfy you? Do you think there is an acceptable answer?"

But there had to be. There had to be a reason some people were bad, a way to identify them and explain their crimes. Otherwise . . . on the other side of *otherwise* loomed a chasm, a deep pit into which I couldn't afford to fall.

The babies lay next to each other on a quilt, their feet kicking. Theo could already rock from side to side, pausing at the farthest point for a long moment when he might have rolled over, but he didn't, not yet. Grace waved her hands at the bright baby toys dangling from a soft padded arch over the quilt. She looked like she was casting a tiny spell, trying to shift the toys despite being unable to touch them.

"It's getting late." Elizabeth put her hands on the small of her back and stretched her shoulders. Between us the stack of books now sprouted tags, each marking a case that was remotely like Brady's: blue for psychology of serial killers, yellow for forensics, red for biographical similarities—suburban, construction workers, married couples. "What should we do with these?"

"Can I leave them here?" I didn't want to ask her to lie to Wyatt, and I wouldn't lie about them to Michael, but I also didn't want either of them to know. And that made me feel a weight of shame and guilt I hated.

Elizabeth didn't blink. "Of course. I'll put them in the guest room." She didn't say that Wyatt wouldn't see them there, because she wasn't hiding them, but she wasn't going to leave them lying around either. Her profile was inscrutable. She was here, doing something she might never have done, because she hadn't wanted me to be alone. That was more than a spark; that was steel, to put a friend first.

"You never liked Lena." I was testing the waters. It wasn't Elizabeth's way to say something unkind or unnecessary. But I'd be able to tell by the things she didn't say. There was a habit she had of pausing, and I'd grown to see that was her way of mentally counting to ten. My father would like Elizabeth. He always recommended using the three questions: Does this have to be said? Does it have to be said now? Does it have to be said now by me?

And of course, my sisters and I would continue our barrage of accusations and defenses, screaming our inconsequential manifestos at each other, because nothing had to be said by us at any time, so we might as well say it all at the top of our lungs the minute it crossed our minds.

And Elizabeth paused, the stack of books in her arms. I could feel something gathering in her. Did I want her to say she'd never liked Lena? That Lena was too brash, too loud, too judgmental, definitely the kind of person who'd end up on the nightly news? Maybe hearing that would make it okay for me to be angry; maybe it would make me want to defend Lena. Maybe it would be an indictment of me, the kind of person who hadn't seen the real Lena, who'd either been taken in or been complicit.

But all Elizabeth said was, "I didn't really know her."

20

BACK AT HOME, I was on my laptop while Grace pushed up on her forearms and then rocked on her little tummy. I sat on the floor, my back against the sofa.

A text buzzed on my phone. For a moment my heart leaped, as if I expected it to be Lena, but of course it wasn't. And then the wave of grief pressed up, rising in me until I could feel the heat of tears and my vision blurred. It wasn't fair. My best friend was gone. Impatiently, I swiped at my eyes. I was lucky that Michael was alive, that we had Grace and a home and an income. We had been so close to danger, only a few feet away, and we'd survived.

I glanced down and read a message from Elizabeth: *I don't know if this is what you were looking for, but there's an online crime forum discussing the case.* She'd included a link.

And I clicked on it.

I knew there was a world on the internet beyond comments on articles and reviews of restaurants. I'd been in online forums for art historians, but this was something else. Elizabeth had sent me to a site that offered discussions of thousands of crimes—current, centuries old, unsolved, famous, fictional. And it looked like every kind of person had a chat space specifically devoted to them. On my art historian forums, I might have found a neoclassicism discussion and one on Banksy and one on unionizing museum employees, but here there was a discussion group for forensic breakthroughs, another on a new theory of Jack the Ripper, and one titled Serial Killer in Sugar Land. In order to post, or to view the full profile of anyone who did, I'd have to register, but I could view the site anonymously.

At least I hoped I could. The camera on my laptop had been covered up ever since Michael purged every electronic camera and listening device from our home. And surely my IP address wouldn't out my identity. My finger hovered, but I didn't enter the Sugar Land forum. There was a reason I'd gone to the library first. Books were safe, static like a painting in a frame. What lived on the internet was a dangerous mix of investigative photography and in-your-face performance art. It had taken me so long to scrape the stench of internet troll off my soul. Was I strong enough to dive back in?

My lips tightened. I needed to know what was out there. I clicked the link and opened the discussion about Brady.

The first post was an overview, bare bones. *A man was arrested in Sugar Land on charges of homicide. A female body was found in his home. He's being held in conjunction with several other missing persons. His wife has been missing since last week.*

Another poster had linked to an online news story, and I clicked through. First the article stated that Brady was in custody, that he'd been charged but hadn't confessed. Then came a series of quotes from people who had worked with him, the rotating crew of men who had staffed those trucks and done roofing, wiring, plumbing, HVAC, windshield repair, locksmithing. *A good boss. Really skilled. Liked to joke around.*

And then I read about the bodies.

Already they were linking Brady to previously unsolved deaths. A young woman, younger than my younger sister, found in pieces in the soft soil at the edge of the Brazos River. Tortured, then dismembered, just like Brady had done in front of Michael. Another, a Mexican citizen in his forties, had been slaughtered in the "Killing Fields" off Calder Road in League City, left where so many others had been killed since the seventies. How had I not known that the site of this many murders was less than an hour from my front door?

Back in the forums, posters were speculating about other possible victims, including the missing drivers of those abandoned cars. And I wondered how many bodies might be stashed where they'd never be discovered—under the slab foundation of a house in our very neighborhood? In a bayou I drove over on my way to H-E-B for groceries?

Scanning the page, I saw it hadn't taken long for people to jump to conclusions about me.

Turned in by a neighbor. The guy was there for hours, was he helping? Involved?

Do you think the wife was involved?

Which wife? The one that's missing or the one that drove her husband to the police station?

Maybe they wanted out, so they turned Brady in.

Were they defending Brady? Like Michael and I had set him up? This wasn't some creepy episode of *Criminal Minds*, where the truth was always the most extreme explanation. But in a world where dismemberment was only one house away, the truth was extreme.

The same poster who'd opened the thread wrote: *I think it would be more common for Brady's wife to have been involved than for a couple he'd only met like a year previously. We're still waiting on more details about the number of his victims, but IMHO it's likely a serial killer would have been operating for much longer than that.*

Thank you. At least someone didn't think Michael was the devil.

Then the full import of what I'd read sunk in.

Brady's wife. Lena.

Of course she must have been involved. She must have known what he was doing. I shut the laptop and pushed it away from me, but the leaden weight of the truth was cold iron in my gut.

Somehow I'd tamped down the full gravity of that knowledge and fought back against it, but after seeing it printed in the blunt words of an anonymous stranger, there was no way I could doubt it. I'd been so focused on Brady, his voyeurism and violence, and on Michael, the way his trauma had changed him, that I'd been able to skirt the truth.

Lena was another friend I'd never really known.

I must have groaned, because Grace stuck her lip out, her tiny brows drawn together.

When I didn't immediately smile and say something reassuring, her face crumpled and she wailed.

I was being stupid, poking at an open wound. There weren't any answers: not online, not from Michael, not from the police, not if Lena herself rose from the dead. Death didn't have a reason why; no explanation was good enough.

Shutting the laptop, I slid it under the sofa and reached out, pulling Grace close. Her head smelled so sweet, and she turned her face into the crook of my neck and snuffled. My tears dampened her soft hair, and we sat like that for a while. I wished I could be content to keep my eyes closed.

But I knew I wasn't ready to stop looking.

*　*　*

Another evening of awkwardness, another night of restless dreams, another morning where Michael drove away early, leaving me both relieved and bereft.

I was sitting on the couch, turning the remote control over in my hands, trying to resist the urge to surf the news programs for information, when I heard a gentle knock on the front door. I tensed, glancing at Grace kicking on her play blanket. But no reporter would knock so gently, eschewing the doorbell as if afraid they'd wake the baby. I peeked through the window of our front door and saw Rahmia. The beveled glass fragmented and refracted the pale pink of her hijab so that it looked like blossoms on our tree.

I opened the door and motioned her inside. Rahmia was carrying a disposable aluminum pan covered with foil and a gift bag dangling from her wrist, but she was already looking past me. "Where is your sweet girl? I have something for her too. She must have grown so much. It's been too long since we've seen each other. I haven't seen you walking, and I texted, but . . ."

"I'm terrible about checking my cell phone. I'm so sorry."

She waved away my apology. "You had too many other worries on your mind. I brought you chicken pulao. You can eat it tonight or freeze it for later." As she passed the food to me, our eyes met, and I remembered that one of mine was still black.

"Thank you. You didn't have to do this." The pan was heavier than I'd expected, still warm, and a sweet yet savory aroma rose from it. Although it was just midmorning, suddenly all I wanted was to gorge myself on this gift of literal comfort. Instead, I brought it to the kitchen and slid it into the fridge. Maybe this homey casserole was exactly what Michael and I needed to break through the ice that had formed over our evenings. "Grace is in the other room on her play mat."

But Rahmia stayed with me in the kitchen. "This has all been very stressful for you. It's a terrible thing. How are you doing really?"

"I'm okay. I mean, it's hard, I'm not sleeping well, but . . ." I squirmed.

"And Michael, how is he handling all this stress?"

"Neither of us are sleeping well. He's still got work, though, so that helps." I thought about those forums, the newscasts I hadn't watched, the speculation and the reporting all mixed up together. "How much do you know about what happened?"

Rahmia didn't launch into an involved story. Instead, her fingers worried at the cord handles of the gift bag. "It was your neighbors, Lena and her husband. Michael found out about it. That's what the news said."

"That's true."

She took a deep breath and set the bag down on the table. "Your eye—"

"I fell out of bed." The truth didn't sound any more convincing than when I'd said it to Elizabeth. "I really did."

Before I could react, Rahmia reached out and brushed my cheek, so lightly I barely felt it. "If you were not feeling safe, you could tell me."

Why did my eyes well with tears whenever anyone said anything nice to me? "I *am* safe. Brady's in jail, the reporters are gone, there's a policeman right out front."

"Sometimes the danger isn't outside the house." Her hands twisted and untwisted the hem of her hijab. "You could go somewhere better for you. Better, safer, for Grace."

"Michael wouldn't hurt me. Really." And then I remembered Rahmia's work with the women's shelter. "I promise, Rahmia. I'm safe at home. I'm safe with Michael."

"But you have other family too. Maybe this is a good time for you to visit your mother or your sisters."

"I can't leave, not now." All the reasons I'd told my own mother on the phone rose again in my mind: *Michael needs me. The police won't let me leave.* But Rahmia's words had awakened a childlike longing to be with my parents, familiar and loving, where I was always safe.

She nodded, studying my face as if she could read my mixed emotions in it, until a squawk from Grace startled us both.

"Would you like tea?" I asked, but she scooped the gift back up.

"No, no, don't bother. Your princess is calling me." Rahmia went to find Grace, then dropped to her knees beside the play mat.

"You are a princess," she cooed. "Just the most beautiful girl. So much bigger than last time." She reached into the bag and pulled out a small floppy bunny, shaking it to make it rattle. Grace smiled at her, and Rahmia crooned back in a mix of baby talk and Bengali. Grace squirmed as though her joy were too great for her body, and I laughed, almost surprised that I still could.

Rahmia looked back over her shoulder at me. "We should take this princess on a parade. She deserves a little fresh air, and so does her mama."

I hesitated, and she patted Grace's plump little leg. "There is no one out there now. I walked from my door to yours and saw nobody, not a single nosy neighbor or newshound. Is that the word? Put on a sun hat and your glasses, and we'll walk, just for a bit. I won't let anything happen to this sweetheart."

And despite how little Rahmia looked, how round and friendly and no more threatening than Bibi, I believed that she would protect us, that she could.

The next thing I knew, we were stepping out the front door. The sky was the gorgeous cerulean of an Impressionist masterpiece. The shine of light on the trees and the warmth of the sun seemed like a thin screen over the horrible things that could happen behind closed doors.

As we passed Lena's house, Rahmia spoke more and more quickly, as if to distract me from the gravitational pull of the familiar place, now so terrifying. There wasn't any way to tell if someone was inside. The windows weren't dark, but they were shining with reflected light, which made them just as impenetrable. I imagined Michael standing behind that door, afraid for his life, afraid for us. I could picture every inch of the first floor of that house.

The kitchen must look the same as I remembered, but if I stood there now, every shadow on the wall, every smudge on the grout, would be the afterimage of death. Or it could be nothing. After all, that kitchen was just a room. This house was just a house.

Without realizing it, I had slowed down, and Rahmia was a few steps ahead of the stroller. She turned back. "Kacy, are you okay?"

Despite the warm October day, I was cold as if that house cast a shadow. A shadow like the one that must have been underneath Lena's broad smile, our shared jokes. Was it me? Did I attract something dark and dangerous?

"What will happen to the house?" I asked. "I mean, if Brady goes to jail, what happens to it?"

Rahmia stayed at a distance, as though she was also afraid of the thing we couldn't see, unspeakable acts committed within those walls. But it wasn't the house's fault. Its builder was the same as mine, the same as hers, the same as Elizabeth's. Rahmia answered, "I asked Alondra about this. After the investigation is over, and the trial, it might go to family, or it might be sold to pay the lawyers. But the HOA has to discuss things too. There are hundreds of houses in our community. This isn't the first one where something bad has happened, just the worst."

My hands relaxed a little on the handle of the stroller, and I started walking again. The HOA as an agent of justice—that seemed as bizarre as anything else that had happened. And then it was behind us and we were at the corner, just as I had been with Lena so many times.

"Do you mind if we stop by and pick up Bibi? I didn't want to bring her into your home with the baby, but now that she's safely in the stroller . . ." Rahmia's fluttering hands twitched at the canopy, making sure Grace was protected from the sun.

"Sure." The sunlight felt amazing, but I was having the strangest sensation, like I was simultaneously walking with Lena and Rahmia. *That spoiled rat of a dog is her baby*, Lena whispered in my head, and I felt a flash of guilt, as though Rahmia would hear.

But she just kept talking, telling me how much Bibi would love a little walk and how the dog her parents had when she was a baby used to be too delicate for walking and would end up perched on the canopy of her carriage or even tucked in beside her, but Bibi loved walking, she never got tired, even though her legs were so short that they had to move three times faster than other dogs'. Rahmia's words filled my head, pushing the darkness aside.

And I laughed again as she made her fingers flash like a dog's moving legs.

We did pick up Bibi, and after the initial yapping yelps and the spinning leaps with which she greeted us, we continued our walk.

Grace kicked off the light blanket I'd draped over her. Stretching her legs out, she spread her toes, clearly relishing the breeze on her skin. There was also undeserved joy, new life, coexisting right along with violence and death. I'd forgotten how it felt to be with someone like Rahmia, someone joyful. It was like coming up from underwater and drawing a deep breath.

Rahmia quickened her step, pulling the blanket back over Grace's legs. "You'll freeze your toes off, you pretty girl." With a stronger kick, Grace got the blanket off again, and Rahmia rolled her eyes and let it be.

When we reached the cluster of mailboxes, I opened mine and pulled out a sheaf of envelopes and fliers. We hadn't checked in a few days. Now I put the mass of paper underneath the stroller.

Rahmia handed me the leash and bent to open hers. Bibi started to bark, leaping and spinning on the end of the lead like a child's toy. When Rahmia stood, she had a handful of mail. I could see a few bills and some of the advertising magazines that we got almost daily.

As she flipped through them, I noticed something stuck in the grass under the mailbox. I bent to pick it up. A postcard, a real one—not an advertising circular—with a photo of the glass-fronted Martina V. Umana museum.

I flipped it over, and there was Aimee's familiar spiky writing: *Are the police investigating you? Criminal or criminally stupid?*

10

Helen: So the police have Brady in custody, they're keeping a close eye on the neighbor who turned him in, and they're going over the whole house, digging up the backyard, looking for bodies. Arguably, the most important evidence they find in the house is the cameras. They get their tech guys in and there's tons of footage on Brady's cloud drive. Almost every house Brady did any electronic work for, he put in a camera. Voyeur central. Including the neighbor's house.

Julia: Their so-called friends.

Helen: And the baby. But there's also footage of the murders. Now the police have plenty of evidence to charge Brady with a dozen murders, and Lena's right there helping him.

Julia: But no one knows that yet.

Helen: Right. They're only sure about Brady and the multiple homicides. At least, that's what the district attorney says during his press conference. What they don't have is any idea what happened to Lena. They process the entire house, every vehicle in the fleet of vans. Nothing. Not a drop of blood, not a scrap of evidence. The only things they find are Lena's fingerprints, hair—

Julia: Stuff they would expect to be there.

Helen: Now they have this story that Lena was going to visit her aunt. And they have the texts from Lena to her friend. The aunt doesn't know anything about this alleged visit. And then they find

Lena's car under an overpass by the Brazos River. Her phone, her keys, everything's right there.

Julia: So maybe that's proof that she didn't send the texts?

Helen: Not really strong proof. Did she kill herself or stage her death? Did Brady abandon that stuff there? I mean, the two of them had dumped a body in a tributary of the Brazos once before.

Julia: I could buy the story that she was dead and her husband did it, but I don't see how anyone would believe she killed herself. Plus, the whole thing looked totally staged.

Helen: But if she wasn't dead, where was she? And what was she planning to do?

CHAPTER

21

AFTER I PUT Grace down for her nap, I pulled the sheaf of mail out from under the stroller and dropped it on the kitchen table. Between my art books, I had a folder of Aimee's postcards, and I brought it over and sat down. I fanned them out, the mean-girl comments in angular marker on one side, photos of special exhibitions and opening events on the other. They didn't have the sting they used to. In the back of my mind, I had been turning over ideas to reuse them, to create something beautiful from something spiteful. I thought I'd saved them all, but now I didn't see the one with the picture of the modern take on *Winged Victory*. I'd wanted to compare it to my dream, but the memory of dream-Michael's smirk made me sweep all the postcards up and flip the folder shut.

I was also still crafting paper stars, even though no one was collecting them anymore. I'd used up the origami paper I had, and then I'd switched to marketing fliers and ad magazines, the glossy paper of varying thickness making each star a little different. I looked through the mail, tearing apart any pieces that appealed to me and stacking them to put in the shoe box where I kept my star paper. Some of the envelopes were trash credit card or insurance applications, one was a renewal notice for *Smithsonian Magazine*, but the last one was handwritten, personal. Not the fancy square shape of an invitation or a thank-you card, just a basic envelope with a stamp. I opened it and pulled out a piece of lined notebook paper, the edges ragged from where it had been torn from a spiral binding. In blotchy ballpoint, someone had written: *It's people like you who should have been killed. I hope you rot in hell.*

My throat constricted, and I glanced at the windows and the front door. Strangers were attacking, just like before. They'd read the story in some paper or seen it on the news, and we'd been found guilty. They were coming after us, and no part of the new, happy life I'd built was safe. My breath was quick and shallow, making me light-headed. I forced myself to inhale deeply. Nobody was in the house. The curtains we'd chosen hung undisturbed, sheltering us from any passersby. The golden oak of the kitchen table was smooth under my hands. This time it wasn't just me; it was Michael and Grace. I had to be strong for them.

I snapped a picture of the note and the envelope—no return address but postmarked Texarkana—and texted it to Alondra. I could just picture the creep who'd sent it. Some old busybody without the savvy to use the internet or the sense to realize that not everything the media tells you is the truth. Just like the books I'd left at Elizabeth's, I wouldn't lie about this, but I wasn't going to tell Michael about it either. My phone buzzed with an incoming text. Alondra had written: *High publicity case=crazies. Anything personal or specific, send to police. Otherwise hold onto them, but don't let them fuck w/your head.*

Too late for me and Michael, I thought. Our heads were totally fucked.

I added the poison pen letter to the folder with Aimee's postcards and slid the whole thing between two art books. Michael didn't need to know about this either. So much for being totally honest. I'd always been proud of being a lousy liar. Maybe I'd been kidding myself about who I really was too.

Throughout the rest of the day, I went back to the online forum over and over, scanning every new piece of evidence, every missing person or found body or anything that popped up there. And they kept discussing Lena. One poster with the screen name TXsally808 swore up and down that Lena must have been the organized one, the dominant one, the one who'd gotten away. *I'm just saying I heard that they had a neighbor who kept complaining to the HOA about them, and he turned up dead. Looked like a slip and fall accident, but I betcha that woman was behind it.*

I shut the laptop, but the words echoed in my head. The previous homeowner, blood spreading over what was now our bedroom floor, the things Lena had said: *Kind of a pain about us bringing our trash bins in on time and leaving work vans in the driveway* and *pervert.* But he wasn't the pervert; it had been Lena and Brady. The cameras had been there before Michael and I ever moved in. They had been watching that old man, just the same way they must have been watching us. And he'd been alone when they came in that night and attacked, leaving him to bleed out. Had he known what was happening?

Maybe, someday, we would have been next.

*   *   *

I should have known Michael would catch me. I was on my laptop after dinner, and I thought he was asleep. Rahmia's savory rice and chicken had made our kitchen table feel like a haven.

For once, Grace had cooed happily in her bouncy chair while Michael and I ate together, but I found that the list of things I couldn't tell him—the library books I'd consulted, the internet forums, the letter from a stranger—were the only things I could think about. And when I asked about his day, he said only, "I'm just working on the project. They moved me to computer stuff. Spent all day staring at a screen."

Too soon we were finished, he'd rinsed the dishes and loaded the dishwasher, and by the time I'd fed Grace and put her down, Michael was in our bedroom, leaving me alone again.

So I turned back to the internet forums and was soon deeply engrossed in a discussion about couples who kill. A poster speculated that maybe Lena had been the dominant figure and Brady the submissive until he himself snapped and rebelled.

I didn't hear Michael come into the room, didn't even notice him behind me, until he leaned over the back of the sofa and flipped my laptop shut. "Why are you looking at that garbage?"

"I was just trying to understand." I set the laptop aside and stood to face him across the sofa.

"It's disgusting, the way people are talking about this, enjoying it. Vultures. People are dead, worse than dead—" He shook his head like he was trying to unsee something more terrible than I could imagine.

"That's not why I'm—"

His face tight with anger, he jabbed a finger at me. "You ought to know—they did the same thing to you, calling you an art thief, a liar, an embezzler—"

"Stop yelling at me!" I picked up a sofa cushion, holding it like a shield against my stomach. My heart was pounding harder than it had the night we'd fled to the police station. Michael and I didn't fight, not like this. How could I explain with him looking at me like I was someone he hated?

He gripped the back of the sofa. "Speculating, joking and blaming and picking your life apart like you weren't a real person at all. And now you're reading the same shit about me? I thought you were better than this. I thought I could trust you—"

"You can trust me. But you're not talking to me."

"I want to move past this, but it keeps going on and on." He turned away, his shoulders slumping. "I told the police everything I know, I told you everything, I let them search our home, tear up our garden, and it just keeps dragging on. And now this."

Michael had never accused me of anything, not even when I'd looked guilty. This wasn't like him. "I know." I walked around the sofa and laid a hand on his back. "You did everything right; you did." But he hadn't told me everything. That wasn't true at all.

"If I had realized sooner—" He shrugged off my hand and faced me. I could see how deep the lines between his brows had gotten, how bloodshot his eyes had become. I reached up to touch his cheek, but he stepped out of range.

"You couldn't have realized earlier—he's a predator. He was camouflaged." Aimee had already taught me that a friendly face could hide a sociopath. Had Michael thought I was the only one who could be fooled?

"And now you're looking at that trash . . ."

"Not because I enjoy it. I'm trying—"

"I told you what happened." From down the hallway, I heard Grace's tentative cry, sleepy and confused. *Not now. Not now. Go back to sleep.*

"You told me *some* of what happened." I regretted the words even as I uttered them.

"What do you want from me? If I don't tell you everything, every gory detail, you're going to think I did it?"

Grace's wailing was gathering strength, but I said, "You're not talking to me, you're not talking to a therapist, you need help."

"Are you blaming me for all this? I'm trying to keep a roof over our heads. I don't have the luxury of a nervous breakdown."

"That's not fair." My voice cracked a little, and I hated how weak it sounded. Was that who he saw when he looked at me? The broken-down mess whose total collapse had brought us to Texas in the first place? Grace was crying louder now, the sound vibrating through my body.

"None of this is fucking fair."

He wheeled around, but before he could escape into the bedroom, I caught his arm. "You can't just blame me and shut me out. We're in this together. We're a family."

That traumatized woman I'd been before was gone. I was stronger than he knew.

But when he looked back at me, his face was flushed and his eyes were glassy and distant.

"We're not in this together. You weren't there. It's just me."

My breath caught. "You don't mean that."

When his hand balled into a fist, I flinched, ducking away to protect my bruised cheek.

His gaze fell, and he shoved his hand into his pocket, muttering, "Go get the baby already." He strode back into the bedroom, slamming the door.

And I let him go.

Shaking, I went to lift Grace from her crib, trying to catch my breath.

We'd always been in it together. That was our deal. That was what he'd said when we moved. If we weren't a team, why the hell was I still here? Grace and I could be up in New Jersey watching football with my parents as the aroma of Crock-Pot chili filled their home. I could be hanging out with my big sister Charlotte, pretending to watch her kids while really they watched Grace.

Her sobs had subsided, and now she was rooting around my neck and shoulder, looking for comfort. I settled her against my breast as the tears blurring my vision finally spilled over. *You weren't there.* But we had been, hadn't we, Grace and I? Although we'd been safe at home, asleep, as far as Michael was concerned, we'd been in that room with all the blood and death. He'd seen us on the video monitor, and he'd known the danger we were in. *We* were the reason he'd been afraid to challenge Brady. If it hadn't been for us, he wouldn't have had to play along. When he looked at me now, did it put him right back in that room?

Grace was sleeping again, a bubble of milk at the corner of her mouth. I brought her to my shoulder. I knew what trauma felt like, I'd been there before, and I knew the value of space and silence. Healing doesn't happen when you're churning up raw flesh. Sometimes you need to let it all settle down so you can find the bedrock of your soul.

But what if it didn't? What if the man who'd stood by me, my best friend, my husband, father of my daughter, what if the Michael I knew was gone forever?

Eventually, I grew uncomfortable in the chair. I put Grace down in the crib. In our room, Michael had rolled himself in a blanket from head to toe. On the bed stand next to him I saw a foil packet of over-the-counter sleeping pills, but I couldn't believe he was sleeping, not really.

"Michael?" I whispered, but he didn't answer.

* * *

I lay awake that night opposite Michael, my muscles tensed in painful knots. Without the baby monitor, I never really felt like I could stop listening for Grace. My mind wouldn't stop whirling. I should pack in the morning; I should take Grace and go to my parents. I wouldn't really be leaving, just giving him space. *And keeping myself and our baby safe*, something deep inside whispered.

But I didn't want to leave Michael. I wanted him to roll over in the bed and gather me close. I wanted him to kiss me, to smile at me, to make me feel loved again. But instead there was only the barricade of blanket, another rejection like a thorn in my heart.

Somehow I must have fallen asleep, because when I woke, Michael's side of the bed was empty, his pillow and the blanket gone. He couldn't even stand to sleep next to me. All the pain of the previous night returned. And this was a Saturday. Forty-eight hours of avoiding each other, of pretending we hadn't said the things we had, two full days before the Monday-to-Friday routine saved us from each other again.

We used to work on the house together on weekends, walking around furniture stores and plant nurseries, lining up projects and planning for the future. But I couldn't see any *future* with the distant husband I'd faced last night.

I listened for Grace, but the house was silent. I dressed quickly and tiptoed down the hallway. Her door was open. In the gray morning light, I could see her sleeping on her back with an arm outflung. And, on the floor right next to the crib, lay Michael, wrapped in a blanket. The curve of his cheek was a larger echo of Grace's, and his brow was smooth, the corners of his mouth slack.

I hadn't seen him relaxed since before that terrible night in this same nursery. And I wanted him back so badly, that other husband, the one I loved and trusted. I could see him right there in front of me, but I knew that waking him would break the spell. I stepped back into the hallway and pulled the nursery door softly shut.

In the kitchen I opened the fridge, looking past the cartons of yogurt, the leftovers from Rahmia's casserole, and the bag of breast milk. We had eggs. I'd make scrambled eggs and toast. That could be breakfast for one or for two. But when I pulled the carton of eggs out, I caught sight of what was behind it, and I let them fall. Lena's aunt's sourdough starter, its label stained, Lena's loopy writing faded.

Leaving the eggs on the floor, I took it out and dropped it into the trash. Then I washed my hands, scrubbing them as if some fermented component might have infected me.

"What's happening?" Michael stood at the entrance of the kitchen, his hair mussed and the blanket trailing over one arm, the pillow dangling from the other.

"I just dropped some eggs."

He nodded like a sleepwalker. "Grace's awake. I'm going back to bed."

Maybe Michael hadn't gone to Grace's room seeking comfort or wanting to protect her. Maybe he'd just taken too many sleeping pills.

As he walked to our bedroom, I picked up the carton, damp on one side from the eggs that had broken. I could hear Grace vocalizing, experimenting with the sounds she could make. What if he'd acted out another nightmare the way he had when he hit me?

There were two whole eggs left, but I wasn't hungry anymore.

After I changed Grace's diaper and got her dressed, I brought her into the living room to feed her. The nursery felt claustrophobic, overlaid with bad memories.

A call buzzed on my cell, and I groped to answer it before it woke Michael. Grace cried in protest, a bubble of milk forming at the corner of her mouth before she latched on again. I should have started her with the bottle today instead of going into this struggle again.

"Hello?" I hadn't gotten a glimpse of the screen in my one-handed fumbling.

"Michael's not answering his phone." The woman's voice was accusatory.

"Who is this?"

"Alondra. And nobody's picking up your home phone either."

"It rings through to our cells. I must not have heard it. What's wrong?" Grace gave up nursing in disgust, and for a second I risked dropping the phone or hanging up with the side of my face as I tried to maneuver her onto my shoulder.

"The police want to go over some things with Michael. He needs to be at the station in an hour."

My whole body seized up, and Grace arched her back, flailing with her fists. "What kind of things?"

"Hold on." I could hear muffled talking, like Alondra was answering someone with her hand over the phone, and just then my own doorbell rang. I jumped up, tightening my grip on Grace, and the doorbell rang again. Were the police already here, ready to drag Michael away?

Alondra came back on as I was hurrying down the hall. "They've pulled in the FBI. I want Michael to wait in the parking lot until I get there, do you understand?"

I wrenched open the front door, expecting to see the police, but it was just a white van peeling away. On our doormat was a cardboard box, no address, no stamps, not even taped shut, with a card tucked under the loose flap.

Alondra asked, "Kacy, are you listening? Do you understand?"

"Someone dropped off a box at our front door. It looks weird." The cardboard was unmarked, freshly folded.

"Weird how?"

"No address, not sealed up, just dropped off by some white van. There's a card."

"Don't touch anything," Alondra snapped, but my hand was already reaching for what I could see was a postcard. Was it from Aimee?

"Kacy." Alondra was used to being obeyed. "Kacy, get back inside the house. Let the police handle the box."

As I straightened up, a shriek made me jump, but it was just a little boy two blocks away, sprinting across the street to the pocket park, followed by an indulgent grandparent.

I flipped the postcard over, half expecting to see Aimee's bold scrawl. Instead, in loopy black marker, I read, *Working on another surprise for you. xoxoxo.* Despite the humidity, the back of my neck grew cold.

This wasn't Aimee's handwriting. It was Lena's.

11

Helen: So the number of known victims is over a dozen at this point, but only a few have been identified. The police are working on that, they have Brady in custody, and the FBI is involved.

Julia: And they're going over all the information and reinterviewing all the witnesses.

Helen: They're planning to. But on the very day the neighbor, Michael, is supposed to come in for questioning, a package is dropped off at his house. It's got a note from Lena on top and a dead rat inside.

Julia: Ew. Very Mafia. But isn't it a little late for a "don't rat me out" warning? I mean, the neighbor's already turned Brady in, made a statement, taken the cops around the crime scene, the whole deal.

Helen: It's never too late for witness tampering, my friend. Plus, law enforcement now has proof that Lena was complicit, is alive, and is out to save her man. Remember they'd built up this whole contractor business? They had a fleet of vans, dozens of employees, and plenty of cash money. The police never identified which van dropped off the package, because, let's face it, without a business logo, all white work vans look the same.

Julia: Creepy. They all look creepy.

Helen: So the FBI take the nonmurderous neighbors back into the station for more interviews, run over all the details again, and then they break the news: "You're still in danger. We need you to go into protective custody until we lock this thing down."

Julia: Although if you and I had been killing together happily for years and then you blew it by inviting some rando over when I was out of town, I wouldn't be blaming the rando.

Helen: Sweetie, I'd never commit murder with anyone but you.

22

"THE PACKAGE IS from Lena," I whispered.

I turned around, scanning the street, as though the postcard had been handed to me. Brady was in custody; I knew he was safely away. But this card was from the Fort Bend Museum, practically in Sugar Land.

Alondra said, "How do you know it was from her? When was it sent, and from where?"

I said, "Her handwriting, and it's the Fort Bend Museum."

The museum postcard was more than a callback to the card I'd received the first time Lena and I went walking, the first time I'd told a friend about my past. The postcard, the location, was a threat.

Then Alondra started to curse, slowly and deliberately, the way some people might take a deep breath to clear their head. Finally, she said, "Okay. When Michael goes to the police station, you and Grace go too. I'll meet you there. But I want you to pack first. Do that right now. Pack for a week or so. I'm going to call that station and make the situation abundantly clear. They should've sent someone to escort you."

"I could call the local constable, the one assigned to our neighborhood."

"Do that. And I'll call the station." She spoke to someone in the room with her; I couldn't quite hear what she was saying. Then her voice came through clearly again. "Check your doors, call that constable, and don't open up to anyone but him. When he arrives, have him follow you to the station. You and Michael."

"Wait." But she had already clicked off.

I stepped inside, leaving the box where it was, and locked the front door behind me. With Grace up on my shoulder, I hurried to the back door and double-checked that it was locked. She gave a milky burp that left dampness against my neck. I held her close and glanced up at the security box against the back wall. I knew all the cameras were gone, and the morning light shone clearly across everything in my line of sight, from the living room sofa and Grace's play mat to the gleaming kitchen counters straight to the front door.

But I still felt watched, as if Lena could surveil me without any equipment at all.

Even the tone of the postcard, unafraid, cheeky, sounded like Lena, and I was flooded with a mix of contradictory emotions. This Lena was simultaneously the friend I'd loved and the wife of a murderer, at the very least. With her vitality and her strength, there was no way she'd been a passive victim in thrall to her husband. She'd been the planner, the organizer, and that meant that every dead runaway, every terrified old man, had to be laid at her feet. I knew that.

And she was reaching out to me.

Unlike Aimee's note, this postcard wasn't mocking; it invited me to participate. It was an outstretched hand, not a raised middle finger.

Slipping into the bedroom, I started to set the postcard down on the dresser, but I didn't want Michael to see it and suffer another shock. He wasn't asleep, but he was engrossed in something on his phone, the light of the tiny screen casting his face in relief. He took one look at me, and the lines of resignation deepened around his eyes. He didn't even have to ask, *What now?*

I just told him. And we started to pack.

*   *   *

At the police station, they separated us, sending Michael and Alondra with the FBI agent and his partner to go through another gauntlet of questions. Lugging Grace in her carrier, I followed

Detective Clark into another room, where a selection of items was spread out on the table. Even out of context, a jolt of recognition pierced me.

"Can you identify any of these?" Detective Clark asked.

Of course I could. Lena's phone in its battered utilitarian case. Were my last texts to her still on it? A pair of oversized sunglasses in a brand she used to call "drugstore not designer." Her wallet, which I knew would be neatly organized with a few bills and carefully folded receipts. I had been so sure that postcard meant she was alive, but now, seeing her personal items lying there on the table . . .

"Where did you find these?" I asked Detective Clark. There was something else, a torn piece of paper, behind the sunglasses.

"Do you recognize them?" she countered.

"They're Lena's. Her wallet and phone." And I remembered that the cops had found her car abandoned by the river. It must have been staged. Lena was alive, I *knew* she was. "Can I see that paper?"

Detective Clark slipped on a thin latex glove and moved the piece of paper closer to me. "Don't touch," she warned me.

I didn't bother to answer, bending closer. Half of a torn postcard, its glossy picture one I knew all too well. *Winged Victory*, the statue from my old museum. The only postcard from Aimee I hadn't found in my collection. "Can you turn it over?" I whispered, and Detective Clark complied.

On the ragged portion that remained, I read my own name and address in Aimee's spiky handwriting. Lena had taken the part with the nasty message. If I could only ask her, *What the hell is going on?*

"I don't understand." I stepped away from the table. "That's a postcard that was sent to me by someone I used to work with. The picture is from the museum where we worked. But I don't know why Lena had it." Unless . . .

Detective Clark started slipping the items back into plastic evidence bags, but something in the angle of her body let me know her attention was still on me. She was waiting for me to give her something more.

Feeling my way tentatively through my thoughts, I said, "The half that's missing has the message."

"Any reason she would have wanted it?" Detective Clark's tone was studiously casual.

Heat rose in my face. How many times had Lena taken my side? How often had she said Aimee should pay? But that was stupid. I'd just gotten a postcard from Lena from right here in Texas. "I don't know. The part that's missing has the address for the museum on it."

Detective Clark gave me a blank look, and I felt like a complete idiot. Nobody needed a postcard to find an address. That's what the internet was for. "If you think of anything else," she said, and I could almost hear the subtext: *I'll be shocked. What a complete waste of time.*

*   *   *

We'd been arguing with the detective and someone new, an FBI agent, for a while. Michael was their primary witness, an important part of their case. When they thought Lena might be dead, apparently they'd been willing to harass him, imply they thought he might be involved, tighten the proverbial screws. But now that Lena was out there, really and truly, suddenly they wanted to protect us. Even though this might be the last straw that cost Michael his job. Even though being shut up together in a tiny hotel room might kill what was left of our marriage. They needed Michael's testimony. And Alondra seemed to agree with them. "You'll be safer," she told me.

"Where exactly do you want us to go?" I asked again.

The detective gave me a reassuring smile, but I wasn't buying it. "We have a safe house, we can put him up, all of you up, there."

Michael sat with his arms crossed, the way he had since I'd been allowed back into the interview room. "I don't want Kacy or Grace involved."

"I don't want to be away from you," I said, but he didn't even look at me, keeping his gaze on the detective. I could see the same tension in his jaw and shoulders that he'd had on the worst parts of our drive from New Jersey, when a phalanx of trucks enclosed us. He was focused on the road ahead now, just trying to get us through safely.

Alondra asked me, "Is there a place you could go where Lena wouldn't know to find you?"

In the back of my mind, I'd been thinking about this, going over and over the things found in Lena's abandoned car. Her phone, her wallet, and the last thing, just a piece of trash to the detective but everything to me. Lena didn't leave trash in her car, and she didn't make mistakes. She'd sent me one message: *Working on another surprise for you.* Was the torn postcard some other communication I was supposed to understand?

It wouldn't be hard to find my parents; my maiden name was out there on the internet. But my younger sister was subletting a basement apartment not too far from their house. Molly's name wasn't on the lease or the utilities, and she'd been on tour with her band for the last month. Her landlord lived upstairs, but supposedly he was out of town almost every weekend. Nobody would know we were even there. I'd be close enough that my parents could watch Grace, which I knew they'd love to do, as long as I could convince them to keep their visits to the sure-to-be-crappy apartment rather than bringing us back to their house.

Would I be going exactly where Lena wanted me to go? Because this was it, the moment when I could make a choice to get answers, save a friend, or catch a killer. That torn postcard might be a clue, a winking invitation. Of course, it could also be nothing at all.

If I told Michael what I was thinking, he'd be angry or afraid. He'd ask me not to go. He might even tell the police what I was planning. And he'd be right. My plan was reckless, but I wasn't going to put Grace in danger. I'd do everything possible to hide where she and I would be staying, my parents would be there to look out for her, and once I got up there, once I was in the right area, I was sure I would find Lena. We'd been fated to be friends, at least it had felt that way, and now it felt like I was fated to be the one to find her.

I had to find her.

What was the alternative? Lena never caught. Michael and me living in fear, always terrified that Lena would be circling us, a shark prepared to strike.

Michael was thinking about all the ways he could keep us safe. I could tell from the tension in his shoulders and the grim set to his mouth that if he needed to, if he thought it would make a difference, he'd divorce me, he'd swear never to see Grace again, he'd go into witness protection to save us from the danger he thought he'd brought down on us. But he couldn't stop me from wanting to keep him safe. I slipped my hand into his chilled one and twined my fingers with his, pressing our palms together.

"It's okay." I tried to put all the certainty I didn't feel into my voice. "Grace and I will go to my parents'. We'll hide out at Molly's place. There's no way anyone can trace us there. We'll be safe. You do what you need to do."

He tried to smile at me, but only half his mouth could manage it. "Thanks." He squeezed my hand. "I'll feel better knowing you are both someplace else."

The detective was watching me closely, too closely. I knew I had no poker face, but surely there were enough emotions—terror, love, grief, an attempt at bravery—that she couldn't detect the vein of sick anticipation running through it all.

Maybe this would be my new round of affirmations. *I am brave. I am smart. I am going to save us.*

And somewhere in the back of my mind, Lena whispered, *You are going to kick ass.*

*   *   *

I boarded my flight in a blur of juggling the stroller, the diaper bag, and the carrier, followed by wiping everything down, taking advantage of the empty seat next to me to buckle in Grace's car seat, and giving her a bottle during takeoff. Once she settled, I felt a strange relief in the sterile cabin thirty thousand feet off the ground. At least here, Grace and I were safe. I'd been deluded to think that a torn postcard was some kind of secret communication. Too many sleepless nights and internet forums had made me hallucinate a message from Lena.

I rested my hand on the edge of Grace's car seat, where the hum of the plane had already sent her to sleep. The police, the FBI, Alondra, everyone was so sure Lena was in Texas. Her aunt was there, all her employees, Brady. There was no reason to think she'd be anywhere else. Instead of racing off to find her and put an end to this nightmare, I was really just running away from danger. All I wanted was safety for Grace, a stable home with two parents who loved her and each other. I could still feel the phantom pressure of my last embrace with Michael, but even as I noticed, it faded away.

When we landed at Newark, I was so relieved to see my parents waving by the baggage claim. Only three months had passed since their visit, but as I set Grace next to them in her little seat and sank into my mother's embrace, I felt decades older. They looked exactly the same, my mother with her feathery ash-blond hair and oversized earrings, my dad with his steel-rimmed glasses.

Was it my imagination, or were they studying me a little too intently? Then the first bags appeared on the baggage carousel, and I started sprinting back and forth, gathering the portable crib, the stroller base, and our suitcase, while my parents cooed over Grace.

Then my dad picked up the crib and stroller. "Your sister's place in Hawthorne is just a fifteen-minute drive. Might as well get this show on the road."

Molly's sublet was nicer than I'd expected for a basement apartment, like student teacher digs rather than a troll's cave. The windows were large, even if they were high up on the walls, and the inexpensive furniture was sturdy and undamaged. I could see signs of my younger sister, the framed album covers and a specially matted concert poster I'd given her, the tins of exotic teas, a blanket crocheted by our grandmother with primary-colored flowers edged in black instead of the gray she had used on mine.

Grace took to my parents as if she remembered them, smiling and reaching for my mom and allowing herself to be passed to my dad without a hint of protest.

Once we were settled on the IKEA futon in the tiny family room, my mother asked, "So, have you heard anything else?"

I ran a hand across the crocheted blanket draped over the back of the futon. "Not from the police. They just want us to lay low until they find Lena."

"You said you got a postcard from that woman?" My mom's mouth twisted like she could taste something bitter, and I knew she'd put Lena's name next to Aimee's in the vault of words she'd never utter again.

"Yes, the police and the FBI are looking into it."

My mother was no fool, and I'd never had any luck trying to hide something from her. She asked, "Where did the postcard come from?"

"A Fort Bend museum." But the only postcard I could think about was the one Lena had taken, the one Aimee had sent. Alondra had said the police were pretty sure Lena was still in Texas. Obviously, I hadn't known her as well as I'd thought. But I still couldn't shake the feeling that I knew Lena better than anyone else except Brady.

My mom's eyes narrowed as if I were a teenager evading a direct question. Instead of challenging me, she turned to my dad. "I think we should stay here with Kacy and Grace."

He nodded, lifting Grace over his head and pretending to snap at her toes. "I can stop by our house and pack."

At that, Mom rolled her eyes. "You'll pack what? A toothbrush and an extra pair of socks. You can't pack for me. You have no idea what I need."

"So write it down." My dad cut his eyes at me to see if I was enjoying the show.

Mom didn't notice. "It'll just be easier to do it myself."

"I'm not letting you go back there alone." My dad stood up, holding Grace closely. "And if we both go, then Kacy and Grace will be alone."

As they went back and forth, I felt a warm glow of gratitude. There was evil in the world, vast and malevolent, but there was also this: love that did the work needed, love that came together, even when it was in the ordinary task of packing a suitcase, or grudgingly allowing one's spouse to pack it.

Finally, Dad promised to stay on the phone the whole time so my mother could tell him what to pack. He handed her Grace and left. The door had scarcely shut behind him when she said, "We shouldn't have let him go alone."

"He'll be okay. Alondra says Lena's still in Texas."

She shut her eyes and rested her cheek against Grace's head. "I just wish I could be sure."

"I know." And in that silent moment I wished I could promise my mother that I was done making her worry. Almost two years ago, my mother had suffered with me through my public humiliation, professional ruin, and private breakdown. I knew she'd cried on my behalf, had longed to make things better, had endured the same hopeless frustration I felt when I saw Michael's pain. If I could spare her now, I would. So I said, "She doesn't know where we are, Mom. Molly's last name isn't on the lease or utilities or anything. And the postcard Lena sent wasn't actually threatening."

From the look on my mother's face, she didn't find it comforting that a serial killer was communicating with me for fun. Any communication—friendly, threatening, even promotional—was bad. But she changed the subject. "Your hair's gotten so long." She reached out and tucked a strand behind my ear.

She stayed on the phone with my father while he packed, running through the minutiae of things she might need ("No, Bill, not the drawer on the left, the one on the right") and occasionally throwing out a question to me ("Do you think he should pack a cooler of food?" "Would you want cereal for breakfast?").

Then suddenly she turned to me, and her countenance made me tense. "What does this woman look like?"

"Is she there?" My lungs froze, and I couldn't catch my breath. I'd been stupid to come here, stupid to put my family at risk.

"No, no." My mother waved her hand. "I only thought we should tell your father, in case he noticed someone following him."

I exhaled hard. This was just my parents being prepared. "She's tall with red hair. Here . . ." I grabbed my phone and scrolled through the photos. I hadn't deleted them, and after I scanned through months of Grace in every permutation of expression, there was Lena in a selfie with me, our foreheads together, both of us smiling. I knew my smile had been genuine, but Lena's looked just as real, radiating joy from the curve of her lips to the crinkles around her eyes.

My mom squinted at it, and I realized she didn't have her reading glasses on, but she turned back to the phone. "Red hair. Curly. Kacy says she's tall. Well, I don't know if she's in disguise, Bill; how would I know that?

"Okay, keep me on speaker as you drive home." She clicked her own phone over to speaker and set it down next to her on the end table. Then she turned the full force of her attention on me. "So how are you doing, really?"

"I'm okay. In shock, I guess." The enormity of Michael alone sixteen hundred miles away and of Grace, so helpless and trusting, sleeping on a collapsible temporary bed in a strange apartment, settled over me, and I twisted my fingers in the crocheted blanket. I didn't want to lay all this on my mom.

"Are the police going to check in, at least?"

I wished I could just tell her everything, the way I'd done as a kid, but worry lines creased her forehead, and her hands looked so thin. I was too old to make myself feel better at my mother's expense.

"I don't know." Outside the bubble of my planned community, there wasn't a designated constable ready to stop by and check on me personally. I had texted Alondra to let her know I'd landed in Jersey. She was my liaison with law enforcement. And I'd called Michael, but he hadn't picked up. Instead, I'd left him a voice mail and sent him a text with a picture of Grace in her car seat from the plane. And he'd texted back: *Stay safe* and heart emojis. But it wasn't the same. Neither of us had the comfort of a real voice, real conversation, only a recorded message and fragmented sentiments on a screen.

Half an hour later, Dad came back with a cooler and a wheeled suitcase. "Where should I put this?"

"Let Kacy and Grace have Molly's room. We'll sleep on the futon."

"Mom, I'm up and down a lot in the night. Why don't you and Dad take the bedroom?"

"We'll be fine out here for a few nights. Not another word." My mother put her hand over mine, either to comfort me or to make me stop messing with the crocheted blanket.

And that was the end of the discussion. I felt simultaneously irritated and adored.

* * *

As I huddled alone under the covers in a bed that sagged too much in the center, Grace's rhythmic wheezing put me to sleep, but my dreams were fractured scenes of running through empty rooms in terror.

I woke with a start, disoriented. Apparently, my sleep problems weren't something I could leave behind in Texas. The slight scent of patchouli and dust pervaded the room. Molly had been on tour for almost a month, and little things—a spider web in the corner of the bathroom, a whiff of mold by the refrigerator—made me feel her absence even more. She was probably crashing on the sofa of a friend of the band or sharing a dingy motel room with three other people. And Michael must be alone in some spartan bed with nothing to distract him but his own fears. Even my parents were sleeping on a crappy futon instead of their own four-poster with its pillow-top mattress. No one was snug in their own home.

Grace was stirring, making little sounds. If I nursed her now, she would probably drift off without waking my parents. She ate quickly, without opening her eyes, and before half an hour had passed, I was placing her back in the crib.

But I was brutally awake.

The television was in the other room. I hadn't brought any earbuds, and the sound on my phone might wake Grace up. My fingers itched for movement, something to tear and fold, something to do. And Molly hadn't left so much as a spare scrap of paper where I could find it.

So I pulled up a game, swiping colored squares on my phone with the sound off, hoping the repetition would put me back to sleep. But whether it was the light from the screen or the mild competitive thrill I got from winning, the endorphin rush of doing it over and over again, I was getting further and further from sleep.

An old impulse pulled at me, born from the dark, the phone in my hand, the feeling that what I did here in this strange space didn't matter. I opened up Aimee's social media accounts. Her Twitter hadn't been updated for a couple of days and included just a cryptic quote designed to make her sound deep: *Life is the Medium; Living is the Art*. Her Instagram featured an artfully arranged photo of a coffee shop I knew well, one right around the corner from the museum. The filter was set to blur everything except the close-up of a mug of coffee—which I knew was black with cinnamon—and a folded arts page of the paper over the caption *Old School Monday Morning*. Almost a week out of date.

Then on Facebook, I struck gold. A story was still up, something she had to have posted within the last twenty-four hours. Aimee at a club, leaning against the bar, cocktail in hand, between two people with their backs to the camera. Her angled bob was a little shorter, her lipstick a little darker, and her pose was a little overly theatrical. There was the time stamp. Four hours ago.

I waited for the bitter taste of envy or anger, but that poison seemed to have drained away. Even those postcards were almost quaint, relics of a bygone relationship, designed to hurt me with paper darts in a world where real bullets had grazed my head.

But I still kept flipping back to the story over and over, until finally I just took a screenshot and enlarged the picture. Was that also a club I'd been to? Was Aimee still living the same life she'd been before—same breakfast, same museum, same lover, same cocktail in the same nightclub? Despite myself, even though I didn't want her friendship anymore, I did feel another lingering pang for those glittering nights when it seemed like we might live forever. This picture was full of purple, pink, gold, all the vibrant colors of a fairy carnival, and the people in the photo . . . I squinted, my pulse quickening.

On one side of Aimee was a young, dark-haired guy in a white shirt leaning over the bar to place an order. On the other side, a woman, also in a white shirt, also with dark hair, also with her back to the camera, was looking off the side, so that she and the man made a perfect frame for Aimee in her sapphire sheath. But something was sparking my memory, something about the edge of that woman's face, her hair—the wrong color but the right texture—a certain out-of-placeness to her.

I was paranoid, seeing Lena everywhere.

I dismissed the picture and switched back to my game, but no matter how I tried to focus my attention on the flashing shapes, I lost over and over. It was four o'clock in the morning after a day of travel with a newborn. I just wanted this to be over, and that was why I'd thought I'd seen Lena. I'd conjured her out of my head.

I couldn't stand it. I opened the picture again just to be sure. Aimee kept smiling, confident and polished, next to maybe-Lena. Maybe just another anonymous city girl, slightly awkward in her pressed white shirt. Maybe a cocktail waitress at the bar or an off-work hostess.

If I'd still had my old phone with all my old contacts, would I have texted Aimee and warned her? Maybe she had other pictures from the bar, ones she'd rejected before she posted this one, ones that would dispel the illusion, revealing a more narrow nose, a heart-shaped face, a woman younger or older or just *other* than Lena.

I needed a second opinion, from someone who wouldn't judge me. Michael had enough to worry about. I had to keep any additional burdens away from him. Like I'd said to him in the voice mail message, Grace and I were good, we were hidden away, and my parents were looking after us. Safe and snug, that's what we were. Not post-stalking one ex-friend and hallucinating another.

I was caught in a state of suspension, torn between what I thought I'd seen and what I knew. My whole body was buzzing.

Nobody I knew would be awake now, but sending a text would be okay. Anybody worried about being woken up would have their phone on silent.

Holding my breath, I sent the picture separately to Elizabeth, Alondra, and to Rahmia.

No explanation. No commentary about who Aimee was or how I'd found this or even a *Didn't want to bother you, but . . .* I didn't want to cloud their judgment or color their response. I just sent the picture and the words *What do you think about the woman on the right?* A puzzle I couldn't solve alone.

In only a couple hours, Grace would be awake again. My eyes were dry and tired from staring so hard at the screen in the dark. Hitting send seemed to have sent my worry out into the ether. It would be waiting for me in the morning.

12

Helen: Investigators are looking for Lena in Texas. They've reinterviewed the aunt—

Julia: The one she was supposedly visiting.

Helen: And they're not buying her "my niece wasn't supposed to visit, I never saw her, this is all a total shock" story. They start pulling footage from traffic cams, and lo and behold, there's Lena's car on the interstate the night before everything blows up with Brady and the neighbor.

Julia: So he didn't kill her.

Helen: Nope. And all he would have had to do was not kill anyone else or at least not invite anyone else into a crime scene until she got back. But he screwed that up.

Julia: If he wasn't in jail, she'd probably have killed him. I might have.

Helen: Seriously. So the cameras also show her driving back towards Sugar Land, presumably to abandon her car by the Brazos. But after that, there's no trace of her. She's got cash, access to properties under construction all over Houston, and nobody knows what she plans to do next. She could just disappear, start a new life as someone else.

Julia: Kill more people.

Helen: Maybe. When you look back at her life, there were a number of deaths even when she was young. A local kid drowned in a creek, a great-uncle fell down the stairs.

Julia: If you look far enough back in anyone's life, there are *some* deaths.

Helen: The most suspicious one is a neighbor from the year before she met Brady, a young woman found dead in her apartment below Lena's.

Julia: Dead in her apartment like Lena and Brady's neighbor was found dead in his house?

Helen: What?

Julia: Both living alone, both found dead from a slip and fall, and both living next door to Lena.

Helen: Damn, I think you could be right. But without a confession, I don't see how they'd ever prove this. But it all adds up. You have to wonder if those neighbors saw something or knew something—

Julia: So they were "business" kills, while the ones she and Brady did and recorded were for fun?

Helen: If you add up the victims we think Lena killed on her own and the victims she and Brady killed together, the number jumps to serious double digits.

Julia: We might never know how many she really killed, because she didn't hack them up, like, "Look over here, y'all. These are some murder victims!" She was sneaky.

Helen: And the victims she and Brady chose were so random, so dissimilar from each other, that it seems deliberate.

Julia: No way Lena would let Brady accidentally kill two white teenage runaways instead of just one.

Helen: So she was hard to predict. Her early crimes, if they were crimes, were opportunistic ways to get rid of people she knew, while the later ones were highly planned, but the victims were random. Only the timing—six months apart—was regular.

Julia: So now that the pattern was disrupted, would she keep killing solo? Would she feel compelled to keep killing someone at the six-month mark? Or would she go back to sneaky kills whenever she felt like it? Had Brady messed up the whole system? Would she blame Michael and come after him? How many people would Lena kill?

Helen: Take a breath, honey. We'll get to everything.

CHAPTER

23

WHEN I WOKE, Grace wasn't in her crib and sunlight was streaming into the basement windows around the edges of the woven bamboo blinds. I sat up, calling out, "Mom?"

I could hear my parents' voices in the other room, and then my father crooning in his talking-to-a-baby voice. They had Grace. Everything was okay.

Swiping the sleep from my eyes, my head still heavy, I glanced around the room. No clock. I picked up my phone to check the time, and texts were waiting, even though it was an hour earlier in Texas. I had a reply from Elizabeth and another from Alondra. Nothing from Rahmia, but it was a weekend, and she probably hadn't gotten up with Emir yet.

Alondra's read *What am I looking at?*

I answered: *The woman with her back to the camera. Lena?*

Her reply took just seconds: *Don't see it. Will forward to police. Stay put.*

Then I opened Elizabeth's: *Is that Lena? Where are you?*

Not my picture. Saw online.

Did you send it to the police?

Alondra's on it.

Do you know the other woman, the one next to her?

Yes, from a long time ago.

You should warn her.

If I warned Aimee, would she even believe me? Then I thought about the postcard Lena had sent. *Working on another surprise for you.*

A year ago, I might have jumped at the chance for Aimee to be beholden to me. She'd be in danger, I'd save her life, and then she'd confess everything and clear my name. But now I hesitated. I could pretend I was wrong about the picture, that the postcard meant nothing. But I wanted Elizabeth to think I was a good person. No, more than that, I wanted to *be* a good person.

I will. I'd warn Aimee, I would. But even as I typed my answer into the phone, my skin prickled. What if I was too late?

In the gritty light of morning, I went back to Aimee's page. She hadn't posted anything new, but the story was still there, time-stamped seven hours ago. Lena could have done a lot in seven hours.

I enlarged my copy of the photo again. The woman with her face turned away from the camera looked like Lena. But was she really? Even though nearly two years had gone by, Aimee was definitively herself. No question, positive identification, that was the bitch who'd wrecked my life. But the woman next to her was like a police artist's sketch. My head was comparing her height, her hair, her build and not coming up with a conclusive answer. Yet my body tensed with certainty. Wherever the police thought Lena was, I believed she was here.

I slid out of bed, dropped the phone on my pillow, and started throwing on clothes. None of the victims I'd heard about on the news had a personal connection to Lena or to Brady. Maybe that had made me feel strangely safer, as though our relationship would keep me alive, but that was stupid. Killing random people instead of neighbors was just another way of not getting caught. It was calculated, not compassionate.

And I couldn't shake TXSally808's suspicion. If Lena and Brady had killed the man who'd previously owned our home, there was something different about it. Not just that it was personal, petty, a violent reaction to a few HOA complaints. The other crimes, the ones getting publicity, were splashy, obvious murders. This other one had been stealthy, carefully orchestrated to look like an accident. So sad. Could have happened to anyone. Just like . . .

My stomach clenched, bile rising.

Just like Sandy.

No. But even as I tried to reject the idea, my mind kept whispering. *Lena was working on her house. Lena hated her. Lena was so much taller and stronger than Sandy. Sandy was threatening not to pay Lena, was going to badmouth her business.*

A second death in our neighborhood, another older person living alone dead from an apparent slip and fall. A person who just happened to have had a run-in with Lena.

I'd still been hoping, somewhere deep inside, that Lena had been an accomplice, afraid or cowed or under Brady's spell. Because I could see her standing at the doorway with a pitcher of margaritas, still feel the freedom when she hurled a glass in solidarity, still somehow credited her with lifting the depression I'd been under. And she wasn't dead, but now I didn't know if that was better or worse. Because she was absolutely a killer. She knew my maiden name, so I couldn't let my parents go back to their house again. She knew I'd been fired from the Martina V. Umana. And she knew how badly Aimee had hurt me.

My phone vibrated with another incoming text. I scooped it up. This one was from Rahmia, with a link to a local news story.

I clicked on it, and a rushing sound filled my ears.

The story, titled "Army Veteran's Struggles End in Tragedy," was an in-depth profile of one of the victims, Marcus Fontenot, an older man in a military jacket. The pullout quote from one of the man's daughters read, "We never stopped looking for him, trying to bring him home for good."

I knew that man. In the photo, he was standing against a pale-blue background in a professional photographer's studio. But I could still see him half in shadow, no medals on his distressed green jacket, a jacket that was too warm for the Houston humidity, even in the shade of the underpass.

And then I shuddered with a cold that radiated outward from my bones. I'd seen him with Lena. Not with Brady, just with Lena. She'd noticed his army jacket. I'd given him my tacos. His eyes had looked so much like my father's.

He'd been slaughtered.

I read the words *dismembered* and *decapitated* and *disposed*, horror blurring the screen of my phone. This man, the man I'd seen with Lena, had been carved into pieces and discarded in the bayou. He was dead, worse than dead. Had I drawn Lena's attention to him? Maybe I was the reason she'd plucked him from the street.

My phone vibrated again with another text from Rahmia: *Be safe. She's dangerous.*

Shaking, my stomach roiling, I sat down on the edge of the bed. Lena was dangerous, I knew that; some part of me had always known that. Wasn't that why I'd wanted her on my side? Wasn't that the feeling she'd given me, that I was powerful, could be dangerous too? I'd been so scared—of Aimee, what she'd said, what people would think, what people might post. Now all that seemed like playground gossip.

And my friendship with Lena left me feeling like an accomplice.

Working on another surprise for you.

What surprise? My baby shower hadn't been a surprise. Maybe the baby monitor she'd given me? But that was naïve. I turned the phone over and over in my hands. *Another surprise.* Was Sandy the first surprise? She was the only person in Texas I'd had any trouble with, but I'd never wished her dead. Had Lena seen something in me that made her think I longed for violence? No amount of bitchiness meant Sandy deserved to die naked and alone in a pool of her own blood.

A sob built in my throat, but I tried to choke it down. I didn't want my parents to hear.

If Lena thought Sandy deserved death, her next surprise must be Aimee.

Lena might have sliced Aimee up and murdered her on a whim. For a hot second, I almost burned with something like joy. All that agony over, my tormentor dead. But the feeling was gone in a flash, leaving me sick to my stomach. Revenge was one thing, wanting vindication or restitution, but death was something else, something vile and permanent, a stain on the new life I was building, an affront to the joy I had in Grace. If I really was brave, if I really was strong, I couldn't just cower in this basement and let bad things happen to someone else.

Even someone I thought I hated.

Alondra was notifying the police. Nobody here would be convinced by an almost-out-of-frame profile on a screenshot from a social media story. And Aimee wouldn't be convinced by a simple message from me. If I just knew she was alive, maybe that would be enough.

I'd deleted her cell phone number ages ago, so I called the main number for the museum. Most museum employees took Sunday off, but Aimee preferred to work long hours, weekends, even holidays. Maybe when she was home alone, she couldn't stand her own company. The automated message ran with choices for tickets, hours, exhibitions, special events. I bypassed the directory and entered Aimee's extension.

My pulse was so fast I could feel it in my throat, but the number went to voice mail. I listened to Aimee's familiar voice saying her own name, and then the robo-voice invited me to leave a message, but I hung up, shaky and cold. Even if she had answered, I might not have been able to speak. What could I say that wouldn't sound insane? And why would she stay on the phone with me at all?

No, this was crazy. I'd have to see Aimee in person. Maybe to warn her, maybe just to reassure myself that she was alive.

* * *

After nursing Grace, I left my folks to finish their coffee and play with her and took the travel breast pump out of my suitcase. Somewhere, a part of me I'd almost forgotten was making a separate plan. I'd need my parents to be able to feed Grace. That was crucial. And I couldn't alarm them by racing out of the apartment. They'd come after me or call the police or somehow bring Lena's attention to them. I needed them to stay here, stay safe, and let me go.

I could hear their soft voices. My dad must be looking up from his book while my mom talked to Grace. Safety, comfort, and family were all in the next room over, and I was going to leave it behind just to prove to myself that someone I hated wasn't dead.

Once I'd pumped a full bag of milk, I pulled myself together and brought it to them. Dad was sitting with Grace on his shoulder, patting her gingerly, one of his cotton undershirts serving as a burp cloth. I put the bag of milk in the fridge and took the pump to the sink to clean it.

"So when Grace goes down for her nap," I said, trying to keep my voice neutral, "if it would be okay, I'd love to go get my hair trimmed, even at one of those clip-'n'-go places. You noticed how long it had gotten."

My mother frowned. "Is that safe? I thought the police wanted you to stay inside."

My face felt flushed, and I swept my hair behind one ear, just the way I'd done as a teenager. "Nobody knows where we are; nobody will be following me to a haircutting place. It's just so nice to have you and Dad here with Grace. And she usually naps for two hours. If she wakes up before I get back, you can give her a bottle." I knew how tempting that would be for my mom.

Dad stopped patting Grace's back. "How would you get there?"

"I can call a car—"

Mom shook her head. "No, you'd have to give your name."

"She can take our Subaru," Dad said. At my mother's expression, he added, "We're staying in a place Molly sublets from some guy who doesn't even own the building in the first place. All her mail's been going to us anyway, so she's probably not affiliated with this address in the least. Kacy'll duck out, get her hair cut or whatever, and be back before you know it." He gave me a wink. Grace's head was drooping on his shoulder. The calm rumble of his voice had put her to sleep. This was my moment.

Mom stood. "I just don't think you need to be taking any unnecessary risks."

I took Grace gently from Dad. "It's not a risk. Just an errand. I promise, Mom."

I was pretty sure Dad knew I'd been lying, and I wondered if he chalked it up to my being stir-crazy or needing a break and using the haircut thing as an excuse. I wasn't even thinking about what I'd say when I came home with the exact same hair as when I'd left. Those were problems for a future Kacy. Right now I had a mission, and if I told my parents, which I wanted to do, they'd argue with me, they'd be afraid, and they'd probably be right.

Once Grace was safely in her travel crib, I almost changed my mind. My mother was reading a book, my father was stretched out on the futon, and my heart contracted a little. I knew how awful it would be if anything happened to them, and it would be just as bad for them if something happened to me. It was my responsibility to be okay, to be careful. I owed that to my parents, to Grace, and to Michael, who'd sent us here to keep us safe.

But Lena was out there *working on another surprise* for me. I could picture Aimee, her wide eyes glassy and her lipsticked mouth slack, lifeless in the bowels of the museum. I had to know if she was alive, I had to warn her, and as I pulled the door shut behind me, everything else fell away.

My hands trembled as I entered the destination into my phone's GPS. Just because I'd been to the Martina V. Umana every day for two years didn't mean I knew how to orient myself in this unfamiliar neighborhood. About half an hour from Hawthorne to Montclair, if I took the Parkway and got lucky with Sunday traffic.

On the drive, I moved with a steady stream of cars until I reached the Montclair/Nutley exit. Now, as the green lawns rolled past me, it was almost as if the years could roll back too. I was alone: no baby, no husband, ready to hop on the transit or take a bus to the city. I could still be that woman, going to meet her best friend, their whole futures ahead of them. And then with a bump, I drove under the rail bridge, and as I approached the familiar landscape of Bloomfield Avenue, the fantasy fell away.

I wasn't that person anymore.

My pulse quickened as I caught sight of it, the soaring concrete wall running along the building until it reached the roof, then arching up and away. The museum itself was a simple glass-fronted rectangle except for that single wing, miraculous in its weight, its size, and its unsupported grace. I'd loved that building, loved going to work there. As I waited for the crosswalk to empty of pedestrians, that love felt like an old bruise. It was Aimee's fault I wouldn't be welcome there, Aimee's fault I'd lost it all.

I took a ticket from the automated dispenser and drove into the parking garage, not the familiar employee lot behind the museum.

Would I even get through the door? I might have been blacklisted as a disgruntled employee or theft risk. My hair was longer now than it had been, lighter from all my walks in the sun; my body was shaped differently, softer, rounder; and I wasn't wearing the hip contemporary clothes or polished makeup of a museum docent. I looked like a mom. Maybe my blandness would give me the anonymity I needed.

I entered through the side door from the parking garage, and the first person I saw was a familiar security guard, Jared, still working the morning shift. I hurried toward the atrium without looking at him, afraid that if I smiled in greeting, it might trigger his memory. To my right, a hallway branched off to a large community room used by caterers prepping for events. Weddings, corporate parties, fund-raising galas—those were all big bucks for our small museum. On this holiday weekend in October, odds were good there'd be something going on tonight.

Walking straight, I entered the atrium, where the ceiling soared over two stories high and a broad stairway led to the galleries on the second floor.

Through floor-to-ceiling windows, I could see the concrete steps leading from the main entrance to the sidewalk and the street. Above me, ribbons of blown glass hung from steel wires, and when the daylight moved across them, they seemed to spin like paper stars on Grace's mobile. This was a new installation since I'd last been in the museum, and I felt a pang at how beautiful it was, and how much I must have missed.

Clenching my purse, I skirted the main desk, where a stranger, a woman who looked too young to be out of school, was rearranging the brochures in their plastic stand. Not Lena and not someone who thought of me as a criminal. Just an ordinary girl, like I used to be.

A voice echoed from the galleries above me. Yonas, who I'd always considered a friend. His passion was problem solving, using math and engineering to calculate the support necessary for an art installation of hanging steel furniture or to estimate the space needed to safely maneuver large groups of people between glass sculptures.

Now I could hear him giving orders, the tone clear although the words were indistinct, and even as fear flooded me, my heart yearned to see him, to catch up on the gossip, just to laugh together again. Not that it would happen like that. He'd been there on my last day, watching with thinned lips and pinched nostrils as Jared removed me from the museum. However fondly I thought of my former colleagues, that wasn't the way they thought of me.

This open space seemed too big now, the handful of weekend museumgoers nowhere near enough to hide me if Yonas looked over the railing or Jared recognized me or Lena was lurking. My breathing was quick and shallow as I looked for a safe space. Down the hallway past the public restrooms was an entrance to the corridors with the offices where people behind the scenes decided on policies and programming and applied for grants and allocated funds. That was where I'd find Aimee, and I wouldn't need an entrance ticket to get in.

Heat was rising in my face, and I hurried out of the atrium just as a trio of women emerged from the restroom. I ducked past them and barreled through the bathroom door. Resting my hands on either side of the sink, I took a deep breath, then another.

These feelings were like a wicked hangover, stomach-churningly awful but temporary, brought on by events of the past. I could endure them now, and they would fade. I was stronger than I had been.

I caught sight of myself in the mirror, my expression so serious that I smiled in response. I could do this, not because Aimee mattered to me, but because it was the right thing. All I needed to do was make sure Aimee was alive, and then I could go back to my real life.

Walking with a confidence I almost felt, I exited the bathroom. At the end of the corridor was an unmarked door with an electronic pad to swipe a key, but it was always unlocked when the museum was open to the public. I pushed right through it.

The corridor smelled the same, as if the deliberately neutral scent of the larger museum was concentrated, revealing notes of musty paper and linen, pungent glue and disinfectant. That was something I hadn't even thought about. If I closed my eyes, it might have been any day at all, any day from *before*. I dashed past the first two offices until I reached the one I used to share with Aimee. Now the oversized table at which we'd worked together was piled with boxes and papers, and the whole thing felt like an unused storage room. Empty.

Of course, she'd probably gotten a raise.

There were only two offices bigger than this one. The one at the end of the hall that had belonged to the museum director and was almost always vacant, and the one to my left with a view of the sculpture garden. Now I could almost smell the jasmine and cedar notes of her perfume.

I felt sick.

Either Aimee was dead, violently, viciously murdered, or she was alive and I'd have to face her. I raised my hand to tap on the door but stopped. This corridor, this closed door, this building, featured in every nightmare I'd had for the last two years, but I had bigger fears now. I didn't need to force myself to face this one. I'd just ask at the desk if Aimee had come in. I didn't have to lay eyes on her. This was stupid.

But before I could flee, the door opened and she was right in front of me, perfectly polished, from her sleek angled bob to her glossy plum lipstick. Instead of the sapphire sheath, she had on a white silky blouse, an A-line skirt in a Rorschach print, and curvy heels that had probably cost a mortgage payment. Guess she was still making plenty of money on the side.

When she saw me, her mouth sagged open. "Kacy? What are you doing here?" Through the floor-to-ceiling windows of the office behind her, I could see a piece from the sculpture garden with rough metal spikes arching away from a polished basalt center, as dark and glossy as Aimee's modern desk.

My mind went blank. After almost two years of poisoned memories and social media photos, now Aimee looked smaller than I'd remembered, or at least no taller than me. Her skin stretched taut across her collarbones, and concealer couldn't quite hide the shadows under her eyes. Maybe her life wasn't so perfect after all.

"There's a woman," I blurted. "The police are looking for her, and I think I saw her in your picture, your story last night."

"Why are you here, Kacy, *really*?" Aimee's tone was stagy, the way she'd talked when we were at a bar and she wanted the guy two drinks down to hear us.

"Brady Voss was on the news, the serial killer from Texas." But Aimee *knew* this. She'd taunted me about it in a postcard.

Now she tilted her head, her eyes bright and blank as glass gems, waiting.

"His wife is here, and she was right next to you at the bar last night. I saw it in your feed. She knows about the museum. You're in danger." I sounded crazy, and I hated it. She'd think I was looking for a way to get back in, but all I wanted was to convince her so my conscience would be clear.

She arched a perfectly shaped brow. "You were post-stalking me? Sad."

"No, I came to warn you—"

"Is this a threat? Is that what's happening here?" She slipped her hand into the pocket of her skirt. "You found some other unhinged lunatic and sent her after me?"

"They thought he'd killed her, but she sent me a postcard, like you did." I spoke sharply now. How had I ever put up with the drama and the game playing? Gossip at work, drunken nights and crowded clubs, hangovers that made thinking harder and emotions more raw.

"I didn't send you any postcard." Her voice had a singsongy tone, light, like a child's playground chant. She was lying, and she didn't care if I knew it. Why should she? The director was never on-site, and in his absence, she was queen.

"Quit playing games. I'm trying to help—"

"Oh, please." She rolled her eyes. "Only an idiot would come back after what you did."

"I didn't do anything. I . . . you . . ."

"I . . . you . . ." she mimicked, and then the smirk vanished from her lips. "You're crazy. You'd have to be. After all you've done, you have the nerve to show up here?"

Screw this. "Fine. I'm leaving. I just came to warn you. You're not safe. There's a killer after you, and you're not safe. Do you understand?"

Our eyes met, Aimee's brow furrowed, and for a moment I thought my friend, the one who'd laughed with me on rooftop bars and pulled all-nighters in our office, might still be there under that painted mask. But she widened her eyes and said, "I don't know what you mean. It took me ages to trust again. After all your lies, the way you hurt me, I'm lucky I didn't lose my job too."

My hands were clenched fists, and I burned to smash the smugness out of her. "I hope Lena does kill you."

Aimee pulled her hand out of her pocket, and I saw her phone was lit up. "Oh, I'll be fine, Kacy. But thanks for your concern."

A man spoke behind me. "Everything all right in here?"

Jared. That bitch had called security.

She looked past me. "Took you long enough. Escort Ms. Tremaine out."

Jared took my arm; then recognition flashed over his face. "Kacy? Is that you? It's been a while." He sounded almost pleased.

Then he glanced at Aimee and said firmly to me, "How about I walk you to your car?"

"I'm going." I pulled my arm away and turned to follow him, saying over my shoulder, "She's a killer, Aimee. And she's coming after you."

Jared and I walked in silence through the hallway and back into the atrium. I couldn't hear Yonas, so maybe he wouldn't see me getting thrown out of the museum a second time. Finally, Jared asked, "What was that all about?"

"I wanted to talk to Aimee. Did you hear about Brady Voss?" Heat rose in my face, but this was my second chance to warn someone. Even if I sounded like a lunatic.

"That guy down in Texas?" He kept his hand on my arm as we passed the front desk with its metal spinner of postcards.

"He's my next-door neighbor."

"No shit." Jared opened one of the heavy doors, and the hush of the museum dissolved in the noise of traffic echoing through the parking garage. "You can never tell about people."

I stopped walking, letting him stand there holding the door, and for a second it was just like it had been the day I'd been fired. Jared had been kind then, too, as if he had just been walking me to my car out of courtesy. And I'd been too stunned to make a scene, stumbling, desperate to wake from the nightmare. Once I'd reached my car, I'd sat blinded by the tears I no longer needed to hold back. Finally, I had wiped my face and raised my head, only to see Jared still there, watching like he hadn't wanted to leave me in that state.

Had he pitied me then? Maybe he still did, but if Jared would only listen to me, I could live with the mortification.

"Let me show you a picture." I opened my phone. The first picture that came up was the one of Aimee at the bar, but it was hard to see anything but that sapphire dress. I totally looked like a stalker. "Not Aimee. The woman next to her with the dark hair, see?"

Jared nodded, but I couldn't tell if he'd really looked or if he was just humoring me. I scrolled through my pictures until I found the one of me and Lena, our heads tilted together. "This is Brady's wife. I think she dyed her hair. The police and the FBI, everybody's looking for her, but I think that was her in the other picture. She sent me a postcard. That's how they knew she wasn't dead. Look out for her. I think she might come here."

He was definitely giving me *humor the crazy lady* eyes. And he started walking again, his hand on my arm bringing me through the door and out of the museum. "Listen, Kacy," he said. "I don't know everything that happened back then. But you don't want to mess with her."

"Aimee?" I'd just told him a serial killer was on the loose, and he was worried about the mean girl in management?

He hunched his huge shoulders and whispered, "I'm not losing this job. That's all I'm saying."

We entered the parking garage, and I realized Jared was seriously going to escort me all the way to my car. I was almost out of time to convince him. I pulled my arm away. "I'll go, I'm leaving. Just promise me if you see that woman, the one I showed you, you'll call the police."

In the dim light of the garage, he studied my face like he was trying to gauge my truthfulness. Probably just the same way he looked at his kids when they promised they'd done their homework or swore they were meeting their friends at the library. I knew he had teenagers; I knew his wife was a nurse and his brother ran a bakery known for its incredible Portuguese custard cups. Jared was kind, soft-spoken, physically imposing yet slow to anger. But I had no idea who he thought I was.

Finally, he sighed and stepped back. "Okay."

"Okay, you'll be careful?" Maybe he just meant it would be okay if I left. I needed to be sure I'd warned someone, that I'd made some kind of difference.

But he just nodded and turned away, leaving me alone. Acutely aware of the echoing garage around me, I strode to my car, each footstep slapping frustration and fear on the concrete.

I hadn't saved Aimee's life. She hadn't believed a word I'd said. If Lena killed her, it would be her own damn fault. I wanted Lena to stab Aimee right in her stomach. But I'd still feel terrible, the worst mix of guilt and fury.

"What would your world look like without Aimee?" Dr. Lindsey had asked me. Well, I knew what it looked like. I'd been living it. Without her, my world was calmer and more predictable, with friends I could trust who trusted me back. It wasn't glitzy, with techno beats and an alcohol haze. I'd thought living in that world had changed me, but coming face-to-face with Aimee had sent all my certainty topsy-turvy. She could look me right in the eyes and lie, knowing I *knew* she was lying, and leave me helpless and incoherent with rage.

If anybody had ever deserved to be killed, Aimee did.

It would serve her right.

13

Helen: So what would you do if the person you hated most in the world—

Julia: My ex-boyfriend—

Helen: Your ex-boyfriend was in danger. Would you care? Would you try to save him?

Julia: Maybe *I* would be the danger.

Helen: I just got chills. And that's exactly what we're talking about here. The other half of our serial killer couple is in the wind. There's a concern that she's in Texas, so they've put the only eyewitness to her husband's murders into protective custody, and his wife—

Julia: Our killer's BFF—

Helen: Is in hiding. And just a reminder, it's because of the postcard that the police even knew Lena was alive in the first place. Or at least, that's what this friend, Kacy Tremaine, said.

Julia: So I know we went into this with Brady, but why do you think Lena sent that postcard? *Allegedly* sent.

Helen: I know Kacy turned it in to the police; they tested it and did handwriting analysis and everything, but it wasn't introduced at trial. And that makes you wonder.

Julia: It's kind of old-school, isn't it, a postcard? I buy a few at every CrimeCon, but I never mail them. They just pile up in a drawer.

Helen: I don't think this one reads like a cry for help or a confession. It reads like some kind of inside joke. We asked about why Brady would reach out to Michael, but I think it's equally interesting why Lena reached out to Kacy. Because she really could have just disappeared.

Julia: Do you think she was hoping to get a new sidekick or a partner in crime, since her husband was out of commission?

Helen: Maybe. *Now* we know about Kacy's past with the allegations of art theft and embezzlement. Maybe Lena thought there was a chance to tempt Kacy to the dark side.

Julia: Like if you, Helen, were a serial killer who'd been working with a partner, maybe you wouldn't want to go it alone.

Helen: And if I wanted to entice you to join me and be my very best butcher buddy for always, I know exactly who I'd kill for you.

Julia: [laughing] Somewhere my ex is getting very nervous.

Helen: Double-lock your doors, you cheater!

Julia: So when this postcard first shows up, nobody except Kacy really knew what it meant, but later, it's so obvious that Lena was referring to a woman from Kacy's past.

Helen: Lena's "surprise" is Kacy's worst enemy.

Julia: Wouldn't you want to kill her?

CHAPTER

24

ON THE WAY back to the apartment, I passed a strip mall and
glimpsed a salon. I didn't have an appointment, but maybe they
could lop off an inch and my story about getting a haircut wouldn't
be a lie. But when I pulled up in front, I could tell it was too busy.
Each stylist was working on someone, and there were three more
people waiting. But next to it was a drugstore. I could do this myself.

I went in and bought a pair of scissors. Outside my dad's car,
so I wouldn't make a mess, I gathered my hair into a ponytail and
flattened the end with the fingers of one hand. The bundle of hair
was almost too thick, but the scissors were sharp, and I chopped as
if I were cutting Aimee's throat. I brushed the cut end a few times
to get any stray hairs and then let go. My hair fell loose around
my face, and I exhaled. Aimee wasn't my problem anymore. I'd
warned her, for what that was worth.

In the car's side mirror, I checked my work. Not elegant, but
shorter. Shorter was all I needed now. Elegant was overrated. I
didn't have to squeeze myself into a pencil skirt or take my blouses
to the dry cleaners. I didn't have to impress donors or patrons or
even strangers at nightclubs. My Texas friends didn't even know
the me-from-before, and Grace didn't care what I looked like.
Maybe some part of me would always mourn that long-ago life,
but I didn't wish I was still living it now. I'd built something real
and lasting, something to experience rather than exhibit.

I dropped the scissors into my purse and pulled out my phone. *Miss you*, I texted Michael. Then I started the engine.

The drive back seemed quicker, and I was almost home when the gas light came on. I didn't want to leave this for my dad, so I pulled into a filling station. As I waited for the attendant to notice me, I caught sight of a white cargo van parked over by the side of the convenience store. For just a flash, I thought it might be Lena, but then a young guy in blue coveralls approached it, carrying a wrapped sandwich and a fountain drink, and my tension drained, leaving me cold. I was seeing her everywhere.

The attendant tapped on the window, startling me.

As the tank filled, I had a sudden vision. Back in Sugar Land, driving at night with Michael, and running out of gas. We'd pull over on the side of the road and call for a tow truck, but then a van would pull up. There'd be a couple inside, a man and woman, friendly, offering to help, the woman smiling at me. Michael and I would get into that van . . . and we'd be found hacked to pieces in the underbrush weeks later.

My hands shook as I gave the attendant my credit card. Those abandoned cars, that couple murdered in Brazos Bend State Park; I hadn't connected it before. What were the odds there'd be two sets of serial killers working the greater Houston area? Brady and Lena snatched people standing on the side of the road—homeless or lost or working. Other times they might have found people stranded. And sometimes Lena killed people right where they lived. No place was safe.

And it didn't matter if you were a stranger or a neighbor or even, possibly, a friend.

* * *

When I walked through the door of Molly's apartment, I realized I'd completely forgotten my plan to pick up lunch, but it wouldn't have been necessary anyway. The apartment smelled invitingly of toast. The warmth, the smell of food, and the roar of a football game on the television took me back to any number of Sunday afternoons growing up.

Mom was on the futon sofa with Grace on her knees, while in the kitchenette, Dad added another slice to a towering stack of toast.

"Is anyone joining us?" I asked, locking the front door behind me and setting down my purse.

He looked at me blankly, and I added, "That's a lot of toast, Dad."

"Ah." He grinned. "I'm making some omelets too, but they're fast. Didn't want to start until you got back."

"Your hair is cute." Mom studied me. "Kind of choppy, like that actress from that movie." She looked at Dad. "You know, the one with the elevator."

He turned back to the stove. "I can't remember any of their names."

I went over to Mom, and the sight of Grace softened any remaining frustration and paranoia. I was safe here, part of something amazing, something Aimee could never tarnish. "How was Grace?"

"Perfect angel. She woke up about an hour ago, had a new diaper, then a bottle, then another new diaper, and we've been talking ever since. I told her all about the garden club—"

"What did she think about that?"

"She agreed with me that the selection committee has gotten really political, but there's no call for the drama about mixing wildflowers and cultivars in competition."

"You've got a smart girl there," my dad called out. "She knows when to agree. And she's pulling for the Giants over the Cowboys."

"They're playing at the MetLife Stadium," Mom said. "We went a few weeks ago, but that place is just too big for me."

Grace's gaze had been fixed on my face since I'd come in, and the longer I stood and talked without picking her up, the more vigorously her arms and legs moved. She reached for me, grunting, and despite my mother's clinging arms, I gathered her up and cuddled her close.

The entire morning had been like a bad dream, returning to the museum to warn somebody who meant nothing to me. And what was I warning her about? Alondra hadn't gotten back to me. I'd probably hallucinated any resemblance between Lena and that mysterious profile of a stranger's face. The door was locked, we were in an anonymous sublet apartment, and Lena could be miles and miles away.

"Smile for me," Mom said, holding up her phone to snap a picture.

I let the warm glow of this safe space spread through me, enveloping me and Grace. When my mom checked the screen and nodded in satisfaction, I said, "Send it to Michael." We'd all be together soon.

* * *

After we'd eaten and the leftovers had been cleared away, Dad settled in next to Mom to watch the game.

My phone buzzed with an incoming text. Elizabeth: *Did you warn your friend?*

Former friend. I could feel my body getting hot, and I felt too petty to write the words. Instead I typed: *She didn't believe me.* And she'd called security and had me thrown out. But that wasn't something I wanted Elizabeth to know.

I'd been a fool, extending myself out of some childish desire to be vindicated as a hero. Not that it had worked. Suddenly, I wanted to hear Elizabeth's voice instead of hunching furtively over my phone.

When I stood, my mom looked up. "Everything okay?"

I nodded. "Need to make a quick call." On the quilt in the middle of the floor, Grace arched her back, craning to see me. Dad was sitting on the edge of the coffee table so he would be lower, closer to Grace, without actually getting down on the floor.

With a pang I remembered how he used to crawl on his hands and knees, chasing us through the house and roaring like a lion. Now my sisters and I were grown, with kids, jobs, busy lives of our own, but we were all still weighing my parents down. I wished I hadn't put this burden on them.

Mom stood up too. "I should probably check in with your sisters. The Giants have pretty much won this anyway."

She smoothed Dad's hair down, but he batted her away, saying, "Don't jinx it. Grace will be heartbroken."

While my mom took a seat at the tiny table in the kitchenette, I stepped out the front door. The street was lined with older homes. In one yard bounded by a chain-link fence, a black-and-white shepherd mix worried at a toy; in another, an older man wearing a barn jacket raked leaves.

I sat on the concrete stoop, hoping that Molly was right and her upstairs landlord was out of town this weekend too. Even though the air was warmer than the Octobers of my youth, cold seeped into my jeans.

Elizabeth answered right away. "Are you okay?"

"She didn't listen to me. If something happens to her . . ."

"It won't."

"How can you be so sure?"

Elizabeth was silent, and I waited, giving her the time to craft her response. Why couldn't I be calm and measured like Elizabeth? Instead I kept making stupid mistakes, not seeing the danger when I'd lived next door to it, then rushing to warn a total bitch who hadn't believed me anyway. I wanted to scream, right there on that quiet street. Why did Aimee make me so crazy?

You know what, it was the principle. Bad people shouldn't be able to lie and cheat and be rewarded. And if you tried to help a person, they shouldn't be an ass about it.

Then Elizabeth said, "I got a postcard today. I'm sorry I didn't tell you right away. The police said not to tell anyone, but I didn't want you to worry that Lena was there when I think she might be down here."

"What postcard? What did it say?" My breath was shallow.

"I'll show you."

After a few excruciating seconds, I got two photos of a post-card. On one side, an old-fashioned Model T hearse, and on the other, written in Lena's distinctive hand, *See you soon. xoxo.* And, I noticed grimly, there was no stamp and no postmark. Another hand delivery.

Working on another surprise. My own arrogance twisted in my stomach. I'd assumed Lena would go after Aimee because I hated her. I never imagined she'd go after my friends. "When did this come?"

"This morning. It's from the funeral museum downtown," Elizabeth said. "When I went to check the mail, it was sitting in the middle of the doormat. I took the pictures and called the police. The neighborhood constable's parked outside now."

"They should put you somewhere safe. You should leave—"

"I'm not the only one. Alondra told me that at least two other people have received postcards. She won't tell me who. She says she shouldn't have told me at all."

Then the real truth hit me. "Lena's in Texas. So I just . . ." I had just made a fool of myself for no reason. The people I needed to protect were over a thousand miles away.

"You just did the right thing."

"But Lena's nowhere near here. You're in more danger than Aimee is." Immediately I wished I could take it back. Lena had been a little jealous of my other friendships. Michael was in protective custody, but Elizabeth . . . "Seriously, maybe you should stay someplace else for a few days."

"If everyone who had anything to do with Brady or Lena moved into a hotel, the whole neighborhood would be empty." Elizabeth's tone was light, but I could hear how serious she was. More than serious. Brave.

Then she added, "But I'll think about it. We're not taking any risks. Don't worry about us, Kacy. You stay safe."

Across the street where the man was raking leaves, a white-haired woman in a shawl-collared sweater came to the door. He looked up and gestured—*a few more minutes*. Maybe I had been hallucinating danger here as a reaction to all the months I'd been living in blissful ignorance under surveillance by killers. "Promise me you'll be careful," I said.

"You promise me the same thing."

"Deal." We hung up.

My breath was coming quickly again, and the cool calm I usually absorbed from Elizabeth was gone. A mail truck came down the street, and when the driver reached through her window to stuff mail into a neighbor's box, the black-and-white shepherd became frantic, barking and leaping inside its fence.

Why wasn't Lena just disappearing? She shouldn't be sending postcards; she should just have driven over the border and lived her life. When she and Brady killed together, it was violent and bloody and gruesome. But on her own . . .

No one would ever know a murder had happened. Maybe a year would go by, maybe two. One day Elizabeth would put Theo down for a nap, go into her kitchen for a mug of tea, and something would hit her on the back of the head. She'd bleed out on the creamy tile floor of her kitchen, her blond hair matted and stained, unable to rise when she heard Theo crying. "Did you hear?" the neighbors would say. "What a tragic accident." And the

Bluebonnets would drop off meals and Wyatt would raise Theo alone or maybe move back to Canada and Elizabeth would be gone. I'd always know she was a terrible footnote in Lena's story, and that she might have been safe if she hadn't been friends with me.

Aimee wasn't in danger. Elizabeth was, and so were those mysterious "others" who had received postcards. Maybe Rahmia or Rachael or Inés or even Alondra. Just like Sandy, they might be gone in an instant, and I was helpless to protect them.

And the person I most longed for was also in Texas, and also in danger. Voice messages weren't enough, texts weren't enough, even a phone call wasn't enough. What I needed was Michael's embrace, pulling me close, a wordless promise that we would be okay even if the world burned down around us. Holding on to each other was all we'd ever had, from the moment we'd met to our first tiny apartment and the long drive across the country.

But the call went straight to voice mail. So did my next call to Alondra. No contact with him, no answers from her.

I wrapped my arms around my stomach, a meager substitute for what I really wanted. Michael had been strong for me when I hadn't been able to stand up for myself, but I could now. I had stood up to Aimee. Maybe I hadn't persuaded her, but I'd been strong enough to try. And if Lena wasn't here, if Aimee wasn't at risk, that meant the police were right to protect Michael. He was the only eyewitness against Brady. It was my turn to give him strength, but I was too many miles away.

Here on the front stoop, I could admit how scared I was, how much I wanted to cry, how hard it was to act normal when terror fluttered around my lungs with razor-edged wings.

My head was bowed when a pickup truck pulled up right in front of me. Before the engine stopped, I was on my feet, backing up, my hands raised to ward off whatever was coming.

An older man in a flannel shirt and a green cap got out of the cab, hesitating when he saw me. Then the door behind me opened and my dad shouted, "Jim! You found us."

I turned to look at my father and then back at this new arrival, my body still tensed for flight.

The man, Jim, grinned at my father. "No problem at all, Bill. Enjoying that grandbaby?" He had a sheaf of mail and a newspaper in one hand and a cardboard box in the other. Now I could see the *NJ Osprey Project* decal on the back of his truck and the rod holder on the rack. This must be one of my dad's fishing buddies.

"Sure am. And this is my daughter, Kacy." Dad put a hand on my shoulder and maneuvered us both off the steps.

"Nice to meet you." Jim handed Dad the mail and stood for a minute, looking at us both. "I can see the resemblance. You fish, Kacy?"

"Not if I can help it." My response was automatic, and both men laughed.

Dad held up the box. "Well, I appreciate this, Jim. New phone. My old one just doesn't hold a charge, so Charlotte ordered me this one. I was hoping it would come early yesterday, but you know, the minute you're waiting for something . . ."

"That's how it always is. Like I said, no problem. On my way. Sure you can't play hooky? I've got an extra rod."

"Next time." Dad didn't even hesitate.

"All right then. Just one more thing." Jim went back to the truck and pulled something out, a glass jar with a big black bow. "This was sitting on your front stoop, so I brought it along." He passed it to me. "Take care."

But I didn't hear Dad answer. I was holding a mason jar, filled with something like paste. Turning it my hands, I found the label.

I cried out and the jar slipped from my fingers, clipping the edge of the concrete step and rolling into the street.

A preprinted label said *Friendship Starter.*

CHAPTER

25

THE YOUNG POLICEMAN who showed up seemed unfazed by my frantic explanations about Lena and Brady and the FBI, but he wrote everything down. Jim explained how he'd seen the jar on my parents' front step when he was picking up Saturday's mail last night.

My dad kept shifting from one foot to the other, his arms folded across his chest. I knew how much he wished he could fix this, just step in and handle everything. It wasn't supposed to be this way. I'd come here to shelter from danger, but I'd brought it right to my parents' door.

Even to my eyes, the little jar looked anticlimactic, but the policeman took it with gloved hands and dropped it into a plastic bag. Then he spent a long time talking to someone higher up. Where was his sense of urgency? This was a message from a killer.

Standing on the front lawn of this rented house, I felt so vulnerable and exposed. I didn't know anyone here; no one was looking out for us. It was just me, my parents, and Grace.

I called Alondra for the fifth time, but it went straight to voice mail again. *Emergency*, I texted. *CALL ME*. If Lena had found my parents, maybe we weren't safe here either. Nothing, not the apartment nor the utilities nor even the mail, came here in my sister's name, but I didn't want to take a chance.

As the policeman came back, I asked, "What did they say? Can't you stay here or send someone to watch the house?"

He shifted from one foot to the other. "They said to bring this in. It wasn't left here, though, so if they sent anyone out, it would probably be to that other house."

"But *we're* here!" He was going to leave us unprotected, and there was nothing I could do to make him understand. My dad put a hand on my shoulder, but I knew its weight and warmth was a false comfort.

This guy looked so young, probably used to straightforward speeding tickets and noise complaints. I knew the operator hadn't understood when I'd told her about Lena. This wasn't some random stalking or a paranoid delusion; it was a message from a killer. They should have sent FBI agents or a SWAT team, something serious. Instead I had a kid whose furrowed brow said he felt sorry for me, he wanted to do the right thing, but he'd been told to collect the evidence. "I hear you," he said. "I tell you what. Let me take this in, and I'll see what I can do." He shook my father's hand, nodded to me, and headed to his car.

I was about to shout after him, to ask how long it would be, should we move to a hotel, when my phone rang. Alondra. Finally, someone who could light a fire and get us protection.

She said, "I was on another call. Are you okay?"

"It's Lena. She—"

"Lena is in Texas, Kacy. There have been some developments, but she's here in Texas."

"I know about the postcards, Alondra. But Lena left something at my parents' house. The police were just here."

"What?"

"She left a jar of sourdough starter. At my parents' house! My mom and dad, Alondra." I'd been holding it together, trying to appear credible to the police officer, but now my body started to shake.

"You're not making any sense."

"She knows where they live. And I called and called you." Studiously ignoring my phone conversation, Jim waved good-bye to Dad and got into his truck. I didn't even know where he was headed, but his little "no big deal" errand had ended up taking all afternoon and included a brush with a serial killer. I wished my dad would drive off with him, someplace remote and unfindable, out of harm's way.

"But this is about sourdough starter?"

"Lena gave me some back in Texas, and when my dad's friend picked up the mail, this other jar was on the front step." I could hear it now, how banal and unthreatening this sounded, like all the stress had sent me around the bend, but I didn't know how to convince her.

"And you're sure it's from Lena? Not just some neighbor or something?"

"Definitely." I couldn't offer the other jar she'd given me as proof; I'd thrown it out. I couldn't point to her handwriting or a threatening message or so much as a smudged fingerprint, but I knew, *knew*, it was from her.

"And you reported it?"

"I called the number you gave me. They sent someone to pick it up, but I don't think they understood about it, and about that picture I sent you, the one where I thought I saw Lena—"

"Kacy, I shared it with them. Take a deep breath. The feds are handling this. Lena is in Texas."

"How do you know?" Dad was casually leaning against the front door of the house. He didn't want to leave me alone out here, and that thought, that he was as scared for me as I was for him, pierced me. If Lena was really in Texas, we were safe here, and that was all I wanted. Just to rest together without fear. "Are you sure?"

She was silent for a minute. Then she said, "I'm going to send you something, and I swear to God, if I see it on the news or online, I will make you regret it."

"I wouldn't share it." *Please let it be proof that Lena's in Texas. Far, far away from my parents and Grace.*

"Okay. I'll send a picture. Take a good look, then delete it. I'm not even supposed to have it, but I want you to believe me when I say the best thing you can do is stay put. Will you do that for me?"

"I will." *Send it. Send it now.*

"I'm not gonna lie to you. I'm ninety percent sure Lena's in Texas, but a few weeks ago I would have been ninety percent sure I didn't know any serial killers. I'm going to call the FBI office up there. You need someone watching you, just to be sure."

"I asked the cop who was just here, and he said he'd see what he could do."

"Not good enough. Let me make some more calls. I know you're going crazy waiting. I know this is hard, but if you just hang tight, I'll let you know as soon as there's news, I swear." She spoke to someone out of range. "Okay, I have to go. Stay safe."

"Wait . . ." But she was gone, and I was alone, and certain that eyes were watching from behind the curtains of every house on the street. After all, I was a stranger here, squatting in a sublet apartment, and the police had just left. Good. I hoped they were watching, and that if they saw Lena, they'd call the cops.

My phone buzzed with the picture Alondra had promised and a single word: *Laredo.*

Cupping my hands over the screen of my phone to reduce glare, I squinted at what appeared to be a security shot of a woman approaching the counter of a convenience store. Tall, broad shouldered, with her hair crammed under a baseball cap. A Skeeters cap. The color in the photo was washed out like a snap from the seventies, but her hair was somewhere between brown and red. This woman looked a lot more like Lena than the photo from Aimee's feed.

And the time-stamped date was yesterday.

My shallow breathing slowed. Not Houston. But Texas. Laredo, five hours away from Michael. Almost two thousand miles away from me and Aimee. Right on the way to Mexico.

Could I believe this?

Maybe. I could picture Lena backlit on a beach, a sunset reflecting in her blazing hair, a margarita in her hand. Mexico sounded right.

That would mean we were safe here in this house. For now. But then this nightmare would never be over. Lena could always come back from her tropical vacation and get right back to work. Our home wouldn't be safe, our friends, our family.

There'd be no end.

* * *

That night after pizza that nobody ate, Dad turned on the news. When the anchor announced, "New details in the story of a Texas serial killer," my mother opened her mouth to protest, but then said nothing. Grace was in her bouncy seat in the kitchen. She wouldn't understand anything she heard, I told myself. But it still felt wrong.

In silence, we watched the segment detailing the bodies found. Familiar places flashed across the television screen—the bridge I took to get to H-E-B, the new construction where Rachael had been looking at houses, my own street and even my own home—and over it words like *found dismembered, buried remains,* and *grisly discovery.*

Worse still were the pictures of the victims, photos taken in happier times. Marcus Fontenot in his military uniform, Shelby Jackson seated at a picnic table between two friends with their faces blurred out, Jessica and Damen Weber on their wedding day. The police had connected Brady and Lena to the abandoned-car killings, bringing their joint total to double digits. Together Brady and Lena had plucked these people from the side of the road or out of their own cars and butchered them.

And the news didn't mention the man who'd owned our house before, or Sandy, or any of the people Lena might have killed in their own homes. Those deaths weren't as grisly, but that almost made them worse. Sandy should have been safe, relaxing in her shower, but Lena had taken her life and for all I knew, no one was even looking at it as more than an accident.

My mother was twisting her hands together on her lap, the same way I did sometimes, and my dad's mouth was a tight line by the time the program ended.

I stood up abruptly, and my parents looked at me like they expected me to make a speech. "I'm just . . ." I didn't know how to finish that statement, so I gestured at the front door.

"Don't go out alone," Dad said.

"Just taking a look." I cracked the door and peeked out. No sign of the police, no note or jar on the stoop. The sky was a brilliant cobalt, and the shadows were deepening.

"It'll be okay. Just shut the door, babe," my mom said over the opening music for the game show that followed the news.

I hated this. I hated watching my parents protect me, I hated leaving Michael alone. I was tired of being the fragile flower, the one nobody thought was strong or brave, the one nobody listened to or believed. I texted Alondra: *No police yet. Is someone coming? Call me.*

While my parents took turns shouting out answers in chorus with the contestants, I brought Grace into the bedroom to nurse her and put her down for the night. Once she was settled in my arms, I pulled out my phone and called Michael again.

Voice mail. Was he ignoring me? Maybe he thought I'd taken the easy way out, leaving him in danger. Maybe he thought if he pretended we didn't exist, he wouldn't miss us so much. Maybe he was hurt, or even dead. No, someone would have told me. But I felt sick and afraid.

Awkwardly, with one hand, I texted *Call me ASAP*.

Grace had one hand up against her forehead and the other flexed open, her tiny fingers spread wide. Despite the toxic mix of worry, irritation, anger, and fear, despite every dark possibility my mind could conjure, I could feel deep peace, untouchable, in these moments when she and I were alone.

But I'd felt the very same way on the night when everything started. I shivered. Would I ever feel safe again?

On my phone, I pulled up the article Rahmia had texted earlier. Studying the picture of Marcus Fontenot, I could almost conjure the day Lena and I had driven downtown. Like the other victims, he'd been part of a vulnerable population, but that hadn't meant he was unloved or forgotten. His family knew he was missing, and they'd been working to bring him home. All the other victims had been real people with a network of relationships cut short at the moment of their death. Cut short by Lena and Brady, vicious hunters who preyed on the unsuspecting.

I dropped my phone on the bed beside me and caressed Grace's warm head. I'd never be so trusting or unprepared again. I'd fight to preserve this undeserved peace, this uncomplicated love.

And my anger at Aimee, my wish that she "get what she deserved," seemed like the petty thought of a child. Aimee had parents, I knew that, and an older brother. If the friendship I'd had with Lena wasn't a total lie, then she might want to kill Aimee in some twisted solidarity. But human beings weren't things to be smashed.

Grace relaxed, her rosebud mouth slack. I gathered her onto my shoulder, burping her with a gentle firmness, fighting the urge to clutch her tightly. If anything happened to her, I'd never recover.

And then my phone rang, and her body went stiff for a second as she startled. I shushed her, groping for my phone. A number I didn't recognize with a Texas area code. A jolt of fear pierced me. Grace squirmed again, no longer asleep, as I raised the phone. "Hello?"

Michael said, "Kacy, it's me."

Relief at hearing his voice, familiar and unchanged, ran hot through me. "What number is this?"

"They took my phone. Alondra picked up this burner."

"Who took your phone, the police? Why?"

He sighed. "The FBI. I guess they want to verify my story or something. It's been a long day."

I'd been imagining him safely in a hotel room, maybe watching football like my folks, maybe chatting with the cop protecting him. But instead he'd been back in the station under the fluorescent lights, being treated like a suspect.

"What happened?" And why hadn't Alondra given me a heads-up?

"The same as before. How about you? How are your folks?" His questions had the easy flow of normalcy and routine, but this wasn't the time for either of those, much as I longed for them.

"Loving the time with Grace. Did you get the picture? I guess it went to your phone. Couldn't they forward your messages?" My last question was sharper than I'd intended. I couldn't help thinking about all the things I'd done that Michael didn't know. I'd been post-stalking Aimee, thought I'd seen Lena, had told Rahmia, Elizabeth, and Alondra, had gone to the museum alone, and had been thrown out by security. If he'd been sharing secrets that big with someone else, even his best friend, it would gut me.

"I'm not really in a position to make demands. They were questioning me for another couple hours at the station."

"Alondra—" Alondra knew what was happening with my husband. But she hadn't even given me a clue. She'd just let them grill him like he was guilty. She was supposed to be protecting him; so were the police. What was wrong with them?

"Alondra was there. Apparently, Brady started talking, lying about me."

We'd done everything right, told the police everything we knew, completely cooperated. They wouldn't even know about

Brady if it hadn't been for Michael. Lies and secrets were poisoning everything. I couldn't stop Brady from lying. I couldn't make the police do their job. I couldn't catch Lena myself. I couldn't do a thing to save my family. "There's no way the police would believe him—"

"I don't know what they believe. They didn't charge me with anything." He lowered his voice. "But it's not like I'm free to go, either. And they moved me to a different apartment."

"Did Lena find you?"

"No, no." He spoke quickly, but I didn't believe him. "At least, they didn't say so. I think they're just covering all their bases."

I should tell Michael everything, or at least that I'd seen Aimee. But then I'd have to tell him I had thought I'd seen Lena and I hadn't stayed safely at home. The words caught, like when a hard candy gets stuck, not able to be coughed out, not able to be swallowed down.

Instead I said, "Someone left a jar of sourdough starter at my parents' house. I gave it to the police."

"Sourdough starter?" I should have known it would sound as stupid to Michael as it had to the cops. He'd spent his day at the police station, defending himself, and I was miles away making up stories.

"Like the kind she gave me from her aunt's starter. But Alondra's pretty sure she's in Texas. Elizabeth got a postcard, dropped off, not mailed. And there's security footage."

"This is insane." I could picture Michael running a hand over his head, ruffling up the hair the way he did when he was frustrated. "And you thought she was leaving your parents a message? Where is she?"

"I wish we knew. If they'd catch her, this whole thing would be over." At least we'd be safe. If Brady and Lena were both behind bars, Michael and I could go home together.

Finally asleep, Grace seemed to get heavier on my shoulder. Carefully I lowered her to the bed. She lay on her back with her arms relaxed, the only good thing I knew I could offer my husband. "Your girl's asleep. When she wakes, I'll send you a picture on this phone."

"I'd like that. I miss you both so much." His voice was in my ear, as intimate as if he were beside me.

We were talking but leaving so much unsaid. That was the way we had been in Texas, walking through our days closed off and mute, isolated even when we were together. I wanted to know, really *know*, everything he wasn't telling me. "What did you *really* do all day?"

He was silent, and I couldn't stand it. If I wanted honesty, I'd have to go first. I blurted out, "Before the whole sourdough thing, I went to the museum."

"Really?" He sounded shocked. "What for?"

Maybe this was a bad idea. He'd think I was obsessing or worse, regressing. But I was tired of letting my fear widen the gulf between us. "When I was looking at Aimee's pictures online, I thought I saw Lena. I went to warn her."

"You thought Lena was up there, and you went out alone?"

"It doesn't matter. She's in Texas anyway."

"You didn't know that, Kacy. Damn."

"But you're safe? I mean, if she's down there—"

"I'm safe, I swear. There's someone here all the time. We split a pizza for dinner. Nice guy. But, Kacy, promise me you'll stay put. That was the point of going up there, so you and Grace would be safe."

"You have to promise me too."

"I'm in a safe house with an armed officer. How much safer do I need to be?"

"No, I mean, promise that you'll *tell* me when something big happens. Just because I'm up here doesn't mean you're on your own."

He was silent again. I'd pushed him too hard. He didn't want my help, and now he was withdrawing just like he had before. I started to say, "I'm sorry," but he spoke at the same time, and I couldn't understand him.

We both stopped, and then I whispered, "Go ahead."

"I'll go to therapy."

I must have misheard. "What?"

"When this is over." He spoke quickly and quietly, his words running together. "I'll talk to Dr. Lindsey or anyone you want. And you and I, we'll take Grace to the zoo, and we'll visit the River Walk, and it'll all be okay. We'll be okay."

"I know, sweetheart. We will be." He yearned for me too, and the way things used to be. I wasn't alone; he wasn't the cold stranger I'd been living with. My Michael was there, and he would fight for our future.

"I love you," he whispered.

"I love you too, so much."

I would have stayed on the phone with him all night, holding it close and listening to him breathe, but instead we hung up with promises to talk again tomorrow.

Grace was snoring softly on the bed, her little chest vibrating like a purring cat. I wished I could believe that the world was as safe as it seemed to her. A full belly and her mama's presence were all she needed. I caressed the top of her soft head.

If I could go back to the beginning, if Michael and I had bought a different house, if I hadn't gone to the Bluebonnets, if I'd recognized Lena for what she was, if I'd heeded any of the warning signs—the cameras, the bitter comments, Sandy's death—then that awful night in the nursery would never have happened. I'd feel just as content as Grace did. Instead I was tense, my shoulders unyielding knots of stress. If Lena was in Texas, maybe we were safe here, but she might be creating a fake case against Michael, stalking Elizabeth, or something worse than I could even imagine.

Around the edges of the woven bamboo blinds, I could see that the world outside was almost completely dark. I gently lifted Grace into her portable crib, sliding my hands out from under her warm back without waking her. I turned off the light and slipped out the bedroom door, ready to rejoin my parents for a quiet evening.

As I sat on the end of the futon, my mother asked, "Everything okay?"

"Just catching up with Michael."

She nodded, clearly waiting for more information. So I said, "The FBI questioned him today, but Alondra was with him. And he's doing okay in the safe house."

Mom looked back at the game show, where a contestant had just blown the big question and was hiding his face in his palm. She said, "Texas seems so far away. I've felt that ever since you moved."

I reached out and took her hand. If I hadn't met Aimee, would Michael and I ever have left the Northeast? Maybe not. Maybe we wouldn't have met Brady and Lena, I'd still be working, my parents would spend every weekend with Grace, and we'd watch this true-crime story unfolding from a safe distance, disturbed but not distraught.

I texted Alondra. *When are the FBI or the police sending someone?*
Her answer was quick: *Working on it.*

Maybe Lena would retreat, there would be no more sightings, no more postcards. But I knew that wouldn't make things better. The FBI would keep looking, but Michael and I would either have to enter witness protection or go back to our lives, never able to relax or feel safe again.

"Did you know Shakira just finished an ancient philosophy course?" Mom held up her magazine so I could see.

I nodded, and as she flipped the page, my breath caught. Maybe Lena wasn't running around Texas faking a case against Michael. Maybe she was faking her presence in Texas altogether.

The box left on my doorstep and the postcards in Texas could have been dropped off by any of Lena and Brady's subcontractors. That security camera footage had been fuzzy. Maybe someone else was in the footage. Maybe Lena had used technology to alter the feed.

Maybe . . . I pulled up the search engine on my phone. The last time I'd seen Lena, she'd said she was visiting her aunt. The aunt who had given her the sourdough starter. The aunt who'd raised her. Was there a picture of this woman?

In a news story titled *Local Woman Questioned in Serial Killer Case*, there was a photo labeled "Courtesy of the Texas Department of Public Safety," a terrible driver's license photo of a grim-faced woman with Lena's unruly hair and strong build. Lena's aunt might be the one caught on the surveillance camera, trying to help out her niece.

My brain wanted to argue, but my body was certain, ice-cold with fear. Lena was still here. That jar on my parents' front steps couldn't be a coincidence.

But it wasn't proof. Not the kind anyone would believe.

When Aimee destroyed my life, Michael and I had run away and started over. But there was nowhere we could run from Lena. She'd pick off the people I loved one by one, and then she'd just disappear again. Tension tightened every sinew in my body as my mind flipped between the options.

Lena was in Texas. Michael was in so much danger that they'd switched his secret apartment. Elizabeth was getting threats. Lena could cross the border into Mexico, Brady would keep lying about Michael's involvement, and our home would never be safe again.

Lena was here. Grace was in danger. My parents—I'd brought a killer right to them. Lena wasn't going to forget where they lived. They would never be safe, not while she was out there. Molly would come back from her tour, my parents would return to gardening and fishing, and then one day . . .

I couldn't even think about it, but it was the only thought in my mind. Their house empty. Their bodies gone. Their blood on my hands.

Surreptitiously, I looked down at Aimee's social media feeds, still open on my phone. There was an event at the museum, an annual benefit for education and the arts where every local celebrity, from restaurateurs to fashionistas to politicians, would be in attendance. Not only wasn't Aimee worried about the warning I'd given her, she didn't even care that I could stalk her. She hadn't blocked me or hidden her post or anything. She wasn't scared at all, not like me.

I was holding the phone in my hand when it buzzed with a text from a number marked *Unknown: Hey girl, what's taking you so long? Get your ass over here.*

The sound of the television faded away. All I could hear was my own breath roaring in my ears. The tone of the text, it sounded like . . .

I watched my shaking fingers type *Who is this?*

My mother touched my arm and asked, "What's wrong?" Her words were garbled and warped as if I were underwater. Lena was in Texas. That's where the police were looking for her. We were safe here; we had to be.

I shook off my mom's hand, gripping the phone until the next text appeared: *Come find me . . . or I'll come get you. Who do you know in Hawthorne? One of your sisters?*

My dad was standing now.

"We have to go." I was on my feet, dizzy with adrenaline. "She knows. Lena knows we're here."

My mom stood, her magazine falling to the floor. "Where are the police?"

Another text: *Not the one with kids. She's in Cherry Hill . . .*

"I'll call them." My dad already had his phone in his hand. My mind was whirling through the choices. The police, Alondra, Michael, someone. How did Lena know where we were?

My phone buzzed again: *You're not answering. You were way more fun before you had a baby.*

I knocked over the end table, rushing to the bedroom. Over my shoulder I said, "Get in the car. I'll get Grace."

"Where are we going?" Dad asked as Mom swept everything into their suitcase.

Another text: *Better meet me before midnight, Cinderella. I'll know if you try to screw me. You know where I'll be.*

And I was in motion, scooping Grace up so abruptly that she woke with a cry. In a blur, I snatched up her stuffed rabbit, pulled one-handedly on the portable crib to collapse it, and whirled out of the room, leaving a T-shirt and yesterday's socks on the floor.

Nothing mattered but getting away. Lena knew we were here, and my family wasn't safe.

"Let's go," I called to my parents, but my dad had already started the car, and my mom was waiting by the front door. She took Grace so I could carry the crib, the diaper bag, and my own suitcase. With a jolt, I thought about my phone, but its weight was in my pocket. My hands full, I staggered to the car and swung my baggage into the trunk.

My mother buckled Grace into her car seat but paused before climbing into the passenger's side. "Did we lock it?"

"It doesn't matter," I told her, but she was already running, key in hand, alone through the dark. Watching my mom, my back pressed against the car, I pulled out my phone to see if any other texts had come through.

And then my stomach flipped. The phone. That's how Lena knew where I was. She and Brady had installed cameras in our home; why wouldn't she have put a "track my phone" alert on mine? Maybe in her backyard when I was swimming while she lounged by the pool, my phone unattended beside her. Maybe at my house, when I was in the bathroom and Grace was the only witness. A hundred opportunities came to mind, and I wanted to fling the phone from me like a venomous spider.

My fingers tightened, and I raised my hand, but then I remembered: *I'll know if you try to screw me.* What kind of spyware might Lena have installed? Had she listened to my phone calls? Could she read my text messages? Had she seen every website I'd visited and every app I'd used?

I looked at the screen as I had so many times, but there was no glowing light or indication that its camera was looking back at me. Still, I could feel Lena's calculating gaze.

If she got angry with me, she'd come after my family. After all, she was willing to wait, to play, to hunt us. She knew I post-stalked Aimee. She'd planned for me to see her in that photo. Whatever was happening in Texas, whoever was on that security footage, it wasn't Lena. She was waiting for me here in Jersey. And I didn't know if she was monitoring my location, my calls and texts, or every single thing I did.

Mom ran back to the car. "Ready?"

I'd have to be. Just like when Michael and I had sneaked out of the house with Grace, I'd have to escape without making Lena suspicious.

I slid into the back beside Grace's car seat, the phone still clutched in my sweaty hand. "Dad, we're going to the police station. The one in Montclair."

"I'll need directions," he said, pulling away from the house.

"Exit 148." No need for a GPS, since my recent trip to the museum had refreshed my memory. I didn't want just any police station, or even the closest one. I wanted the one on the way to the museum. The one where I'd been taken after Aimee framed me. Where I hadn't been believed, where I'd been so afraid I'd be charged, where a local reporter had caught wind of the story and my old life had ended. That was fear, but what I felt now, choking me, making it hard to breathe or even think—this was terror.

"How do you know that woman found us?" my mother asked.

"Alondra," I lied. If my parents knew I'd gotten texts from Lena, there was no way they'd let me protect them. They would die to keep me safe, and I couldn't let that happen. My voice sounded shrill and fake in my ears. "She told me which police station to go to. Let me see your phone for a sec."

Mom passed it over. In the darkness, I couldn't see her face, but the faint scent of her gardenia perfume mingled with Grace's sweet baby smell. If we just kept driving, we'd be safe. This was a place where Lena couldn't touch us. We'd outrun her, and then . . .

And then she'd bide her time and strike us later when she chose. Nobody could run forever. My mother, bludgeoned, beaten, dead.

I opened my contacts and entered Alondra's name and number into my mother's phone with the designation *lawyer*. Leaving that screen open so it would be the first thing Mom saw when she unlocked her phone, I clicked it off and passed it back to her.

My father's silence became heavier and heavier. As he signaled our turn off the Garden State, he said, "Kacy, exactly what did this lawyer say to you?"

Heat rose in my body. "She texted that Lena was in our area and we should go to the police station." The words sounded like something from a script, so fake. But he had to believe me. I couldn't let Lena come after him.

"Did you call her?" he asked.

At the same time, my mother said, "Why the police station?"

"No, I didn't call her."

"Try her now." My dad merged the car smoothly with traffic, thick and slow, off the exit.

My mother twisted around in her seat, even though it was too dark for us to see each other's expressions. "Are they going to put us in a safe house?"

"I don't know, Mom, maybe." Looking at the last text—*I'll know if you try to screw me*—I tapped the word *Unknown*, but there was no way to call it back. I held the phone to my ear, as if waiting. After a few seconds, I said, "Alondra, we're on our way to the station. Call me."

My mother sighed and turned back around. "It'll be okay," I told her. "Once we get to the station, we'll be safe."

And I imagined the relief. Running into the building, all of us together. I'd call Michael and Alondra, the police and the FBI would converge on the museum, and . . .

And Lena would be gone. She'd disappear again, and my family would stay in purgatory, never safe, never at ease, never truly free. And if Lena did kill Aimee, they'd think Michael and I were both in on it, especially with the lies Brady was telling now. Grace could grow up with this shadow blighting her life. No playdates, shunned at school, pointed out by strangers. *Her dad's a killer, her mom's a psycho.*

Maybe I could ask the police to take my phone and go after Lena. But if she was using the camera or listening in, she'd know it was a trick. And she'd disappear to plot revenge.

At least I should tell my parents what was happening. They were going to be so terrified, so guilty, so angry that I was doing this alone. But it was worth it to keep them safe.

I pulled up Aimee's social media feed, the one I'd been examining when Lena's text came through. Coincidence, or had Lena been waiting? As I swiped through the photos now, scrutinizing the backgrounds, trying to focus on the shaking screen, I felt an absolute certainty that Lena was there. Now I remembered the way Lena used to watch people, even me, with a cold steadiness when she thought herself unobserved. She'd been quick to anger, showed absolute disdain for pretentious "stupid" people, and was as ready to fight my battles as her own. At the time, it had felt like validation, like someone on my side. I'd been the one who was stupid.

If Lena really was there, she'd be watching Aimee and relying on my phone to let her know where I was. I'd find her, distract her, and then contact the police. The station was so close.

I'm strong. I can do this. But the affirmations were just covering up a deeper whisper. *I'm going to die.*

We pulled into the dark parking lot, and I lifted Grace's car seat out, leaving my phone and purse on the back seat. We were still really near the interstate. Maybe I could get away with this detour.

The limestone building seemed to glow in the dark like a fortress of safety. My parents waited for me, and I sped up. Dad held the door and we entered a lobby, older than the one in Sugar Land but with the same elements: locks on the doors to prevent entry farther into the building, a display case with medals and awards, and the officer seated behind a protective barrier.

I set Grace's seat on the floor, her eyes wide as she took in the bright lights of the police station. I had to be the kind of person she'd look up to, the kind of person who was brave, who rescued others, who took action. But I didn't want to leave.

You were more fun before you became a mom.

My heart beat a staccato rhythm in my chest. Grace. I'd do whatever Lena wanted, sacrifice myself, as long as Grace was safe.

The car keys were still in my father's hand, and quickly I took them. "Left my phone in the car." Before he could insist on going with me, I darted out of the building, hurled myself into the driver's seat, and started the engine.

I didn't look in the rearview mirror as I pulled out of the parking lot.

CHAPTER

26

THE MUSEUM WAS strung with fairy lights in the trees and around the entrance, reflected in delicate patterns through all the windows, making it impossible to see through them.

In my slouchy athletic pants, T-shirt, and cheap cardigan, I wasn't dressed for a gala, or even dressed to *cater* a gala. These events were highly orchestrated down to the last detail. If this were a movie, I'd sneak into the kitchen, pick up a platter of canapés, and waltz into the crowd, perfectly in disguise. But I knew that everyone on the floor would be wearing a uniform, that in the kitchen each team would be so well organized that they wouldn't hand a platter to some random person, and in the sea of hot boxes and prep tables I'd stick out just as much as I would in the midst of the glitterati.

And if I stuck out, Lena would see me before I saw her.

There would be security working the event. I bit my lip, the pain focusing my mind. Well, there would be security at the entrances, but this museum wasn't the Met. I wouldn't need an *Ocean's 8* maneuver to get in. I just needed to get a look at the people there, make sure Aimee was still alive, scan for Lena. Call the police. I'd slipped the scissors from my purse into my pocket as backup, and now I clenched the cold steel, my only weapon.

As long as Lena knew I was here, she'd stay. Hopefully long enough to get caught.

The scissors pressed painfully into my hand. I wasn't strong enough to fight Lena. I'd survive only if she didn't see me.

The front steps of the museum were illuminated, although guests weren't arriving yet. I darted into the shadows at the side of the building and went around back, where catering vans were parked by the loading dock. I recognized Tyler, the service captain standing with his clipboard, from countless other events, big, small, and esoteric. I'd seen him fire a cook on the spot for wearing a long-sleeved T-shirt. No way I was getting past him. But I couldn't see another way in. There were three vans, all the standard white, with several people unloading plastic tubs, aluminum trays, and milk crates like a reverse game of Tetris. Inside the prep area, knives must be flying and proverbial plates must be spinning.

I wrapped both arms around my knotted stomach, trying to calm down enough to assess the situation. After all, I used to be the one coordinating these events with Aimee.

Together we had tasted rock shrimp on corn madeleines, lemon and rosemary macarons, flower petals and gold leaf suspended in champagne gelee. We'd designed menus and called donors and stretched our budget, calculating whether the expense would encourage donations and publicity. Aimee adored parties, not the food as much as the glamour and the attention. I was always on high alert, gauging our guests' reactions, coordinating with Tyler or the service captain from whichever catering company was there. I knew exactly how many of the secret vegan options we had, and when some skinny socialite said, "Oh, that looks good; can I have that instead?" I was the one who added the cost of having her to my mental tally.

"But she's part of the publicity," Aimee had pointed out. "A vapid, selfish part of the publicity, but still . . ."

"It should be about the art. That should be what people care about."

I had forgotten how it felt to be that certain, that idealistic. Now as I looked at the museum, I felt that it contained in brittle glass, fragile paper, and inflexible stone the fears and desires of a hundred human souls, each so easily destroyed.

Death was the opposite of art, and here I was, seeking it out.

Terror made it so hard to think, but I had to. Grace's life, Michael's, my parents'—everyone depended on me. I had to make sure Lena was captured. If I waited by the vans, maybe when the last of the catering crew went in, I could enter through that back door. If I did, and I managed to get through the kitchen, I could use the service elevator to get to the upper floor. From there, I could see everything.

My hand touched the scissors again, a comforting weight in my pocket. Comforting, until I thought about using them. Then rational thought faded and my body tensed, trying to override my plan and *run, run, run*.

When I saw Lena, I'd find someone else's phone to call the police. No heroics. Nothing like that. I'd get in and get out. Michael would be cleared, and the three of us would be back where we were supposed to be. *I swear*, I promised, *I'll never take a single normal day for granted again. Please, please . . .*

Moving like a marionette, I walked along the edge of the parking lot. One of the catering guys looked up, and I waved at him in a *nice evening, nothing to see here* kind of way. He nodded and dragged a loaded plastic bin off the van parked by the door. As he joined the ranks of cooks lugging equipment into the museum, the service captain checked his clipboard and followed them. They must have been cleaning out the final bits and pieces.

At the far end of the parking lot, three empty vans afforded me some slight cover. The gala would start in the next hour or two, the front of the museum would be lit and crowded, but back here there was a soft darkness, diluted by the lights at the edge of the parking lot and the light coming from the back loading door. I wrapped my arms around my stomach, trying to ease the knot of terror. Back here, I couldn't go look for Lena, but I was safely hidden. I'd just wait for the right moment.

Only three guys were left, messing around with the van. They were almost finished, and when they were, I'd sprint to the door. I shifted from one foot to the other. It was colder up here than it would have been in Texas, but I hadn't thought to bring more than a light cardigan. One of the guys pulled something out of a pocket and offered it to the other one.

They were going to smoke before going in. I almost groaned aloud. They leaned against the back wall of the museum. If I could see them, they could see me, so I drew back a few more steps, concentrating on the distant sound of their muffled laughter. It was warmer between the two vans, as though their engines had just been turned off or they'd been transporting hot boxes and the residual heat still glowed.

I was almost holding my breath, straining to hear the sound of the door shutting, my signal that the coast would be clear, when a hand clamped over my mouth and a familiar voice whispered in my ear, "Took you long enough."

I struggled, twisting in the iron crook of that arm, until I could see Lena. Her wavy hair spiraled out from the knot she'd made of it, but it was dyed a dark black, which threw her pale skin into relief. The pressure of her hand kept me from opening my mouth enough to try to scream. She was strong, strong enough to break my neck.

She threw me sideways, slamming my head into the side of the van. The pain stole my breath and my vision. I closed my eyes and tried to shout, but her hand was back, sealing my mouth as she loomed over me, pressing me against the van. I could scarcely breathe.

"Shut the fuck up," she hissed at me. "What's the matter with you? It's *me*." She wore tailored black trousers and a button-down white shirt slightly too large, bagging under the arms and sitting too wide on her shoulders. Unlike me, she was dressed to cater.

Somewhere in my terror, what she'd said sunk in. She wasn't planning to kill me. Which meant if I could buy some time, I could get away and call the police. I could get out of this.

I stopped struggling.

She squinted at me, the expression so familiar, the exact way she'd looked back when she'd said, "You're on the benefit planning committee?" like she was trying to evaluate me from the inside, to see if what she thought about me matched who I actually was. I slipped a hand into my pocket and grasped the handle of the scissors.

I opened my eyes wide, trying to project innocence, and she frowned. Why did I have to be such a crap liar? Why couldn't I be more like Aimee, with a poker face that exuded warmth when all I had inside was ice?

I couldn't just pretend. I was going to have to feel it. And at the thought of the Lena with whom I'd made bread, these same strong hands that held me captive once pounding the dough, another friend who'd just been an illusion, I let my eyes tear up.

Slowly, she took her hand off my mouth. "Just be cool. Don't freak out."

"You *lied* to me."

"I didn't want you to be involved." Her clamp on my arm was so tight I could feel my blood throb underneath her grip.

"You *killed* people."

"Not anybody you knew."

I didn't have to pretend. I could feel my brows draw together, my face contort. How could anyone be like this, so cruel and yet so normal? A killer should be crazed, evil, hate life. But Lena loved the sunshine and good food and laughter.

And she was still standing too close for me to run and get away.

"Why are you here?" I demanded.

"You even have to ask? Brady screwed up; he ruined everything. And I know that made things harder for y'all. So I thought I'd make it right and do you a favor before I took off."

"I don't want you to kill Aimee."

"Why the fuck not? The bitch ruined your life."

"Yes, but . . ." What could I say that was true, that Lena would believe? "But if she hadn't, I wouldn't have moved, I wouldn't have met you."

"Is that a vote for her or against her?" The smile, the laughter in Lena's voice, was so infectious I would have laughed, if this had been just another evening by the pool. And then I saw the black cloth bag at her feet. Those people she and Brady had killed, they'd been tortured and dismembered. And any illusions I'd had about how much she'd been involved were dispelled by what must be a bag of tools at her feet.

If I couldn't break free, at least I had to lure her away from the museum, away from Aimee and closer to help. "They've got security all over here. You're not safe. Let's just go."

"I'm not going to let her get away with what she did."

"Forget her. She's not worth it. And there's so much security."

Lena smiled, her lips stretching wide in a grin that didn't touch her eyes. Her voice was soft. "You said that already. What are you trying to do, Kacy? Are you trying to play me?"

"No, I—"

Her other hand shot out and grabbed my wrist, hard, forcing my fingers to open, releasing the scissors. "You're not worried about me at all," she hissed. "Are you trying to save this bitch? Why do you still give a shit about her?"

"I don't. But you're going to get caught." I was almost shouting, and Lena's gaze went past me, evaluating who might have heard.

Her hand closed harder around my arm, and I cried out as her other hand reached into a pocket on her pants. She had a weapon, I knew she had a weapon. I froze again, my whole body stiff.

She bent her head close to mine, whispering with fierce intensity. "I don't get caught. I've never been caught. If Brady had been able to control himself for a few goddamn days—"

"You really were going to your aunt's house?" I croaked. I could hear the noise of the street, but I couldn't see more than a sliver of the parking lot. If only one of the catering crew would come out now, they would see us, they would call for help.

"Of course I was. I was there when I heard the news that my dumbfuck husband had blown everything. I'm so sorry he dragged Michael into this. I didn't mean for you to get involved."

I could almost believe she *was* sorry, that she'd tried to shield me from her own heinous crimes. She'd been watching us on those cameras, she'd been destroying innocent people, and I couldn't hold my tongue, not even with my life at stake. "Why? Why did you do it?"

"I'm trying to make it up to you. Just quit freaking out." She gave me a little shake, almost playful.

"What are you talking about? You killed people."

"Oh, that." And I could have sworn I saw something moving in her eyes, something dark and hungry, but what she said was, "It was Brady. He was obsessed. God, I love that asshole."

She was lying, I knew it. "But he's not here now."

"No," she said slowly, "he's not, is he?" I tried to withdraw my arm gently, but her grip tightened. "I can't fool you, Kacy, can I? But it's true, I did try to protect you."

"Let me protect you. Just go. They won't find you." I'd sprint to the street and call the police.

"I can't." She looked almost sad. "This is who I am, and you know I always finish my jobs."

Then she raised her hand, and I felt a sharp sting, an injection in my shoulder. As my vision narrowed to a pinprick, she whispered, "Sorry, sweetie. I just need a head start."

14

Helen: Okay, so there's a lot to unpack here at the end.

Julia: Like, fifty suitcases' worth.

Helen: But we're going to keep it tight on logistics. First, that woman on the security footage? Lena's aunt. She muddied up the timeline, lied her ass off about seeing Lena, and generally caused havoc.

Julia: I would do that for you, totally.

Helen: You cause havoc recreationally.

Julia: Truth.

Helen: But the FBI is not taken in by all these Texas shenanigans. They're following up with Lena's extended family in Louisiana and Arkansas and they're keeping tabs on Kacy and her family too.

Julia: As victims, witnesses, or suspects?

Helen: My guess is yes to all three. Secondly, Lena has been monitoring Kacy's phone. She knows where this "safe house" is, she knows Kacy's been to the museum once already, and when everything's just the way Lena wants it, she knows Kacy's taken the bait.

Julia: Because there's no point in preparing a surprise party if the guest of honor doesn't show up.

Helen: Happy birthday, baby.

CHAPTER

27

I CAME TO ON the ground in the shadow of something large, my cheek pressed into the rough asphalt, the stench of oil and trash in my nostrils. I sat up, my head swimming, trying to make sense of what I saw. A wooden fence, a dark alley, a bit of the parking lot, and a dumpster. I'd been lying almost underneath it.

"Help!" My voice cracked. I staggered to my feet, my hand on the filthy metal for support, my stomach queasy. I crept around the dumpster and scanned the parking lot. Despite the nearly subaudible hum of the surrounding city, everything was quiet. I didn't see Lena anywhere.

The catering vans were gone, the museum dark. The gala must be over. I raised a hand to my aching head. I had to call the police. I reached in my pocket. Empty. No car keys. No scissors. No phone.

I scanned the asphalt. Nothing. Lena must have taken everything.

A car was approaching on the main street, and I ran toward it, waving my hands. I could have sworn it sped up. The darkness thickened around me. Lena could be anywhere, in any doorway, watching me. But she wouldn't watch for long. That wasn't her style. Maybe she pictured me as a wounded animal she needed to stalk.

But that wasn't what she'd said. Lena had threatened Aimee, but she'd talked to me like we were friends.

I looked over my shoulder at the front entrance to the museum. Of course. The security guard. He'd have a walkie-talkie and a phone. He'd call the police. My next breath drew bile into my throat.

Lena knew I was here, and she could figure out where my family was. My parents. Grace. They were at the police station now, but they couldn't live there forever. When they left, Lena would hunt them down.

Although she hadn't hurt me yet, every little remark she'd made about babies and Stepford wives ignited a panic that burned through the foggy pain in my head.

I sprinted across the parking lot, along the side of the museum, and up the concrete steps of the entrance. The main glass doors were locked, as I knew they would be, and no one was visible. I banged on the doors with my open palms, shouting, shrieking. When I heard a car behind me, I turned and screamed at it too, waving my arms frantically.

Why didn't pay phones exist anymore?

I heard another vehicle on the road and turned to see a garbage truck. I raced to intercept it, hurling myself into the street in front of it. The driver slammed on his brakes, and I threw my hands up and closed my eyes as it stopped right in front of me.

The sanitation worker on the back of the truck hopped off and loped toward me, his yellow vest reflecting the streetlights. "What the fuck?"

"Call the police. I need you to call the police." I reached out to him, and he slowed, as if worried I might be dangerous.

The driver opened his door. "I could have killed you, lady."

From a safe distance, the worker squinted at me. "Are you okay? Are you hurt?"

I held up my open hands. "It's an emergency. Please, can I use your phone?"

He might have wanted to refuse, but I was already closing the distance between us, reaching out. Surely he could read the desperation on my face. Every second we wasted here was another second Lena could be on her way to Grace.

As the driver switched on his emergency flashers, the other worker dug in his pocket and offered me his phone.

"Thank you, thank you." I fumbled to dial 911.

The dispatcher asked, "What's the nature of your emergency?"

"Lena Voss, the fugitive, the killer. She was at the Umana museum."

"What's the address?"

I gave it and my name, tripping over my words.

"Spell that for me." Could I see movement inside the building? Maybe Lena was still here, still hunting.

"Are you injured?"

"No, I mean, it doesn't matter. If you call the Sugar Land Police Department in Texas or the FBI or my lawyer—"

"Description of the suspect?"

"She's been on the nightly news." I was almost screaming. "Dark curly hair, midthirties, tall."

"Where is she now?" The dispatcher's calm sounded patronizing. I wasn't some child who'd seen a bogeyman.

"I don't know," I snapped. "She knocked me out. My parents are at the police station in Montclair."

"Are you in need of medical assistance?"

"Just send the police." I definitely saw a faint light moving inside the building. A flashlight or maybe a phone? The only thing worse than knowing Lena was lurking somewhere in the world was the realization that she was here, right here. And the only way to pin her down was to play her game. I stopped listening to the dispatcher's instructions.

Lena had my makeshift weapon, my car keys, and my cell phone.

I hung up and dialed my own number.

And Lena picked up. "Hey, girl, what's taking you so long?"

"Where are you?"

"Right in front of you, Sleeping Beauty." The warmth in her voice was a wicked contrast to the coolness of the emergency operator.

In front of me the museum waited, its glass-fronted entrance an impenetrable pool of darkness.

"The police are coming." Was I warning her or threatening her?

"Like I couldn't be done and gone long before they get here. Don't pretend you don't want me to."

As long as Lena was in the museum, Aimee was the one in danger. But the minute Lena left, my family could be in her sights. Even if she disappeared, Michael and I would never feel safe again.

Maybe I could keep Lena talking until the police arrived. "Is she alive?"

"For now. Think you can talk me out of it?" Of course, she could see right through my futile hopes. Then she whispered, "I left the door open for you . . ."

And she hung up.

The silence in my ear was like a flashlight being turned off. If I couldn't see her, couldn't hear her, I wouldn't know where she was. To keep her from vanishing, I had to go after her.

The museum's front doors were locked, but Lena had gotten in somehow. The caterers must have been among the last to leave, and they would have used the back door. I hadn't even tried it when I'd woken up on the pavement. The alarm should be set, but no security system would be a match for Lena. She'd probably disabled it. But maybe I'd catch a break and by entering the museum I could silently trigger it.

I handed the phone to the sanitation worker and said, "Stay here with your truck. The police are coming. Call them back at 911 and keep them on the line. I have to go in."

"What's in there?" he called after me.

But I didn't slow down to answer.

I sprinted around to the back door. It *was* unlocked. Inside, I dashed up the narrow stairs into the room where we'd staged events. The smell of food and antiseptic cleanser lingered in the air.

"Lena?" I called.

No one answered. I ran into the atrium, my steps echoing, the only light the occasional flash of red or orange in the ghostly glass ribbons overhead. From somewhere, I heard Lena call, "Cold."

I stopped short. Crossing that expanse felt like being on stage, with the galleries looking down on me and the glass wall at the front of the museum exposing me to the street. From here I couldn't see the red flashing lights of the garbage truck. Would the men stay there until the police came? Were they even there now?

I paused by the front desk, fumbling under the edge of the counter for the panic button. I pressed it hard, over and over, but it had no more effect than the crosswalk button when the light's still red.

"Ice-cold." Lena's voice filled the space around me, blithe and playful and impossible to locate.

But I stayed behind the desk for a moment and looked up, scanning the darkened edges of the museum. Light from the street filtered in through the front windows, and the emergency exit signs still glowed red. I couldn't see Lena at the edge of the atrium, on the broad staircase, or in the shadows of the overhead galleries.

"Come out. I'm here," I shouted, and the echoes insisted *here, here, here.*

"Not the way the game is played," Lena answered, but I still couldn't pinpoint her whereabouts. Maybe above me? She was definitely watching. Then I thought of the security monitors. Had she disabled those too? I had to take the chance. The security office was across from the bathroom, and I sprinted toward it.

"Cooler," Lena's voice urged, and then I stepped on something large and uneven and flew sprawling. A crumpled mass, a human form. I crawled closer and saw a security guard, not Jared, an older man with his hand outstretched and his hat lying next to him. I took his wrist, feeling for a pulse. His skin was warm, and I thought I felt a flutter against my fingertips, but I wasn't sure. His face was in shadow, but I could tell his eyes were closed.

"Hello," I whispered. As my eyes adjusted, it seemed the shadows around him grew deeper. I put a tentative hand to the side of his head and felt something sticky matted in his hair. I jerked back, and my knee hit something hard. A darkened flashlight. I picked it up but didn't turn it on, clenching it like a handrail for stability.

"Quit fucking around and get your ass up here, Kacy," Lena called, and then there was a long scream, echoing through the rooms. Aimee.

I slipped off my cardigan and pressed it tightly against the man's head. I didn't know if he was alive. But I knew Aimee was. For now.

I took the stairs in huge leaps, my feet slapping against the polished marble, the flashlight a comforting weight in my hand. There were three galleries up here, fronted by a balcony that overlooked the first floor. As I reached the top of the stairs, Lena shouted, "Warmer."

I darted into the closest gallery, filled with statues constructed of something brittle and light. I grazed one, and it moved with a brushy sound like ash blowing across pottery.

I heard the sound of scuffling feet behind me, and I paused. Each of the three pathways connected at the back and opened out onto the same balcony. Lena could have been ahead of me, entered the central gallery, and now be behind me again. As long as she was moving, she wasn't enacting horrible torments on Aimee. And the scuffling—surely that was the sound of more than one person's feet.

But I was afraid to ask if Aimee was okay. Asking would only draw Lena's attention to my interest, make her wonder how much I cared, maybe piss her off. It didn't matter that I didn't want anyone to be murdered, that somewhere a part of me was still kneeling by the security guard as he lay bleeding, maybe dead. She would misread my interest in Aimee and react to it, and the last thing I wanted to do was give Lena something to push against. She was the equal and opposite force, the inevitable reaction. That was how we'd first become friends, wasn't it? I'd hurled a mug and then she'd matched it, shattering another against the wall. But this time, it wouldn't be an inanimate object that she broke.

"Come find *me*," I called, my voice stronger.

"I don't think you want to see what I have with me." Horrible mirth ran like a dreg-filled current through her voice.

"Forget about Aimee. Let's talk, just the two of us." With effort, I kept my tone light. At any moment, Lena might decide the fun was over and she could kill Aimee. I knew she could.

"We *are* talking. And Aimee's fine. She's just listening now. Aren't you, bitch?" she hissed.

There was a thud, like a piece of furniture being knocked over. Aimee must be struggling, but now I had a better bead on her location. Right next to me, one gallery over. I put on a burst of speed, running lightly, silently I hoped, past the fragile statues and down to the end of the gallery, the security guard's flashlight in my hand, still turned off so it wouldn't give me away.

I rounded the corner into the central gallery, the one that had featured in so many of my nightmares. *Winged Victory* was still in the center, a form as dark as if all the shadows had fused into the shape of a looming angel.

And just beyond it, Lena was waiting for me, silhouetted against the feeble light from the front of the museum. With her preternatural instincts, she'd heard me, of course she had. Actually, thanks to the security cameras in my house, she'd always known where I was, every second of the last year. There was no point in pretending to hide.

I switched on the flashlight.

She was smiling, the same way she had when meeting me for a walk or handing me a margarita poolside. Even with her newly dyed hair, she looked like the same woman who'd sat next to me at Bluebonnet meetings and picked me up for impromptu lunches out and spent so many hours talking. She looked delighted to see me.

But she wasn't alone.

Aimee's arms were twisted behind her back, a strip of silver duct tape across her mouth and Lena's arm around her throat. Aimee's metallic champagne cocktail dress was wrinkled and askew at the neck, and she wore only one shoe, its stiletto heel throwing her further off-balance. Tears shone on her cheeks in the flashlight's beam, and smudged mascara bloomed around her eyes. When she saw me, she struggled more, but Lena pressed the tip of a knife right against her jugular.

Maybe I had imagined vengeance and humiliation for Aimee, maybe I'd thought *she'll be sorry*, but I'd never wanted to see Aimee afraid for her life. I didn't want to watch her die.

How long had we been here? Surely the police would arrive soon. Warily, I approached, stopping next to *Winged Victory*. Cold seemed to radiate from its raised wings, but they offered the illusion of shelter.

And now I could see more clearly how the sharp point of the blade indented the skin of Aimee's throat. No, not a knife. Scissors. The ones from my purse. My breath caught.

Lena watched me, her smile unchanging, a challenge in her eyes.

"What do you want, Lena?" My voice was colder than I'd intended.

But Lena only grinned, the warmth and friendliness of her expression chillingly at odds with the situation. "It's what you said, Kacy. Remember? 'The world should be fair.' This is our chance to even the score."

Hearing my own words pierced me, and I couldn't help myself. "Just let her go. You're better than this."

"But I'm not." Now her grin was wolfish. "You don't have to be either. You don't have to be hurt or angry or patient. You can get even. Being a good girl for so long, what did that get you? Just another wife and mother. Another automaton moving from the house to the grocery store to lunch with the girls. Fuck that shit. You don't have to be good anymore."

My hand trembled, and the oscillating flashlight beam made Lena and Aimee seem like a flickering film projection. "I'm not good," I whispered. A good wife wouldn't have left her traumatized husband alone; a good daughter would never have put this burden on her elderly parents; a good mother would never have abandoned her daughter to chase a monster.

Lena shook Aimee by the scruff of her neck, and a whimper escaped from behind the tape. "This stuck-up liar pretended to be your friend, but she was just using you the whole time, laughing at you. Even after she got it all—the job, the money, the prestige— she couldn't let you go."

All the times I'd complained about Aimee flashed through my mind. The way Lena had taken my side when I'd received Aimee's postcards, how good it had felt to have someone angry on my behalf. Had I set these events in motion? And mixed in with my guilt and fear, was there the tiniest thread of satisfaction? I felt sick.

Lena's hand moved, and instead of the point pressing against Aimee's jugular, now the open blade rested straight across her neck. "She thought she was untouchable. She's too stupid to be afraid." With the other hand, she jerked Aimee closer and started walking backward toward the balcony connecting all three galleries. Lena was so much taller that Aimee struggled to remain upright.

I wanted to stay in the shelter of the statue. I wanted to turn and run, leave the museum, ask the sanitation workers to take me home, never leave Grace for a second ever again. But if I left, Lena would definitely kill Aimee, and then she might wait months, even years, before striking again. I just had to stall her until the police arrived. Could I see something on the street outside the museum? I wanted help so badly that it might be my imagination.

My whole arm was trembling now, the flashlight bobbing like a buoy on choppy water.

Aimee's wide eyes were locked on mine, but my full attention had to be on Lena. "What are you waiting for?" Lena called softly. She'd dragged Aimee all the way out of the gallery until they were standing together against the balustrade. "Get out here, Kacy, or I'll just toss her over."

Did she mean it? Cautiously, I approached, stopping just out of reach. The front windows provided enough light that I lowered the flashlight, but I kept it on. The weight of it made me feel stronger.

Lena kept the blade of the scissors tightly pressed against Aimee's throat. If the police were really out front, this might be almost over. But whether they followed me up the back stairs or broke down the front door or even landed with a SWAT team on the roof, the moment Lena saw them, I knew she'd hurl Aimee to her death.

I had to make her believe I was playing along. "What do you really want, Lena? Why am I here?"

She smirked. "I'll make you a deal, Kacy. If you stab this bitch like she deserves, I won't kill her. I'll let you both go. How about that, bestie?"

And she *was* my bestie, my soul sister, my fearless leader. I'd missed Lena, my best friend always right next door, only a text away, ready for any adventure. Now my heart was breaking. How could I know her so well and have missed everything else that she was: methodical, voyeuristic, deadly?

There was no way I could stab Aimee. She was right there, between Lena and me, the corners of her eyes drawn down, pleading, begging me not to hurt her. I'd thought I'd wanted her humiliated and penitent, but now I just wanted her safe.

I took a step and reached out my hand. If Lena gave me the scissors, I'd have some power back. Maybe I could cut Lena, then Aimee and I could run, maybe . . .

But Lena had always been able to read my expressions.

"Just so we're clear." She yanked Aimee so she was bent backward, hanging over the balcony. "If you decide to screw me, she's going over. Those tile floors will smash her skull."

For a second, I saw that she really wanted to throw Aimee over, that the sight of a broken body bleeding in the middle of the pristine museum was exactly what she wanted. But then she looked at me, and like a screen coming down, the mask of "my friend Lena" fell back into place.

I stretched out my hand, edging closer.

"Christ, you look like you're going to touch a snake." One hand still wrapped around Aimee's neck, she stretched the other out to me. There were the scissors, the same stainless-steel ones I'd used to cut my hair just hours earlier.

My fingers wrapped around the open shears, and I took them gingerly. Lena laughed again. "You're not going to do much damage way over there. Get closer."

I took another step as slowly as I dared. "So I stab her, you let us go, and what, just disappear? You had disappeared. You were free. Why come back for me at all?" *Take your time answering.*

From the corner of my eye, I could see smaller lights through the large windows, flashlights like policemen would have. They were here, but if I really looked, Lena might turn around and see them too.

Her mouth twisted in amusement. "Nice try. You know, we could have had the best fucking time if you weren't so weak. Thelma and Louise–ing our way all across the country. And forget that blaze-of-glory bullshit. I'm talking down in Mexico, drinking real margaritas on the beach."

And I could see it—sitting shotgun beside her like I had so many times. Riding a buzz as the sun went down over the ocean instead of her swimming pool. That feeling of finally being on the inside, having the full force of Lena's attention, becoming unstoppable.

I must have hesitated, because she said, "It's not too late to say yes. I love Brady, but that man's a walking id with no fucking impulse control. But you and me, we'd be smart. We'd pick the bad guys, make the world a better place, and you know we'd never get caught."

Even in her escapist fantasy, Lena was killing people. I *knew* her, but I'd never *understand* her. And even without the brutal undercurrent, blowing off my life for a never-ending vacation wasn't me. It was all a lie. My life wasn't my own any longer; it was Grace's and Michael's and my parents'. And, God help me, Aimee's.

I glanced down at the scissors, then back up at Lena. "Actually, you and Aimee are a lot alike."

"The hell we are," Lena shot back.

"Waiting for your moment, biding your time." I regretted the words the moment they were out, but there was no going back.

The creases around Lena's eyes deepened with irritation. "Quit fucking around and stab the bitch. Or do you need me to get you in the mood?"

She ripped the tape off Aimee's mouth, but instead of screaming, Aimee squeezed her eyes shut, a whimper escaping her lips. "Isn't this everything you dreamed about? She stole, and she fucked your boss, and she lied, and she set you up. And when they were firing you and smearing your name, she didn't just stand there, did she?"

Lena gave her another shake. "No, she joined in with her bullshit and her froufrou little lies. I know this type. She hates other women. You were her competition and her fall guy. Are you going to let that stand?"

My hand was cramping around the blade of the scissors slick with my sweat. "I don't want—"

"You *do* want this. You're just too nice to say so."

I heard the faint sound of a door closing, and the relief almost buckled my knees. I wasn't alone. The police would be here soon.

"Last chance, Kacy. You do it, or I'll have to. Either way it's on you." Lena braced herself, and I knew how quickly she could bend and slide her arm behind Aimee's knees to flip her over the railing.

I stepped forward, my hand still outstretched, and the point of the scissors hit Aimee under her arm. She screamed, and in the depths of the museum, the noise swelled. I dropped the scissors and the flashlight, both clattering on the floor.

Lena gave me a look of utter disgust. "You are a weak-ass bitch."

Then, just as I had imagined, she bent to slide her arm behind Aimee's legs. Before Lena could flip her over, I lunged, grasping at Aimee's bound arm. I missed, but my knee caught Lena in the nose. She staggered backward, losing her grip on Aimee.

I grabbed at Aimee, trying to catch her shoulder, her arm, her dress, finally gaining purchase on the duct tape that bound her arms together. For a horrible moment I thought we'd both go over the railing, but my clenched hands wouldn't let go. Then I threw my weight backward, and we crashed to the ground together as the police entered.

*　*　*

The cavernous museum was suddenly filled with people and shouting and noise, but Aimee and I were still on the ground. She rolled away from me, and when I reached out to help her up, she flinched. I rose to my knees, but then an officer's hands were on me, pulling me away, and an EMT knelt beside Aimee. I caught a glimpse of a small dark stain against the shine of her dress.

"Your name?" the agent asked.

"Kacy. Kacy Tremaine."

My hands had been the ones on the scissors, and I didn't see Lena anywhere. On the ground floor, I could see FBI agents and police fanning throughout the museum. The EMT had checked Aimee over and was freeing her hands. His head was close to hers, but I couldn't hear what he was saying. Then he helped her to her feet and led her away.

"Kacy, I'm Agent Castillo. I need you to walk with me."

"Where's Lena? Did you catch her?" Through the blood and the confusion, the medics and the police, Lena might be long gone.

Agent Castillo didn't answer, instead scanning the room while somehow giving the impression that she was completely focused on me. Her dark hair was pulled back in a low ponytail, and her bulky FBI vest covered a fitted black top.

I had only seconds before I'd be escorted out as well. I would have seen Lena go down the main staircase; the police would have seen her.

"We have to go," she said again. She wore a thin silver chain around her neck with a wedding band hanging from it. I wanted to let her hustle me down the stairs, back to my parents and Michael and Grace, but if Lena was still on this floor, lurking, like an angel of death. . . .

"Lena's still up here. She has to be." She wouldn't panic or flee. That wasn't Lena's style. She'd wait and watch, somewhere we wouldn't look for her. I knew this museum, maybe not the changing exhibits and the new employees, but I knew its bones.

Where could she be? The elevator in the front opened in the lobby, full of people. Both the freight elevator and the fire escape would have put her out by the back door and the loading dock, where the emergency vehicles must be. There was no place to hide in the gallery with the papier-mâché statues and mixed-media portraits.

From where we were, I could see into the gallery, where another agent, a tall black man, walked past the gleaming onyx angel. That statue was big enough to hold Lena, but the base was solid stone.

There was another option. A room for staging installations, full of empty crates and bits and pieces of hardware, bases and supports and plenty of places to hide.

"The exhibition preparation room, just off the last gallery," I said, pointing.

Agent Castillo spoke into her walkie-talkie and gestured to her counterpart. He nodded and called out to two police officers who'd just reached the top of the stairs. Together they entered the third gallery.

I edged closer, only to have them wave me back, but not before I could see the display inside. More mobiles with glass twisted into impossible shapes, smaller versions of the one hanging over the atrium, hung down from the ceiling or rested on invisible shelves. On two sides the walls were draped with black fabric, gathered and pleated until it appeared to flow like water, pooling onto the shelves and merging with the shadows, distorting a viewer's depth perception. With the right lighting, the glass pieces would seem to move freely, their cords and metal wires invisible.

In the center of the room stood the biggest piece, a woman raised as if standing on a cliff, larger than life, three-dimensional and translucent, catching and refracting the light. When the agent strode past, the separate leaves of glass shivered apart on their metal strands and then came together again. Despite how light it looked, how easily it moved, I knew how deceptively heavy glass could be. The base looked like a sandstone cliff, rising from floor level to waist-high, the shimmering glass woman poised as if to leap.

She was still trembling, although no one was near.

The officers opened the door at the end of the room, shouting their identification before entering. But I didn't hear a commotion or anything that sounded like an arrest. I could have sworn I felt Lena's eyes on me, watching me.

I glanced up, but the red eye of the security cameras was still dark. The glass sculpture in the center of the room stilled, and the glass woman seemed to be looking right at me, challenging me. There was nowhere for Lena to hide in the first gallery or the second or in the base of this glass statue . . . then I knew.

Gently I touched Agent Castillo's arm and pointed to the dark drape over the side wall. In the corner, where the fabric was bunched and gathered, a person with steely patience could hide, waiting for a quiet moment to slip away. The agent looked at me, and in her gaze, I felt myself weighed and judged. Complicit, stupid, attention seeking? No, the agent motioned for me to get behind her. She believed me, trusted me, and she drew her gun.

Approaching slowly, Agent Castillo reached out and flipped back the edge of the fabric. Lena stepped from behind it, knocking over a few of the smaller pieces and sending the glass mobiles clinking against each other.

Agent Castillo shouted and Lena raised her hands, grinning that huge smile that lit up her whole face. As she slowly dropped to her knees and the agents swarmed into the room, her eyes never left mine.

That smile stayed with me like a splinter of ice until I was reunited with my furiously relieved parents at the police station and finally called Michael. With his voice in my ear and Grace in my arms, I could believe that we were truly safe.

15

Helen: And now Lena and Brady are both locked away. Separate prisons, maximum security, awaiting trial on multiple counts. Best-case scenario for them: life in prison.

Julia: But this is Texas, so death is on the table.

Helen: Excellent point. And even though Kacy lied, snuck off to meet a murderer, and actually stabbed someone—

Julia: Just a little bit . . .

Helen: She's in the clear. The almost-victim tells the police Kacy saved her, and everything works out . . . after hours of questioning and fact-checking and face-saving.

Julia: The almost-victim who got her fired from the art museum in the first place? That's a revenge fantasy come true, getting to save your archnemesis. Think she's a little bit sorry now? Just a tiny bit ashamed?

Helen: She's probably just as sorry as Lena and Brady—not at all. Different shades of psychopath.

Julia: [Sighs] Anyway, I love a serial killer story with survivors.

Helen: This is about as close to a happy ending as we ever share. But don't get too comfortable. Next week we'll be starting a new series about an orthopedic surgeon, a childhood secret, and a string of suspicious deaths.

Julia: Remember, we always have *"Crime to Chat"* with you!

28

As the podcast fades to a musical signature for its production company, I turn it off. Three episodes in this series, one each week, and I've finally reached the end.

These episodes felt different from all the other cases Julia and Helen had covered. Maybe because I didn't have the distance to listen dispassionately while evaluating the evidence. I wasn't in suspense about the facts of the case, only about what conclusions they would reach about me. But to be fair, I'm not sharing my story with the press or authors or even my favorite podcasters. We screen our calls stringently.

Now that the series is over, I'm still left without an explanation for Lena's compulsion and her cruelty. More importantly, I also have no explanation for why I've survived.

My doorbell rings, and I answer it with Grace charging behind me on one side and our golden retriever, Lancelot, on the other. Elizabeth waits on the front step, precisely on time, with a binder under one arm. Next to her, Theo stands in a little button-down checkered shirt and khakis. The juxtaposition of his baby-round cheeks and his preppy outfit, missing only a bow tie, slays me. I'm lucky if Grace keeps any outfit on longer than twenty minutes. She's in her nudist phase. Theo barrels past my legs, and I hear the squeals as he and Grace take off with Lancelot in hot pursuit.

Elizabeth looks exhausted, the only sign that she's in the first trimester of her second pregnancy. While I love the idea of Grace being a big sister, I don't think Michael and I are ready to dive in again yet. I say, "Come on in. You're the first one here."

She looks like she might apologize, but then she relaxes and quips, "Always." Elizabeth doesn't have to be careful and precise with me.

But I don't lead her into the house, because behind her I see a familiar figure in a peachy hijab approaching my front walk. With a grin, I say, "You're just barely the first one here."

Elizabeth turns to see Rahmia and waves. We're planning another fund raiser, this one a family carnival to benefit the International Women's Resource Center. I've been spending time every week there, doing art projects with the kids and practicing conversational English with their moms. Volunteering is more than atonement, it's a mission, and I feel so grateful that these women allow me to get to know them. They're survivors, and sometimes I think I might be one too.

As Rahmia comes up the front walk, I see her glance at the house next to mine, Lena's house. Or, as she's noting, Lena's former house.

I know some people were surprised we didn't sell our home. Finances aside—and the finances of selling a house so quickly after buying it aren't trivial, especially with the added burden of legal fees—this is our first home. This is the kitchen where Michael and I learned to cook, the yard where we learned to garden, the home where we conceived Grace and where we're raising her. We've repainted the walls, changed the decor, filled it with things we love. I've seen its insides, behind the plaster and beneath the flooring.

People might look askance at this place, but they might look that way at me too. Nothing that happened was this house's fault. I hope it wasn't mine either.

Something inside crashes, and Elizabeth blanches and ducks past me, shouting, "Theo!" He's in a "knocking over lamps" phase, but it upsets his mom more than it does me.

Rahmia's talking by the time she reaches me, gesturing to the SOLD sign in the yard next door, but all I catch is the last question. "Who bought it?"

I shake my head. "No idea. Michael thinks it could be an investment firm." The house has been on the market for over a year, almost unheard of in our neighborhood. I don't know how much money Lena and Brady had, but their lawyers can't be cheap. The pool is filled in, the floors are redone, and both the number of drive-by gawkers and the price have decreased.

"Do you think anyone will live there? Maybe the company will rent it out or do short-term leases?"

"Probably someday." I don't tell Rahmia, but I looked into it. Even murder houses sell eventually, and people live in them. From Dahmer's midcentury ranch to the Menendez brothers' Mediterranean-style residence to the *Blood and Money* mansion in River Oaks, real estate recovers, and there's always someone looking for a bargain. That SOLD sign is proof that the world keeps turning.

"I'm so sorry, Kacy." Elizabeth has returned to the door, a table lamp in her hand, its harp and shade bent at a right angle. "Somehow he didn't smash the lightbulb, but it won't turn on anymore."

"No worries. Michael will look at it later." And Michael is recovering too. We visit Dr. Lindsey separately and together, groping our way out of the darkness. Once Michael decided therapy was the logical and necessary step to fixing our problem, he was on board. He still has nightmares, but now he turns to me and lets me wrap him in my arms. We share this life raft, and only by holding on to each other will we survive.

Rahmia and I follow Elizabeth into the kitchen and sit around the table. I've added a leaf so we can fit everyone who's coming. Inés and Alondra are always late, but Rachael and her little girl Caryn should be here soon. And I've invited someone new, a woman I met at the last Bluebonnets meeting. Something about the guarded way she scanned the room, her tentative smile when I patted an empty chair next to me, the catty side-eye her nose ring was getting from some uptight women, made me think she needed a friend. Or at least the chance to make one.

Rachael lets herself in, and as her daughter Caryn twirls through the kitchen in a princess dress, I realize I didn't lock the door after Rahmia. Some part of me still thrums *danger*, but there's no point in locking it this second, when two more people are about to arrive. Rachael drops into a chair beside us and checks her phone. "Alondra said to call and she'll video in when we're ready to start."

Once the three of us had toddlers, planning meetings downtown became a thing of the past. My house's open floor plan and a few judiciously placed child gates mean we can watch toddlers race from the back door to the front while still getting work done at the table. "I'll use my phone," Elizabeth offers, and I shoot her a grateful smile.

"It's okay," I say. "We'll use my laptop." And it is okay. Because Grace is growing so fast and our parents are so far away, Michael and I video chat—we use our camera and we call our friends and family. But we do check our phones for malware weekly. We're not total Luddites, just careful. Because that's a choice we've had to make. Cut ourselves off completely and live in fear, or move on. Our phones are links to the world, and they strengthen the relationships that matter.

Plus, it's how I listen to podcasts.

The doorbell chimes again, and Lancelot gives a lazy woof, like he knows that bad guys don't ring the bell. The most comforting sound in the world is the clicking of his toenails as he makes the rounds every night, touching each doorknob with his nose. "Maybe he's a shepherd in golden retriever's clothing," Michael said. I think Lancelot is circling the flock, protecting our family.

I open the door, and the new girl, Jenny, stands there, one hand clenched as if she's forcing herself to wait. This is the moment, the threshold, when she doesn't know me and I don't know her. Her face is narrow, her razor-cut hair emphasizing her sharp cheekbones, but her eyes are wide and vulnerable. She looks so young. Maybe in a year I'll know all her secrets, maybe she'll text me a dozen times a week, or maybe I'm opening the door to my next nightmare. But a door that never opens is just a prison. "Come on in," I tell her.

I show her to the kitchen, and as the conversation eddies around me, I realize that the last episode of *Crime to Chat* did leave me something. It framed my time with Lena as a story with a beginning, a middle, and an end. Michael and I will keep going to therapy, we'll take trips to San Antonio and Austin and South

Padre, Grace will get older, she'll go to school, our story will keep unfolding. Even if we need to testify, even when the next tragedy hits us, we're going to be okay.

I once thought Aimee's betrayal would ruin all my chances at a happily-ever-after, but I've found friends and a purpose and built a new life, one I won't let my past with Lena destroy.

Grace and Theo and Caryn tear through the kitchen with Lancelot bounding behind them. The room echoes with laughter, and I wonder: if Lena was the bad fairy surrounding our home with bloody thorns, maybe family and friends have broken the spell at last. Now our real story, a better one, begins.

ACKNOWLEDGMENTS

O NCE AGAIN, I couldn't have written this book without the encouragement and love of my husband, Tim, and our kids. This past year when we were all working and learning in close proximity to each other, I was especially grateful that you are awesome coworkers as well as wonderful family members.

To my parents, who are not the inspiration for these parents, and to my sisters—I love you all and count myself lucky to be related to people I enjoy so much!

I am so thankful for my dedicated agent, Melissa Jeglinski, for her expertise, advice, and encouragement. Her warmth, humor, and unflagging support have been incredible gifts.

Editor Terri Bischoff's insights made this a much better book, and her words of praise helped me power through revisions. I'm especially indebted to Madeline Rathle for her marketing magic, Melissa Rechter for making everything run smoothly, Rachel Keith, Melanie Sun, and the whole team at Crooked Lane Books for bringing this book into being.

Many thanks to all the friends with whom I've traded pages and critiques, commiserated and rejoiced, including Erin, Kena, Bill, Chuck, John, Melissa, Rodney, Alice, Anne, Betty, Cheryl, Alisa, Grace, Angélique and David. Thanks to Lisa for her friendship and her geographical advice. Special thanks to Heather and Barbara, for telling me everything would be okay (and then reading my pages just to be sure), and to my dear Stacey, for dragging, bullying, and forcing me to create the book I dreamed about writing. I'm eternally grateful to be in the writing trenches with you.

And this book is especially for the friends I've made in groups including the New Territory Women's Association and the Blacksburg Newcomers' Club. None of these organizations are at all like the Bluebonnets, save in a single respect. Much like Kacy, I met some of my closest friends by taking the first step and walking into a roomful of strangers.